Praise for
A Lakeside Reunion

"I was entranced by Reese Devlin and her gorgeous, complicated life at the Shores. This tale of debutante balls, lasting loves, and family pride was delightful…and important."
—Nancy Thayer, *New York Times* bestselling author
of *Summer Love*

"This beautiful book introduced me to a new, fascinating world and then wrenched at my heartstrings. A tribute to the power of hard-won love and deep-rooted family ties, this book will linger long after you turn the last page."
—Alyssa Day, *New York Times* bestselling author

"Once you dip your toe into *A Lakeside Reunion*, you won't want to leave this perfect escape read! Chilove weaves Southern charm and elegance with real-world commentary in this sparkling enemies-to-lovers romance."
—Dylan Newton, author of *All Fired Up* and *How Sweet It Is*

"C. Chilove's *Lakeside Reunion* is an elegant, steamy, and soulful telling of a woman's journey of self-discovery through a mountain of family secrets. This second-chance romance proves the great equalizer between the haves and the have-nots is love."   —LaQuette, award-winning romance author

"The chemistry between Reese and Duncan is powerful.... Chilove captures complex family dynamics and evokes a strong sense of Southern culture, with special attention to the history of debutante balls. This sensitive romance is sure to please."

—*Publishers Weekly*, starred review

Unexpectedly
YOURS

Unexpectedly YOURS

C. CHILOVE

FOREVER

New York Boston

Forever
Hachette Book Group
1290 Avenue of the Americas, New York, NY 10104
read-forever.com
@readforeverpub

First edition: December 2024

Forever is an imprint of Grand Central Publishing. The Forever name and logo are registered trademarks of Hachette Book Group, Inc.

The publisher is not responsible for websites (or their content) that are not owned by the publisher.

The Hachette Speakers Bureau provides a wide range of authors for speaking events. To find out more, go to hachettespeakersbureau.com or email HachetteSpeakers@hbgusa.com.

Forever books may be purchased in bulk for business, educational, or promotional use. For information, please contact your local bookseller or the Hachette Book Group Special Markets Department at special.markets @hbgusa.com.

Print book interior design by Marie Mundaca

Library of Congress Cataloging-in-Publication Data

Names: Chilove, C., author.
Title: Unexpectedly yours / C. Chilove.
Description: First edition. | New York ; Boston : Forever, 2024. | Series: Shores of Dora ; book 2
Identifiers: LCCN 2024024659 | ISBN 9781538705643 (trade paperback) | ISBN 9781538705650 (ebook)
Subjects: LCGFT: Romance fiction. | Novels.
Classification: LCC PS3603.H5647 U54 2024 | DDC 813/.6—dc23/eng/2040603
LC record available at https://lccn.loc.gov/2024024659

ISBNs: 9781538705643 (trade paperback), 9781538705650 (ebook)

Printed in the United States of America

LSC-C

Printing 1, 2024

For my daddy, the man who showed this Florida girl orange groves and dock fishing... Thank you, those experiences helped me imagine the Shores...

Unexpectedly

YOURS

Chapter 1

"CARRAH BRIGETTE CHÀVOUS Andrews!"

Carrah's spine went stiff. She took one last glance at the email from Hurston House Publishing then slammed her laptop shut. She sprang from her desk chair and dashed across her bedroom to the door to cease the pounding knocks from the other side. Before she could turn the knob and open it, her sister, Aubrey, barged into the room.

Carrah folded her arms and made her face tight, successfully camouflaging the anxiety eager to spiral out of control. "You've got some nerve, barging in here and calling me by my full name like you're Mom. My door was closed."

She evil-eyed her sister. Only for a second, though, since she became captivated by the way Aubrey pranced into the room. Their mother called it the beauty queen charm that had been passed down from mother to daughter. Aubrey was a spitting image of their mother. Above-average height, thin with high cheekbones that accentuated her medium brown skin and made her look like a *Vogue* cover model. Aubrey embraced their gene pool and used it to her advantage in all facets of life; Carrah was the opposite.

She preferred to wow people with her brains, not beauty. It was already hard enough that people compared her to their great-great-grandmother, who had been known as a beautiful, yet infamous, voodoo queen in New Orleans. Beyond the comparisons that were hauntingly real, and most times hard to accept, because ignorant people claimed she was the woman born again. Beyond the Haint Paint believers, Carrah struggled with traditional conventions applied to beauty. Aside from her long, silk-pressed tresses, she was short and had to count calories while working out like a maniac to maintain her hourglass figure.

"True, but it wasn't locked." Aubrey stuck her tongue out at Carrah, releasing a giggle. She then stepped past her, commanding the space as usual while poking her nose around Carrah's desk. Aubrey's presence seemed more overwhelming than usual since she had tossed the business suits she normally wore for a more relaxed summer wardrobe that showcased all of her assets.

Typical, they were in the Shores. This was the place her family came to year after year to rejuvenate. The glow radiating from her sister was new, unmistakable, and simply divine as highlighted by the white linen romper she'd paired with dangling gold and diamond-encrusted earrings framing her heart-shaped face.

Aubrey picked up a stack of papers as a questioning expression furrowed her brows. "You should've been downstairs twenty minutes ago—you are not even dressed. People have already started to arrive, and we are lining up soon. Please don't mess around and be late, Carrah. You know our mother and her grand entrances." She sighed. "Why are you working anyway?"

Carrah moved at the speed of light and snatched the papers

from her sister's hands. What Aubrey held wasn't exactly work. It was Carrah's first completed manuscript. A dream she'd forgotten she had until last year when she needed a way to express the suffocating effects of life and the demands her family placed upon her. It was by chance that the universe had wanted her to remember the way she crafted words onto paper and imagined different worlds, and was now ready to grant her wishes true.

"I didn't have a choice," Carrah lied. No matter how close they were, Aubrey wasn't allowed to see the desires lurking in the shadows of her heart because nothing was ever more important to her oldest sibling than Noir Cosmetics, their family's business. "Dad and Beau have been after me to review the product performance from the trials on the new anti-aging serum."

Her sister chuckled. "Well, that is important. I decided not to ride your ass because this is supposed to be our downtime and of course the acclaim you garnered from *Aimer*. Sales have been through the roof on that fragrance. The company hasn't seen a product command so much attention from the beauty industry in a long time. We waited too long to give you free rein in developing a pipeline." Aubrey frowned and looked off for a second. "I know how hard you work. Besides, we are all counting on that genius brain of yours to develop the next big thing. Maybe even finally surpass the Olina Chennault Cosmetics Company."

Carrah held in her sigh. The business rivalry between the Andrewses and the Chennaults started over forty years ago. They were fierce competitors in the industry as two of the most respected Black-owned cosmetics conglomerates in the world. Right now, Chennault had the advantage. They often outspent Noir's advertising campaigns, gained access to the top shelf for many retailers, and were the preferred choice for Black skin care products.

She was also willing to bet that the person heading their R & D division didn't have as many restraints. Freedom to innovate could've enhanced Noir's pipeline two years ago. Beyond business, the tension between the two families always seemed to impact Carrah's summers the most since they all vacationed in the Shores.

Of all the children between the families, she and the oldest Chennault, Christopher, were the closest in age. They shared many friends and were often invited to the same functions. It was hard not to be in the same space. Still, whenever possible, the Andrewses and Chennaults didn't attend the same parties, mingle in public, or pretend to like each other. This was the way it had been since she was old enough to remember. Hell, she and Chris Chennault had even kept their distance a few weeks ago when they went out on the boat with their mutual friend Duncan McNeal, to Dorian's Cove.

"It won't be the serum," Carrah mumbled, clutching the sheets of paper within her hands that told a love story. The happily ever after she'd written had been the inspiration for *Aimer*, a fragrance that evoked emotion from a heroine who had loved one man through many lifetimes. "The skin-correcting foundation is going to be the blockbuster product, and it's far from being ready for trials. Chennault Cosmetics doesn't have anything like it in market, and if they are considering a formulation, it may be prepping to enter research and development. That is according to a little birdie I know that works there."

"Honestly." Aubrey paused, shrugging her shoulders as though nothing Carrah said were important. "It doesn't matter. You'll figure it out."

Carrah blew a long breath, went to her desk, and carefully put the manuscript away. Her family always seemed to need something from her. "Aubrey, you do realize that isn't fair, right? It can't only always be me. Mom and Dad have four kids, but I'm the one that has this pressure to produce a blockbuster product that turns the industry upside down and puts us back on top." *Or care for Mom when she's sick because all of you are too afraid*, she wanted to say but didn't.

"We are heiresses to one of the largest Black-owned cosmetics companies in the world. You sound foolish." Her sister's words bit. "Don't let Mom, Dad, or Beau hear you say that. We all have a part to play that ensures the longevity of this company. Yours is developing new and innovative products. I mean, you are the chemist. You've always wanted to do this. You even traded your crown."

Once upon a time, Carrah thought, and then nodded, knowing that chemistry had really been the equivalent of true love's kiss. It had freed her from the pageant circuit along with the extra pressure and expectation to fill her mother's shoes.

Besides, it wasn't her fault she fell in love with mixing essential oils in Erlenmeyer flasks before pouring them into test tubes or visiting a greenhouse to sniff out the fragrant properties of flowers. Apprehension relaxed and unknotted in her belly as happy thoughts rushed in while she recalled how she used to blend her mother's old eye shadows together and create new colors. Unintentionally, she had chased her father's legacy and followed in his footsteps by becoming a chemist while shattering her mother's dreams for her.

Her mother managed her bitterness by always saying that her father had orchestrated Carrah's interests by taking her along to his lab, where she had discovered and memorized the periodic chart by thirteen, mixed chemical compounds at fourteen, and created fragrances by sixteen. In truth, Carrah was tired of being dolled up and put on display for people to judge her beauty in a Little Miss This or Miss Teen That Pageant.

Being in a lab behind the scenes was much more appealing than running for Miss America. It was the reason she wasted no time declaring her intent to major in chemistry and becoming the first of her siblings to decline admission to an Ivy League.

She opted to follow her parents' legacy and attend the historically Black college, Xavier University, before she completed her graduate studies at MIT.

The unfortunate consequence of falling in love with chemistry play sets, blending essential oils, and graduating from her parents' alma mater was that her siblings believed she was their father's favorite child. It ruffled her older siblings' feathers. Especially her brother Beau. The only saving grace was they each believed in her abilities and had confessed that Carrah was the only one who possessed the innovation needed to guide Noir into the next one hundred years. The success of *Aimer* and the pipeline Carrah had identified proved as much.

So, Aubrey was right. If Carrah had not been distracted with chasing unrealistic dreams, both the serum and foundation would be near ready for market.

"But…" Carrah held her tongue, debating her words. "Haven't you ever dreamed of doing something different?" There, she finally said it.

"I have only ever imagined working at Noir Cosmetics, being at my father's side, marketing what you create, watching Beau manage the money, and eventually having Dominic review our complex contracts." She smirked then stared Carrah in the face. "We planned this out in our tree house and now it's all come true. Well, almost. Baby bro still has to finish law school. Now isn't the time for dreams when we have a reality to fulfill." Her sister's lips pressed together.

Carrah huffed cynically. She didn't have the energy to try and explain that life sometimes uncovered and made you remember hidden treasures within. "I'm not sure why I expected a different response from you. Maybe I just hoped that the last year of seeing Mom sick or the joys you've found in motherhood had shown you that the life we planned as kids may not be the one we live now."

A tense silence hung between them, corroding the jovial nature that usually surrounded their relationship. Aubrey looked away for a second, swallowing hard as if she were searching for the right words. The sharp decline in their mother's health last year had caught them all off guard. It made Carrah reflect on the possibilities that were slipping through her hands. Now, she hoped for something more.

Apparently, it was not the same for her sister. Carrah had decided the unfortunate outcome as Aubrey offered nothing except forcefully brushing past her. "It's Mom's birthday. Get dressed. You're expected to enter with the family."

The door should've slammed behind Aubrey, given her icy words. Except all Carrah heard was the latch clicking against the faceplate, reminding her that there was no escape. She was a fool to think she could change course now. So much had been invested in her to become who and what she was today. No one in her family would understand her contemplation over a glimmer of hope that held no promises.

Not when they were all counting on her genius. Carrah understood she was born into a life full of expectation. There-fore, she removed the last pages of her novel from her desk and packed them away. Maybe one day she would try again. For now, she had to get ready to celebrate her mother and accept that the path she had chosen all those years ago was not one she could abandon for fear of letting everyone else down.

Chapter 2

CARRAH DARTED OUT of her room like the March Hare, afraid of not making teatime. She was about to be late, and if she were, she would never hear the end of it. Aubrey had jinxed her, she thought as she raced down the stairs and considered ignoring the ringing of her cell phone.

Carrah relented and pulled the phone to her ear. "Hello."

"Where are you?" Carrah's big brother, Beau, shouted in her ear.

"I told her not to be late," Aubrey hissed in the background.

Carrah paused at the bottom of the stairs and kicked off her shoes then snatched them up into her hands. She sprinted down the west hall of the house. It was the fastest way to get outside to the carriage house from her room. "I'm coming," she panted. "Be there in a second. Don't start without me."

"Ridiculous," Beau barked before disconnecting.

Carrah disregarded her brother's palpable disgust and continued moving toward the meeting point for their mother's second line birthday entrance. After grabbing a Cajun shrimp skewer from a moving appetizer tray while almost bumping into the service staff, she sped up. Once she'd made it to the door that led to the portico, where everyone was staging, she dropped down and quickly put her shoes back on. Just as she was about to exit outside, movement caught her peripheral vision.

"I'm now certain that I am not the only one to have raised the ire of our big brother." She had turned to gain a better view and watched as her youngest brother, Dominic, emerged from a closet buckling his belt as a girl adjusted her dress. Carrah breathed a little easier knowing she wasn't the only one who would owe Beau and Aubrey an apology. Her lips curved until a smirk rested upon her face.

Dominic flashed a smile whereas the girl, who turned out to be the younger sister of her friend Peyton Daniels, darted away in the other direction. "You know I'm irresistible." He winked and then adjusted his bow tie.

Dominic was a charmer. He stood tall like their father at a good six feet three inches with an athletic build he attributed to football. His wavy hair and ebony eyes were his icing on the cake, and there was never a shortage of girls willing to throw their panties his way. "I know you need to learn to keep that thang in your pants, Nic."

"Mannnn, watch out!" He chuckled. "You talki—"

A trumpet blared to life. Carrah and Dominic scrambled to the side door, pushing and shoving each other to be the first one out. Carrah was the victor and she gloated by quickly snatching up a parasol and leaving Dominic with a handkerchief. They disregarded the glares from Aubrey and Beau while blending into the sea of family members giddy with excitement.

The Grand Marshal who had been procured to lead their

elaborate entrance adjusted his sash, gazed over everyone before he lifted his Stetson, and turned to the front, blowing his whistle. They all began to move forward, following the man's fancy footwork, as the band's zest filled the notoriously quiet, sleepy lakeside town with melodies of the Crescent City.

Carrah danced around, twirling her hand-decorated parasol as she kept in step with the brassy sounds of her hometown. There was an unclaimed joy she experienced as she looked over her shoulder, seeing family and friends swing handkerchiefs to the beat of the drum. Her happiness became almost uncontainable when her attention landed on her mother, Camille Andrews, at the front of the processional, waving a feathered fan. The smile upon her mother's face matched the energy of her body as she strutted toward the event tent, where guests were waiting. It was a glorious sight after months of helping her get around with a walker.

The solid timbre of the trombone ripped through the air and replanted Carrah in the moment. Never had a brass band blared this much to life in the Shores. Mount Dora was unlike the Garden District in New Orleans, which was her primary residence. Life in the Big Easy was fast, colorful, and sadly demanding. By contrast, the Shores offered a slower pace that lingered in nostalgia and allowed time for her mind to rest, reflect, and discover unspoken possibilities.

The bucolic views of green, rolling hills and Lake Dora made the world stand still, and the pressure to be her family's savior faded away. This was the place she had escaped to summer after summer to leave the cares of the real world behind. Her true friends were here, and they had been since she was old enough to walk.

After all, this was where other like-minded families of the Black elite congregated from May through the end of July. A great sense of belonging always seemed to settle her thirsty spirit during the annual reunions, which were full of lakeside shenanigans. It was the reason she came back even though she was old enough not to.

A flash of royal blue went up into the air before the Grand Marshal buckjumped for joy and caught his snazzy hat. The festivities were in full swing as he continued leading the second line in jubilation fully showcasing the sights and sounds of New Orleans, courtesy of Carrah's mother. This one time, Camille had decided to liven the night and bring the flavor of her Creole roots to their summer haven to celebrate making one more, hard-fought trip around the sun.

"Happy Birthday, *ma mère*," Carrah shouted over the music, laughing as she jumped to her mother's side. They stood still, indulging in the delicious sounds of rhythm and blues as their hips swayed in sync. There was an undeniable energy and connection that flowed between mother and daughter. She planted a huge kiss on her mother's cheek. "I love you."

"Ahh, *chérie*," her mother sang through a wide smile before wrapping her long, fair-skinned arms around Carrah. "What a blessed day it is. This time last year I wasn't sure if I would make it." The smile tightened upon her mother's face as water started to well in her eyes.

Carrah fought the emotional roller coaster that would gladly take her to a peak then zoom in and out of loops and bends before dropping her down in a valley she didn't have enough energy to claw out of. "You're not allowed to cry tonight, Mama." Carrah forced a smile upon her face, thumbed a tear from the corner of her mother's eye, pushed her parasol in the air, and then began twirling again. "It's your birthday! We're going to celebrate."

"You're right." Her mother linked elbows with her. "Thank

you for being the only one of my children that let me live even when I thought I was dying." Their eyes met with understanding, and this time it was Carrah unable to control the water pooling in the bottom of her lids. "Sorry, now come, dance with me. *Joie de vivre*," she cried out.

Carrah shuffle-stepped with Camille and vowed to forget the way lupus had ravaged her mother's body last year...at least for tonight. While everyone in attendance this evening would believe the over-the-top festivities were to celebrate Camille's penchant for the flair on her fifty-sixth, Carrah, her father, and siblings knew tonight honored her strength for being a survivor. And it wasn't a far-fetched decoy.

Camille, once coroneted as the famed Zulu Queen of Nawlins, was the definition of pomp and circumstance. Hailing from one of Louisiana's most prominent families that were descendants of the *gens de couleur*, she lived for ways to expose her rich culture and influence her family still wielded over the place many had nicknamed the Paris of the South.

An earsplitting shrill from the Grand Marshal's whistle elicited cheers from the crowd of two hundred awaiting them in the distance underneath the event tent. They were already on their feet clapping and swaying to the beat of the music. Laughter and cheers swirled, while handkerchiefs darted into the air to welcome their mother.

Not one person had been able to resist the beat of the bass drum framing the rhythm for the brass instruments that sparked joy, life, and fond memories of growing up in one of the lushest estates within the Garden District of New Orleans as a Creole elite. After a few minutes, the music mellowed until the sounds of the second line faded into applause.

"They're all here for you, darlin'," Melvin, Carrah's father, said as he carved a small space between Carrah and her mother.

He kissed his wife on her temple and then winked at Carrah before signaling for her siblings to come to their side. He then turned his attention back to the crowd and gestured for them to reclaim their seats. "Thank you all for joining us this evening. You know my wife loves a good party. This one is extra special." He paused, swallowing hard as he pulled her into his side and held her tight. "Happy birthday, Camille. Me and the kids love you so much."

Aubrey grabbed Carrah's hand tight. Beau and Dominic followed suit. Carrah looked down the line at her siblings and could see the same pride she felt for their parents. Camille and Melvin always commanded their respect and admiration. They had defined love, showed them a healthy marriage, affection, and trust between a man and a woman. However, it was a lesson Carrah had no interest in mastering.

Unlike her sister, who had dutifully married right after graduate school and produced a grandchild, or her oldest brother, Beau, who had tied the knot with his college sweetheart, Carrah simply wished for the scars from her last relationship to heal.

"There is plenty of food, spirits, and the band will be here awhile longer. Enjoy yourselves!" Their father then turned to them. His hard dark eyes skipped over her and Aubrey, and landed on Dominic. "Be on your best behavior. This is a special night, and we don't need any distractions. Got me." It wasn't a question, and yet he still waited for Dominic to acknowledge his words. "Oh, Carrah, I believe Trent will be here tonight. Do show him your best Southern hospitality." A half smile played on his lips before he spun their mother into the crowd and disappeared.

Carrah battled a wave of nausea at the mention of her ex before turning to her siblings. Aubrey and Beau's deadpan expressions chased the bile in her throat away. Why hadn't she escaped like Dominic? "What'd I do now?" Carrah asked, silently counting to twenty to keep her hot head from exploding at the judgment she sensed her older siblings were prepared to cast her way.

"You were almost late," Beau snapped.

"But I wasn't," Carrah quipped back, unable to contain the way her voice had risen a decibel. She never almost did anything; she always gave it...them...her all. "You really want to do this now, big brother?" She gestured to their guests. They had all learned long ago that eyes were always on them. Especially in a place as small as the Shores.

Beau raised his arms in defeat. "Fine. Just make sure the product performance review is in my in-box by the morning. I've tolerated you being on your own time long enough."

Her brother turned on his heel and walked away. Before Carrah gave her sister an open door to echo Beau's sentiments or coax her into playing nice with Trent, she ducked into the crowd. The dust hadn't settled from their earlier exchange, and the resentment over being boxed in and denied the chance to chase her own dreams was still too raw.

On her quest to find the friends she knew were in attendance, Carrah was roped into hostess duties. She bided her time exchanging pleasantries, highlighting her accomplishments that unfortunately left out aspiring to be a novelist while pretending that all had been perfect in the Andrews household despite the battles her mother had fought. By the grace of God, her mother had won. Only, now Carrah realized the fear of not having enough time to accomplish her own dreams.

Once Carrah broke free of her duties, she made a beeline to where Reese Devlin and Peyton Daniels were standing together. They were friends from her family's inner circle whom she had adored for as long as she could remember, particularly during the summer months when they all came to the Shores. They also shared being legacies of Jack and Jill, and were part of a famed sisterhood that formed when they were presented to society ten years ago as debutantes in the renowned Lakeside Debutante Ball.

A sense of relief passed through Carrah. These were girls, now women, who had been raised like her and understood the complicated world of the Black elite. They understood the high value placed on legacy and family loyalty above all else. It was the only reason she freely contemplated sharing the unsettled emotions doing battle within her to gain Reese and Peyton's perspectives. Carrah needed assurance that the thoughts plaguing her weren't as irrational as they seemed since she'd never deviated from the path she was expected to follow. Never mind the fiduciary duties that bound her to Noir.

Except this was one time that her decision to stay on the straight and narrow and remain in her families good graces didn't feel right. She didn't know exactly what she was hoping for, but she knew it felt like something was about to slip through her hands. So she had to ask them if forgoing notions of chasing unicorns in order to fulfill family ambitions was foolish or best left deferred?

"Reese, Peyton," she called. They waved as she began walking to where they stood. She greeted them *faire la bise*, air-kissing each of their cheeks before looking over her shoulder to make sure her ex hadn't shown up. "Glad you both could make it!"

"Do you really think my mother would've let me miss her favorite soror's birthday party?" Reese laughed, prompting the same from Carrah. Their mothers were two peas in a pod. It was the very reason Reese and Carrah had become friends as toddlers. "Besides, Ms. Camille would've told me about myself at the next debutante activity. She looks great, Carrah."

Carrah would never confirm the battle her mother endured last year even though she suspected Reese knew since their mothers were close. The secrecy she was sworn to preserved her mother's frail vanity. Camille cowered at the thought of anyone thinking of her as sick and shut in. She only wanted people to associate her name with strength and beauty.

And while Carrah understood her mother's sentiments, the mental toll it placed upon her had been unimaginable. Having a friend to confide in would've been helpful. Thank goodness she'd rediscovered her ability to craft words.

"Thanks. She has a lot to be happy about." The smile stretching across Carrah's face as she spotted her mother dancing with friends was priceless.

"I'd say! Your mama still moves like one of those Silas Green showgirls." Peyton made them chuckle as they gazed at the center of the dance floor and watched Carrah's mom. "For real! And is there a such thing as reverse aging?"

"*The Curious Case of Benjamin Button*," Ava snickered, magically appearing as part of the circle while prompting them all to fall out in laughter before she hugged and kissed them. "Real talk, Carrah. Peyton is right. Ms. Camille looks like she's no more than thirty years old."

Carrah's cheeks remained full. "Good genes, girl."

"Black don't crack," Reese mumbled through giggles.

"Of course it doesn't. Especially when your daughter is an alchemical genius." Peyton winked at Carrah. "Did you bottle up the Chàvous DNA? Is that the secret life-prolonging elixir you were pulling all sorts of crazy hours in the lab to create?"

No, was the honest answer. Those wee hours in the night were spent writing her first draft after she had finished work and caring for her mother. However, they should've been used to perfect the serum or review products that would define the future of Noir. Carrah forced a smile. She was appreciative of their admiration, but not certain on how to respond because it meant she would have to tell another white lie to cover for the first.

"Ha! Secret life-prolonging elixir." Reese threw back the last of her wine and flashed a grin that went from ear to ear. "Is that what we're calling it now? At ten, it was that purge potion you created and made a jack-o'-lantern throw up at Ava's slumber party."

A bubble of laughter managed to escape Carrah. "You remember the vomiting pumpkin?"

"Of course we do—it was the highlight of my party," Ava teased. "I tried to do it again after all of you left. All I got was fussed at for the mess I made, and that I used my mom's new kitchen towels to clean it up."

They all fell into a fit of laughter, and then a slow creep down memory lane began with the girls reminding Carrah of how she always brought a lab set to playdates and oftentimes made them her guinea pigs. It was just the right dose of cheer to make Carrah's heart feel lighter about the work she did compared to how she felt when she'd dashed out of her room to line up for the party.

"Hey, you three." Quinn popped into the circle they were standing in. She kissed each of them on the cheek and then passed Carrah a small wrapped box. "Sneak this into your mother's gift stash," she whispered. "Sorry I'm late. I'm mad I missed the beginning. I heard Madam Camille's entrance was to die for!"

"You already know." Carrah chortled, tilting her head at her mother. "However, she won't know you missed it unless you tell her." Quinn brought her fingers to her lips and did an invisible zip. "Why are you so late anyway?" Carrah asked.

"Because she's been politicking like her daddy." Ava signaled for a waiter to bring over the tray of appetizers and wine for Quinn. "Guess you can't help it since your dad's up for reelection."

"The dark side of being a senator's daughter with an unmarried brother eager to follow in his steps." Quinn took the wine from the waitstaff and gulped. "But...I was actually or rather unofficially meeting with Chris on behalf of the Juneteenth committee. He's sorta helping me tie up a loose end for the annual Red Party."

Carrah rolled her eyes. Chris Chennault was the last person she wanted to hear about. His family's cosmetics company had recently launched a beauty campaign that outshined Noir's, and placed more pressure on her to complete the serum, foundation corrector, or anything else that could expeditiously move through the pipeline and be in stores by the end of the year. The stress of the competition had recently turned her oldest brother into the worst CFO, and placed a strain on the family that had not been felt since the passing of her grandfather.

She dared to not be selfish and consider how it was negatively impacting her ability to take advantage of a once-in-a-lifetime opportunity. "Chennaults don't sort of do anything, Quinn. They are deliberate. I'm certain there is something in it for Chris."

Reese, Peyton, and Ava all shot wry glances her away. As their lips pursed to reply, Quinn's hand shot up while she shook her head no. She frowned at Carrah. "Just because you and your family don't mix with the Chennaults doesn't mean the rest of us should feel the same." Quinn paused for a second and took the boudin ball and second full glass of wine that was being offered to her. "For the record, his mother used to co-chair the Juneteenth committee. We called in a favor to him for help with securing new entertainment after the band we booked backed out."

"That makes sense. He's well connected in the entertainment industry. His roster is stupid impressive," Ava offered, half glancing up to meet Carrah's eyes. "Heck, I'm still sometimes shocked to see my name by all those big-time celebrities. But he's been my attorney since before he founded his own firm."

Reese cleared her throat. "Didn't you tell me that he recently helped you land a publishing deal for a photographic arts journal with *TIME*?" Ava nodded yes and Reese cast her judging gaze onto Carrah.

"So basically, he's beyond qualified and a logical choice for the committee to seek help from," Peyton chimed in, cutting her eyes at Carrah.

Carrah ignored them and gulped down the last of her merlot. She needed to remember that these friends didn't take sides, which was why she sometimes found herself coexisting at a distance with him. They had all been friends with Chris for as long as she had been friends with them. It wasn't their fault the Chennaults and Andrewses were like oil and water. Now was starting to feel like the perfect time to leave.

"Anyhow," Quinn said, regaining Carrah's attention. "One of his clients agreed to perform at th—"

"Excuse me." Trent's deep voice cut off Quinn's words and made Carrah's skin crawl. "Carrah, darling, can we talk?" His words were sweeter than syrup. Only Carrah knew better.

Carrah's teeth clenched together. She slowly turned her head to see Trent standing mere inches behind her. Her ex-lover may have had a face carved by the angels, but his soul was vile. She wanted no part of him, and he knew it, which was why she couldn't believe he had come to her mother's party. The fact that he'd apparently received an invitation was even more alarming.

"There's nothing to talk about, Trent." Carrah refused to mince words with him. She'd been clear when they broke up three months ago. The audience of her closest friends empowered her to remain true to her feelings. Her line of sight met each of her friends' before she looked off into the distance. She hoped he would get the hint and disappear.

He gripped her arm then tugged her toward him. "Let's not make a scene. We need to discuss a few things." He inclined his head to the front of the room, where her father stood smiling at them. "Your father wants us to talk."

"What about what I want?" She cleared her throat and snatched her arm away from him, all the while fighting back the discomfort from having to be in his company.

"How about you tell that to your father," he whispered.

The sureness of his words made the hairs on her arm stand up. He was not above starting an argument with her tonight to get his way. And while she was ready to give him a piece of her mind, this wasn't the time. She would never taint the celebration honoring her mother.

"I'll catch you ladies later." Carrah offered a tight lip smile and then turned away from her friends.

She moved through the crowd, never checking over her shoulder to see if Trent followed. Based on the fact that he boldly showed up demanding they talk, she knew he would be behind her. When she got to the edge of the tent, she made the rash decision to step outside, away from the perimeter where people lingered, and faced Trent.

Logic had battled spontaneity because she knew having any eyes was better than none when dealing with a man with questionable integrity. Yet this was the Shores, and she wasn't ready to become the subject of gossip among their crowd of people.

Trent relaxed into an unwelcome smile then reached for her hand. Carrah took a step back. Boundaries were important here. Her ex had crossed every line that would deem a relationship healthy, happy, or loving.

After a tense silence, he finally spoke. "You look beautiful."

"Is that what you told Oliva and Ebony? Oh, wait, I forgot about your assistant. What was her name?" Carrah's throat burned with shame as she swallowed the hurt and pain from being made to feel inadequate. All those dollars in therapy seemed useless as she stood in front of Trent.

He took a step toward her, and she took another one back. "I've apologized. I even proposed. What more do you want?" His jaw ticked. "You've had more than enough time to get over my indiscretions. Your parents want this wedding, and so do I. I need you. I'm sorry I fucked up."

"You only need me because it boosts your image and helps with your aspirations for public office. Like I asked you earlier, what about what I want? How will I ever achieve my hopes and dreams if I'm drowning in yours." It wasn't meant to be a question, but a statement she left him with as she took off back toward the main house.

Once inside her room, she locked the door and scatted over to where she'd stowed her manuscript away. The second it was in her hands, the anger, anxiety, and pain that were bearing down on her were replaced with hope, joy, and freedom. She saw possibilities, not a dead end. She couldn't give up the chance to change her life.

The evening had delivered the unexpected. And yet there was a silver lining. Her friends had unknowingly provided an answer to her dilemma, and it was Christopher Chennault.

She said his name under her breath as she sat at her desk, opened her laptop, and typed his name inside the Google search bar. A record of his success was plastered across the web from various articles to photos with him alongside famous celebrities. She didn't discover anything she didn't know. However, she had not fully comprehended his reach in the entertainment world, which on his bio included literary representation.

Hope bloomed to life. Chris would understand and could explain the offer extended by Hurston House. With his counsel, she could logically deliberate her options and decide if she was ready to walk through a new door. The alternative was to remain stuck in a place where what everyone else wanted for her was not what she desired for herself.

Carrah had a life to figure out. One that had been in constant reflection since her mother took ill and she'd rediscovered a lost passion. It was time she took a chance and did something for herself. And so she swallowed her pride, shook off her apprehension, and quickly filled out the online query form for Chris's firm. The bad blood between their families dictated her formality. However, just maybe her enemy could become her ally.

Chapter 3

CHRIS TOOK IN a deep, hard breath then sprinted the last one hundred yards up the shore-lined path. He was free to chase twilight even though he knew he would never catch it. His timer beeped along with his heart rate monitor, forcing his feet to stop beating the dirt underneath.

He bent over to catch his breath then came upright and laced his hands behind his head. He walked in a circle, slowing his racing adrenaline, until his line of sight went back to the horizon, where the sun was breaking dawn by scattering its light into the upper atmosphere.

He walked another few feet before disregarding the NO TRESPASSING sign at the base of his parents' lawn and then cut across to the dock. The world went still and a modicum of solace that often evaded him courtesy of his career found him. He could only capture moments like this here, in the Shores.

The little enclave was a slice of heaven. The best-kept secret of the Black elite, where he'd formed lasting friendships

and spent summers fishing, boating, and enjoying life without distractions. He chuckled, thinking back to skate nights
with Gavin and Duncan, or getting frozen cups from Uncle
Willie's Sweet Shop. Of course, he would never forget the time
he spent with his mother on their evening walks or how she
baked cakes and cooked his favorite candied bacon.

She was always supposed to be here, and now that she
wasn't, he seemed unsettled, unbalanced...not grounded. It
was the very reason he still came this summer even though the
expansion tried to dictate otherwise. He needed to feel close to
her. And so despite the sacred oath to never bring work to the
Shores, he did.

The ringing of his cell phone ceased his introspection.
The intrusion on his peace introduced thoughts of leaving city
life behind.

"Chennault," he answered, somehow managing to present his crisp legal tone after a 5:00 a.m. seven-mile run with
thoughts weighing him down like a rucksack.

"Good morning." Shayla, his assistant, sounded as perky as
ever. Which was odd, considering she had never been a morning person in the last three years that she'd been a part of his
team. "Who do I have to thank again for giving you the bright
idea to set up a temporary office in this little Southern town."

They both chuckled. "I take it you are enjoying the
Shores?"

"I haven't felt this relaxed in a long time, and I'm still
working. Jordyn and Dion said they're never going back to
New York, and Mike is upset that in my years with you this is
our first time here!" She continued sharing more of her husband and children's recent excursions across the town.

"This place has that effect." He gazed back out onto the
water and couldn't help the smile curling his lips. "Thank you

for being willing to come here and set up shop with me. For the first time in my twenty-eight years of life, my mother won't be here. Her passing has made this summer challenging, and with my father's recent sentimental displays, this was definitely not a time I could miss being in the Shores."

Chauncy Chennault had maintained a strong front for Chris and his siblings after the passing of their mother. However, as the summer began closing in and he started packing up his Louisiana residence to make the trip to Florida, he came from behind an invisible veil and showed how much he mourned his wife.

Chris cleared his throat. "Well, I'm certain you're not calling me this early to chat about our temporary work location. Let me guess, Miller-Godwin?"

Shayla snickered into the line. "Bingo! They've called and emailed several times since late last night, demanding a meeting today."

"I figured. Gerron's publicist and agent have already pinged me. If the rumors floating around social media are true, he may have breached the character clause within his contract and that's grounds for them to write his ass off the show. They've been looking for a reason and he's given them one." Chris sighed, massaging the back of his neck. "You can put them on midmorning. I need time to chat with him and his team first."

"Got it. I'll slide them in as early as permitting since you're only working a half day. One more thing," she mumbled. "Does the name 'Seraphina Charles' ring a bell? She submitted a new client inquiry."

His mental Rolodex went to work. He'd met a ton of people recently with the expansion of his offices to the West Coast. Maybe the name should be familiar, but he couldn't place it.

Nor did he care to. His client load was beyond full. "No, it doesn't, and honestly it doesn't matter. You know all initial consults are done in person. Beyond that, I'm not taking on any new clients."

"What if I told you Ms. Charles was referred by one of your longstanding clients, Ava Hamilton, the photographer, and is willing to be here by the afternoon."

"Hmmm, that's a bit odd." Chris shook his head. He wished he didn't feel the confusion that scrunched his face. "Ava would've mentioned something like this to me. Seraphina Charles," he whispered twice to himself, still drawing a blank while noting to shoot Ava a text.

Shayla yawned into the line then offered apologies. "She was delightful over the phone. I called to make her aware that we received her request since she sent it multiple times through the online portal and indicated it was urgent, and of course since Ava referred her. I did take the liberty of explaining your initial consult policy. She had no problem with finding her way here to this little sleepy town. She's eager to have a contract reviewed."

He paused, upset that something so insignificant was intruding upon his quiet time. This was generally the only part of day that his mind wasn't consumed with the needs of his clients. And now it was being hijacked by someone who wasn't. "This piece could've waited until we were at the office later."

"Not exactly...I confirmed the appointment. You don't have to accept her as your client. Pass her to one of the other attorneys without a full roster. But at least meet the woman. She's gone above and beyond to get your attention, and her referral speaks volumes."

Chris relaxed a bit and released a light chuckle. "You're going soft on me, Shayla. You used to bite like a bulldog."

She sighed into the phone. "Blame it on the Shores." She giggled. "Our morning is full. See you soon, boss."

The line went dead as Chris gazed back out onto the lake and began bidding it farewell. He was somehow intrigued by the prospective client's connection to Ava, and her determination to meet him in his very inconvenient summer space. Mount Dora was not an easy location to get to. There were no direct flights, the closest airport was over fifty miles away, commercial hotels were limited, and Ubers were unheard of, which was what the summer residents preferred. The exclusivity of the Shores had made it the playground for the Black elite for a long time and nothing would change soon. So if Seraphina Charles was willing to jump through a few hoops to get here, he would meet her to satisfy his curiosity and keep the peace with Ava and Shayla.

He turned away from the water and went up the backyard and entered the house. Everyone was still asleep except for the head of house staff, Ms. Watson. He saw her moving about, preparing for when all of his family would finally greet the day.

"Morning, Ms. Watson."

"Morning, Christopher." She smiled at him. "Oatmeal this morning?"

"You know it!"

She laughed. "Boy, your mama would be tickled pink to see your grown behind demanding oatmeal. Your sister and brother haven't touched it since middle grades."

"Ahh…is that why I'm the favorite?"

The old woman swatted at Chris. "Gone and get your hips upstairs and get out of them wet clothes. I'll get your breakfast started. Should I make some for Heather?"

"No." He paused for a second and then started up the stairs. He didn't want her to see his regrets or ask about the argument from last night that he was certain they all heard. "Don't forget the brown sugar and crushed pecans on top. Some sausage patties, too, please."

"I been cookin' for your family for the last thirty-odd years. I'm the one who started you on hot cereal." She puffed. "You think I don't know what you like to eat?"

"No, ma'am." Chris chuckled, raising his hands to cast the white flag before a war could start. He was not doing battle with the woman who was like a second mother to him. She knew the good, bad, and ugly. "Thank you!"

He dashed up the stairs and quickly ducked into his room. He froze by the foot of his bed and scanned Heather, his girl-friend of a little more than a year. Had he heeded his mother's warning, perhaps Heather wouldn't be here now. The impromptu weekend visit was all wrong, and the sudden ulti-matum of propose or break up validated why he had never con-sidered asking.

Logically there was already an answer, since demands were his Achilles' heel. His parents had learned the hard way when he denied the family business to pursue a career as an attorney. Chris knew his father allowed him to chase law only because it could still benefit the Olina Chennault Cosmetics Company. Just like deep down he knew Heather wouldn't give up until he placed a ring on her finger.

However, last night unveiled clarity that a warm body and pretty face could no longer hide. Heather confessed she loved him, but he did not love her. The more he thought on it, their relationship felt transactional. She attended an event with him, they went to dinner, did what lovers do—repeat.

There was no warm and fuzzy, no prioritizing her above his work, and he never had that feeling of wanting to move heaven and earth for her. His mother had promised he'd know the feeling, and after more than a year of being in an exclusive relationship with Heather, he didn't.

He moved away from the bed, not yet sure of how he would sever their relationship, and he got into the shower. No less than an hour later, he stood in front of his closet mirror, perfecting the knot of his tie. He was grateful Heather was such a sound sleeper. He didn't feel like another argument over his refusal to discuss a future with a woman he finally understood he didn't see in it. Not before going into the office. He needed his head on right.

Despite being in the Shores, the expansion forced him to keep some office hours. They were shorter than normal, but still jam-packed. There were agents and managers to chat with, litigators to renegotiate contract terms with, insider meetings to get the scoop on the projects that were happening at Amazon, Disney, Netflix, and other streaming platforms in addition to Warner Brothers and the major studios. The level of interaction that he expected from himself, but also knew was demanded of him, contradicted summer in the Shores.

Even still as he mentally prepared for his day while dressing in his signature three-piece bespoke style, he knew his mother would not have accepted less. At an early age she had drilled into him the importance of upkeep and appearances. When she dressed him for church, events, and parties, she often explained that dressing nice would make him behave well, stand a little taller, and act like a big boy. By the time he was a teenager, and participating in oratorical competitions, Men of Tomorrow, and serving as a Regional Teen Officer in Jack and Jill, she helped him to understand that the way he presented himself communicated who he and his family were in society.

His grandmother, the great Olina Chennault, didn't bother to sugarcoat like his mother had. She cut right down the middle and told him plainly to dress to impress for it was a game of respectability politics. It was how Martin Luther King Jr. and his crusaders changed the way people viewed their protests, and it was the same logic Chris used every morning he stood in front of the mirror to prepare for his day.

He smoothed his hand down his tie, missing his mother. There was no doubt in his mind that if she could see him now, she would be proud of the man he had become. *Dignity and respect*, the words echoed in his head, knowing that was what she would say to him if she still were here in this world. However, now was not the time to ponder the mysteries of life and death. He snatched his suit coat from the chair, grabbed his laptop, and left the room.

The sweat cream of Ms. Watson's famous oatmeal combined with the hickory and pepper he scented from the fried pork made his feet move a little faster until he reached the breakfast table. "Smells delicious," he broadcasted to her as she stood at the stove plating his sausage. "You know I've asked my dad if you could come stay with me permanently."

She shook her head. "No thank you. Ain't nobody tell you to put your main office in New York." She gestured for him to take his seat at the table. "Besides, I can't be nowhere with all that concrete…and those women wear white shoes after Labor Day."

The seriousness of her words forced deep-bellied laughter from Chris. His mother, grandmother, and younger sister were all staunch believers of no white after Labor Day. As a result, he found himself silently condemning women in the city for committing fashion crimes against the South.

"Thanks to all of you, I find it odd myself." He slid into a chair at the table and she put a plate in front of him.

"As you should, my dear brother. Although I don't think your girlfriend feels the same." Chloe, his sister, side-eyed him while adding her two cents as she entered the kitchen refolding a newspaper. "Why are you taking breakfast in the kitchen instead of the dining room?"

"Why not?" he retorted.

Chloe waited at the counter while Ms. Watson poured her a cup of coffee, and then pulled out the chair across from him. "Must you always be the rebel," she mumbled then took a sip from the steaming mug. "I thought you were spending the day with us? Dad mentioned golf at the club today."

"I'll be there." Chris shoveled a spoonful of oatmeal into his mouth, and savored the taste.

"Don't bring Heather," his sister said boldly. "I don't feel like hearing her complain about the heat or her dress being ruined. Why are you with her anyway?"

Chris stared at his sister. He didn't owe her any answers. Besides, he was doubtful Chloe would empathize with his need to fill a lonely void. She still resided at the family home in Louisiana, where she was surrounded by love, support, and the memory of their mother.

Whereas he was in New York, navigating grief on his own. Heather had been a reliable distraction—that was the conclusion he'd arrived at before he made it downstairs for breakfast. So his sister was one hundred percent right for asking him why he was with the woman. However, if she knew, she'd never let him live it down. Chloe had been a pain in his right side ever since she was born. And yet he admired her. In a male-dominated business field, she managed to be the absolute best in school and now for the family business.

"She's leaving today," he grumbled before taking another bite of his breakfast.

A loud yawn captured their attention before the swing door to the kitchen flung open and their baby brother, Carter, walked through. He walked directly to Chris, threw a news-paper down on the table, and then plopped into a seat.

"You beat me to it." Chloe smirked, eyeing the newspaper and then leaning back in her chair. "They love to exclude us."

Chris now regretted the extra mile he ran and the phone call he'd taken this morning. If he had kept to his normal rou-tine, he'd have missed both of his siblings at the breakfast table lamenting over their fear of missing out. "So what." He dropped his spoon on the table, unable to control the gruff tone of his words. They would not let him enjoy his damned oatmeal.

Chloe smacked her lips. "I'm sure Carter was the only escort for the Debutante Ball not present at Camille's little soi-ree last night."

"Put a handle on that woman's name, Chloe. That is not how you were raised, young lady." Ms. Watson moved to the table, placing a plate of eggs, bacon, and toast in front of Chloe then Carter.

"I'm not eating carbs." Chloe pouted.

"Fine." Carter reached across the table and grabbed the toast off her plate. "Ms. Watson didn't do anything to you." He finally made eye contact with Chris. "Chloe is right, I was the only one not there last night. All my friends and the girl I'm escorting were present, living it up, and here I was sitting in the house wondering where everyone was."

Chris folded his napkin and relaxed back in his chair. He looked from his brother to his sister. This was the story of his life. For as long as he summered in the Shores, he would never forget the lengths everyone went through to keep the two fam-ilies from each other's spheres. "Are you both really so bothered by the Andrewses not extending an invitation to our family that you bring these shit attitudes to the breakfast table?"

In an instant both Chloe and Carter sat up a little

straighter. Chloe opened her mouth to respond. Chris halted her. "Have we ever invited them to any of our functions? Do we mingle with them when both families are invited guests? It's been like this for as long as I can remember."

"Doesn't make it right," Chloe uttered, barely above a whisper.

"Try telling that to Granddad and Dad." Chris gave her a pointed look before taking a bite of his sausage. "Your perspective will be missed."

Carter cleared his throat. "You know the one your age, Carrah, she's nice. I mean, I know she knows my last name, but she doesn't treat me any differently than the other escorts during rehearsals."

Chris paused. He let go of his spoon, finally deciding breakfast was a lost cause. Carrah Andrews had been the bane between him and his friends every summer since they first started coming to the Shores. When his mother was alive, it had been more intense. Everyone walked on eggshells to appease friendships.

For the most part, he and Carrah had an unspoken agreement to exist with distance. However, there were times that if Carrah were present, he couldn't be, and if he were present, she didn't come. One exception had been a few weeks ago when they all went out on their mutual friend Duncan McNeil's boat.

"Cue the world of the old guard. She will be polite in public and so should you," Chris finally responded as he got to his feet. "As Mom used to say, it's for appearances sake." He left the table and grabbed his jacket and bag.

"Is that why all of you looked so chummy in that picture at the cove?" Chloe asked before he could leave.

Ms. Watson looked at Chris and then turned away. That

day was awkward as hell being in the same space with Carrah. The forced proximity had challenged his notions of her,
her family, and the way his parents raised him to view the
Andrewses. It also provided a glimpse into aspects of his life
he missed because their grandparents had decided over forty
years ago their clans couldn't mix. However, rules were rules
and he would not be the one to break them.

"Right!" Carter exclaimed then gulped down some orange
juice, pointing at Chris. "Forget all that craziness. You looked
like you were having fun. That girl is fine as hell. If she were
my age, this little feud between our families wouldn't matter."

Chris shrugged. Maybe Carrah was beautiful, but she
wasn't his cup of tea. Her attitude toward him had never been
peachy. Perhaps it never would be, and she had proven that on
more than one occasion over the years. The day at Dorian's
Cove had been no exception. Besides, the last time his family
was close to hers, they tried to steal everything.

"Do you ever think our families will get along? I mean,
we have a lot in common." Chloe's fiery attitude had calmed.
He sensed the genuineness of her question and could tell she
wished things were different. He had, too, once upon a time.

However, his sister needed to remember. Actually, both
siblings did. Maybe since he was the oldest and it had been
etched into him longer, he didn't have a hard time realizing
their worlds would never collide in any manner that resembled
something pleasant.

"Never forget why Olina Chennault Cosmetics is the
number one cosmetics company in the world for Black women.
The Andrewses are our rivals, and so I would tell you that hell
would freeze over before our families got along."

Chapter 4

"CHRIS." SHAYLA BUZZED his desk phone.

He disconnected the virtual call and sank back into his chair, then swiveled just enough to sit looking out onto his view of downtown. Hill House sat at the top of the hill whereas Donnelly Park was in the near distance at the bottom, and the quaint shops that lined the city streets were as charming as they had been when he first learned to appreciate the history of the place his family called home three months out of the year.

"Yes," he finally responded. The hustle and bustle of New York City streets may be missing from outside, but not within his office walls. This was the life he chose, and he wouldn't trade it no matter how much his father had recently begun painting the legacy picture for him to head up the family business.

"I couldn't get Gerron. His assistant said he was on location shooting so expect a return call tomorrow. I was also unable to reach Ms. Hamilton." She paused. Chris sensed there was something else. Instead of asking, he waited. "However, Celeste Demi is on the line regarding Alonzo's contract."

Boom. There it was. His corporate nemesis on a day when he somehow felt a little off-kilter after having his schedule highjacked and being sabotaged at the breakfast table by his siblings. Most irritating was that he still hadn't made contact with Ava to confirm the mystery referral. He didn't do surprises in the business world. That was what made him good, hard to poke holes in. Shayla's hesitation was from knowing him the way she did. "Very well," he exhaled loudly. "Shayla, have you found any information on Seraphina Charles?"

"I, uh…No, Chris I haven't yet."

Without another word, she disconnected and his line began ringing again. He shot Ava another quick text. Then he sat up in his chair, cleared his throat, and answered the line.

* * *

Carrah pulled up to the red light at the intersection of Fifth Avenue and Donnelly Street. She gazed at the corner, admiring the Chennault Building with its stately arched windows and the painted brick exterior as if she had never seen it before when in actuality she had driven and walked past it more than a million times. The building had been the first bank for the town of Mount Dora, and thus a cornerstone. No matter where you were in town, at some point you would pass by it.

The light turned green, and Carrah eased her foot off the gas. She made a slow turn onto Fifth, and then searched for a parking spot. Less than three shop doors down from the Chennault Building was an empty space. She cut the engine to her car, but then pulled down her visor mirror and took a deep breath.

She wanted—no needed—something from Chris. Not

anything big, just a simple review of her contract and advice on her rights was all. It would help her make a decision that could change the rest of her life.

"Will he help me?" she asked herself out loud.

Afraid to ponder the answer, given their families' rivalry and the way she had treated him over the years, she simply grabbed up the items his assistant had asked her to bring and exited the car. Her pace up the sidewalk to the entry doors was slow. There were so many thoughts running amok in her head that when she raised her hand to pull the handle of the door, she dropped it back down and turned away.

What was she doing? She was an Andrews and he was a Chennault. This was more taboo than asking for unsweet tea or missing first Sunday communion. Forget that his client roster included movie stars, athletes, models, and singers. Not to mention that he only accepted referrals, and that didn't guarantee representation.

A pinned-up breath finally escaped her lips. None of it mattered. She only wanted him. Based on the research she'd stayed up doing last night, she learned that he was a mover and shaker in the industry. He'd negotiated significant contracts that had launched careers. It was possible he could do the same for her and then she could discover the life that was waiting for her if she took a chance and followed her own dreams.

Carrah closed her eyes, inhaled deeply, and then turned to grab the handle. She stepped inside, swallowing her pride, and became captivated by the way the marble on the floor was also on the walls as wainscoting. Then, of course, there were original gold chandeliers, trim details that rivaled buildings in the French Quarter, and preserved teller cages that were bronze with brass grilles. She had heard the rumors of how consideration had been given to safeguarding the past without

compromising the foundation or opulence of the old structure. This was her first time inside, and she was upset that
she'd allowed family prejudices to delay her experience.

The awestruck feeling subsided when an older man
bumped into her making his way into the real estate office that
occupied the first floor. Carrah scanned her email from Chris's
assistant once more and then bypassed the elevator for the
stairs. She climbed the steps one at a time, taking in the full
details of the elaborate metal filigree railing while attempting to ignore the subconscious thoughts flooding her mind.
The second she entered the door labeled CHENNAULT GROUP,
her contemplations ceased. There was a sense of security that
wrapped around her as she made way to the receptionist desk.

"Good afternoon," Carrah said as she walked past a few
chairs to the small reception desk.

The dark-haired woman looked up from her desk and
smiled. "Afternoon!" The woman stood and made her way
around the desk. Her designer digs screamed high fashion and
were indicative of the high-profile clients the firm serviced.
She extended her hand to Carrah. "You must be Ms. Charles."

"I...uh, yes." Carrah recovered fast. For a second she'd forgotten that she used a pen name in hopes that Chris wouldn't
automatically dismiss her request to meet. "Seraphina Charles."
She gripped the woman's hand and shook it firmly. "And you
must not be from around here, Shayla?" They both snickered as
the woman nodded, confirming she was who Carrah had spoken
with over the phone. "Assistants from these parts don't dress in
Armani blouses and those killer Louboutin heels."

Shayla blushed a little while sizing Carrah up from head
to toe. "I guess a woman like you clad in an ensemble that
could only come from Neiman Marcus easily recognizes these
labels. I hope it was a compliment."

"It is!" An awkward pause filled the space between them. "Again, my apologies for all the messages and emails. I'm on a tight timeline and I wanted to meet with Mr. Chennault as soon as possible."

"No need." Shayla returned to the other side of her desk. "You're here. This isn't the easiest place to get to and he's made the time. Did you bring the materials I requested?"

Carrah dug into her bag and pulled out the manuscript and a copy of the offer that was sent from the publishing house and handed it over to Shayla.

"Thank you. He's running a little behind. Have a seat, and as soon as he's ready, I'll come and grab you."

Carrah turned and claimed an empty chair in the lobby. She pulled her phone out to check her messages and saw tons of notifications from Beau, Aubrey, and Trent. Instead of swiping up to read, she threw the phone back in her purse. She suspected Beau and Aubrey were calling to harass her over the email she had sent this morning further delaying the product review. She was too busy researching Chris and how she could explore options with her manuscript to prepare the specs on the product.

As for her ex, she cared not to think about him. She was still baffled that her father had invited him into her sacred place and more confused by his wanting to reconcile. Carrah would never go back to Trenton Thomas Butler. Not after he went out of his way to make her feel inadequate.

The door to the office opened and saved Carrah from reliving the nightmares she associated with Trent. She then watched a tall, mocha-skinned woman with a pixie cut obnoxiously dripping in Gucci sashay in and go to the desk. If her mother or her sister had seen the woman, they would call her a wannabe. Camille had a firm belief that people who broadcasted designer labels like a mannequin in a department store had new, little, or no money. She had taught Carrah and her siblings at a young age to mix and match iconic fashion brands without being ostentatious.

The only exception was a purse. However, there were limits. The woman standing at the desk going back and forth with Shayla hadn't got the memo.

"I said, I need to see Chris now!" Her haughty voice rang loud in the small space before she proceeded to pass Shayla.

Shayla jumped up from her chair and blocked the woman's path. "I'm afraid it cannot be this minute, Heather. He's wrapping up a call and is late for his next appointment." She gestured at Carrah.

Heather whipped around and met Carrah's line of sight. Any other day Carrah might've asked the woman what she was looking at. Today, she forced herself to play nice and picked up a magazine from the table next to her.

"If ever something is to get done, I have to do it myself," Carrah heard Heather scold Shayla. "Why he pays you to do a job, I'll never understand." She huffed loud and then proceeded to make her way back into the seating area. "Excuse me."

Carrah flipped to the next page of the magazine, intentionally disregarding the woman. She saw under her lids that Heather was now standing in front of her expecting her attention. She'd make her wait as payback for the nasty attitude she witnessed toward Shayla and saturating the air with negative energy when Carrah was desperate for good vibes. Once she finished reading the caption of a picture that was less than memorable, she glanced up.

Heather recoiled. Her pretty face scrunched as she scanned Carrah. In spite of the expression resting on her face, Carrah thought the woman reminded her of the models in magazine ads. It was possible she was, given the talent Chris represented.

"I'm in that issue." Heather pointed to the magazine Carrah was holding. "I believe it was a Lauren ad."

"I beg your pardon," Carrah replied with the amiability of a saint, despite the woman committing one of her most egregious pet peeves of being braggadocious. As if not being rude was enough, Heather displayed a self-satisfying ego that reminded her of Trent.

"Hi," Heather clipped. "I'm Heather Jensen."

Carrah stood, tossing the magazine back to the table, and extended her hand. "Seraphina Charles."

Heather cleared her throat while taking time to complete a full body scan of Carrah. "I'm sorry to do this, but I need to see Chris. I'm his girlfriend and it's urgent I speak with him. Do you mind if I take a few minutes before your appointment to see him?"

It was Carrah's turn to assess the woman in front of her. She'd never been around Chris enough to know the women he dated. For all she knew, he was like Gavin, who dated countless women. He had the looks, smarts, and wallet to be a playboy. Yet here was this woman he'd brought to the Shores. That seemed more committed than she would have expected from him.

"I still have to check with Chris, Heather," Shayla called from her desk.

"Shayla," Heather snarled, "mind your place. I told—"

"It's fine, Shayla." Carrah spoke to Shayla with an even tone before cutting her gaze back to Heather.

"Thanks," Heather offered in a nonchalant manner as she took an empty seat in the lobby. "Do I know you from somewhere?"

Carrah couldn't resist walking through the door Heather had opened. She knew better, but old habits sometimes died hard with people like this Heather Jensen. "Ah, no, I don't believe we mingle in the same circles."

"You seem familiar. Are you a model? Is that why you're here to see my Chris?"

"Modeling is seemingly uninteresting to me. I'm here on professional business."

A snort from the opposite side of the room made Carrah's lips curl into a small grin as she sat crossing her legs. Minutes passed and the tension in the air crackled. There was something about the woman in front of her that raised the hairs on her arm. If Chris had been her friend, she would tell him. But since their relationship was not on those terms, it wasn't her place.

"He just got off the line," Shayla announced. Heather got to her feet and started toward her. "A minute, Heather. I need to speak with him first."

Heather plopped back down into a chair as Shayla slipped down a small hallway. The anxiety Carrah had escaped outside returned. She didn't know Chris well enough to predict how he might react to her making up a name or asking for a favor. One thing she knew was that, like her, he was raised in the ways of the old guard. He wouldn't create a scene that neither of them couldn't recover from...or so she hoped.

Chapter 5

"FUCK!" CHRIS PUSHED out of his chair, slamming his hand on the desk. "Celeste has the studio unwilling to renegotiate Alonzo's contract."

"You always use the harshest expletives when ending a call with that woman." Shayla sighed as she moved through his door and to his desk.

Chris smirked. "She brings out that side in me." He pulled his attention from the window and looked at Shayla. "Ava never got back to me. Did you find anything on Ms. Charles?"

"I'll do you one better." Shayla passed him a folder. "Inside the folder is her manuscript and a contract from Hurston House."

His head tilted to the side. "Hurston House?" He wouldn't pretend not to be intrigued.

He sat back down at his desk and opened the folder. Before he could read, Shayla said, "I know we're in the middle of expanding the firm and you wanted time with your family before heading out west, and that you aren't taking new clients. But her Letter to Acquire is unlike anything I've seen come over in a while. She seems really nice too."

"Nice." Chris frowned. "That won't commit me to a client."

"I know, but before you determine anything about Ms. Charles, Heather is here demanding to see you. She even asked the woman if she minded taking a few minutes of your time."

"What?" He got back to his feet, running his hand across his face.

She nodded. "Yes, and you're almost thirty behind schedule. I may need to reschedule your call with MGM since you're close to quitting time."

Chris closed the folder on his desk. He wished that leaving Heather this morning had been as easy. He took in a deep breath and smoothed his tie. "I can't deal with this shit today. Damn Ava. If she hadn't been the referral, I would've declined this meeting." He started then stopped on his way to the door. "You saw the contract. Who can it be assigned to?"

Shayla became the night before Christmas silent. Completely out of character for his assistant, who always had something to add when he considered new clients. He turned and looked at Shayla.

She finally shrugged. "I don't know, Chris. I think you should grant her more serious consideration. The woman is being offered a six-figure contract after submitting a story to a contest. You and I both know that is beyond rare, and the story is probably worth more. Seraphina also has that look. New York will love her."

Chris folded his arms. "Seraphina," he questioned, weighing her words, and he could see that somehow the woman on the other side of his office door had impressed Shayla, which was hard to do. "How'd you get on a first-name basis so fast? You've never had a problem reassigning before."

"I told you she's nice." She paused. "Do you want me to send Heather in? She seems a little needy."

He shook his head. Lately, everything with Heather turned into an argument. He didn't want his professional space tainted with the negative energy he was sure would permeate after they spoke. "No, I need to at least address Ms. Charles. She's waited patiently. Afterward, I'll walk Heather out and come back for the consult."

They walked out of Chris's office and proceeded down the hall. Before Chris could step out of the corridor, Heather rushed him. Her smile greeted him bright and wide. However, he knew better, and it couldn't erase their blowout from last night.

"Baby." She pouted so loud, he drew back. She wanted something, ideally to make up. Only he wasn't in a forgiving mood, considering the words they'd exchanged last night when he refused her ultimatum. "Can we talk?"

"I need to address my waiting client." He peeked over Heather and saw the woman seated with her head down, long silky hair curtaining her face as she furiously typed on her phone. His gaze narrowed. Something about Seraphina Charles seemed familiar. "Give me a second and then I'll walk you out." Heather's brow cocked and her lips pursed. It was exactly the reason he would chat with her outside.

He sidestepped Heather, and strolled over to the sitting area. Before he could greet Ms. Charles, she lifted her head and looked him in the face. He went bone-rigid still.

"Carrah," he whispered. A puzzled expression settled on

his face and he glanced over his shoulder to where Shayla sat and then turned back to a girl who had always been on the outside looking in. Or was it the other way around?

Carrah stood, adjusting her dress. She avoided looking him in the eyes. Her attention floated behind him as her fingers fidgeted before she extended her hand and smiled. "Seraphina Charles, pleasure to meet you, Mr. Chennault." Her words were soft, even though her eyes pleaded hard with him to continue her charade.

But why? Instead of questioning her in front of Shayla and Heather, he played along. "My apologies for keeping you waiting." He extended his hand to hers and gripped it firmly.

"Please don't apologize. I'm just happy you agreed to see me."

But I didn't, he wanted to say, despite the sincerity of her words. She'd made him an unwilling accessory to her scheme. This wasn't anything resembling nice. She'd fooled Shayla.

His heartbeat sped up, pumping anger with adrenaline to remain alert. He was wary of this visit and the lengths she had gone through, and still was to maintain this façade. He knew the day was off. Never in a million years did he expect this.

Chris schooled his face clear of any emotion. "Do you mind if I take a few more minutes to resolve a personal matter? I don't want our appointment interrupted."

Carrah nodded. He spun around, took Heather by the hand, and exited the suite. Heather's mouth was moving and words were coming out as he passed the elevator doors and quickly led her down the stairs to the outside of the building. Unfortunately he heard nothing. His mind was still upstairs.

A number of scenarios began playing in his head. However, none could justify the way Carrah Andrews had slithered her way into his space.

"Chris," Heather barked, snatching her hand from his. "Are you listening to me?"

"I am not," he responded with calm and honesty while pointedly staring her in the face. He was never one to mince words...or feelings, especially once he understood what they were. "I just got off a call that didn't go in my favor. There is a prospective client upstairs. She helps me to continue making my goal of expansion reality, but I'm down here discussing personal matters that could've waited until I was done with work for today."

"You're always working," Heather snapped. "So tell me when would've actually been a good time for you."

"I asked you to stay in New York because now wasn't a good time to come visit, but you still came. Now here you are wanting to discuss the ultimatum you delivered last night of propose to you or else." He stepped back from her and slid his hands into his pockets. "My head is up there in my office. I don't have time to deliberate a marriage you know neither of us are ready for...which is why we agreed last night that you would leave this morning. Yet you're still here."

Heather rushed to him and he promptly took another step back. "I'm sorry things got a little heated last night. Sorry, Chris, how many times do you want me to say it?"

He hesitated for a second because he didn't care to become the subject of small-town gossip in case she pitched one of her fits on Main Street. However, it was time. They'd run their course. "You don't ever have to say it to me again. It's over. I really do wish you the best— Goodbye, Heather."

Chris turned away from her and quickly made his way back to his office all the while ignoring the mean-spirited words she hurled at him. The blinders were off. Grief had stalled him from seeing that they were never exactly compatible. At least all she had required up until now were fancy dinners and luxury gifts.

He couldn't give her his time, wouldn't miss the sex that was oftentimes bland, and he never considered more. Shame on him for believing she had filled a void. The truth had been staring him in the face for a while, but the discomfort of removing someone else from his life had made him ignore all the red flags. Until the ultimatum, it forced him to accept the reality that Heather had been a beautifully convenient distraction.

He pleaded with chaos to be still for the rest of the day and reached for the doorknob leading back to his suite. His prayers were rejected, and the weight he'd left downstairs found and crushed him the second he stepped inside and locked eyes with Carrah. Uncertainty halted his steps. He knew relief—it was the emotion he'd felt moments ago after telling Heather goodbye—but this feeling he had as he looked at Carrah was unrecognizable.

Chris cleared his throat. "I'm ready for you, Ca— Ms. Charles." He continued through the lobby, passing Shayla and went down the hall.

* * *

Carrah grabbed her bag, got to her feet, and followed. This wasn't the first time she'd noticed his powerful build, standing over six feet with broad shoulders perfectly proportioned between athletic and lean. The difference this time was that he was clothed in a tailored suit instead of swim trunks that had revealed him as a god crafted for war.

She pushed the image of his chiseled, golden skin from her head and thanked him for holding the door open as she entered his personal space. It lacked many of the normal trinkets that traditionally furnished an office. For the first time that she could recall, she wished to see something that would tell her who Chris Chennault really was. It was the human nature of curiosity to be in one's space and take a peek into who they were.

She wanted that now in an effort to connect with him beyond knowing that they'd spent summers ignoring each other.

"How dare you?"

The door closed behind her and she whipped around to see him staring her down. He was deceptively calm. The tick in his jaw was what gave away his irritation. Only those eyes, she had wished to avoid them.

All the girls in the Shores deemed them beautiful. She had just been too proud to admit it. In this moment that sweet mix of brown and amber seemed to see straight through her, stripping her bare naked. No one had made her feel so vulnerable and perhaps it was because the enemy would now know her battle plan.

"Are you just going to stand there like a deer caught in headlights? You know perfectly well what I mean, Carrah." He popped the button on his coat and slid his hands into his pockets. His eyes never left her.

She raised her hands in surrender and swallowed hard. "I can explain." He gestured for her to do so and then leaned against the wall. He reminded her of the men she saw posing in ads for Armani, not an attorney. Why was this even a thought? "I...I, uh, heard you were the best at contract negotiations, that is."

He huffed. "Maybe I am. That doesn't explain why you lied. Your name is Carrah Andrews, not Seraphina Charles. Why are you playing games, Carrah? I suggest you leave."

Chris pushed off the wall and brushed past her. He sat at his desk, ignoring her presence. She then contemplated leaving, actually running like hell. Except she didn't want to become a coward to her own dreams.

She lowered herself into the chair in front of his desk. His eyes burned into her, stirring regrets to life, but she had to try. "I did something that I don't want anyone else to know about. Not even Ava knows I'm here. I used her name because she's your client and I doubted you would question it."

"So you lied again. Not surprised." He reclined in his seat, never breaking eye contact. "Why me?"

Carrah's teeth tugged at her bottom lip before she glanced down at her fidgeting hands. "Because I'm running out of time and there's no one else I can go to," she said, a little above a whisper. "I wasn't blowing smoke earlier. I heard you're the best. I need your help." She finally looked up at him.

"Our families have history that make it hard for me to engage with you on this level. In this space. Additionally, in order to enter into an attorney-client relationship, there has to be trust. You lied to get into my office today and then made me complicit in your little scheme. I can't trust you. Then again, that is what crumbled the bridge over troubled waters between our grandfathers, isn't it?"

"But—"

"No buts; this is business." A hard edge touched his words. He sat up and steepled his hands atop his desk. "We can pretend this conversation never happened and resume our normal of ignoring each other, not attending the same events, or timing our arrivals to socialize with mutual friends."

Carrah had known Chris was a hard-ass. She remembered hearing over the years how he never gave in and always played to win, not caring about the casualties in his wake. Oddly she hoped this meeting would've yielded a different outcome. However, it seemed the chip on his shoulder wouldn't prevent anything except his dismissal of her.

Chennaults don't mix with Andrewses...Chris excellently upheld old sentiments. Though, if she were honest, she had too. Of all the children between the two families, she and Chris were the closest in age. They also had years of proximity to each other due to their social circles, and that time was spent preserving a generational grudge.

They both festered in the rivalry, and now Chris clung to it with an iron fist. Her desires had clouded her judgment and allowed her to make a fool of herself. No need in further rocking the boat.

Carrah stood, anger boiling over embarrassment, and was determined more than ever to find someone else to review her contract after being brushed off by Chris. She tossed her bag on her shoulder. "You know what, you're right," she spat. "*Connard*," she hissed then stormed to the door.

"*Petit petard!*"

His words froze her hand midair before she could touch the doorknob. Emotions were getting the best of her. She'd forgotten Chris understood. As children from two of the oldest Black families that were able to trace roots back to French New Orleans, quadroons, and octoroons, they had both been raised to understand the old tongue. Not to mention, their grandfathers had been best friends, college mates, and business partners before the fallout between their families.

She owned her rookie mistake and then turned to face him because she wouldn't be known as a coward. But how...how did he know the nickname that only her family used whenever they said she was being spicy?

"How dare you come into my office and insult me because

I don't give you your way," he sneered as he moved toward her. He stopped inches away, eclipsing her five-three with his dominant stature. "Were we not just on a boat together that you went out of your way to avoid talking to me…and now you demand my help? You must take me for a fool."

Her teeth smacked together. "I *asked* you for help, Chris."

"So what? People ask me for help all the time. I have the right to choose who I give it to. You're not getting it."

"Fine!" Her voice was loud, pride hurt, and dreams slipping away.

"Fine!" he shouted back.

"How foolish of me. You're exactly the asshole I thought you were." In one swift movement she opened the door and left his office. She was all out of options and time was not on her side.

Chapter 6

CHRIS PLACED THE phone on the receiver then stood from his desk and removed his glasses before wiping his face clean of the frustration from the day. It was only two thirty in the afternoon, an uncommonly early time for him to consider ending his day compared to the hours he kept while in New York. However, it was the summer, they were in the Shores, and he had promised his dad a round of golf...and Carrah Andrews had got so deep beneath his skin, until he found it hard to focus.

He glanced down at the manila folder on his desk labeled SERAPHINA CHARLES. He wouldn't bother to further review any of its contents. They were unimportant and a waste of his time just like Carrah had been in his office. Although if he was completely honest, a small part of him was curious to know the details of what was inside. What had she written to garner the attention of Hurston House? They were the mack daddy of publishing houses and everyone in the entertainment industry longed to have a client affiliated with them. Perhaps Carrah knew that, too, and maybe that was why she went out of her way to put them both through a very avoidable awkward moment.

In the end, it didn't matter. He was a Chennault and she was an Andrews. He held on to that thought, grabbed his work bag, and picked up the folder. On his way out he tossed it on Shayla's desk.

"Did you even look at it?" she questioned, forcing him to acknowledge the anger he was desperate to be rid of.

"No." He stopped walking to the door and faced her. "Nothing within that folder will make me reconsider."

Shayla shook her head while displaying a grin that mocked his decision. "So you and Ms. Charles have history? Is she an ex?"

Chris pondered her question for a minute. He did have history with Carrah, only it was not in a good way. All their lives had been spent avoiding each other in honor of the old grudge that had begun with their grandfathers. The competition between their families' companies put them at odds in the business world. Then there was the power struggle between their mothers for committee chair positions or board service for various organizations in Louisiana. Summers were always hard since friends were forced to choose who to hang with. Some of the bitterness subsided with age as they formed cliques, and then of course, with his mother's passing, but it never fully went away.

"Her name isn't Seraphina Charles. It's Carrah Andrews. And no, she's not an ex. Our families are longtime business rivals."

"Oh." Shayla recoiled a little. "I, uh...I assum—sorry."

Chris cocked a brow, watching as his trusted assistant quickly put her head down. "Assumed what?" Shayla glanced up, pressing her lips, and shook her head, but Chris wanted to know how she had jumped to that conclusion. In the years Shayla had served as his assistant, she'd ordered a handful of flowers and gifts. Maybe set a dinner reservation or acquired tickets to a basketball game for him to have a night on the town with a woman.

However, he had never paraded any of them in his professional space. He was not the type to publicly display his personal life for the world to see. Therefore, how could Shayla truly assume anything? He had to know. "Can you please answer me?"

Shayla exhaled. "She just seems like the kind of woman you would date."

His gaze narrowed upon her before he moved back to her desk. He was even more intrigued by this observation. "Explain."

"First, the woman is beyond gorgeous. She's stylish, seemingly smart, and she has that air about her like you."

"An air," he questioned, folding his arms, definitely wanting to hear more of how Shayla perceived his personality and taste in women.

"Yeah, you know, kinda stuck up but not. Refined and elegant, yet still a little down to earth. She seems more your type than—" She cleared her throat and looked back down to the folder on her desk.

"Than Heather?" He stopped at the front of her area and rested his elbow on the countertop.

Her head popped up, and they gave each other a look of knowing. "You said it."

They both chuckled. Chris relaxed a little more than usual and then decided to confide in Shayla because she had long earned his trust. He gave her the quick and dirty version of

Heather's pop-up visit and the ultimatum. She was the sounding board he didn't know he needed. "Well, for the record, we broke up."

"I saw this coming after the *Songbird* premiere dinner." She sighed while Chris began thinking back to four months ago. He'd been invited to Los Angeles by a client to attend a celebratory dinner for the launch of his new television show, for which Chris had negotiated a stellar contract. By coincidence, Heather booked a gig the same weekend in Los Angeles and then crashed the dinner. "She wanted more than you could or would give her. No breakup is easy though. Are you okay? You dated her the longest."

"Better, actually. It will be easier to focus on the new office." Instead of dodging marriage demands, he thought to himself.

"And you're really not going to take on Ms. Char—I mean Ms. Andrews?"

He straightened from the counter and firmed the grip on his bag. "That's not good for business. Now, I've got to get going before I'm late for tee time with my old man."

Chris disregarded the disappointment on Shayla's face as they exchanged goodbyes. He restarted to the exit, but before he could leave, he had to ask one last question. She always gave it to him straight even when she didn't agree. "Shayla, am I an asshole?"

She smiled. "Did she call you that?"

Chris nodded.

Shayla cackled, slapping her desk, and then she bent over, covering her mouth. "I knew I liked her," she managed to get out despite the laughter clogging her voice. Her hysterics continued a few more seconds before he crossed his arms, demanding an answer.

She stood upright. Her face tightened to match the seriousness of his. "Umm, well, uh...not to me. You can be, though, especially when you're negotiating."

"The fact you find it funny is concerning." He managed his annoyance and then left the office for the day.

The next twenty minutes Chris took his time, driving along the winding road leading to the outskirts of town. New York and Los Angeles traffic was never this easy, and neither city could compete with the beauty of the Florida countryside. On one side of the road was the lake, nestled against the hills rising to the east. The other side was anchored with canopied oaks full of Spanish moss.

He began to chuckle as he recalled times as a child when he and his friends would climb the massive trees or simply pull moss from the branches and put it in water to watch it turn green. Those were simpler times, full of good memories. His soul settled and he took a deep breath, finding appreciation in the life he always found when he visited the Shores.

Picturesque rural landscapes faded away and the vast golf course of Dogwood Country Club began unfurling. Chris turned off the highway, and rolled over the cobblestone bridge into the entrance of the members-only facility. Irony was never lost on the fact that when his great-grandparents first discovered the Shores, they were denied membership into the prestigious club because of the color of their skin.

Not an uncommon practice for Black people to be turned away back then, but today as he parked and then walked up the steps to the main building, he was given salutations that he wished his great-grandparents could've experienced. Although they may not agree with the exclusivity that was in practice since they had endured segregation of space not just by race but also complexion.

Chris suspended the past, then quickly ducked inside and started toward the men's locker room. He checked his watch and picked up the pace. He wasn't in the mood to endure his father complaining about missing tee time, which would open the door for him to start lecturing on the temporary office for the summer, family legacy, and settling down.

"Hey, Chris!" The bubbly feminine voice he'd tried to reach since this morning called to him. He backtracked a few steps then turned to see Ava waving. Instead of her signature ripped blue jeans and plain T-shirt with two cameras hanging around her neck, she had conformed to club standards and was adorned in a collared shirt that matched her flower-patterned jogger shorts. Her racquet seemed more like a prop, and the only thing that told him she wasn't just at the club for tea or a cocktail.

"Aves! I messaged you earlier." He went and hugged her. "I'd heard you were finally back in town? Surprised to see you at the Wood. Thought this place was too bourgeois for you."

"The ball is in a few days. I couldn't miss." She giggled as he released her from his embrace. "As for this place"—she rolled her eyes—"I was dragged here. You said you messaged me?"

"Yeah, earlier." He cleared his throat. He understood that she had no knowledge of Carrah's machinations. "Don't worry about it now. I got it resolved."

Her hand went to her chest. "Thank God. Super sorry. I dropped my phone last night and cracked the screen. It's being repaired n—"

"Ava, you ready?" Carrah called, interrupting their conversation as she emerged from the ladies' locker room adjusting the pleats of her bright white tennis skirt. At the Dogwood, fashion and etiquette went hand in hand, and a girl like Carrah would never miss a chance to honor the old ways of dressing in crisp whites for tennis. She defined prestige and embodied a confident attitude that commanded the hallways of the club. It was the very same cockiness that let her assume she and Chris could enter into a business arrangement after years of sitting on opposite sides of church.

When she finally looked up, her eyes locked with his. "Chris," she snipped and came to an abrupt stop.

Ava cleared her throat. "Be nice, Carrah," she mumbled.

Chris clenched his teeth together and felt his jaw tighten. It did nothing to counteract the way his temper roared to life. No one should have to tell a grown-ass, well-brought-up woman to be nice. Especially one who had been in his office earlier begging for help.

"I'm used to it." He shrugged, pretending that she wasn't under his skin while prying his eyes away from Carrah, and he focused back on Ava. "Anyway, Belfast, how was it? You wrapped up production early."

"For once," she gushed. "I trekked over to the Dark Hedges and then Giants Causeway like you recommended. It was breathtaking even for me, and I've seen a lot of places in this gig. I'll admit I still haven't found a place that compares to here."

"I was literally thinking the same on my ride over here from downtown," he confessed.

Ava nodded. "Yeah, but everything was good. I think my work may have led to a director of photography role on an indie film. Of course, my agent will be sending the contract over to you if that happens. So keep fingers crossed."

Chris held up his hand and crossed his fingers. His smile went flat as out of the corner of his eye he saw Carrah fold her arms and pout as though he was inconveniencing her. She always did this whenever they were in a space vying for the attention of the friends they shared.

"I'm going to the courts," Carrah announced.

Chris glanced over and watched as she placed the racquet bag on her shoulder and began walking in the opposite direction. "Best of luck, Seraphina," he called, unable to resist himself from taking a dig at her.

"Seraphina?" Ava asked, whipping her head from Chris to Carrah, who became still. "Who's that?"

He could've—should've—outed her. She deserved it. Instead he tilted his head at Carrah. "I'll let her tell you."

* * *

Carrah cut her eyes back at Chris. She balled her fists, turned on her heel, and stormed out the door. She refused to play his game, because if she had, she might've gone to where he stood and slapped the smug expression from his face.

Once outside, she took in the fresh lake air. This was all her fault. Had she just accepted the life she was supposed to lead…or disregarded ancient family advice of always having a legal eagle review important documents and signed the contract from Hurston House, she would've never needed to go to his office.

"What was that all about?" Ava's voice pulled her from a downward spiral.

Carrah looked up from the ground to her friend and then restarted her journey along the path lined with fuchsia bougainvillea until they stopped at the door of the reserved court. It was getting hard to pretend that the life she led and the one she wanted were doomed to collide and leave her damaged.

Make Mama happy. Make Daddy proud. Work by your siblings' side because nothing is more important than seeing Noir survive.

"Nothing." She faked a smile, and again recited the mantra that had been repeated to her a thousand times. Only this time it didn't boost her confidence. In fact, their little family saying hadn't helped in a while. If anything, it reminded her that she wasn't the priority. "Ava, you know Chris and I have never really gotten along."

Ava sighed. "True, except that was different. I know your families have not so good history. But the both of you are usually a bit more nonchalant in honoring that whole coexist-from-a-distance philosophy. That back there was trending intense. And who the hell is Seraphina?"

Carrah gazed everywhere, omitting Ava's direction. She wasn't sure if she could stare her friend in the face and tell her that she'd lied and manipulated Chris's assistant by using Ava's name and client relationship to get an appointment with him, or that it seemed like all the chemistry degrees meant nothing anymore. Of course, there was also the pride she possessed that refused to let anyone, especially a free spirit like Ava, see her cowering to family loyalties instead of chasing her own ambitions.

Only, she and Ava had been friends since they could ride tricycles. Ava wouldn't stop asking. Maybe it was better out than in.

"Promise me you won't tell anyone?" Ava dropped her hand from the court door. "Not Reese, Peyton, or Quinn."

"Ohh, this sounds juicy." Ava stalked her, scanning over Carrah before her face went through a myriad of emotions, which started scrunched and ended with a dropped jaw. "Wait! Did you and Chris...umm...did y'all bump uglies?"

Carrah threw her hand over Ava's mouth. "Why are you being so loud? You want the whole club to hear?" Carrah lowered her hand to see a silly grin all over Ava's face. "No, that's not something we would ever do!" The thought made her hot all over. She had never been allowed to view Chris in that way and she surely wouldn't start now. He'd already dismissed her and moments ago decided ridicule was a fitting punishment for daring to ask him for help. "Why would that be your first thought?"

Ava reached for Carrah's arm to prevent her from moving away. "Because y'all were being weird. He's never goaded you and you've done far worse."

"He's upset because of what I did today, and honestly, I don't know if I blame him." Carrah sighed then gestured to an empty bench that was a few feet away.

For a few minutes they sat in silence. Carrah weighed her words. What could she...or should she say without being judged? Confessing that her earlier manipulation was why Chris antagonized her was shameful.

Worse was knowing that she'd been wrong all those years ago when she'd negatively criticized Ava's decision to follow her dreams and become a photographer. Carrah's young nineteen-year-old mind had determined snapping pics wasn't as viable a career as becoming a chemist. She now knew better.

The friend sitting next to her had always wanted to travel the world and take pictures of breathtaking landscapes. Ava did it for a living and loved being on movie sets in remote locations across the globe, where she captured the imagery that helped tell stories viewed on the big screen. Ava had conquered her dreams. Too bad Carrah hadn't realized hers until now.

"What happens to a dream deferred?" Carrah whispered.

"Are you asking me or reciting Hughes?" Ava replied.

Carrah dropped her racquet bag and slumped in the bench, still refusing to make eye contact. "Mine was put on hold and I didn't even know it. I was so busy fulfilling everyone else's that I forgot about my own until my mother got sick." She finally looked over to Ava, who was already staring at her.

It was clear Ava didn't know how to respond. Carrah didn't

know if she expected her to or not, so she continued. "We didn't know if she would make it. That birthday party meant more than anyone knows, and to cope with it all, a therapist suggested journaling."

"Oh my God, Carrah." Ava grabbed her hand and held it tight. "Why are you just now saying something? I had no idea Ms. Camille was sick."

Carrah released a small, patronizing smile. "You've lived alongside this circle long enough to know the answer."

Ava nodded. "Pride will always come before the fall, as my father says." It was Carrah's turn to nod before she responded with a hushed yes. "Did the journaling help?"

"It did. I escaped from the reality of my mother facing death. Most important, I stopped focusing on what everyone else wanted from me and rediscovered how much I love writing." Carrah felt her cheeks fill as genuine happiness coursed through her veins. "One night after I'd tucked Mom into bed, I went to my computer and realized that I'd written something like eighty thousand words."

"Serious!"

"As a damn heart attack." Carrah giggled. "A few women in my support group that I formed bonds with while caring for Mom read my journal-slash-story and suggested I submit it to this little contest. It was meant for me to get feedback. Next thing I know, an editor from this publishing house wants to acquire my story."

Ava let go of her hand and hugged Carrah tight. A deep-seated joy unlike anything Carrah had ever experienced stirred within her hearing Ava's congratulatory words. There had not been anything in a long time to make her feel so full, but writing did. The hope and satisfaction she'd discovered in creating a happily ever after was the main reason Chris's rejection stung so much. It felt like he was taking something away from her when the truth was he owed her nothing.

Ava released Carrah. She grabbed her shoulders, scanning her a dozen times. Her smile slowly fell. "I think I know what happened. You went to Chris for help and he said no because of all the family drama?"

The hope she'd held on to last night while plotting to visit his office floated into the void. "Yeah, something like that," she confessed. "Only I lied, said my name was Seraphina Charles, and that you referred me. He was totally caught off guard."

"Oh shit." Carrah nodded in agreement of Ava's words. "He's the consummate professional. The moves he's made in the industry at such a young age dictate as much. Now I see why he was so indifferent toward you." Ava shook her head and stood. "Well, it's your fault. Why didn't you say something to me sooner instead of using my name to manipulate him?"

Carrah jumped to her feet. "I'm sorry. I should've asked or told you last night when everyone was singing his praises. I didn't know how."

"Because your family doesn't like his? You've got a lot of nerve, Carrah."

"Our families don't like each other…You're taking his side? Wow, I thought you were my friend."

"I'm friends with both of you. Despite the fact that I've seen you go in the opposite direction of him or avoid being out with everyone because he's there. I also heard he attempted to be nice to you when y'all went out on Dunc's boat, but you remained antisocial. Whatever the grudge is between your families, you seem to carry it harder than he does."

"That's not true!"

"It is, and you know it. And since we're friends, I will say this to you honestly. I'm proud you found the courage to rediscover who you are and write your story. However, you don't deserve his help." Ava turned from Carrah and went to the court. "Come on. Get off your entitled butt, so I can beat it."

Carrah lifted her head as is if the shame suffocating her didn't exist. "You really still want to play? You seem mad at me."

"Humph." Ava rolled her eyes then came back to the bench and pulled Carrah up. "Me being upset over you being your typical spoiled brat self does nothing to help this situation. Had the both of you known each other better, what you did wouldn't have upset him so much and how he reacted wouldn't have you in your feelings."

"Perhaps, but I'm in no condition to play you right now. Let alone win." Carrah winked.

"Precisely why we should play." They both giggled, breaking down the tension that had formed around them. "I've never beat you and this may be my only chance."

"Fine, but if I beat you, no whining." Carrah unzipped her bag and removed the racquet. She twirled it in the air as she stepped onto the court. "I'm sorry for using your name to gain access to Chris in his professional space."

"Don't apologize to me," Ava said over her shoulder as she went to her side of the court. "Say sorry to him. My guess is you called him some mean name or said something spiteful when you didn't get your way after showing up to his office and expecting years of family drama to be brushed under the table for your benefit."

Carrah offered no reply. She had done exactly what Ava said, and had never contemplated giving Chris an apology until now.

"I know you too well, Carrah Andrews," her friend teased. "Now, serve the ball, and apologize later. You owe him that much."

Chapter 7

HIS OLD MAN whistled as Chris brought down the golf club. "Boy, where the hell is your head?"

Chris adjusted the club in his hand before passing it to the caddy. He looked back over the green then peripherally at his father, Chauncy Chennault, rubbing the back of his neck.

"A lot happened at work today, Dad."

"Well, that's the problem," his father grumbled as he moved to take his turn at the tee. He took a practice swing then faced Chris. "The Shores is where we come to unwind. I've brought you here since you were old enough to walk and you never saw me shuffling meetings or pushing paper."

Chris adjusted his cap and glanced back out into the distance. "You did do work here. You still do."

"I take a phone call or two. You brought your whole damn office here like them folks can't live without you."

Chauncy bent at the knees and finally took his real swing. They both watched in awe as the ball sailed through the air, landed, and then rolled into the hole. The smile stretching across his father's face was priceless. He'd take a beatdown on the green from his dad any day to see him this way. "Gosh durn shame your old man whipping your butt." They both chuckled. "Sure it's work? Chloe told me that girlfriend of yours left out mad and in a hurry."

Asshole. The word made his skin burn and irritation was starting all over again. He still couldn't believe Carrah had called him that to his face. His run-in with her inside the club was no better. Heather was the least of his concerns as he pondered the way Carrah had lied, and then waltzed into his office expecting his help. The woman had a lot of nerve considering that, for the better part of his life, he remembered her going out of her way to avoid him. Until now, because she needed something. However, he'd spend eternity in Siberia before she got anything from him.

"Heather and I are done."

"Glad to hear it." His father's smooth fair skin crinkled at the eyes as he traced his silver beard.

"Glad to hear it? I thought you liked her."

"Son, she was easy on the eyes and that's it. That young lady lacked appreciation of the arts, which your mother loved. Her conversation held no depth, she was caught up in thinking designer labels spoke wealth, and she was without the right pedigree." His father frowned. "She would have had you—us—embarrassed around the company we keep. You dodged a bullet."

Chris knew exactly what his father meant. A woman like Heather had not technically been born into the right family by old guard standards. She had not attended certain schools or held membership in social organizations that catered to their kind of people. Heather had surely never summered in the

Shores or on the Vineyard until her pop-up days ago. However, Heather had always been honest to a fault. It was more than he could say for Carrah, who could easily meet his father's lengthy old guard requirements had her last name not been Andrews.

Did pedigree and legacy really matter? For his mother, it was everything. She'd devoted her life ensuring Chris, Chloe, and Carter went to the right schools, had membership in certain organizations, and were prepared to be future leaders. Even if he could convince his father otherwise, he, too, realized he'd dodged a bullet in breaking things off with Heather.

Although, he was certain she didn't feel the same. Heather had called and messaged him nonstop since they parted ways earlier, begging him to reconsider the breakup. It was the most unattractive thing she had ever done aside from the fact that she refused to apologize for the way she had treated Ms. Watson.

Ms. Watson was like a second mom to Chris and his siblings. She had been a rock to them when their mother took ill and after she passed. Seeing Heather treat a woman he loved and respected as a second-class citizen agitated him. Ironically, it was his defense of Ms. Watson that led to the ultimatum Heather delivered since she believed Chris was supposed to take her side after Ms. Watson refused to cater to her beck and call.

Those ugly insults she hurled at him as he left her in the parking lot would not be soon forgotten either.

Something about the way the day started foreshadowed his sour mood. If only he'd known then who Seraphina Charles was. It's possible he could've avoided one ill-fated episode and the overwhelming frustration that rode him like a witch on a broomstick.

Chris went to the golf cart and slouched behind the wheel. He'd known Carrah all his life, albeit from a distance, but she'd never grated his nerves this bad with the little antisocial stunts she'd pulled over the years. He also had an appreciation for the world of the Black elite, which had forced him to engage in her scheme and was now oddly reminding him of why Carrah was the type of girl he was expected to share his father's legacy with. Except, she was not an option…never would be unless he wanted to experience the kiss of death. The same could be said of Heather. So now, he was trying to figure out why his father's words stung?

He gazed out into the distance before watching his father make his way back to the cart. Before his dad could claim the passenger seat, Chris blurted, "Nice of you to finally tell me your true feelings."

Chauncy recoiled. "You stopped listening." They looked at each other. "After Morehouse and Harvard, you thought you knew everything. Need I mention how you turned your nose up at the company to be a celebrity attorney?"

"I'm an entertainment attorney," he corrected his father. It wasn't the first time his father downplayed the serious work he did within the music, film, television, sports, and publishing industries by throwing the *celebrity* word around. Chris enjoyed the thrill of negotiating a deal as much as he did providing legal counsel on asset management, intellectual property, copyright, or trust and estate planning. He had pride in his full-service boutique firm, which was rapidly expanding and growing his reputation in the entertainment industry.

Although he was spread a little thin from dabbling in sports and modeling more than he cared to, the expansion would soon allow him to focus on his passion for television, and film. He longed to represent more clients that looked like

him who created content for consumption. It was the only way
to achieve much-needed diversity.

"Besides, you have Miles," Chris continued as he gritted
his teeth and then pushed the gas pedal down, thrusting the
cart forward while jerking his father back into his seat. "I still
consult for the company and often provide legal advice. Why
is that not good enough?"

"Miles is my nephew. His gifts are in research and development. He lacks business sense but is a chemical genius. You
are my son, my legacy. My father passed the company to me
and I want to do the same for you. Why is it so hard for you
to understand that it would mean everything to me to see you
running our empire?"

Chris held his tongue. He didn't know how to respond.
Lately his father had been making comments over his choice
to pursue law and open his own firm as opposed to taking up
the mantle for Chennault Cosmetics. He knew he was capable of leading the organization. Only, he'd found a sweet spot
with entertainment law. He worked with famous people,
went behind the scenes of production studios, and received
music and books before they went to market. He enjoyed a
world where as one of the few Black men in the field he had
the opportunity to make a difference for inclusion and equity
of minority entertainers. Chennault was old, and stuck in its
ways. And…Chris wasn't sure if he could be in a place that had
taken so much from him.

His mother had lived and breathed Chennault to the point
where she ignored her health. Her creative genius coupled
with his grandmother Olina Chennault's vision for creating
makeup that enhanced the varied skin tones of Black women
while affirming a Black woman's beauty, kept her up many
nights. Days were no better, and the arguments she had with

his father over the direction of the company were never fun to hear. It was the reason she had supported Chris when he decided to forge something new and create his own legacy.

He missed her, and if she had been here now, she would've erected barriers to the *fulfill your family duty* conversation that he felt had been lingering on the horizon.

Silence sat between them like a patient old woman. The quiet stretched on even as they continued the game. After his father took his last winning swing at the eighteenth hole, he strolled over to Chris and wrapped an arm around his shoulders. They started back toward the cart with each one restrained from speaking as though they were afraid of saying the wrong thing.

Finally his father broke the silence. "My dreams are not yours. I know that." His father's arm slid from his shoulders and they faced each other. "I promised your mother I would not force you into the company, and I won't. I'm sorry, it's just I can't help wishing you were there with me, especially now that she's gone."

"I understand. I miss her, too," Chris admitted. "Maybe one day." He shrugged and it produced a smile from his old man.

"As long as you continue to review our important contracts—"

"You have my word, Dad."

His father nodded, gesturing for them to make their way back up to the clubhouse. "Let's go grab dinner. Maybe make some trouble at the card table?" Chauncy nudged Chris with his elbow.

Right after they loaded up and were preparing to take off, the blaring sound of a horn came from behind. Chris and his father turned around only when they heard his name being called. To his surprise, he saw his brother Carter, riding along with his best friend, Gavin Lancaster, and his younger brother, Xavier. They zoomed up beside them and slammed on the brakes.

"What in God's green earth are you fellas doing riding around the course like that?" Chauncy puffed, abandoning his passenger seat and going to stand in front of the other cart. Chris didn't miss the menacing stare aimed at his brother. "You gonna have them white folks ready to toss us out of here."

Carter climbed down from the cart. "Chill, Dad. We pay our money just like them." He then pointed into the distance where a golf cart full of white boys were riding around being loud.

Chauncy watched. Instead of this relaxing him, his frown became harder. "We aren't them, Carter. Have you learned any—"

"Dad," Chris barked, leaving his seat and going to his father's side. He motioned for his brother to stop talking.

"Sorry, Mr. Chauncy, you're right. My parents would say the same." Gavin offered an apology, attempting to smooth over the tension as he gave Chris a sideways glance.

Everyone held their breath and watched as Chris's dad mumbled under his breath while making his way back to his seat. Carter made praying hands and mouthed, *Thank you Jesus*, while Chris and the others held back the urge to laugh. This was not the day to antagonize Chauncy Chennault.

"What's up?" Chris finally asked Gavin over a bubble of laughter.

Gavin cleared his throat, hardly able to suppress his humor. "Typical summer shenanigans. You down for a guys versus girls kickball game?"

Chris cackled. "What? We haven't done that in like ten, maybe eleven years."

"I know." Gavin released a chuckle. "The girls thought it would be fun. I mean, the whole gang is here. Quinn texted us all, but you didn't respond. She's trying to round up the girls now. We're thinking the south lawn. You in?"

Not this time. The words almost rushed from his mouth while he ignored his brother's cheesy grin. If the girls were organizing, then Carrah would be there and she'd been more than exhausting for one day. Then, of course, in front of all their mutual friends, he knew they would slip into that *our families are rivals* mode and have everybody on eggshells.

Chris glanced over his shoulder at his father. He'd promised to spend time with him. Therefore, he'd sit this one out. "Nah, I'm good. Dad and I were about to grab something to eat."

"Bruh," Carter boasted, "they're in tennis skirts." He slapped fives with Xavier.

"Who is they?" Chris asked flatly. "Gav mentioned Quinn, and I've only seen Ava and Carrah here. Are you trying to keep their company?" He snickered. "A little old for you, don't you think?"

Chagrin flashed across his brother's face. "Age ain't nothing but a number," Carter said boldly. "The girls y'all's age are fine. Especially Carrah!"

"Don't forget Chareese and Ava. That whole little crew," Xavier added.

"Don't let Dunc hear you say that. You're literally escorting his sister this weekend at the ball and Reese is his girl even if he hasn't said it out loud." Gavin side-eyed his brother longer than what was normal before he focused back on Chris. "It's the usual suspects plus a few girls these knuckleheads' age like Destiny, Alexandria, and Whitney."

Chris heard Gavin, but he was still processing his brother's bold proclamation. He refused to look over his shoulder at how his father might have reacted. Thank God the words Chauncy probably had for his youngest son would be on reserve until they were home out of the public eye.

While it was true that all the families that summered in the Shores annually were aware a rivalry existed between the Chennaults and the Andrewses, most attributed it to business competition. Chris had naively assumed the same until he was a teenager and made the mistake of saying that Carrah was pretty. His mother quickly told him that pretty things were poisonous like their father. From that moment, he understood that the distaste his parents held for Carrah's family extended beyond the backstabbing that had occurred over three decades ago.

The summer months had always placed them in proximity due to their closeness in age. Hence, they were forced to share friends or sometimes miss experiences. The limited interactions untied the blindfold of youth and proved his mother right. He'd learned to keep his distance, and Carter needed to as well. There were rules he need not forget.

"Chris." His dad called him closer to the cart. There was no surprise that Carter's comments had drawn his ire. Chris released a long breath and went to his father's side. "It takes more energy to stay mad than it does to have fun. I don't want you boys to end up like me...or your mother. Grudges of the father don't have to be weights for a son. Family pride aside, gone on and have fun. You just said you had a long day and maybe time with the people you've got into trouble within the Shores may help you unwind. This is why we come here and have every year since you were old enough to walk."

"But—"

"*Pas de mais.*" His father's hand sliced the air. "Gavin," he called around Chris, "your old man here?"

"Yes, sir. He's up in the lounge," Gavin replied.

Chauncy and Chris met eye to eye. "See, I'm good. Besides," his father chuckled, "if that girl is anything like Camille, she doesn't have time for Carter." He howled in laughter, slapping his leg as he moved from the passenger side and sat behind the wheel.

"I'll see you back at the house tonight. Thanks for the round of golf...and make sure your brother doesn't make a fool of himself. You hear?" He pointed at Chris, winked, and then pulled off.

Chris wished to ride his father's train of thought. The man loathed everything about the Andrewses, and yet he was encouraging them to spend time in a place where they were knowingly present. He doubted old age was making him soft. If anything, he was willing to bet that his actions were senti-mental, considering the impacts left behind by his mother.

"Y'all ready?" Chris asked the lot of them as he made his way to Gavin's golf cart. The second they confirmed, he hopped on with them and said, "We better win."

"They're girls," Xavier and Carter said at the same time.

Gavin slammed on the brakes. He and Chris turned, look-ing skeptically at their younger brothers. "Do me a favor baby, bro," Gavin said. "Never repeat that sexist shit again. The women you reference are not at all average."

Chris shook his head as Gavin began driving again. "Nooo. They're like that tribe Wonder Woman hails from when it comes to competition."

"Hell yeah!" Gavin burst into laughter. "Kickball is just the start. They may act all sweet and proper, but they go hard. Be prepared."

Chapter 8

CARRAH STRETCHED HER eyes to the other side of the field and saw all the guys in a jocular mood, including Chris. His disposition clearly seemed to have improved from when she'd run into him earlier, and she was grateful because her intuition had already told her he would be present. After all, every friend they shared stood somewhere on the grassy plain. This would be one of those rare occasions where they silently agreed to coexist from a distance for their friends.

She wondered if Chris was thinking the same. Either way, the thought made her ponder Ava's criticisms. Especially as she studied the guys and noted his younger brother, Carter, was also present. She had helped Carter several times in preparation for the Debutante Ball, and had never once felt the urge to avoid him in spite of the differences between their families.

"We're two girls short," Reese huffed as she came to Carrah's side.

Carrah shifted her line of sight. She scanned the other

recreational areas, but didn't see anyone they could ask. "Chloe and Summer were at the tennis courts when Ava and I were there earlier."

"They're still there. Gav doesn't want Summer to join and I assumed that two of the Chennault crew may be more than enough for you."

"Gav doesn't dictate who plays on our team." Carrah glared over at Gavin slapping fives with Reggie, the youngest of the Caldwell bunch, and Lockhart, scion of the oldest Black-owned newspaper in the Southeast. They were friends who Carrah had played with forever, but they always preferred the boys' team for these competitive games. "What did Summer do to him?"

Reese shrugged. "I think Gav thinks she wants him. But homegirl is after Chris." Reese hit Carrah with the *girl let me tell ya* look. "Has been ever since our debut."

A pulling sensation sat at the bottom of Carrah's stomach. She spotted Chris on the other side doing high knees then whipped her attention back to Reese. Summer Bradshaw was pretty, but only cared about landing a rich husband. A Southern socialite in her own right after abandoning her professional career to be a permanent fixture at every gala and fundraiser. Essentially any event that allowed her to orbit money daddies while riding on the coattails of her family's society status. Summer wanted to be the epitome of the old guard Black elite, and some rich boy's trophy wife.

No wonder she had her sights set on the oldest of the Chennault siblings. Christopher was a prime candidate. Aside from his successful firm, his family had been millionaires since before Jim Crow. The Chennault family's generational wealth was as iconic as Madam C. J. Walker's. It had been the subject of case studies, and always made Chris, Chloe, and Carter well-desired plus-ones.

However, it was none of her business who liked Chris. And yet she found herself comparing the woman from his office to Summer and then to herself. Model chick and the social-ite were tall whereas Carrah was short. Heather was a mocha beauty with short hair. Summer could've passed for white with her mid-length brown hair while Carrah embodied the shades between at a solid caramel color with jet-black hair that fell down her back. All different.

Why Carrah's mind began contemplating complex scenar-ios was beyond her. She shook her head from its trance.

"That long?" Carrah finally asked. "But Cameron escorted her for debut and Gav for the Links ball."

"Cam and Gav were her parents' choices after Ms. Clau-dette said no. The woman had high standards when it came to Chris. No girl was ever good enough. Maybe Summer thinks there's a chance now that his mom is gone. She's been stalking him on social like a hussy needing new panties." They both fell into a fit of laughter. "If you're cool with Chloe, then I'm going to ask them to play." Reese waited until Carrah nodded and then they fist-bumped in agreement before Reese took off to get the extra players.

Thirty minutes later after a coin toss that gave the guys the chance to kick first, and then nearly annihilating the girls in the first inning with seven runs, the girls were eager to make a play and give their male foes some competition. The 7 to 3 score in favor of the guys had the girls on edge. They had to put some runs on the board or risk trash talk and brag-ging rights that would endure until they were probably all old and gray.

"Roll the ball, Xavier," Reese shouted, anxiously waiting her turn to kick from the home plate.

Carrah's adrenaline pumped hard. The bases were loaded

and she had to score. If Reese kicked a bomber like she was notorious for doing, then Carrah, Quinn, and Alexandria all had a chance to score. The second Carrah lunged into racing position, Gavin sent Xavier a signal that made Carter, Reggie, and Lockhart back up in the outfield while he and Chris crashed forward. She read their strategy like a bestseller.

They wanted to catch Reese's ball and then cut Carrah off from making it home. It was smart and achievable since the girls had only one out.

"Tag up!" Carrah called back to Quinn. "Give it to him." She then yelled to Reese from third base, "We're ready! They aren't winning today."

"Okay, Seraphina," Chris jeered, mocking Carrah from second base and then clapping his hands, "let's go."

Carrah's eyes narrowed at him as she bit her tongue and focused on the pitcher. She would claim a run today.

Xavier released a bumpy ball that zoomed down the line to Reese. Without hesitation, Reese ran toward the ball, kicked it with all her might, and sent it up into the sky behind the outfield players.

Carrah took off running down the base line. The girls behind home plate were screaming cheers and frantically waving her in. She pumped her arms harder, pressing forward, and then all of a sudden it felt like her feet were pedaling air, and before she knew it, her face was in the grass. Carrah rolled to her back and looked up at the sky before her vision was clouded by her teammates and a few of their opponents.

Tears filled her eyes, but she didn't know if it was from the pain throbbing in her right ankle or the embarrassment of everyone seeing her eat dirt. She turned her head to the side, wiped her eyes, and spit. Yes, she wanted to answer them that she was physically fine. But she was also mad as hell. When she finally sat up, she saw that Reggie was kneeling over her and Chris stood in the distance holding the ball.

Her nostrils flared, blowing steam. She evil-eyed Chris and then adjusted to get to her feet, but Reggie gently pushed her back down. He began asking a ton of questions in a voice that was unfamiliar to her as his fingers pressed and touched along her lower limbs. She giggled for a second as she came to realize he'd gone full-fledged MD mode.

"Does this hurt?" He pressed at her ankle and she howled to the moon. "I thought so," he mumbled, "but why are you laughing?"

"Never," she gritted through her teeth, "heard you like this. You have a sweet bedside demeanor." She giggled again, poking fun, and he rolled his eyes.

"Carrah, quit, he's trying to help. Your ankle looks bad," Quinn scolded her.

"Who's fault is it?" Her snide tone made everyone look the other way except at Chris.

He moved closer toward her. "It was me. I threw the ball. Sorry."

"Sure," she spat back.

Reggie stood stretching his arms between them as Chris opened his mouth to respond. "Blame game won't help right now, Carrah. I need to get you up to the main club and wrap your ankle."

Pride had her in a choke hold. Everyone had just seen her crash to the ground and the bright-eyed jerk that made her feel Tiny Tim small in his office earlier had done it again. Except this time he had an audience. She pulled away from Reggie and anyone else who came to help her as she struggled to stand.

* * *

Chris had heard that Carrah was stubborn. As he watched her reject help from everyone, he came to the conclusion that her pigheadedness was unlike anything he'd ever seen. She continued to defy Reggie's medical advice and assistance from their friends. Worse was that the grimace marring her pretty face told him she was in pain. Hell, her ankle was the size of a racquetball and she was trying to walk.

The guilt over being the one to make her fall encapsulated him, and for the second time, he found himself saying sorry. She turned her nose up at him again but not before throwing daggers through his chest and then hobbling a few inches more from where they stood before she collapsed back to the ground.

He went to her and extended his hand. She slapped it away then tried getting to her feet again. "Are you going to listen to anyone?" He sneered, cursing under his breath.

"For what? The damage is done." She slowly balanced the weight of her body on her right leg until she was back upright. "I don't need Reggie's doctor's orders to see that," she yelled, pointing to a red knot that was the source of her pain, and then started limping away again.

"Let me help you." Chris shot in front of her, making himself an obstacle while trying once more to assuage his guilt.

"Absofuckinglutely not!" She shoved him hard until he was out of her way. "You could've helped me earlier. You didn't. Why now?"

The color red took over his vision. He tossed his invisible white flag in the wind. How could he keep it up after her schemes in his office and now seeing such unsavory sportsmanship coupled with spoiled behavior? Besides, she'd discarded their truce the second she placed her hands on him. So much for coexisting for the sake of their mutual friends.

"Fine." He huffed, scooping her into his arms, and continued walking in the direction of the carts. "You are seriously hard-headed. I had no idea."

"Put me down," she hissed. He shook his head no as she squirmed in his arms. "Put. Me. Down," she growled loudly.

"No!"

"I can take care of myself. I don't need charity from a guilty conscience. You did it on purpose."

"What?" He stopped and looked down into her face. Their eyes locked and then she turned her head away. "Yes, I did try to get you out." He restarted his steps. "No, I did not mean for you to get hurt."

She smacked her teeth. "You were taunting me on the field, Chris. I don't believe you."

"Then don't." He tossed her inside the first golf cart he came to and walked away.

Reese and Peyton rushed past him mouthing, *Thank you*. Ava stopped running and slowly approached him, meeting him a few feet from where the girls were clamoring around Carrah.

"Thanks for getting her butt in that cart." Ava breathed a sigh of relief as she looked around him to where all the commotion was coming from. "I know you didn't do it on purpose."

"Seriously?" Chris recoiled. "Why do you even feel the need to say that to me?" He sidestepped Ava. He didn't need an answer because it wasn't a question. And right now, he didn't have words for her or anyone else who would even think so low of his character.

Unfortunately, this was the norm or, better yet, the consequences of him attempting to please other people. He should've listened to his instincts. They'd been in overdrive, warning him to proceed through the day with caution ever since Shayla called him this morning. Had his father not jumped on the summer fun bandwagon with Gav and Carter, he'd be enjoying a meal with him now instead of loathing the very existence of Carrah Andrews.

"Chris," Chloe called to him. He gazed to where she stood next to Carter at the edge of the field. Without him giving the order, they knew they'd outlasted their welcome.

He pulled the small hill and continued past them. "Let's go."

Chloe ran to his side. "Did she at least say thank you?"

"Of course not." Chris looked over at his sister and then pressed his lips into a firm line as the three made their way to the main building.

"Was she supposed to?" Carter challenged. "I mean, bruh, you hit that girl pretty hard."

"Why are you taking up for her?" Chris blew his lid, tugging his brother by the arm so they could face each other. "You did it earlier today at breakfast and then again before the game in front of Dad, and you know how he feels about that family."

Carter snatched away from Chris. "Dad and Grandad messed it up for all of us, especially you. Chloe and I don't exactly share an age with an Andrews, but you do. And it isn't fair that they are off-limits because of junk that happened before we were even born." Carter restarted his steps. "Say what you want, Carrah has been nothing but nice to me."

Chloe and Chris looked at each other for a second and then moved to be next to their little brother. "You're just wrapped up in thinking she's some beauty queen, Carter," Chloe spat.

"Right," Chris agreed, "you need to grow up. You've got a lot to learn about women. A piece of tail shouldn't make you second-guess our family."

"It isn't. Ain't no ass that fine." Carter's nonchalant tone made Chris raise a brow. "I see where you and Clo might think that. I'm young, not dumb." He glanced from Chris to Chloe and then settled on the path ahead of them. "When I went to that first debutante practice as Alex's escort, all the women who were Mom's friends looked at me with pity in their eyes. I didn't know how to process their reaction to me or the overwhelming sadness I felt walking in without her."

Chloe reached for her brother and hugged him. The three stood in silence for a moment, tears welling in each of their eyes until Carter cleared his throat.

"Mom always talked about you being an escort at one of the most legendary debuts for the Lakeside Debutante Ball, and how beautiful Clo was during her presentation to society. She couldn't wait for me to honor our family tradition." Carter choked up and waved his siblings off. "I'm good. But I want y'all to know that the one person who gave me confidence instead of pity and pushed me to live up to Mom's legacy... even helped me practice the waltz, was Carrah. So I'm saying it again, we shouldn't suffer relationships with Carrah, Dominic, Beau, or Aubrey because Granddad and Dad didn't have good ones with their family members."

Chloe linked her elbow with Carter's, and they restarted their steps up to the club. On the other hand, Chris remained behind. He understood the emotions his brother experienced and had relived them hearing him confess to the overwhelming sadness he faced upon submitting to a time-honored tradition. The void their mother left behind could never be filled. However, he was content in knowing that someone had shown his brother an ounce of respect for how Claudette Chennault had raised them and helped Carter embrace his legacy.

Irony was not lost on the fact that it was the very woman who seemed determined to cross boundaries that had been set so many years ago. He glanced back out at the field, spotted Carrah, and the disdain he'd held for her since this morning began to morph into gratitude.

Chapter 9

"BREAKFAST IS READY."

Carrah's eyes popped open and went to the intercom speaker on the wall. Someone had been in her room. Last she checked, she'd cut off the intercom to avoid amplified commands from her parents or the house staff.

She cursed, debating a hot meal to fill her empty stomach or submission to the grogginess that wanted to pull her back under. Sleep seemed better since it had subdued the pain that was now beginning to radiate from her ankle. Only, she didn't want to further irritate her family. After sneaking into her room last night and missing family dinner, she'd received her fill of messages condemning her avoidance of them.

In slow motion, Carrah tussled with the covers as she rolled from her side to her back. The blank white canvas of the ceiling was in complete contrast to the animation of her mind. Of all the mornings she woke up in the Shores, she couldn't remember ever feeling so restless. The basement of her mind couldn't stop contemplating the contract offer about to expire from Hurston House, her ankle ached, and when she finally did drift off into sleep, her dreams were haunted by bright eyes that belonged to Christopher Chennault.

Ava was right—Carrah owed him an apology for the way she went to his office. Maybe one was in order for how she had reacted to him on the field…and she still didn't understand why she'd been so upset over him getting her to a cart when she truly couldn't stand upright. The loop of what-ifs restarted. Instead of riding it again, Carrah threw the cover off and got out of the bed.

She made quick work in the bathroom of becoming presentable for the breakfast table and then threw on a pair of sweats and fuzzy socks. She had to conceal the aftereffects of the disastrous kickball game with her friends in an effort to sidestep retelling her embarrassment. Besides, a story featuring her injury thanks to the son of her father's longest-standing rival might really trigger an all-out war.

"Morning." Carrah attempted to camouflage her grimace with a grin while wiping the perspiration from her forehead. It had taken her more than five minutes to make a one-minute journey down the stairs.

"Good morning, Auntie," Carrah's little four-year-old niece, Zoe, singsonged as she entered the full dining room.

"Smells delicious." Carrah sniffed the buttermilk of the hot biscuits at the middle of the table, kissed Zoe's cheek, and then gingerly moved to her seat at the table. The only empty chair belonged to her younger brother.

"Glad you could finally join us," her father said sweetly, smiling as she scooted in to the table and reached for the orange juice. "You disappeared after the party and then stayed hidden all of yesterday."

"Yes, I, too, am glad you could finally join us. I wanted to know if you and your friends enjoyed the party." Her mother smiled before taking a bite of creamy cheese grits, which made Carrah's mouth water.

However, the cross expression that came from Aubrey accompanied by the clink of Beau's fork being purposely dropped to his plate before he gave her a death stare made Carrah's appetite retreat. She was acutely aware that leaving the party before the cake was served and purposely avoiding them all of yesterday would draw criticism. She didn't care at the time because she had a life to figure out.

Even now as her little niece sat humming "Shoo Fly," demanding everyone's attention, Carrah felt the lyrics in her soul. She wished she could tell her siblings not to bother her. Since she couldn't outright say it, she began singing along with Zoe while fixing her plate and hoped her siblings would catch the hint.

The second Carrah opened her mouth to devour the warm, flaky biscuit she'd loaded with jam, Beau sneered, "I told you I needed reports yesterday. You didn't send them." Her hint was clearly missed and his curt tone made her wish she'd have simply told him not this morning before she sat down. Carrah set her biscuit on her plate and focused on Beau since it was clear he had more to say. "What were you doing that was more important? I've been after you for weeks to complete the product brief. I told Dad you weren't ready for this position."

"Zoe." Carrah's mother stood and walked to her granddaughter's chair. "Come with Glammy." The two made a quick escape from the room, leaving Carrah with her father, Beau, Aubrey, and Aubrey's husband, Sean, who helped manage company operations.

Beau blew a hard breath. "In case you were unaware, Noir needs this product to go to market ASAP."

Before Carrah could really feel bad for neglecting her corporate responsibility by spending the entirety of yesterday consumed by her own selfish actions, her father tossed his napkin on his plate and leaned into the table. His stern demeanor stifled the air around them, creating pin-drop silence.

He cleared his throat. "You tiptoed from the party. Disappeared all yesterday, didn't even care to reply to our messages, and then you arrive late to my breakfast table."

"Since when do you keep tabs on me?" Indignation had Carrah in a choke hold as she raised her chin in defiance before she snatched the napkin from her lap and threw it on the table.

"Since your brother told me that he's been waiting three weeks for you to submit the specs and formulation for market. Perhaps Beau was right. Maybe we promoted you too soon. I don't think you grasp how important it is for Noir to have another product ready for retail distribution right now."

"I understood the importance of new products four years ago when I started working for the company. If we are being completely honest, the epiphany hit me way before then in undergrad when I knowingly chose to use a competitor's products. Correct me if I'm wrong, but I've pitched several new cosmetics that were shot down by *all* of you."

Melvin pushed his plate to the side and scanned the table before focusing back on Carrah. "Drop the attitude. You're twenty-seven, not ten, and should be able to endure a business discussion without becoming so defensive. The bottom line is that you are brilliant at innovating and forecasting the needs of the beauty population. However, the follow-through on the admin side has not met my expectations."

"Have you stopped to consider that while everyone at this table continued with their normal day-to-day, I completed my job functions in addition to caring for Mom? Let's also remember that three years ago I recommended diversification of product lines. Had we started then, we would not be scrambling to develop and deliver. Your expectations are unreasonable."

"My darling daughter, you have always had your own opinions and I respect them. However, regardless of the way you feel, the company requires more of you right now. So, if you don't mind pausing your summer to get the product brief over with the R & D approvals, I'd appreciate it. I'm certain Aubrey would as well. There is a tremendous amount of work that goes into the product packaging and marketing campaign."

Carrah released a long, hard breath. She was deflated by the inequality of expectations. Her privilege had allowed her to leapfrog more tenured chemists and become the head of R & D. The promotion was meant to be a pacifier...a distraction for her to overlook them saying no to her concepts for new fragrance, hair, and skin care products. If only they had listened then instead of granting her false authority now.

The reality punctured Carrah and forced her to accept that her family's business was taking priority over her life, again. She shouldn't care more for a manuscript that hadn't given her anything. Not when the essence of Noir, which is what gave them everything, relied upon her for the future. She conceded. "Of course, Daddy, right away."

She avoided eye contact with her siblings, who wore self-satisfied grins from witnessing her submission to their father's authority. Any other time she might've argued and told both Aubrey and Beau how to go to hell with gasoline draws on, but this was different.

Her father nodded, accepting her response, and then pushed his chair back from the table to get to his feet. "Oh, one more thing. Trent mentioned that you hardly had two words for him. Are you purposely trying to sabotage your future? The boy begged for your hand in marriage, he's your brother's friend, a great young man from a good family who—"

"Why are you playing so hard to get?" Beau huffed, cutting their father off with his false authority. Of all her siblings, he was the one with the grudge. He'd always been annoyed by the closeness she had to their father from sharing a love of chemistry.

It wasn't a coincidence that he questioned her promotion or failed to support the products she pitched. "You embarrassed Trent at our mother's celebration in front of your friends. Then again, I guess I shouldn't be surprised since you were late to lineup, missed the cutting of her cake, and can't seem to follow standard operating procedures for helping us get a product to market."

Carrah pushed up from her chair. "I'm not interested in marrying a man that can't keep his dick in his pants. Is that why your wife is asking for a divorce, Beauregard?" She mocked him, "Birds of a feather."

"Carrah!" Aubrey exclaimed while gesturing to their father. "Must you have such a filthy mouth?"

"Stop trying to dictate what and how I say it, Aubrey." Carrah glared at Aubrey. She then closed her eyes, took a deep breath, and faced her father. "You and Mom have always shown us a loving, faithful marriage. He cheated on me an—"

"Once," Beau uttered with nonchalance that made Carrah's blood boil.

"Is that what he told you?" She huffed then took in a deep breath and released it slowly to steady her rising blood pressure. None of them knew how horrible Trent really was, and she was still too ashamed to confess the emotional abuse she survived. "Why do I deserve less?"

"You don't." Her father's chin lowered to his chest as his hands slid into his pockets. His line of sight met her brother's, and it seemed odd. Like they were communicating something she wasn't allowed to know. "However, you do have to play nice. At least this weekend...your brother invited him to a seat at our table for the ball."

She swallowed hard, wishing she could sprint from the room, except her injury made it impossible. Her ex's judgment had given her body confidence issues and sexual insecurities. She would not ever return to a man who belittled her to ensure his ego remained large.

"I will not!"

Beau's hand slammed against the table and shot to his feet. "You will because the survival of Noir depends on it. The alternative is watching the company be sold off piece by piece or us submitting to a takeover, and then you, my dear little sister, will have nothing left to inherit."

A bark of laughter escaped Carrah. She looked around the table, unafraid to challenge her brother's insanely cruel joke until she noted everyone's face was pinched tight. Aubrey glanced at the ground while Beau pressed his lips into a firm line as if to double down on his proclamation.

Carrah's knees buckled and then her ankle gave out. She gripped the edge of the tabletop, refusing to fall back into her chair as if she didn't command a seat at this table. After finally having a chance to reinvigorate the pipelines with the development of new cosmetics, she refused to be reduced to a trophy for sale.

"Explain how we are in a position where you're attempting to auction your sister to the highest bidder. Is that what financial gurus do?" Tears pooled in Carrah's eyes as she awaited his reply. "Tell me," she shouted.

Beau offered nothing. Not even an ounce of remorse etched into his face. At least her sister shed a tear. However, it wasn't Aubrey who owed her an explanation. Carrah turned to their father. He looked off for a second then manned up and met her line of sight.

"In order to keep the company afloat until you revamped the product lines for distribution, we cut a deal with BSB, and allowed them to inv—"

"Time-out." Carrah cleared her throat as her brain scrambled to catch up. "You cut a deal with Butler Savings Bank… Trent's family's bank?"

Her father nodded in slow motion. "I had to or we would've already been taken over. Everything that your mother's family worked hard to build—gone."

Beau got to his feet and moved to Carrah's side. His hand rested on her shoulder. "That arrangement was made two years ago. I'm sorry we should've told you sooner. No one expected Mom to get sick. It would've been too much at one time. We all saw how her health affected you and we couldn't demand more. But they are a bank and they want return on their investment before it is completely lost."

Carrah shrugged away from her brother. She began filling in the words he failed to say and clutched the bottom of her stomach. "I think I'm going to throw up."

"They are willing to allow time for your innovation to redefine product lines if you accept Trent's marriage proposal. The alternative is a hostile takeover. People do change, Carrah. The boy has apologized and promised it would never happen again."

Finally, after the intensity of silence constricted the walls around them, her father said, "Aimer showcased your genius while proving we were wrong to table your ideas. Only, it was already too late. Had I disregarded your sibling's jealousy of giving you too much power too soon and allowed you the creative freedom you requested, we might not be in this situation." Both Aubrey and Beau tucked their heads down, avoiding their father's gaze.

Carrah shed one tear and refused to offer more. She didn't want to sacrifice anything else. "Why me?"

"Because"—Aubrey leaned over the table—"you're the wholesome HBCU, STEM girl grad that reigned as a Zulu Queen and could've been crowned Miss America, but chose to work for the family company. You hail from one of the South's most influential families and our connections run so deep that they blanket his family's tarnished brand and messy divorce. Trent would launch into the political spotlight with instant capital with you at his side."

Aubrey's marketing prowess was undeniable. Like Jesus turning water into wine, she'd make shit smell good. Only, if Carrah hadn't ventured into therapy while caring for their mother, she would've never discovered her hidden talents. She realized her potential and wouldn't sacrifice it ever again. "Daddy, I love you and Noir. But I love myself more." There was a quake in her voice she struggled to steady. "Ironically, Trent taught me that lesson the hard way." She took a few steps back, withstanding the pain coiling around her lower leg, and turned to leave because the burden they wanted her to carry was breaking her. "Ask him how many women he slept with while we were a couple. Trent is without integrity and definitely has no loyalty, so whatever schemes you're cooking up, I hate to tell you that he isn't the man." She left the table, but then stopped as disgust nipped away at her flesh. "I won't ever compromise myself again," she called over her shoulder without looking back, "especially for an inheritance."

Chapter 10

THE DIRE STRAITS Noir faced seemed unreal. Yet, for the better of three years, Carrah had been passionate about redefining product and fragrance lines. Every idea she pitched was shot down, citing funding or bad timing. Even after the rejection, she still managed to tinker around in the lab with hopes of developing something they would greenlight for production.

And that was what happened with Aimer. Carrah had been experimenting while responding to market demands. She considered her needs as a young consumer while preserving the old ways of Noir. Through trial and error she re-created a scent she'd remembered upon her grandmother and then infused it with an exotic blend of plumeria and hints of vanilla.

Carrah gave her mother a sample for Mother's Day, and the next thing she knew, the fragrance had a limited-quantity product run. Camille had loved the scent so much that she pulled her heiress card and demanded Aimer be brought to market, where the perfume became an overnight sensation.

Its success opened everyone's eyes, especially her father's, who was blinded by Beau's ambition. Unfortunately, as Carrah found out today, it was too late.

Although now it all made sense. She understood why they had been pressing her to complete product mocks and briefs. Only, her attention was on the manuscript she'd written. Besides, there were conditions she disagreed with that linked her to a man she wanted nothing to do with. How could she possibly create?

The right thing for Carrah to do was to sit at her desk, finalize product specs, ensure the concentrations of ingredients were accurate, and double-check the suppliers of raw materials list to make the product brief complete before sending the final draft to Beau. Instead, she stumbled around getting dressed for a debutante function that wouldn't start for hours and left the house with nowhere to really go until much later.

After her mind stopped tussling with the precarious situation the company seemed to be facing and her thoughts of Beau's archaic ideal of a bride price were overridden by the lingering pain at her ankle, she found herself driving along the hidden path to the Caldwell mansion. She removed her foot from the gas and quickly texted Reggie to avoid breaking etiquette of showing up unannounced.

Once Carrah received a thumbs-up reply, she drove forward, admiring the picturesque curb appeal of the rosebushes anchoring the massive circular driveway. She parked and sat in the car, taking in the stately home until she saw Reggie dart out of the front door and down the steps toward her. His concern was evident as he popped open the driver side door.

"I told you yesterday to let me wrap your ankle. You refused and now look at you."

"Reg, could we not do this? I need your help, please. I'm in pain and the ball is in two days. I need to get into my shoes."

Reggie shook his head while extending his hand and helped her from the car. "So some high heels made you come to your senses. You absolutely have the hardest head, Carrah Andrews." He kneeled down and pressed his fingers to the soreness surrounding her foot. "Had you let me properly take care of this yesterday, maybe we wouldn't be here now...and then Chris wouldn't be all worried," he mumbled.

"Chris Chennault, worried about me"—she sucked her teeth—"hardly. He tossed me in the cart like I was a rag doll." Reggie chuckled, maneuvering Carrah until he became her crutch. "What's funny?"

He shook his head in laughter as they began making way to the steps of his home. "You were being quite ornery. I mean more than your normal. Somebody had to get you off that ankle."

Carrah wanted to pull away and get right back in her car. She didn't have time for Mister Goody Two-shoes to criticize her behavior while condoning Chris's. Except, there was a pair of Valentino heels she was desperate to sink her feet in and strut with the evening gown she'd picked for the ball. She needed Reggie to use all his medical training to help heal her foot. Therefore, she pushed his comment out of her head and hopped on one leg up the stairs, balancing against her human crutch until they got through the front door.

She plopped into the first chair she came to inside Mrs. Caldwell's opulent foyer. The space was an ode to the Southern gentry, a class their ancestors were excluded from and yet rose above. The scent of honey tickled her nose, redirecting her attention from the old-world charm of Mrs. Caldwell's blue-and-white porcelain plates hanging on the wall to an oversized pink Depression glass vase. It was full of flowers she hadn't seen in the Shores since they were teenagers.

"Your mother still grows butterfly bushes?" She pushed up from her chair, waving Reggie off from assisting her, and struggled to make way to the foyer table. She tipped her nose down to the stems and sniffed. "Mmmm...I change my mind, fresh lilac with this," she said under her breath. "I thought the Florida sun was too much for them?"

Reggie shrugged, chuckling. "I have no idea, Carrah. You really haven't stopped putting your nose into flower blooms?"

"Occupational hazard, I guess." She giggled and went back to smelling the flowers.

"As a kid, I thought you sniffing everything was cute. Grown man–physician status, please stop doing that shit before you have an adverse reaction."

She rolled her eyes at him while keeping her nose in the buds. "How else would I create perfume?" She lifted her head. "People like you think I pick flora because it's pretty or smells good and then decide to mix. It's not that simple. I have to be able to distinguish properties, fragrance, and ingredients. In your mom's arrangement, there are hints of honey and earth, which if paired with verbena, becomes a rich lemon blossom. I doubt it would become a bestseller because no one wants to smell like they're in a lemon grove. However, it could work for a home fragrance," she mumbled as her fingertips played at the blooms.

"Well, that was insightful." He huffed a chuckle. "Still doesn't change my mind."

Carrah waved Reggie away at the thrill of rediscovering a flower she had forgotten because it was like being five in the sweet shop. The lighthearted aroma seduced her muse in an unexpected way. In a moment of self-reflection, she realized she didn't want to mix the essence of flowers in her lab. She wanted to write about them being an intoxicating fragrance that made a man weak in the knees before he kissed all over his lover's body.

Romantic fiction allowed her to escape her mother's pain and her own heartbreak. It was why she wrote it. Although if she were honest, it left her with more questions as she came to realize she'd never loved Trent. He had never been a knight in shining armor or Don Juan. Carrah could count on one hand the times he'd sent her flowers and barely recalled foreplay or experiencing pleasure. Intimacy with Trent left her numb.

"Well, what do we have here?" Mrs. Caldwell's elegant voice nudged Carrah from la-la land. She untied the ribbon from her sun hat, removed her gloves, and then smothered Carrah in a hug that lingered in spicy, yet fruity notes warmed by amber. "Last time you were in my house, young lady, you started a ruckus in the parlor over a card game against Christopher and my son. What brings you here today?"

Oh, that night, she thought to herself of the first party of the summer. Carrah had almost forgotten about the way Chris and Reggie purposely teamed up against her in a game of spades. Their plan was derailed by Peyton's younger brother, who they paired her with because they thought he was a beginner. To their surprise, the boy's card IQ matched hers, and together they ran a Boston that effectively booted Chris and Reggie from the table. Needless to say, they didn't go easy and the trash-talking she instigated made it worse.

"It was all in fun, Ma," Reggie chimed in. "Carrah's always been extra in spades. She's not here for that today. She hurt her ankle yesterday and I was going to take another look at it."

Mrs. Caldwell's smile was replaced by mild panic as her

eyes scanned the length of Carrah's leg. "Oh, certainly. Why are you standing up over here if you're hurt?" She tugged Carrah by the hand, leading her to an empty chair.

"I was admiring your flowers. It's been ages since I've seen butterfly bushes." She reluctantly went, watching Reggie grin as his mom became an enforcer that allowed him to disappear from the room. "Do you grow them?"

"I do! Only in my greenhouse, though. That flower is invasive and doesn't do well in natural landscape." The older woman tilted her head and began eyeing Carrah's ankle. She stooped down to do her own examination. After all, Mrs. Caldwell had once gone by Dr. Caldwell, until she preferred duties as a mom over being on call by the hospital. "How'd this hap— You know what, never mind." She huffed as she stood back up. "Let Reggie wrap it good. Ice and elevate, take ibuprofen for the pain. You do that and you'll be able to get into your heels for the ball." She winked at Carrah and they both struggled to conceal their laughter.

"How'd you know?" Carrah asked sheepishly.

"Carrah Andrews, in two days the event our kind of people live for every summer in the Shores is happening, and you always come dressed to impress! You have since your debut. Still wish you and my Reggie had formed something beyond him simply being your friend." The older woman looked Carrah dead in the face.

Carrah had no reply. She and Reggie had been friends for so long and had never thought of each other in *that* way. Given that he was roughly two years older, he had been the kind, considerate big brother she didn't find in Beau. Clearly Mrs. Caldwell didn't see it like that.

Besides, Carrah wasn't Reggie's type. He was typically attracted to tall, thin women who valued being a trophy wife over having an accomplished career. It was a known fact that he suffered from generational delusions of being the provider.

"Nah, man. Give me thirty." Reggie's voice boomed as he reentered the foyer on his cell phone, ending the awkward moment between Carrah and Mrs. Caldwell. "Carrah's here now, finally letting me tend to her ankle."

"Who's that?" his mother snapped.

Reggie's face scrunched up at his mother and then he finally replied, "Chris."

"Oh, hello, Christopher," Mrs. Caldwell said as if Chris were standing inside her house. Unexpected knots formed inside Carrah's belly before she watched the woman point at her son and whisper, "Need I remind you that we don't tell other people's business in this house." His mother's piercing stare lingered until he nodded. "Now, I'm going to get some sweet tea and head back to my garden. I'd take you, Carrah, if you could walk good. Maybe next time."

Mrs. Caldwell winked. "Make sure it's wrapped snug, Reg. She needs the compression to drain the swelling."

"I'm aware." His gruff response was followed with a frown that only Carrah saw as his mother sauntered off. "I'll message you when I'm on my way," he said back into the phone. "Yeah, I'll tell her." Reggie ended the call then slid the device in his pocket.

He dropped down to one knee in front of Carrah and opened a large first-aid kit. A few minutes passed with him kneeling in front of her adjusting a pad under her anklebone before he pulled tape to start wrapping. While she was grateful for his care, patience was never exactly her MO.

"Tell me what?" she finally asked, schooling her voice to appear as nonchalant as possible when deep down she was curious to know what her nemesis had said.

Reggie grinned. "Doesn't matter." He huffed a slight chuckle while pulling the tape in a figure eight around the bottom of her foot. "Let's just say you may have managed to crack that hard-ass's wall."

* * *

Why did he say sorry, again? Chris pulled the phone from his ear and threw it onto his desk. Carter's unexpected confession of the kindness Carrah had shown him and how she'd lifted his spirits in the absence of their mother made him vulnerable.

In two days, his little brother would escort one of the South's most promising debutantes into society, like he had, and their mother would not be there to see it. A stuttering breath escaped him as the memory of his mother ached. Claudette Chennault hadn't lived to see her youngest son's rite of passage, which she'd carefully orchestrated to ensure the prestige associated with her legacies remained in high esteem.

In one motion he pushed up from his desk, pressed the button to ring his assistant's direct line, and said, "Cancel all meetings and no calls for the rest of the week."

The line went dead and in a heartbeat Shayla was pushing the door to his office open. "What happened? Gerron, Alonzo, MG—"

"Neither. I'm starting my weekend early. My family needs me and I need them. My mother not being here—" He cleared his throat and released a deep breath. "I may look at a few things. Don't expect any emails or calls."

"Understood. Is there anything I can prep for you?"

Chris looked around his makeshift office then down to his desk. Under a stack of papers he spotted the one folder labeled SERAPHINA CHARLES. Odd, he'd given it to Shayla the other day. She must have put it back.

Regardless, he still refused to accept the guilt that had attempted to latch on to his conscience from the second he witnessed Carrah fall to the ground. It taunted him in a way he'd never experienced before. In the same way his curiosity was now at work. Was there any escape?

"Nope," he answered Shayla—and himself—as he reached down and grabbed the manila folder and its attached documents and placed them in his bag. "I'm good." He proceeded to shut his computer down before snatching up his car keys.

As soon as Chris began moving toward the door, his office line started ringing. Shayla shot past him and answered the phone. She quickly relayed his out-of-the-office status, scribbled a message, and then set his desk phone to auto voicemail.

After which she stopped at his side and offered the Post-it she'd taken the message on. "You can deal with this when you get back. Sounds like they're finally ready to negotiate." Chris nodded, accepting the message, and then said goodbye as he left the office.

Once out in the fresh air, he relaxed as he strolled to his car and opened the door. He tossed his briefcase on the passenger seat, shrugged out of his suit coat, and rolled up his sleeves before climbing into the driver's side. The sense of relief that washed over him as he backed away from the parking space was unexpected. Spontaneity took over, and instead of turning right to bend the curve and cruise down Lakeshore Drive to where his family estate stood nestled on millionaire row, he took a left.

He skipped the fame and fortune for simplicity, crossed over some train tracks, and journeyed to where his great-grandfather had settled their family long before he built the family's summer compound. Roughly thirty minutes into the drive, the wheels of his Bentley Continental met the old dirt

road leading to his grandfather's fishing cabin, and he regretted not being in his Jeep Renegade. It was made for the rugged,
outdoorsy life. More than that, it was a symbol of freedom and
adventure, which were all he ever experienced when he came
here.

When he stepped out of the car and took in the nature surrounding him, he texted the guys a rain check, and all regrets
faded. The anxiety he had been desperate to escape retreated
and his mind settled. Only, the normal urge to suit up into
fishing gear and cast a line was replaced by an impulse to look
beyond Carrah's shenanigans and read what Hurston House
wanted. He went around to the passenger side, grabbed his
briefcase, and then went inside.

He would thank Ms. Watson later for prepping the cottage. He had not yet made it over since arriving into town and
it was clear she'd come to ensure that, when he did find time,
it was ready. After he settled in, he carefully pulled Carrah's
manuscript from his bag.

"*My Soul Remembers*," he whispered to himself, reading
the title. The hairs on his arms stood up as he slumped into
the couch and traced a finger over her pen name, Seraphina
Charles.

Chapter 11

EXCITEMENT SWIRLED AROUND the ballroom, sprinkling specks of pride, joy, and adoration. This was the night that royalty in the South gathered to celebrate a long-lived tradition. Nineteen young ladies from the most influential and elite families under the Mason-Dixon Line had made their debut into society, and the thunderous applause bringing everyone to their feet confirmed the proper occasion.

Carrah searched the room for her favorite debs: Chareese Devlin, Ava Hamilton, Peyton Daniels, and Quinn Hightower. They were all standing at their respective family tables, basking in the pomp and circumstance of the Lakeside Debutante Ball, admiring the young ladies that had come after them and joined the ranks of their unique sisterhood. It was indeed a rite of passage that was unmatched for the young ladies and their beaus.

The thought immediately refocused Carrah's attention back to the dance floor, where she found Carter Chennault.

Like many of the boys invited to be escorts on this famed night, Carter possessed the résumé. He had the looks, wealth, connections, and had long mastered the waltz along with the chivalry expected in presenting a deb. However, when the season first began, his morale had been low due to the absence of his mother.

While Carrah didn't know what it was like to have a deceased parent, she understood what it could feel like after almost losing her mother this year. Perhaps the sadness she witnessed in Carter was why she went out of her way to encourage him to do his best in a space where his mother held so much prominence. It was his duty to make Claudette Chennault's memory proud.

And then it dawned on her…*Why Carter, and not Chris?* She didn't even recall sending condolences when Ms. Claudette passed away. She was uncertain if her parents had expressed any, given the resentment her mother carried for always being outshined by the matriarch of the Chennault family.

The echo of applause began to die down and so did her smile as she watched her father wave Trent over to an empty chair at their table. Her ex was notorious for leeching away her happiness and tonight should've been off-limits. She deserved this time to be with people she had been around and respected her entire life.

"I'll see you all back at the house." Carrah snatched her purse up as Trent prepared to sit. She would not stay on the sinking *Titanic* or pretend to be accepting of backroom deals. "I'm not for sale," she hissed, looking both her parents in the eye. She cut her eyes at Trent and then left.

Carrah carefully pushed through the crowd. Only two days had passed since Reggie wrapped her ankle, and while she no longer had a limp, there was still a hint of soreness, especially in heels. Therefore, she took her time, and once she was on the other side of the ballroom doors, she released an audible sigh of relief.

A gentle evening breeze entered from the balcony and nudged her as she strolled down the hall, debating on whether to go home or rejoin the festivities. Political correctness entailed her conforming to the societal expectations of the social class she was raised within. That was only if she cared, and right now she didn't, so she made a beeline for the view of the lighthouse nestled on the shore of Lake Dora.

The solace was much appreciated until low, muffled giggles accompanied by footsteps came at her back. Carrah glanced over her shoulder and saw Summer clinging to Chris's arm as they walked toward her.

She quickly turned her head back, pretending as though something in the distance had captivated her as she tried hard to ignore the two people she least liked.

"Carrah!" The shrill of Summer's voice was hard to ignore and it grated her nerves more than usual. "What are you doing out here? I saw Trent inside." She pulled up to Carrah's side like they were friends.

Carrah refused to acknowledge her because that meant she would see Chris standing beside Summer. She continued her gaze into nothingness while weighing the other girl's words and then replied, "I don't think that's any of your business, Summer." She then backed away from the rail and finally faced them. Her eyes locked with Chris's for a moment before she darted her attention to the open doors leading back to the ballroom. "Enjoy your night." Carrah started back inside.

"How's the ankle?" His deep voice froze her. His words seemed sincere. The expression she found on his face once she turned around indicated the same, but she couldn't be sure. "I'm not joshing you, Carrah."

Her lids fluttered and she looked up at him. He'd caught her off guard with his old-fashioned words and it made her think back to youthful sunny days when they coexisted for the sake of their friends.

Summer smacked her teeth. "I mean, it's been three days. Clearly it's good if she's in heels." She moved closer to Chris and linked her arm within his.

Carrah bit her tongue. Her gaze lingered longer than she would've liked at the knot Summer's elbow created with Chris's, and oddly it rubbed Carrah the wrong way. She'd never really liked Summer, and tonight the comments from the peanut gallery solidified why she hadn't embraced her as a friend. Meanwhile, Chris shrugged away from his date and took a step closer to Carrah.

"I didn't mean for you to get hurt." His lips pressed into a firm line.

"So you say." Carrah shook her head and held her hand up to keep a significant distance between them. Something about his closeness suffocated her. "Don't worry about it. It's not like I'll never walk again."

Chris's face turned red. His jaw ticked as he looked off for a second. Carrah didn't care. She was never one to sugarcoat, and she wouldn't dare for the man that had dismissed her twice. Even if his current demeanor contrasted against the one she met in his office and at the club.

Summer blew a breath of exasperation. "My God, Carrah! How hard is it for you to accept an apology? Everybody that was there knows it wasn't on purpose except for you."

"Good night." Carrah turned to leave. This was neither the time nor the place to say things to make her become the subject of the summer gossip column. She would never stoop that low and embarrass her family over a Bradshaw. They had a reputation for being petty and lacking couth that their old money hid.

"Wait." Chris skid closer to stop her. "Summer, would you mind giving us a minute?"

Summer folded her arms. She sized Carrah up and then looked at Chris. "Only a minute. I'll be inside." She winked at Chris and then turned an evil eye on Carrah as she left the deck, sashaying so hard that her bony hips might break.

"She wants you," Carrah said the moment Summer crossed the threshold and reentered the corridor. "Bad." She focused back on the man standing across from her, forgetting he was not Gavin, Duncan, or Reggie, who usually asked for her womanly advice.

Just as she opened her mouth to apologize, he shrugged. "Perhaps... You do know she's right, though?" His hands slid into his pockets. "Is it really so hard for you to accept my apology?"

"It's not. It's simply unnecessary. Is there anything else?"

"Dammit, Carrah, why must you be so, so—"

"Me." She was grateful he hadn't said "complicated." That was Trent's go-to. Then again, her ex had forced her to erect barriers between them that had made their relationship anything but easy.

"If that's what you want to call it." A frown creased his face.

"It is. You'd know that if we hung out but..." She looked down at her feet. "Our families' history has made that difficult." She shifted the weight of her body and started walking off. Her conscience screamed at her to stop and she did and then faced him once more. "I'm sorry for the way I came to your office...and thank you for getting me off my ankle the other day." Before he could reply, she started off again.

"'If I walked away this time, my soul would be broken beyond repair.'"

Carrah whirled around. It was a moment in time that could never be reclaimed. Once the weight of his words settled upon her, she took a step forward, for once closing the distance between them. "Those are my words," she whispered. "I wrote them."

He nodded. "You did." A self-satisfied grin curved his lips. "I read them, Seraphina." He sidestepped her and went to the balcony rail.

"How come?" she snapped, hating that he'd taunted her and that he'd used a window to her soul, but she couldn't resist moving like the Flash to be at his side.

"You brought them to me."

"You turned it down."

"I've changed my mind," he countered, finally turning his head to meet her eyes, and it took her breath away, but why? "The story was mesmerizing. It should be read by more than your attorney and acquiring editor."

Carrah gasped, "What?" She stumbled backward in disbelief. "You'll represent me?" Chris moved until his back was against the rail, and he watched her. He seemed anxious and she wanted to ask why. Only, she didn't want him to take the offer back. Her natural curiosity overruled caution, and she took the risk. She had to know why he stared at her the way he did. "Why are you looking at me like that?"

A deadpan glare formed and quickly removed the apprehension she thought she saw upon his face. "Because I don't want you to fall again and then blame me."

"Oh." She straightened and went back to the rail.

"To answer your question, I will review your contract and submit on your behalf. If there is negotiation, I will take care of that until you find an agent. I have contacts I can share with you."

"Chris...I, I don't know what to say. Thank you."

"You were there for my brother when he most needed it. This is the least I can do. Let's plan—"

* * *

"Carrah!"

Both Chris's and Carrah's heads went to the voice shouting from behind. Chris's eyes adjusted to the dim light until he recognized Trenton Butler. A long time had passed since Chris last saw Trent. They had hung out a little as preteens, but the boarding school Trent attended often kept him away from the Shores once they were teenagers. If there were ever a family that could compare to the Chennaults in terms of generational wealth, it was the Butlers.

Their family had founded the first Black-owned bank south of the Mason-Dixon Line in 1902. It was still open for business and had a stellar reputation. However, after Trent's parents' scandalous divorce, the Butlers lost prominence with the summer crowd since many didn't want to take sides.

Trent came to where they stood. His attention went from Carrah to Chris. "'Sup, Chennault! Been a long time." They gripped up and then came apart. Trent's attention landed back on Carrah for longer than a few seconds. He reached for her and she wriggled away. A flash of malice crossed the other man's face before he acknowledged Chris again. "Surprised to see the two of you out here together, given the whole Andrews versus Chennault drama."

"You being where you aren't wanted is the biggest surprise." Carrah cocked her head at Trent and then stepped closer to Chris when Trent attempted to claim the space between them. "We were in the middle of a conversation."

Chris assessed Carrah. He noticed an unnatural stillness fall over her body as she clammed up and shied away from the other man's touch. Her body language contradicted her sassy words, and a part of him wanted to know what had happened to Mr. and Miss Perfect. After all, ten years ago on this night, Trent had escorted Carrah as she debuted into society. It was the type of match every parent in their sphere wanted to unite power and prestige.

Yet this wasn't Chris's business. "I'll let you two be. We can catch up later, Carrah?"

"Now is better." Carrah looked him in the face, her eyes pleading for him not to leave.

"Catch up on what?" Trent flexed his cool words with whatever made-up authority he thought he had by directing his question at Chris.

It was a mistake—Chris Chennault cowered to no one. He had been raised to be an alpha male, and thus situations like these only provoked his dominance. Instead of his initial thought to politely excuse himself and allow them privacy, he flexed.

"I'm certain if Carrah wanted you to know, she would tell you." He stretched a little taller into his full six-three frame and for some reason became protective of someone who wasn't family and had been on the opposing side for as long as he could remember. "Carrah?" He peered down at her, watching as she shook her head no in slow motion. "There's nothing for you to know. Now, if you don't mind, we were in the middle of a conversation."

"We need to talk." Trent raised his voice a decibel and lunged to grab Carrah.

Alarm bells rang. The plea Chris saw in her eyes now made sense. He stepped in front of her and cut the other man off. "That's not what she wants. You need to respect that."

Trent's nostrils flared as he glared at Chris. After a few heated breaths, he spun on his heel and darted back inside. An awkward silence swarmed them for longer than a few minutes while Chris attempted to rationalize what had just happened. One minute he simply wanted to show gratitude for how she'd helped Carter, the next he wanted to protect her.

"Thank—"

"I'll message you later this week." He moved from her, albeit chasing the cloud of confusion away then inspected the walkway that would take him back inside. "Give me some time to review the contract and speak with the acquisitions team at Hurston House."

"Why are you mad?" The inflection in her voice evidenced a timidness he'd never seen in her, but it also revealed frustration. "You don't have to help me because I showed your brother kindness."

Hell, he honestly had no idea why he was upset. All he knew was that he was for some strange reason. Mention of his brother forced him to consider if his logic was flawed. Did he really need to jump through hoops for Carrah Andrews because she'd given Carter compassion instead of pity?

Sure, that was what she was thinking. Anyone with a brain and background on their frenemy status should arrive at the same conclusion. And they would be right. Only, Carrah had rescued them without knowing or wanting anything in return.

They'd spent a year lamenting that Claudette wouldn't be here tonight to see Carter escort Alexandria Devlin. He owed her for being there for his brother even when he couldn't be.

He just had to remember their well-established boundaries and all would be fine.

"If I don't help you, who will? You don't have much time left to respond to the contract." He turned to leave then stopped and glanced over his shoulder. "One more thing… Me helping you needs to remain between us. I cannot risk my father finding out. He's had a lot thrown at him in the last year and a half. And…whatever drama you and Trent have, settle it ASAP. You don't want that while launching your new career."

He strolled off before she could reply and reentered the interior space. He hadn't had a chance to collect his thoughts before Summer came racing to reclaim him. Only, he was no longer in the mood to entertain a woman. Let alone one begging to give him things between her legs. He didn't need to get on top of one woman to get over another one. However, he did need to calm his racing mind from feeling as though he might be betraying his family.

Just as he was about to make up a lie and claim a rain check that he had no intent on using, his brother and Alexandria came and ushered him away. Without hesitation he gave Summer the church finger, never looking back. Any other time he was reluctant on being roped into Carter's schemes since it usually involved him doing something that inconvenienced his plans. However, on this night he would've gladly played Uber driver to get outside of the Lakeside Inn.

"Where are we going?" Chris asked as they continued to pull him.

"My mother wants us all in a picture. Your dad, Chloe, you, Reese…she's determined to capture this moment." Alexandria giggled. "You know how we do."

Chris huffed a dying chuckle because he knew exactly how their kind of people did. This was the clout play. There wasn't another pairing tonight more prominent than his brother, a Chennault, with a Devlin.

"Some things never change," he whispered and allowed them to lead him.

On the way to wherever Mrs. Devlin was coordinating a picture of their families, he saw his father in a corner, puff-chested and pointing at Melvin Andrews, who was doing the same. He broke free of Alexandria's clutches and dashed over to the two older men.

"Dad." Chris stepped between them and gently moved his father backward. "This is one of the most publicized events of the year. What are you thinking?" Chris ground out harshly, then narrowed his eyes on Melvin.

"He's not," Melvin Andrews grudgingly replied. "He's still stuck thirty years in the past."

"Tell that to Hannah!" Chauncy huffed. "You son of a bitch! You never cared to apologize and now you want my help."

Chris tugged his father by the arm. He was unmovable until Carter popped up at his dad's other side and helped. The corner they were in was starting to attract attention, and this would be the last thing Olina Chennault Cosmetics needed since the board had started questioning Chauncy's ability to lead in the wake of Claudette's death.

"I'm fine, boys." Chauncy snatched his arms away from his sons. He began buttoning his jacket and made way toward the ballroom.

Chris reached out and grabbed his father by the hand to stop him. "Are you sure? We don't have to go back in. Besides, Mrs. Devlin wants us to take a picture with Carter and Alexandria."

Chauncy heaved a sigh of relief. He didn't need to admit why his entire mood was off. There was still plenty to process as a result of his mother no longer being here, and Chris knew it was a one day at a time sort of thing for his father so he didn't push. He simply gestured for Carter to lead the way to where his escort and her family might be and Chauncy followed.

Their family's dynamic in this space was forever changed, and so was his and Carrah's. The same couldn't be said for the relationship his father had with Melvin Andrews.

Chapter 12

"WELL, I DECLARE, Claudette and Genevieve planned this night a long time ago." Camille dropped the Sunday paper—with the front page featuring a photograph of the Chennault and Devlin families together from last night at the Debutante Ball—into Carrah's lap. She then shed her robe and went to the edge of the pool and dipped her toes in. "Alexandria is no Reese, and yet she was anchored by the youngest scion of the Chennault family, who presented her to society."

Carrah scanned the photo. She had already seen a version of it circulating on social media, and she had not been able to stop looking at it...or Chris, rather. His offer to help still seemed surreal. A few more seconds was all the photo got from her before she folded the paper and tossed it to the empty lounge chair at her side. "It's a nice photo, Mother."

"Of course it is!" She cleared her throat. "You better believe last night was orchestrated a long time ago. That picture is proof that all of our summers here make dreams come true."

"Is that what you and Dad told yourselves while arranging a marriage for me to Trenton Butler?" Carrah tried, but couldn't hide her contempt. "For the record, my dream is not to become that man's wife. I went along with your game ten years ago for debut so that our family could be coveted by society. I will not subject myself to becoming his bride to remove Noir's debt."

Her mother turned her nose in the air before she eased down the steps into the water. "Your father made me aware of your sentiments. I guess that's why he had a not-so-nice run-in with Chauncy last night."

"Wait, what?" Carrah sat up in her chair, her mind racing down an empty alley full of side streets. Did Trent mention to her parents that she was outside with Chris? Would the argument between their fathers change his mind? She hadn't heard from Chris since he took off last night, and while he said to give him time, too much may set her back...again. This was not good.

"You heard what I said. Your father had no business approaching Chauncy at the ball. Wrong place, wrong time. The man is still grieving. They all are. I saw that last night."

Carrah scooted from the chair to the deck of the pool and dropped her legs into the water. She wished she knew what had triggered an exchange of words between her father and Mr. Chennault. Chris had made it clear, almost as if she didn't know that their arrangement needed to remain private. For the sake of her future she prayed nothing had been compromised. "How can you be so sure? You don't talk to them."

"Maybe not anymore, but I've known Chauncy since we were children. Claudette was my sorority sister, and we moved in the same circles. She was a big presence at the Lakeside Debutante Ball, and is missed by many. Hell, if she were here,

I probably wouldn't have been tapped to chair. Chauncy is not the same without her. Summer Bradshaw on the arm of their oldest further illustrates my point."

"Did you send condolences?" Carrah pulled her shades down and analyzed her mother, who seemed to become speechless with her question. Later she would assess the surge of annoyance at the mention of Summer being with Chris. Right now, she needed to better understand her mother's sudden change of tune on Claudette Chennault. It seemed friendlier than it had been in years. "I mean…it's okay if you didn't. Not like we socialize with them."

"Once upon a time we did." Her chin lowered to her chest as she flicked at the water. "How could I not offer my condolences? You know the many boards and committees we sat on together. Not to mention the positions we competed for or friends we shared." Camille turned her head to the heavens and released a long, audible breath. "None of how our families are was my choice…It was hers." Her mother's last words reeked of bitterness before she took the final step and submerged herself in the water from the neck down. "I attended Claudette's funeral…sick and all. It was the least I could do," she mumbled as her expression became vacant.

Carrah pushed her sunglasses to the top of her head. She'd only seen the expression cross her mother's face last year as she battled for her life. "Why do you say that?"

"*C'est tout.*" Camille slipped into the old tongue when she had a point to prove or one to evade. In this case, it was the latter based on the way she dismissed the conversation without an answer to Carrah's question. Carrah didn't understand why she had been willing to say so much and then pull back harshly. She'd never heard her mother speak so freely about Mrs. Chennault, except when they were vying against each other for a membership or position in some organization. "Now, please tell me you've sent Beau the reports he requested? If not, he's going to keep using your exit from the table last night after being privy to the company's situation to highlight your obstinacy and make it cause for your father to limit the powers he's given you at Noir."

Carrah pushed her shades back down over her eyes. She'd spent years being the dutiful daughter, only to be met with consequences that suggested otherwise. The anger rolling over her body wasn't meant for her mother and she didn't want to say something she couldn't take back. Just as she swung her legs out of the pool and pushed to stand up, water splashed all over her. She looked straight ahead and saw her mother's teasing smile.

Random, lighthearted acts from Camille had been nonexistent the last year, and Carrah missed them. She took a deep breath, remembering the affirmations she'd learned in therapy, and made the conscious decision to ignore the machinations of her brother, her father, and Trent. Her choice was to be happy and enjoy the sunny day she'd planned by the pool. She then splashed her mom back, which prompted them both to fall into a fit of laughter. Their giggles faded when Camille pushed out of the water and joined Carrah on the deck. She took her daughter by the hand and they sat in silence for a while.

There would never be enough words to communicate how much she loved the woman who gave her life. Only, her mother had to stop being the go-between. "Your son should've checked his email this morning before he came whining to you about the product brief."

"Noted," she responded, patting Carrah's hand. "What about Trent? I'm not sure his family will remain agreeable once they learn you're not accepting his proposal."

"He's a serial cheater. That relationship—or whatever it was with him—cost me a couple thousand dollars in therapy before I was willing to admit that to myself." An ache in her head started, but she closed her eyes and released a breath. "I can't stand to be around him."

Camille sighed. "Maybe…he's changed. Honestly speaking, I think he has. Trent is twenty-nine, and poised to become one of America's youngest senators. People love his ideas, and having a woman like you as his wife would boost his public image. There's no coincidence that he chose you, Carrah." She squeezed Carrah's hand.

"You're joking, right?" Carrah snatched her hand away from her mother. She then left her side and went to gather a towel off the chair. Her eyes squinted at her mother, who was shaking her head no. "He chose me or our families chose us for each other?"

"There's no need in me answering what you already know. You and Trent were matched ten years ago for your presentation to society. You dated in college. You've been a part of each other's lives a long time. This is natural."

"Mom, stop!" Carrah swallowed hard to prevent screaming. "Do you hear yourself? Did you come out here and pretend to lounge by the pool so you could convince me to reconsider his proposal?"

Camille Andrews stared her daughter in the face before she sank back into the water. Carrah hoped her mother hadn't stooped to such a low, but Noir was involved and there wasn't anything they wouldn't do to preserve the origins of their wealth.

"You know more than anyone that Trent is not the man for me. I literally just told you that I can't stand to be near him."

Carrah snorted. "Another mutually beneficial relationship. Is that what you want for me, Mother, because we couldn't very well call it a marriage."

"Carrah," Dominic called, standing in the open French door. "Reese and Ava are here. You want me to send them out?"

"Yes." She sized her mom up. "Mother was just leaving." Carrah grabbed a fresh towel for her mother and held it up.

Camille acquiesced and exited the pool. "Can you at least think about what I said? Not only would Noir have another chance to survive, you would be placed back on a national stage. You've always enjoyed that, and it was unbelievable to see you reign as Miss Louisiana after you had been crowned Miss Xavier University, and the Queen of the Juneteenth Pageant. I'm still uncertain why you chose to work for the company instead of pursuing Miss America after being coroneted the Zulu Queen."

"Because I'm more than a pretty face." She paused, weighing her words. "You enjoyed it much more than I did."

Camille clicked her tongue. "Nonsense! The way you woo crowds is unlike anything I've ever seen before. You've been raised to be in the limelight and could take it all back after revamping the product lines. The visibility Noir would get with you as the wife of a rising political star would be priceless. At least then you would never have to go back in the lab...I mean, it no longer interests you the way it used to, right?"

The way her mom arched her brow before she proceeded to leave didn't sit right with Carrah. How did she know? She started to ask then stopped herself and waved to Reese and Ava, who were now walking on the deck. Besides, one question for her mom would lead to another answer she probably didn't want to hear and it could finally force her to admit that the life everyone else wanted her to have was not the one she imagined.

"Hey, gurl!" Reese snickered, dropping her beach bag down on a lounge chair. She then kissed Carrah on the cheek before Ava. "What's wrong? Don't say nothing, 'cause it's written all over your face." Ava rested a hand on one hip then took her free pointer finger and traced a circle around Carrah's face.

Somehow Carrah was able to release a little giggle before she crashed back down to her seat with Reese and Ava huddling around her like they did when they were little. She could've never imagined the closeness the three had forged as tots playing duck-duck-goose would wrap her in a blanket of security, shielding her from the collateral damage of their world, at age twenty-seven.

Carrah didn't exactly know how to feel when so many things were wrong. She didn't want to see Noir fail, but she couldn't rationalize marrying a man to save it. There was no way she could forget or forgive his past indiscretions and believe he would never come home to her not smelling like Chanel No. 5 or Jo Malone's Peony & Blush. She despised those fragrances as competition in more ways than one. Most importantly, if she gave everyone else what they wanted, she was left with nothing. Her life and the future she imagined was worth more than Noir's chances of survival.

"Better?" Carrah forced the fakest smile she could muster. Both Reese and Ava shook their heads no. She waved it off and then said, "Mama drama. That's it. That's the tweet."

At once Reese and Ava fell into laughter. Carrah tried resisting, but ended up joining in. If she didn't laugh, then she would spend the rest of her poolside hangout stewing on the dense encounter with her mother.

"Mama drama." Reese cackled so loud. "Trust, I know. Genevieve is the queen!"

"That may be you one day, Reese." Ava giggled.

Reese shoved Ava. "Hardly." She cleared her throat and looked at Carrah. "You want to talk about it?"

Short answer: no. Long, unshareable answer: the agreement with Chris needed to work so she could escape. She was done living for everyone else.

"I'm good," she chirped, removing the sunglasses from her face and tossing them onto a towel. A huge grin curved her lips as she started backing away from her friends. "Last one in the pool is a rotten egg!" She darted to the deep end and plunged in.

Her toes grazed the concrete bottom of the pool. She pushed off, accelerating up through eight feet of water, and finally came up for air. Reese was next to break the surface, and Ava was still on the deck tucking her hair inside a frilly swim cap that looked like it came from 1950.

"Seriously." Carrah giggled, treading water. "You're natural."

"Girl, just because I don't have that creamy crack doesn't mean I want to spend my evening washing and blow-drying hair."

Ava's sassiness lasted less than a second before Reese sneaked up the steps and yanked her into the water. A splashy catfight ensued as Carrah hung back strangled by laughter. The second she moved to join in, squeals of laughter came from behind. She watched Peyton zoom past Quinn.

"Y'all started without us," Quinn shrieked.

Carefree silliness that they'd missed for ten summers while Reese was away returned, filling them with nostalgia as they all decided to re-create childhood memories. Carrah paired up with Peyton and maneuvered her way onto her shoulders and then Quinn did the same to Reese, for a rematch in the ultimate battle of Chicken Fight. A moment that had been missed was reclaimed. Life felt good, free without judgment, and one day, Carrah would thank them for saving her.

Chapter 13

THE TWO-STORY YELLOW brick building came into view. Much like Hill House, the Witherspoon Lodge was a permanent fixture in the Shores. For years the old place had been the meeting location for Masons in the tradition of Prince Hall Freemasonry. At one point in its long history, it had served as a church and then during the era of segregation as a school. There was purpose in the place Duncan had asked to meet at.

Only, Chris never had the chance to experience it. More than fifteen years had passed since he'd set foot inside. It was all because his father refused to fraternize with Melvin Andrews. Given the puff-chested altercation he'd witnessed the other night, it had probably been for the best.

Chris lifted his foot off the gas and slowly turned into the side lot of the building, where he parked between Duncan and Gavin. As he eased from his car, he admired the lodge and how it and the men who called themselves Masons stood for liberty, equality, and peace. In a small way, it made him reflect on the work he had been doing with Gavin and Duncan by investing in the community to keep it relevant and safe from overeager developers. He cherished Mount Dora and the time he spent in the Shores, even if it was three months and a few weekends of the year.

In moving toward the entry of the building, he recalled the times he came to the lodge before his father stopped visiting. Alongside his friends, he watched his father and other men put aside divisions created by their individual journeys across the burning sands and socioeconomic status. They came together for the greater good of the community. Beyond social justice issues, they visited the sick and shut-in, fed the homeless, and gave to those less fortunate.

A sudden thought halted Chris's steps inside, making him wonder what life would've looked like had his father and Melvin remained friends. Maybe he would be as excited as Duncan was to meet here today...and he very well may not have been a stranger to Carrah.

The last thought creeped inside his head, lingering, and he didn't know why. Not caring to venture down that rabbit hole prompted him to reclaim his steps and enter the building. The guys were already seated at a round table with a bottle of bourbon and three glasses in the middle.

"What are we celebrating?" Chris called making his way to the table. "A little early in the day for drinks?"

"It's four o'clock Sunday afternoon, and it's summer. I daresay we can partake in spirits." Gavin stood from his chair and gripped Chris up. "Just don't tell my mama. That Southern gal don't believe in alcohol on the Lord's day."

Laughter consumed them for a minute as Duncan poured drinks. "I appreciate y'all for coming on short notice."

Chris sipped his drink, groaned at the strength of it, and then set it back down. "I had the time. Surprised you did. Thought you would've been with Reese after seeing you together at the ball last night."

"Ditto," Gavin chirped.

Duncan shook his head, holding back a laugh. "She's with the girls. They went swimming at Carrah's."

It was as if a sinkhole had opened wide and swallowed him down the one he'd evaded outside. The simple mention of Carrah's name forced recall of their time on the balcony last night. He had not forgotten that spellbinding scent that reminded him of orange blossoms and roses in bloom before observing her shock from learning that he had read her manuscript. Nor could he let go of the disgust that marred her pretty face when Trent popped up and interrupted them. His instincts told him they were not the couple their families showcased them to be.

Gavin waved his hand in Chris's face. "Damn, man, what are you thinking about? You legit tuned us out."

"My bad." Chris cleared his throat. "Off topic, what brought Trent Butler back to town this summer? He's been gone as long as Reese, if not longer."

Duncan shrugged before taking another pull from his glass. "My guess, Carrah. He's probably trying to get back in her good graces. Reese told me Carrah turned down his marriage proposal. Something about the apple don't fall far from the tree. Of course, me not being in y'all's little circle, I have no idea what that means."

Chris relaxed into a smile then reached over and patted Duncan on the back. "You love to say you're not in our circle. And yet you somehow always seem to know what's going on."

They all laughed. "Apple doesn't fall far from the tree...I wonder if Reese is referring to the fact that Trent's dad got caught
having an affair?"

"Oh yeah, with the nanny." Gavin's nonchalance swirled
over the table. He stopped associating with Trent after the guy
turned into a sore loser during a Sonic the Hedgehog game
battle. Their hostility for each other grew after they both
crushed on Zeta Graham, who became Gavin's girl but then
had sex with Trent on the side. "I know Trent will fuck anything, and I heard that hasn't changed much, so I'm not surprised. Carrah is a good girl; she wasn't shakin' nothing when
we all left for college. And based on the fact that he's our age,
he was there two years before her. That's a helluva lot of time
to be a good boy waiting for your high school girlfriend to
graduate." He ended with that *if you know, you know* look.

Thinking back to that age, Chris remembered not wanting the hassle of having a girlfriend. He had just pledged. Girls
were throwing their panties at him, and he took the ones he
liked without question. He hadn't wanted anything serious or
committed because he knew he was incapable of giving that to
a girl. He also understood that when he was ready, he planned
to be a one-woman man.

His father taught him that being in a relationship with
someone was supposed to mean something. He'd seen the love
between his parents and grandparents. It was unwavering, faithful, and happy. That was not what he'd witnessed on the balcony between Carrah and Trent. She had been awkward, almost
apprehensive, and it had made him become protective of her.

"Maybe that's you and Trent, Gav. Had I been with Reese
back then, I would've waited." Duncan relaxed into a lazy
smile. For a second it seemed his thoughts might have been
elsewhere.

Chris chuckled, watching his friend float on cloud nine. "My God, she has you whipped already."

"Say whatttt," Gavin snickered and then gave Chris a five. "Grinning ear-to-ear and shit. But real talk, happy for you, Dunc."

Duncan's smile was contagious. Chris knew how much he and Reese had liked each other all those years ago. He was happy Reese finally stopped giving a care about the way their crowd judged people and chose happiness. Few of them were able to break free of the confines forged by family legacy and status. Even Chris hadn't yet figured out how to completely remove the shackles that kept him bound to Chennault Cosmetics.

The clean break he'd been planning from the company with the West Coast expansion had been stalled by his mother's passing. He could not abandon his father now nor would he publicly showcase betrayal in helping his rival's daughter. It was the reason he silently vetoed asking anything more relating to Carrah, despite his curiosity being aroused. Too many questions would peak Gavin's interest and he was notorious for getting to the bottom of things in the most unsavory ways.

"Same, bro." Chris relaxed back into his chair. "Is Reese why you've decided not to use Hill House for the youth village?"

Duncan cursed under his breath, scrubbing his face clean of emotion. "That's why I called you both here. I knew the news would travel fast, but damn, I thought I had time to get to y'all first."

"Mannnn…" Gavin shook his head. "We are in the Shores. You were sitting at a table with the Caldwells and Devlins. That was already reason for people to talk. My mom knew 'bout you, Reese, and Hill House before we got in the car to leave last night."

"And neither of you said anything to me?" Duncan pointedly asked before picking up the bottle and refilling each of their glasses.

Gavin and Chris looked at each other for a second and shrugged. "For what?" Chris retorted. "We trust you. Besides, we know where you live and hide your spare key." A round of laughter filled the hallowed space for more than a few minutes as they cracked jokes, reminding each other of the secrets they shared. "Seriously, though, we've had each other's backs a long time. Ain't no new girlfriend gonna change that."

"Appreciate it because Hill House is a delicate matter." Duncan took a swig from his glass and reclined back in his chair, matching the calm energy surrounding him. "Reese and I want to renovate and reopen it as a bed-and-breakfast. Which raises the question, where does the youth village go?

"Even before I acquired Hill House, my firm scouted the area and there was nothing that met the conditions for proximity, size, or budget. My father reminded me what Witherspoon Lodge used to do for the people here in Mount Dora, before it fell into inactive status...I mean I remember too. Both your fathers and mine used to come around."

Gavin cleared his throat. "Only for three months out of the entire year. They belong to lodges where we permanently reside and can make an impact year-round."

"That's why this place would be perfect." Duncan stood up and turned in a small circle, scoping the perimeter of the building. "Given the history and purpose this old lodge gave to the community, wouldn't this be a prime location for the youth village?"

Chris got to his feet and went to Duncan's side. He

assessed the building, noting the cracks in the walls, brown stains on the ceiling, warped wood floors, and more. He didn't have a gift like Duncan to see beauty in a building when it was presented ugly. However, he grasped the meaning of paying it forward. "It's definitely meaningful and in the spirit of Prince Hall Freemasonry. I like that we can honor the past while building a bridge for the future."

"You get this building looking good again and those old men might just come back." Gavin sighed. "They should've never let it get this bad. We shouldn't have let them."

Duncan nodded in agreement. "The building has sat empty too long without any upkeep or utilities. The mayor informed me that the only thing that has saved it from being condemned is that it's in the National Register of Historic Places."

Gavin finally got to his feet and did a panorama of the space. "Layman's terms. We're not all land use gurus."

"In acquiring the property, I agree to preserve it for the distinction that placed it on the registry. This building cannot be altered but can be updated to become current under new building codes. Originally, I thought the designation was a downfall because of the constraints imposed. Now I see it as an opportunity to blend the old with the new and create something better.

"The land that accompanies the building can accommodate construction of a new structure, or two. The lots surrounding are available as well. My thought is to make this building the nucleus of the youth village and have smaller buildings surrounding it to create a campus-like feel."

"I like the idea," Chris admitted. "Almost like a mini college campus."

"Exactly!" Duncan clapped his hands together. "Reese

suggested auxiliary buildings for the arts, business, and STEM. She's willing to do sewing lessons, and said she could talk Ava into a photography class and maybe get Carrah to host science camps."

"Humph," Chris huffed, "can't imagine." He muttered louder than expected and not on purpose.

Both Gavin and Duncan stared him down. They had always been way too protective of Carrah for his liking. Instead of letting it get to him like it used to when they were teens, he shrugged them off and pretended to give his attention back to the interior of where they stood. Besides, it was best they believe his comment was rooted in their families' longstanding rivalry, not his intrigue.

"Carrah's gifted as hell with science," Gavin chided. "She used to love doing chemistry experiments when we were kids, and then once we got older, she became the supreme mixologist. That girl can make a mean old-fashioned."

"That's a fact." Duncan chuckled before he and Gavin rehashed an experience that didn't include Chris. "But do you remember when she taught us how to make invisible ink?" Chris took a step back, much like he would when they were growing up. It was never a secret that he was the odd man out. It just was never thrown in his face like this. "We spent the whole summer pulling fast ones over our parents until her dad got into her little lab and figured out what she'd made."

Their laughter grated his nerves more than usual as they continued trading all the little things they did with Carrah that he hadn't been allowed because of his last name. At least his isolation never lasted long. Gender always factored in and the guys would ditch hanging with the girls for football or fishing.

Gavin cut his eyes at Chris. "Besides, I know for a fact that she's the mastermind behind Noir's fragrance that recently won all those awards." Chris glanced over his shoulder still more interested than he wished he were. Especially now that he'd found out Carrah was the alchemist behind the perfume that had made his father blow a gasket. "I know the two of you don't like each other, but the girl is a genius who loves science. That's why it's not hard for me to imagine her hosting a science camp."

Truth be told, now that he had a little more perspective on Carrah, he understood their points of view. Only, in recognizing the sentiments they expressed, a cloud of confusion swirled around him. If Carrah was this brilliant scientist, why would she sacrifice the excellence she'd achieved for the unknown? More than that, why did she want him to negotiate it?

Chapter 14

CHRIS GLANCED UP from his computer as Shayla entered his office. He put up his finger, not wanting his train of thought to be derailed. The rumors surrounding his longest-standing client, Gerron Bennett, had not been exactly false. The actor's outspoken opinion on the way a new production cast white actors to play characters of ancient Egyptian origins while continuing to perpetuate racial stereotypes of inner-city gangs had gone viral and restarted conversations on the way Hollywood often culturally appropriated. Therefore, Chris was hard at work substantiating Gerron's criticism as actual civil advocacy that fostered conversations surrounding diversity to ensure he didn't get booted from his highly rated TV series. Once Chris hit the send button, he turned his attention to Shayla, who seemed more than giddy with excitement.

"Been a long time since I've seen you like this." He chuckled. "What news have you?"

She moved closer to his desk, flaunting a giant smile, then

pulled her hand from behind her back and slammed a document on his desk. "They sent the new contract."

He reached for the stack and saw Hurston House on the cover page. Five days ago he'd stood with his friends as Duncan unveiled the future site for the youth village and learned things about Carrah that made him question her pursuit of the publishing contract. Perhaps if he had been willing to listen to her when she first came to him, he might better understand her motivations.

Instead, he felt like he was robbing the world of another STEM girl. His mother had been ahead of her time in formulating cosmetics and it made him wonder if Carrah was that person for this generation, given Noir's most recent success in fragrance. Why was she willing to give up chemistry for writing without first looking for a compromise?

Chris disregarded his personal perspective and focused on the professional duty he owed Carrah. He quickly removed the paper clip, scanning for the updates. He'd promised Carrah at the ball he'd reach out once he heard something. Now he could finally tell her that he had negotiated a higher offer and increased publicity commitments along with more favorable terms for the right to acquire Carrah's next book.

The only thing he wasn't able to remove was the right of refusal for her next manuscript within the same genre. However, he was able to add a stipulation for when she could submit and when they had to reply. In his opinion, it was a win because it was more favorable for her than the original language.

"You're smiling," Shayla said, "which is rare when you are reviewing a contract."

"Not rare when I get what I want in said contract," he corrected, and she blushed. "I'm honestly still shocked, given that this is a debut for her. However, the acquiring editor is also the VP, and she's very excited about this book and its possibilities."

Shayla folded her arms as a small smirk played at her lips. "So are you telling me that you're happy Ms. Andrews wanted you?"

The papers fell from his hands. Chris went completely still. Those words were a double entendre, and if echoed in the presence of certain people, it could make him the second black sheep of the family. Therefore, he wasted no time advising Shayla on the need to remain discreet with Carrah's representation and then decided they would only refer to Carrah as Seraphina moving forward, to avoid any potential slipups.

As Shayla retreated from his office, it was natural for his overanalytical brain to begin running scenarios. For one, he had to consider if his father might feel betrayed...how his mother might be turning in her grave. There was also the issue of the nosy summer residents and how they might respond to seeing them alone together. Beyond the practical nuances, he still needed to not be so confused by wanting to protect Carrah from Trent. He also hadn't found a rational explanation for why he had wanted Summer to leave the balcony so that he could be alone and free to speak with Carrah.

Chris cursed himself for still feeling like he owed Carrah something for being there for his brother when he couldn't be. Had her compassion blinded him? He had to ponder the notion because helping Carrah Andrews, the pretty girl who always went out of her way to avoid him, seemed like a path no one in their right mind would take. Given where he was in life with his firm's expansion and the extra support his father required, the last thing he needed was another headache.

Only, he was a man of his word. His mother taught him a long time ago that a man who couldn't stand by his word lacked honor and would never command respect. So, while Carrah may not exactly like him, she clearly had enough respect to come knocking on his door for help. He would manage the fallout with his family, if he had to, later.

No longer wishing to partake in the internal debate of should I or shouldn't I, he picked up his phone and messaged her.

Afternoon Carrah, I have an update for you. When are you available to meet and discuss?

* * *

Carrah's phone blared to life for the umpteenth time. She glanced over her shoulder to the other side of the small lab that had once been a pool house and decided against checking the notifications. Her siblings had been hounding her nonstop with questions ever since she submitted the proposal on Sunday, and she was certain they were the reason her device was singing with alerts. She refocused on the beaker in front of her and squeezed the top of the dropper between her thumb and index finger.

The essence of watermelon seed oil dripped into a gel-like substance she'd compounded with anti-aging ingredients, omega-3 fatty acids, and antimicrobials. She then picked up her stirring rod and continued disregarding the chirps alerting her to new messages. Once she was confident that everything was thoroughly mixed, she brought the beaker to her nose. Unexpectedly, she sighed into a smile.

The light fragrance reminded her of when she used to ride her bicycle past an old truck loaded down with watermelons on the way to see Reese at Hill House, where she would then sniff around Ms. Connie's rose garden. The mix was subtle, both playful and beautiful, and it made her think that summer was made for falling in love. These were the moments she lived for in her lab. She had always been able to reimagine new products in the Shores because her mind was at ease.

However, the past few days had been different. For the first time since her parents converted this space for Carrah, she found it hard to create something new. The euphoric high she generally possessed as she unraveled the molecular structure she drew on paper into a test tube was marked by mistakes, which led her to second-guess her abilities. The faith she needed to develop miracle products to transform Noir's sinking status was nonexistent, and unfair.

Another few rounds of mixing and experimenting consumed Carrah. She finally felt like she had made progress when the ingredients synthesized and the gel-like substance permeated the scent she'd created as it became a light shade of pink. The only drawback was that the consistency was more watery than she desired. It had the potential to be an easy fix, but that didn't mean it could be solved in minutes. Sometimes it took hours, even days, to perfect.

And right now she didn't have either. Not while she yearned for the summer she expected to find whenever she returned to the Shores. Therefore, she called it quits for the day. The dilemma Noir had managed to find itself in wouldn't be solved because she'd spent the morning in her lab.

Carrah did an about-face. She moved from her station to the other side of the small space. The pressure to develop products for immediate release were like hands choking her windpipe. How could she ensure quality cosmetics with a burden so overwhelming?

A heavy breath escaped her as she grabbed her phone from the old desk. A mental break was in order before engaging with Aubrey and Beau, since they were attempting to micromanage her research and development due to their ignorance.

It wasn't her fault they were too lazy to look up the science of a product or too embarrassed to seek clarification from their father on what Carrah had presented in the brief. All they needed to know were the benefits and end results, which she had clearly articulated in her product summaries. She would not hand-hold them while explaining chemical reactions or elaborate on the way she engineered synthetic smells so they could pretend to understand. Especially now that she knew Beau wanted her stripped of responsibility. Carrah wouldn't give him anything to make his job easier after being reprimanded and relegated to working during her summer break.

When she finally looked down at her phone she saw a waiting notification from Chris nestled between those of her siblings. She snatched off her gloves and picked it up. There were no words to contain the excitement that rushed over her. He had told her to wait until he had time to make contact with the publisher.

At that moment her mind floated back to one Sunday in church when she was eleven. *She was sitting on a pew with Reese and Ava, and had passed Ava a note for Chris...*

Carrah shook her head, forcing the memory to fade. She was back to glaring at the screen of her phone. "It's just a message," she said under her breath, and pressed her finger against Chris's name to read his text.

Afternoon Carrah, I have an update for you. When are you available to meet and discuss?

Her thumbs were paralyzed, stuck in the air, as she contemplated what should be a simple reply. Was it the shock that he had been in contact with Hurston House, and her dreams were no longer galaxies away from coming true? There was no other viable reason beyond excitement. Well, except for the fact that she had found help where she least suspected it. She took a few deep breaths, anxious to receive the news he had and began typing.

May I call you now? If not, I can meet later today or any-time tomorrow.

She hit send, preferring a phone conversation for more than a few reasons. One, whatever weird energy she had around him was easily avoided from two separate ends of a phone. Two, family history dictated they would become the subjects of gossip if they were seen out without the usual entourage. Three, she really wanted to know what had taken place between him and the publisher.

Almost instantly his reply came back.

This is not a phone conversation. 4024 Hemlock Creek Ln @ 6:00 p.m.

Carrah quickly confirmed her attendance then put the phone down before she slipped up and told him she didn't like his tone. She knew their history, his reluctance, and the distance they'd kept from each other over the years. It still didn't justify his direct, almost nonnegotiable demeanor. All of which triggered the memory from earlier of her passing Ava a note to Chris.

Ava slid down then leaned to the row in front of her and gave the note to Reggie, who passed it to his left. When it got to Chris, he looked over to Reggie. He pointed to Ava, who then pointed to Carrah.

Chris snapped his head back to the pulpit, and after church, Gavin brought her the paper torn into pieces. All she had written on it was "Can we be friends?"

She never asked again. In fact, she held it as a grudge and ignored him—until now. A part of her wondered if Chris remembered because for as long as she'd fought to forget, she couldn't. Though it didn't really matter now because being friends with Chris was unimportant. This was strictly business.

Chapter 15

CARRAH TRAVELED THE less-frequented roads along the outskirts of town. She bent the curve on Lake Ola Drive then slammed on the brakes when the GPS announced she'd missed her turn. A string of curse words escaped her mouth while she drove another few yards until she found a driveway to turn around in.

Her little Benz creeped at a turtle's pace then proceeded to crawl, holding up a few cars once she spotted the turn she missed. It was a dirt road, well, more like tire tracks in grass hidden by oversized trees and wild bushes. A true country road, one way in and one way out with a wooden gate that had been left open.

In slow motion, she cut the wheel and began rolling down the gravel-laden path. The rocks and shakes her sedan endured had her second-guessing this ultra-discreet location he'd selected until she made it into a clearing and saw a cute little summer cottage on acres of untethered land nestled on the bank of a lake she didn't know. This was the scenery that made her jet out of Louisiana every May. Old Florida was breathtaking whenever stumbled upon.

Carrah drove a few more feet forward and pulled up next to Chris's vintage blue Jeep. She'd seen him drive it around town here and there during the summer months. However, it was a complete contradiction to the Bentley he often sported. Whereas the Bentley broadcasted his wealth, sophistication, and command of old guard status, the Jeep was simple, relaxed, and rugged. All the things she knew he was not.

She cut the engine off then checked the mirror and gathered her purse before she moved to tug the door handle. It pulled away from her fingers and to her surprise Chris was standing on the opposite side of the car, pulling the door open. Carrah didn't shy away from his chivalry. She accepted it and climbed out of the car, stutter-stepping until she found balance on the arm he'd extended to help her.

Once her heels rooted within the uneven ground beneath her feet, she looked up into his almost disapproving stare. "Thank you." She finally found words to speak after being unnerved by his actions and damn near seduced by those beautiful light eyes.

"My mother raised me to be a gentleman. Why do you seem so surprised?" A smirk twisted his lips as he closed the door. He then walked off toward the cottage.

"I didn't see you come outside." Carrah followed, adjusting her dress. Glad she'd remembered Ava's words on his professionalism and wore business attire as he was still threaded in his. "You know I didn't mean it in the way you've taken it." She had tried to control her tongue, but ended up snapping a tidbit.

Chris stopped at the door with his hand on the knob as he

looked over his shoulder. "Must you always feel like there's a point to prove?"

Meanwhile Carrah's internal battle systems were roaring to life, telling her to abort the mission. She didn't know how long she would need his help, but if it came at the price of always being made to feel that she'd done something wrong, it wasn't worth it. Most important, she wasn't wired with the patience to put up with a condescending, bright-eyed jerk.

Her lack of patience was one reason she had always enjoyed chemistry. Elements always had a reaction, and mixing them revealed if they were compatible or not. Usually, it was instant gratification and she knew whether to continue or discard an experiment. In this case she didn't know. Beyond the reservations she held for Chris, she still understood that dream chasing came with no guarantees.

"I don't have a point to prove. You caught me off guard."

He shrugged, turned the knob, and pushed the door open. He gestured for her to enter, and she did. The cottage wasn't as simple on the inside nor did it look like it had been standing for generations. The reclaimed wood floors and stone fireplace gave off a rustic charm.

However, there were modern comforts such as a Sub-Zero fridge and granite countertops peeking out from the small kitchen that didn't compromise luxury. There was balance here that was warm and cozy, despite the icy reception she had received.

She looked around noting high-end finishes that still preserved architectural detail of a bygone era. Her guess was their mutual friend Duncan McNeal had helped in renovating the space. Unlike both their homes on Lakeshore, she didn't have to walk very far to be on the opposite side from where she'd come in the front door. The space was quaint and it humbled her in a way she had never imagined while giving her the chance to appreciate a gorgeous lake view.

"Why don't you come have a seat?" his voice called from behind. She turned around, searching briefly before spotting him at the only dining table between the kitchen and sitting room. "We have a good amount to discuss."

Got it, she wanted to say aloud, but didn't as she made her way to where he sat. She hadn't misread his tone. All business, as it was supposed to be, except it seemed cold in this setting. Almost as if he didn't want to be here.

Carrah noticed the chair directly across from him that had been pulled out for her. She quickly moved to it and scooted into the table. The only items on the table were two stacks of papers, his laptop, a pen, and his phone.

"Sorry," she offered an apology. "I've never been to this side of town. It's beautiful here."

Chris nodded and placed his hands on the table. "Let's jump right—"

"Wait"—she held her hands up—"can we at least be cordial?"

He recoiled back in his seat and folded his arms. His penetrating stare caused her to squirm in her seat before he said, "Cordial? Have I not been?"

She gulped hard, fighting the way she seemed to become hot from the way his expressive eyes scanned her. "You just seem so…I don't know, like you really don't want me here."

"I don't." He was point-blank, matter-of-fact, never wavering from keeping her the center of his attention. "I preferred that we have this meeting at my office. However, our families' complicated history dictated otherwise. Furthermore, this is business. There's no need for us to pretend a friendship existed prior to you asking for my help and me giving it to you."

"Yes, you've made that clear on more than one occasion."
His lips pressed together. "Carrah—"

"It's fine, Chris." She stiffened, lifting her chin and making her back a little straighter. "Let's get to it, as you said."

*   *   *

Chris hesitated for a second, but then nodded and reached for the first contract he'd had on the table. It had to be this way between them, black and white with no shades of gray. He'd felt confusion surface that night on the balcony and this distance between them was needed to maintain order. Life had brought him too far to be compromised by a woman who had made it her job to disregard him every summer that he could remember.

"Our first point of business is to officially establish our attorney-client relationship." He slid the document in front of Carrah, offered a pen, and watched her sign without any questions before he did the same. He then shifted a second stack of papers to give her a better view. "This is the revised contract between you and Hurston House. I'll highlight items of note and the changes that were made."

Page by page, he went through every section noting important clauses within her contract while explaining the changes and answering her questions. The flow was intelligent and easy. He appreciated her sophisticated, yet inquisitive, approach that engaged him in a way he had been with few clients, and it made him wonder if the way they were now could've always been had they not been rivals. He dared not ask for he was certain that the Carrah he had now would never be the one he got outside of these walls.

"So if I understand you correctly, they're offering me more money," she asked, beaming a Kool-Aid smile.

Her smile was contagious. Chris was genuinely happy to represent her work. In most cases, he had little interest in the project. He was simply excited to close the deal for one of his celebrity clients. In this case, Carrah had written a captivating story that in some ways exposed the shadows within his own heart. Couple her work with attracting a leading publisher and a deal that could help close disparity gaps Black authors encountered within the publishing industry, and all he smelled was her success.

"They are. You'll receive more on the advance and greater attention with publicity."

"Dannnggg," she drawled, "you really are good!"

A hearty chuckle escaped him. He stood, stretched, and then gazed out the window. The sun would set soon and he didn't want her driving on unfamiliar dark roads so he needed to wrap things up. "Once you sign and the contract is returned with a voided check, they will make a direct deposit to your account. Of course the royalties come after book sales."

His vibrating phone silenced their exchange. Both he and Carrah glanced over to his device. Heather was calling. Almost two weeks had passed since he'd heard from her and he preferred it that way. There was nothing left to say after the spectacle she'd made in front of his family and at his office. Which was why he didn't hesitate declining the call before he reclaimed his seat.

"Oh, I forgot to ask. Does Hurston House send you your fees or do I need to cut a separate check?"

"You were there for my brother when I couldn't be. This is the least I can do." His attention left his phone and went back to the other side of the table. He hadn't brought up fees in the attorney-client contract intentionally. The confidence she gave back to Carter was worth more than anything she could pay him. It was apparent she had not read between those lines and perhaps it was hard, given the distance they maintained.

"I—"

The rapidly buzzing sound of his phone halted his words. He took a second to mute the chat with his ex so that he could respond to Carrah without further disruption. Again, his phone began ringing. This time it was Summer Bradshaw, another woman who wanted more from him than he was willing to give. He'd avoided her since leaving the ball almost a week ago now.

A light giggle escaped Carrah, recapturing his attention. "Quite the ladies' man this evening. Guess I should've known. I mean, Gav is your bestie." She got up from the chair and walked into the kitchen. "I'm thirsty. May I have something to drink?"

"Bottles are in the fridge." He cleared his throat, unable to take his gaze away from the way her curves filled out the pink dress she wore. "Grab one for me, too, please." He then sent Summer a quick "we'll catch up one day" text and made his phone disappear.

Carrah returned with their drinks and sat back down. He watched her for longer than a few minutes before finally deciding to throw caution to the wind. They would have this conversation now since she'd accused him of having a personality he didn't own. "Your logic is that because Gav is my best friend, we are the same?"

Carrah took a sip of water. She set the bottle down as her lips curved into a smile while she leaned into the table. "Are you trying to use that LSAT deductive reasoning on me? Won't work; I took that test for fun and passed it too. Besides, I literally just watched you ignore a call from the girl who was in your office the other day, begging me to disregard my appointment so she could see you, and then there's Summer. They're both women that clearly want you."

"So if Reese or Ava called, am I still this Casanova you wish to paint me as?"

"Reese and Ava are your friends. They have been since we were old enough to ride tricycles. I don't think you see them in a romantic way. Therefore, it's different."

He shrugged. "Perhaps," he muttered as he studied her, curious to know what else she thought of him. Only, he wouldn't ask because he wasn't supposed to care. "I'd very much like it if you didn't assign attributes to me of which you know nothing about."

Carrah shrank away from the table. He hadn't meant to make her uncomfortable. It was just that he valued his character. He'd worked hard to cultivate who he was and how people perceived him. Image had been one of the constructs his mother made him prize above all else. No one would think less of him.

"For the record," he started, staring at her, willing their eyes to meet, but they never did. It didn't stop him from saying what he had on his chest. "I'm a one-woman type of man."

"Not everyone is," she said a little above a whisper. Her teeth tugged at her bottom lip and her gaze shifted to a point beyond him. He sensed there was pain behind her words, and it baffled him because what man wouldn't want only her. Trent had to be a fool. "My apologies if I offended."

He cleared his throat and straightened back up at the table. They were back to business, and this timid, almost shy Carrah was a sight he never imagined seeing. "Historically in publishing, your agent would've landed this deal, and yes, they would receive a percentage. I am not your agent. We'll need to work on getting you one." He paused, scribbling a note on a blank piece of paper. "I will not make future deals. That is not my wheelhouse as I stated to you the other night. However, negotiating contracts are and this is the least I can do after your encouragement of my brother."

"Carter is sweet and—"

"And I'm not?" The words rushed out unexpectedly. He pushed up from the table refusing to swallow the bitterness of how she'd dismissed him all his life yet had somehow managed to give his brother compassion. Their close proximity triggered feelings he'd stowed away and he wasn't sure how long he could pretend her actions didn't bother him.

Chris released a breath of frustration and then peeked out the window. "It's getting late. The roads out here don't have streetlamps, so if you're sure about this arrangement and don't have any other questions you can sign the contract and head home."

"I never said that." Her voice held an edge he wasn't able to ignore. He turned from the window and faced her. "You've never given me the chance to know you."

"Are you serious? Miss, I'll keep my distance and use the disdain between our families as the excuse to cold-shoulder me."

"You do the same," she snorted, pompously tossing the ball back in his court as she rose from her chair.

He did, but it had always been a defense mechanism until he was old enough to heed his mother's words that some pretty things were poisonous. By the time Carrah had extended an olive branch, their worlds were set. He'd torn up a letter from her asking if they could be friends because by then he knew who belonged in his sphere and she didn't.

However, now that they had agreed to enter into a business relationship, he preferred that the hostilities between them fade into something more amiable. The two of them getting along would also be easier on the friend group, especially now that Reese had returned home and their circles intertwined.

"Contrary to what you may think, I have tried. Dorian's, kickball, tonight…"

Her jaws went slack then slowly closed. "You've got to be joking. First, I don't recall any form of amicability from you when we went out on Dunc's boat. You walked off when I arrived. Second, you knocked the wind out of me with that kickball and then all but threw me into a golf cart. And tonight…" She huffed. "I had to ask you if we could be cordial since you were Frosty the Snowman when I got here."

"Clearly our interpretations of those incidents differ." He set his gaze upon her. "But if that is how you view things, why do you want me to be your attorney? Why did you just sit here and sign a document that enters us into an attorney-client relationship? I explained to you that this is a relationship that requires trust. I'll know things about you that your family doesn't, and you'll have to believe that whenever I'm working for you, I am executing at my highest potential with no reservations. Is that even possible given the picture you just painted of me?"

"I need to head back before it gets too dark." She snatched her purse from the counter and proceeded to leave. "You're right. Maybe I should've contemplated this a little more. Sorry I wasted your time." She spun on her heel and made a dash for the door.

Chapter 16

CARRAH MADE IT to the other side of the door. Dusk swallowed her whole while chilling the chaotic rhythm of her heart. What the hell was happening to her? Right now wasn't the time to seek answers. It was almost country-ass dark, the crickets sounded like giants chirping in the night, God knows what else was out in the Florida wilderness, and all she wanted was to get home and hide her face in a pillow.

She fidgeted with her purse until her phone and key were in hand and then made a quick beeline to her car. The moment she closed the door and pushed the button to start the engine was the moment she realized that she'd walked away from her dreams.

Water welled in her eyes. Tears slid down her cheeks and she cursed herself for thinking she had the power to break free of the emerald palace her family had placed her in.

A series of knocks struck the window and froze her still. Despite the night settling around them, Chris's golden skin stood out in contrast as he waited by the door. She unlocked the car, allowing him to pop the door open.

"I didn't mean to make you cry." His long arm reached in and then his thumb pushed the wetness from her cheek. She flinched, scared by the way his touch awakened hidden desires within her body. "I'm sorry."

"Don't apologize." Carrah turned her head until their eyes locked. She then steadied his hand. "This isn't your fault."

He lowered his arm, scanning her as though he were searching her soul. "Then why do I feel like it is?"

"Trust me...it is not." She was honest; he wasn't the reason she was crying. However, the way she felt—as though she could throw caution in the wind along with their rivalry to feel his touch once more—was totally his fault. Trent had never made her want him, and for all she knew that might have been their problem all along.

"Truce." He offered his hand.

Carrah placed her hand in his, accepting the cease-fire for the hope that they could make this agreement between them work. "Truce." She gripped his hand and shook. "I think we need a redo." She cut the engine off and moved to exit the car. Once they stood face-to-face, she presented him with her hand. "Carrah Andrews. Thank you for taking me on as a new client, Mr. Chennault. I'm excited to discuss the contract."

His lips quirked into a smile and he slowly clasped her hand then took a step forward to close the distance. "Please call me Chris. Shall we?" He gestured for them to go back inside and she agreed.

This time when they entered the house her stomach decided to growl. He chuckled, while she wished to disappear. "Excuse me," she said sheepishly, holding her stomach and praying it wouldn't happen again.

"Hungry?"

Her stomach growled again, answering for her. This time they both laughed. "Very."

"I planned to make a burger. Want one?"

She nodded then watched him loosen his tie and roll up his sleeves as he went to the kitchen. He gathered a host of items from the pantry and fridge and set them on the counter before he pulled cooking pans from the cabinets. He whistled as he worked, minding his own business as though she weren't even there.

Except she was very much present and intrigued by this person she'd known all her life from a distance. Not in a million years would she ever have guessed that Christopher Chennault was the type of man who knew his way around the kitchen. His family had cooks and maids that traveled from Louisiana to join them in the Shores during the summer months, and everyone knew that Ms. Claudette spoiled her boys rotten.

"Do you cook often?" she asked as she went to the kitchen and pulled out a stool from the counter and sat. She could only know more if she asked. They'd called a truce, he was officially her attorney, and he said he'd try. It was her turn now, and the only way to know more about a man she at one time believed was her enemy. "Sure looks like you know what you're doing."

A smirk danced on his lips as he shook his head no. "Can I make a four-course meal, no. Do I know how to make sure I don't go hungry, yes." He chuckled. "I think I need to hurry up before your stomach yells at me again."

Uncontrollable laughter hit Carrah. She's didn't know this funny side. He was always so serious, straight to business like he was the first time she'd come in. When she finally gasped for breath, she found him staring at her. Those light eyes seemed as though they'd peeked through the windows of her soul and stripped her bare.

"Here." She left her seat and went to the sink to wash her hands. "Let me help. Many hands make light work."

"True." He stopped looking into a cabinet over the stove. A vacant expression landed upon his face. He may have physically been in the kitchen, but his head was a million paces away. "My mother used to say that."

A pang struck her, hearing the solemnness he spoke with. She wanted to reach out and comfort him, but she didn't. They had raised their white flags, not vowed to be friends. Still she couldn't leave him stranded wherever he was. "Maybe it's generational. Mine says it all the time."

He snapped out of it and went back to reaching over the stove and pulled down a skillet he set atop the stove. "They were friends...once."

"Sorority sisters too," she added, and he nodded. She then wondered if he knew why they'd fallen out. "Do you know why they stopped being friends?"

"I do not. I think it happened long before we were born because for all I can remember, our families have not associated with each other." With the efficiency of a sous chef, he gathered a few more cooking utensils and the meat from the fridge. "Ms. Watson, our house manager, premade patties. I'm just putting them in the pan. If you want to help you can clear the table and set it. Maybe get the ketchup, mustard, and other condiments out."

For the first few minutes they worked in quiet, taking on their assigned dinner tasks. By the time the patties were in the pan laughter filled the cottage as they debated summer happenings in the Shores, mutual friends, and Carrah's anti-fry day. Chris argued in favor of Carrah accepting hospitality and sampling the fresh-cut, seasoned potatoes Ms. Watson had prepped. In the end he stood the victor, making her claim a cheat day as he sat a plate down in front of her with a juicy, mouthwatering burger and a stack of fries.

After Chris sat down across from her and said grace, they picked their burgers up at the same time. Right as Carrah was about to take a bite, she couldn't. At least not like this. She put her burger down and retrieved a knife from the kitchen and cut it into quarters. Snickering came from the other side of the table.

"You're kidding?" He wiped his mouth then gulped down sweet tea. "Burgers are handhelds."

"Maybe when you're home." She finally took a bite of her sandwich. "Mmm...this is good." She groaned then took another bite, savoring the smoky notes from cayenne pepper, along with onion, garlic, and a hint of oregano. Creole flavor was on full display and much appreciated since the Southern culinary found in the Shores was different than NOLA. "She always has ready-made patties for you?"

"Ms. Watson stocks the fridge weekly since she knows I like to hide out here from time to time and go fishing." He snickered then enjoyed another taste of his burger. "Fries." He pointed at her plate. "You're not off the hook."

Carrah picked one up and put it in her mouth. That Creole seasoning did what Chris apparently expected and reeled her in. He displayed a self-satisfied grin watching as she continued going back for more, validating the argument he'd won and totally accepting the hospitality that had been offered.

Small talk continued over their meal, allowing her to learn that the cottage was built by Chris's great-grandfather, Cyrille Chennault. The elder had found his way from Louisiana to Florida after traveling with the Silas Green Show to promote

Noir's cosmetics. It was then Carrah remembered in Noir's history that Cyrille launched the company's original products by giving dancers from the variety show face powder and lipstick samples to wear when they performed.

What she didn't know was that it was also the time he founded his family's summer escape. The Shores was one of the first places Cyrille had come to in the South where there were no plantations or remnants of one. He'd also discovered Black and white communities coexisting. It was a place he believed his descendants should have a stake in.

All the talk of his great-grandfather, of course, led to them dabbling a bit into his choice not to be a part of the family business. It seemed he had been more afraid than she was. However, he had no regrets. He loved his career even though he hated the lifestyle of being so close to the rich and famous.

It was why he only took on celebrities with relatively no drama and who actively gave back to their communities, like him. She had no idea until now that he was a primary investor for Duncan's youth village and had recently established a scholarship in honor of his mother for young Black women who were interested in pursuing degrees within the STEM field.

Instead of stuffing her face with the last of her burger, she dropped it, wiped her mouth, and leaned into the table. "Really!" she blurted out, unable to contain the adrenaline spiking within her. "What made you choose STEM?"

Carrah felt almost bewitched by the man sitting across from her. Her desire to mix ingredients in a lab may have diminished, but not her love of science. She would always have a soft spot for the thing that understood her best and made sure her genius thrived…even if it had been a safety net.

"What do you mean?" His brows creased before he stood up from the table and took his dirty dishes to the sink.

"Your mother was a businesswoman. Why not a scholarship fund for students pursuing degrees in business or entrepreneurship?"

* * *

Carrah had to be pulling his leg. Their family businesses had been rivals a long time and he was sure they would have briefed Carrah when she started at the company. There was no way she didn't know of the force that was Claudette Chennault. The woman was the reason Olina Chennault Cosmetics was in the top five around the world beyond always outperforming Noir in African-American markets. She had been featured in every magazine from *Essence* to *Vogue*, and recognized a thousand times over for her philanthropy to eliminate hygiene insecurity among women and children from marginalized communities.

Needing to know if she were running game or being genuine, he went back to Carrah and looked her in the eyes. "Are you pretending to be ignorant of my mother just to make small talk or something?" Carrah recoiled, scrunching her face so hard that Chris offered an apology. He then said, "You really didn't know that my mom was a STEM girl like you?"

A hard-to-read expression flashed across her face. She raked her fingers through her hair then pulled it back into a bun that accentuated her high cheekbones, almond-shaped eyes, and full lips. She was beautiful. Always had been, but he had to turn away.

"You know what I do?" Her question halted his steps.

Of course he knew. The guys had just rubbed it in his face along with the experiments she did with everyone else. Even before that, he'd heard his parents mumble of how Carrah had taken her father's smarts and her mother's beauty. His mother had even once gone on the record of saying Carrah would've been the perfect girl for him to escort if her last name had not been Andrews.

"We have mutual friends, Carrah. I also assist the company with legal matters, so it's natural for me to know the competition. By the way, I heard you were the mastermind for the only perfume that's ever outperformed us in fragrance."

Her lips twitched. They never formed a smile. It was almost as if she resisted. She then left the kitchen and went to the bay window in the sitting room and gazed out. He followed and stood opposite her in silence. He didn't know her well enough to gauge her thought process. What he did know, however, was that instead of seeing pride, he saw resentment. Unfortunately, it wasn't the first time. He'd seen it one too many times with his mother as she struggled to ensure Chennault remained relevant. He hoped it wasn't the same burden for Carrah.

"My mother attained a degree in pharmaceutical sciences." He broke the silence—safely, he hoped. "She was a woman of science turned business mogul after she came to work for my grandfather's company and pioneered groundbreaking advances in hair and skin care for African-American women."

"I honestly didn't know. All my life I only knew that she ran operations at your family's company. A STEM scholarship makes sense." She glanced over at him and smiled.

He sighed, resting one arm on the wall as he continued staring out into the nothingness of the night. The last year had been difficult without her busying around the house or corporate headquarters. "She was the brains of Chennault and now my father seems lost without her."

Almost like they were told to, they looked at each other at the same time. The agony, grief, and defeat that spiraled inside of him was upon her face, and he wanted to know why. Except they weren't there yet. She hadn't opened up much over dinner and he wouldn't push.

"He'll find his way." Her soft words soothed the chaos within and made him come upright. "We all do, eventually."

"Is that why you wrote the book?" She stiffened and he regretted asking the one question he wanted an answer to since he'd finished the manuscript.

A tear slid down her cheek, her eyes closed, and then she said, "I wrote it because I'm tired of being trapped."

Chapter 17

"TRAPPED?" CHRIS ASKED, echoing her reply.

Carrah wrapped her arms tighter around her waist. She felt like Samson between those two pillars. She, too, wanted them to crumble because then she might be free to escape a marriage being forced upon her and loyalty to Noir. She couldn't explain any of it to Chris for fear that he might pity her or, worse, express ridicule that she didn't deserve.

When he turned to walk away she cleared her throat and finally said, "One of the reasons I came to you despite our families' history was because I admire you." She turned to face him. "You broke free...followed your dreams instead of caving into what they demanded of you. Do they still expect something from you? Something you don't want to give?"

His hands slid into his pockets as a distant expression shadowed his face. "My father expects that one day I'll give up my passion for law to run Chennault Cosmetics."

"But why—why do they want us to accept unreasonable

burdens for the preservation of their legacy?" Her posture strengthened. "I want the chance to define my own."

"What else do you want?" His head cocked to the side as she watched him watch her.

She turned away, afraid he could see all of her fantasies. "To know you," she said a little above a whisper. "We've spent our whole lives knowing each other but not really. I don't want us to be pseudo-strangers anymore."

"Then"—he straightened into his full height as his eyes locked to hers—"tell me something I don't know about you. It can be trivial or serious, good or bad."

For a second, Carrah regretted that she'd allowed the words tap-dancing around in her head to slip from her tongue. Charge it to their proximity or his sincerity to help. Never mind the handsome face that abetted in the conjuring of those thoughts. She wouldn't dare mention how the heady scents of cedarwood, lush vanilla, and something else, which was noble and intoxicating, yet mysterious, clung to him, demanding she know more. More than what she had been allowed her entire life.

Only, she hadn't bargained on him also being inquisitive, considering the uptight attitude he possessed when they sat to discuss everything. At the least, she had to be sure it was a fair exchange. She never put all of her cards on the table.

"Will you do the same?" He nodded, and anxiety bloomed to life as she searched herself for what to share. It couldn't be too deep or too shallow. Nothing that would make him regret helping her. "I'm a terrible cook."

"I don't believe you," he replied, straight-faced, scanning her as though he was still searching for the truth. "*Et le gumbo?*" His brow arched, and she giggled while shaking her head no. "Jambalaya?" he asked, accent thicker than normal and she replied the same. "Fried chicken or collard greens?"

Carrah managed to raise her hand as though she were taking an oath despite her uncontrollable laughter. The scowl upon his face had her in tears although it more than demonstrated his disappointment. "I can boil water," she finally got out, "sometimes fry an egg. At times bacon in the air fryer; that's it. I would've burned those burgers tonight if I'd been cooking."

"Glad you set the table." Chris scratched his head while shaking off a laugh. "What about that old saying you Southern women have about the way to a man's heart is through his stomach? How do you plan to catch your husband?"

"Maybe I don't want a husband," she snapped.

The jocular spirit dissipated between them and she immediately wished she had better words. It wasn't his fault her ideals of wedded bliss had been tainted. Chris had said he was a one-woman man earlier. Perhaps he was.

However, she knew Gavin was not and there was an old adage that spoke of birds flocking together because of a feather. At least a woman knew what she was getting with Gavin. He offered no promises, hearts, roses, or weddings. On the other hand, Trent had been a wolf in sheep's clothing that strayed between multiple women's legs.

Her entire body stiffened at the disgusting thought before her gaze returned beyond the window. Nothing was there except for the dark. It was better than allowing Chris to see the humiliation and insecurity another man had caused.

"You don't believe in marriage?"

Carrah turned her head slightly to him while considering his question. It was earnest and relevant, given the way she had callously responded. Still, it was more than she wanted him to know. "Your turn, Chennault. Tell me something I don't know about you."

He arched a brow at her and then moved to the couch while gesturing for her to take the seat across in the swivel chair. "Trivial or serious?"

"Serious." She lowered down into the chair and sat on the edge.

Chris perched up on the sofa then leaned forward until his elbows hit his knees, and he stared her in the face. "I don't like my questions to be ignored."

Carrah swallowed hard as her line of sight fell to the ground. She failed to calculate how getting to know Chris would expose so much more of her. "Maybe one day I'll get married. My parents have shown me a marriage that is kind, enduring, and full of love. Unfortunately, that has not been my experience and I deserve and want the same."

"Ditto," he said as she lifted her head and met his gaze. "Why was that so hard to say the first time?"

She shrugged. "I don't know. It's a topic that has been very personal for me lately." Her thumbs began to fidget and she glanced down at them, praying he wouldn't ask any more questions that would make her think about the way her family had disregarded her happiness and auctioned her off in exchange for Noir.

"If I ever present a question that you are not ready to talk about, tell me. Don't brush me off. Especially if what I'm asking pertains to the business between us. I hope my request is not too much."

"It's not," she admitted. "Although, you are sort of—" She covered her mouth and looked off for a few seconds. "You're very, uh…assertive."

"Sure that's the word you want to use." A sardonic smile curved his lips as he eased back into the couch.

How had she missed this side of him? The Chris she

usually got was quiet, serious, and dismissive of her. The one across from where she sat was unlike anything she'd encountered. The bad blood between their families had totally clouded her perception.

All these years, and by God, Chris Chennault was hotter than hell. Now was the time she had to keep her wits about her. Too much was at stake.

* * *

Chris assessed how Carrah turned away to cover the flush staining her cheeks. He honestly had not meant to taunt her in a way that might induce reservations on becoming his client or being here with him. He knew he had a reputation of being imperious. However, in this moment that was not how he wanted her to feel about him.

A level of comfort needed to exist between them given their already complicated dynamic...and he wanted to know her in the same way she wanted to know him.

He cleared his throat, garnering her attention. "How about something trivial now?"

"You first." She winked.

"Fair." He surfed his mind for things she wouldn't know unless she had spent time with him. A smile stretched across his face and he said, "I'm a sci-fi junkie. I love *Tron*, *Star Wars*, *Dune*, *Stargate*...I could go on."

"Seriously," she shouted, shooting up from her chair with full cheeks and giggles. "What's your favorite episode of *Star Wars*? No! Wait...wait, don't answer. Let me guess."

He chuckled, seeing Carrah so animated. He much preferred this version to the one standing at the window. "Okay, so you're noble. At times arrogant, a little mysterious, and definitely dominant." She side-eyed him pacing the small living room area allowing her full thought process to be on display.

"You have no idea." His reply stopped her. She examined him until he dismissed her silent inquisition and apologized for the interruption. Just as she hid things behind her veil, so did he. Therefore, he signaled for her to continue as he leaned farther back into the sofa.

"Add ego to the list," she huffed. "You're also still conflicted about helping me because of our history. Yet you deem it right." She stopped again, facing him this time with hands on her hips. "Episode three, *Revenge of the Sith*?"

"'I do not fear the dark side.'"

A little tremble rolled over Carrah's body, hearing the malevolent edge he'd laced his words with. "You're such a Vader." She cleared her throat then broke the connection. "And... for the record it's my favorite episode, too!"

"You surprise me, Ms. Andrews." He grinned from ear to ear. "Do tell why."

She rolled her eyes and plopped down next to him on the sofa. His muscles tensed and he readjusted his legs to keep from brushing against hers. He fought his base nature and managed to steer his attention away from those pretty brown thighs at his side. "You're going to think it's super girly."

His lips pressed together and for once he found himself debating fight or flight. The tightness in his chest finally gave way to an exhale and he crossed his legs, perched his chin in his palm, and attempted to give her his undivided attention. "Try me."

"He...Anakin, was desperate to keep the love he'd found with Padmé. His soul was in limbo the entire episode because he thought the path he was on would remove his pain and fear of loss. Of course it did the opposite, but even after she learned what he'd done, she still loved him. So much so that on her deathbed she stated that Anakin still had good inside of him. It was a love story without a happily ever after."

"Mmmm...yeah, that's a bit girly, considering we watched him kill younglings and choke his wife out." He chuckled as he raised his hand to stop the pillow in her hand from smacking him in the face. "Were you going to hit me?" She gave a mischievous nod and he couldn't help smiling while removing the pillow from her hand. He casually tossed it to an empty chair and focused back on her.

"Anyhow, there is truth in what you said. Had you not tried to accost me, I might have finished." He suppressed his laughter as she cackled out loud and signaled for him to finish. "Ultimately it was the path he chose. Albeit tragic, he stayed on it, owned it, and in the end redeemed himself. Not many people will take responsibility for the lows along the road."

Carrah nodded in agreement before they dove into dissecting episodes and character flaws a little while longer. Once her nerdiness took over, she revealed that she was a fantasy buff who was a sucker for fairy lore. She also admitted to being a *Stargate* fan, citing time travel as a staple within the fantastical worlds she loved.

Her admission led to a debate on the ethics of time travel, which was the basis of the *Stargate* series. Do or don't? Indulge or influence, either had the potential to reshape the future. There ended up being far too many scenarios to consider.

However, the one that challenged Chris's views of not altering time was their rivalry. What if there had never been one? Could a leap back in the past correct what went wrong or change nothing at all? It was not the first time he wondered what growing up as friends would've been like. Tonight was just the only time he ever regretted that they were not given the chance.

Perhaps his thoughts were shared by Carrah. He pondered the possibility when she grew quiet and sat staring at him. She had already made a compelling argument for wishing to shift time to take advantage of medical and scientific discoveries. Maybe she would consider righting wrongs.

A little voice told him no. Her intrinsic disposition was rooted in her belief of fate. In Carrah's mind, even if the past was changed, the future outcome would be the same—so maybe not. Regardless, the depth of their conversation gave him chills, much like her manuscript had when he read about lost souls finding one another.

At once their phones came to life severing the reflective pause in their debate. Carrah unfolded from the couch and retrieved her phone from the table while Chris pulled the vibrating device from his pocket. It was Duncan in the guys' chat checking to see what everyone was up to because he didn't want to watch a cheesy romance with Reese.

"OMG!" His attention flung to Carrah standing in the kitchen looking down at her phone. "Dunc better get it together. They are playing catch-up. He has to indulge my girl."

He saw her thumbs working at the keyboard of her device.

"Not everyone wants to be held hostage by a sappy romance."

Carrah lowered her phone. "There's nothing sappy about *Dirty Dancing*. It's a classic." Her eyes narrowed on him. "Did Dunc text you that?"

"Don't matter." Chris slid his phone back into his pocket. "It's not a movie a man is eager to watch."

Carrah moved back to the sitting area. She folded her arms and stared at him as though she were contemplating next steps. "Have you ever seen it?"

He shook his head no and then he peeked down to his wrist to check the time. Before he could tell her it was late and she should be heading home, the television turned on. She stood with the remote in hand typing DIR into the search box.

"What are you doing?" Chris questioned. He abandoned his seat and got close enough to try swiping the remote from her. She giggled, snatched away, and then aimed the remote back at the television. On his second attempt he grabbed it from her dainty hands. "I'm not watching that tonight. Besides, it's late. I should probably follow you back into town to make sure you get there safe. These back roads can be tricky late at night."

She waved her hand in the air, turning away from him, and went to reclaim her seat on the sofa. "I'm not leaving until you watch. The least you can do is honor bro code and make sure Dunc has a guy to exchange commentary with. We both know Reese; he's going to end up watching." She crossed her legs, patting the cushion where he had been seated.

"You're serious?" He kept it simple for there were far too many thoughts crossing his mind, and this was the easiest to articulate.

"As a damn heart attack." She doubled down and leaned back into the cushion folding her arms.

Chris interlocked his hands behind his head and released a long sigh. The astute side of him demanded he adhere to the lines drawn in the sand, forget the contract, ignore the slivers of camaraderie that threatened betrayal, and get her back to town. On the contrary, he had never been a man to disregard his curiosities, and Carrah Andrews had seemingly become one.

Her visit to his office, reading the manuscript, the night of the ball, and now this evening carved a path opposite of the one they had been given from birth. He was compelled to explore it. And though he would never admit it, he liked her company.

Without another thought he unlaced his shoes, slid them off, and moved to reclaim his seat at her side. He gave her the remote. "Who am I going to tell Dunc I saw this movie with? He knows I'd never watch alone."

"A friend?"

A chuckle escaped him. "I may be going out on a limb, but I'm sure most men who watch *Dirty Dancing* do it because they have a lady friend wanting to." Their eyes met for a second, maybe two. "I'll say I saw it with Chloe. I better not hear otherwise."

"Is that a threat?" Her lips quirked into a smile.

"No," he sighed. He had to be honest. Keep the lines from blurring so neither would be disappointed by the realities of the very public division between the Chennault and Andrews families once they left the safe space of the cottage. "A reminder that technically we shouldn't be here."

Chapter 18

THE MORNING SUN beamed in through the window forcing Chris to slowly open his eyes. He stretched, finally able to extend his legs on the couch until his feet were no longer under the covers. There was no rush to move. He didn't have to play host any longer since he'd already watched Carrah tiptoe out at the crack of dawn.

Besides he'd taken the day away from the office, and thank God, because he was still processing last night. He'd been alone with women before but none had ever made him feel like he'd trekked down the mountaintop into a valley full of dense fog before being tossed in the ocean. If there was such a thing as an emotional hangover, this was it, and he was even more confused than he had been prior to meeting Carrah at the cottage.

It was his fault. If he had stuck to the plan—meet, advise, sign—then he wouldn't have mistakenly lowered his guard. Since it had fallen he found parts of himself unraveling. How long had he thought Carrah was beautiful? What would it be like to be in her company longer? Was Trent the sole reason she looked down on marriage? Why did she feel trapped, and was there a way for him to help her? He shook his head, decapitating the thoughts, and got up from the couch.

On the way to the bathroom he saw that she'd left a paper on top of the counter. It was the contract. Carrah had signed it, accepting the deal with Hurston House. The normal fist pump accompanied by a euphoric high after landing a deal didn't happen.

In fact, he slumped down to the stool. He sat staring at the paper, attempting to rationalize his actions and build a solid defense against his betrayal. One day he would have to present to his father and siblings the taboo he'd invited in, because they were bound to find out. There was no going back for him. Especially after witnessing the turmoil upon her face as she confessed that she was trapped. He couldn't stand by and allow Carrah to be boxed in by anyone or anything.

Uncertain and unwilling to understand why he suddenly felt the need to be a protector, he got up from the stool and took care of his morning hygiene before he threw on running shorts and left the house. His thoughts emptied as his feet began beating the pavement. There was something peaceful about running first thing in the morning. Chris didn't know if it was because the sunrise presented renewal and allowed him to consider possibilities for the day while forgetting the problems of yesterday, or if he simply enjoyed the smell of morning dew, hearing birds tweet, and watching squirrels race up trees as the Shores came to life. Regardless of the reason, a morning run always cleared his head.

Five miles and forty-five minutes later, he hadn't been able to escape his thoughts like he'd hoped he would. Instead he stood on the front porch bogged down in what-ifs while removing his sweat-drenched shirt. His phone vibrated and he found himself hoping it was her. One thing he uncovered during his jog was that he didn't like the way she had sneaked out this morning. Nor did he relish the elusiveness she clung to even after they agreed to divulge lesser-known facts about each other. He wanted to know her and was compelled to understand the experiences that gave her a bad taste for marriage. Simply put, he needed to make sense of what it all meant.

When he finally looked at his phone, he saw that it wasn't Carrah, but his father summoning him home. These cryptic messages often translated to there being a need at the company that required his legal advice. Instead of grabbing his fishing pole and heading to the dock like he planned to, Chris showered, dressed, and tidied up the cottage before he was on his way home.

Upon arriving at the family compound, he noted that his cousin Miles's car was in the driveway. Which was odd, given that Miles rarely made it to the Shores during the summer months. Miles and his mother often visited during the winter months to escape the frigid snow season in the Northeast. Still, Chris was excited to see his big cousin, who was more like his older brother. A year had passed since they last had a chance to get together, and it was nice they could for once in a long time explore the Shores together.

The laughter meeting Chris as he entered the home was music to his ears. Ms. Watson informed him of where his family was gathered and he rushed down a rear corridor following the voices until he stopped outside the sunroom. It warmed him to hear his father in good spirits. The man had been struggling to find his place this summer without his wife.

Surprise overcame Chris as he entered the room and saw Benjamin Peters, the company CFO, and Carolyn Elliot, the chief operating officer, along with Miles and Carter. Irony was not lost that mere days ago his father had stood at the golf course lecturing him about reducing his work schedule while summering in the place they called home three months of the year.

"Good morning!" Chris stole everyone's attention as he entered. "Miles." He chuckled, embracing his big cousin who had taken all the genius scientific genes of the family.

"How's it going, little cuz?" Miles mocked with laughter as they hugged then exchanged the secret handshake of men within their fraternity. They came apart and stood shoulder to shoulder at six-three. "Your pops summoned me here. What's the old man got up his sleeve?"

Indeed that was the million-dollar question. Chris glanced across the room to where his father sat in a comfy armchair. "I have no idea. Sounds like we were both beckoned here."

"Have a seat, Christopher." His father tilted his head to the open seat next to Miles.

Meanwhile, Chris wanted to know what hocus-pocus was being conjured. His father seldom addressed him by his full name and only called impromptu meetings to avoid a challenge. Never mind that two of the company's most loyal employees were sitting opposite of where he stood making small talk with Carter.

Before Chris took his seat he exchanged pleasantries with Mr. Ben and Ms. Carolyn. He'd known them all his life, was friends with their children, and respected their business sense. They'd helped his parents shape Chennault into the company it was today, and so as he sat, he knew this was not an average *I need you to do something, Chris* request.

"Chloe," Chauncy called for his daughter.

"I'm here, Dad." Chloe raced into the room. "Oh." She slowed, side-eyeing Chris. "I see you found your way home." She winked and then claimed a seat next to Carter on the couch.

"Alrighty, we can start." Chauncy perched up in his chair, steepling his fingers. "Thanks to the vision and pioneering efforts of Claudette to develop and manufacture products for all skin types and hard-to-match skin tones, Olina Chennault Cosmetics continues to be an industry leader in makeup, fragrance, and hair and skin care for Black women. Claudette left us a blueprint for how to continue being change makers in an industry that scrutinizes beauty by European standards. Yet there are members of the board whom believe it is not the best trajectory.

"They've believe it is outdated and have expressed that it may be time for a change in leadership." Chauncy looked Chris dead in the face and then continued. "Basically, it seems they want me gone and something quote, unquote, fresh. Of course, these board members do not have the shares or votes to oust me as the president and chairman, but we don't want disgruntled stakeholders. It's bad for business."

Chloe cleared her throat. "Excuse me," she interjected. "What of Mother's plans are they unhappy about exactly?"

"Not unhappy." He released an audible breath as his hands fell to his lap. "More like room for improvement. They feel as though we need to attract a younger audience while also providing products that consider aging. We have a few products that address anti-aging, and of course we use ingredients with antioxidants and free radicals that combat the signs of aging, but we do not have a robust pipeline."

"Because over ninety percent of our customers have skin

with high concentrations of melanin. You know this, Ace." Chris huffed a chuckle hearing Ms. Carolyn address his father by his nickname. He hadn't heard it in almost a year. "Claudette explained the science of this a long time ago. It's a natural combatant of fine lines and wrinkles. Why are we deviating now?" Ms. Carolyn's elegant voice was always strong, and fierce.

"For the reason that competitors are making these products and women of color are buying them." Miles spoke up. "There is a market, an opportunity for us to reclaim those who purchase such products. Many of the ingredients used to formulate anti-aging products often do not support the pH of melanin-rich skin because it's designed for lighter skin tones.

"However, there is a way. I've been experimenting with nanoparticles and I think I may have found something."

Chris read the room. He saw Ms. Carolyn toot her lips, Mr. Ben seemed impartial, his father was in deep contemplation, Miles was confident, and his siblings hadn't offered one word. If he spotted their shortcomings, then by his father's standards, Chloe and Carter were incompetent.

At Carter's age, Chris knew the product lines, domestic and foreign markets, investments, and strategic plans. This was a huge problem for him as he considered the future of being absent from leading Chennault.

Instead of offering his opinion, which was in agreement with Miles, and giving his father a glimmer of hope, he focused to Chloe and Carter. This was when he needed them to show up, prove that the company would be in capable hands. "Do either of you have any questions or feedback?"

Carter gave a slow head shake. "I'm just listening right now."

"No," Chloe replied.

His father made eye contact with him again from across the room. Chris's mind faltered back to Carrah's question from last night about the expectation of giving something to his family. He'd shied away from the business a long time ago after seeing the toll it placed on his mother. Therefore, there was nothing he could give without disregarding the life he chose. However, his siblings' lack of engagement made him question those decisions while possibly serving to validate their father's sentiments on Chris taking the helm of their company.

Feeling trapped was an emotion he understood more than Carrah would ever know. However, for him, it could possibly be worse since he'd experienced freedom, only to have it taken away. Chloe and Carter had to do better.

"You're right, Miles, there is a market. It would be wise to tap into it. This expansion would be a win-win for us since it would diversify our pipeline while reducing the noise from other board members." Chauncy scanned the room as if checking the temperature. Not that anyone here would contest his wishes. "As Miles stated, he has already begun working on a solution."

This was the point where Chauncy solicited approval. However, Chris remained reluctant to engage. He was destined for a different path in life and he'd known it from a young age. Growing up in a Southern state full of old plantations that had some of the harshest accounts of slavery exposed him to the double standards of race.

Advocating for equal access became his passion. The accounts he'd read about or heard his parents discuss where Black men and women in the entertainment industry encountered inequities fueled his desire to make a difference. Becoming an entertainment attorney allowed him to push back and break down biases to give Black celebrities more opportunities.

The work he did to create and ensure access for entertainers of color was gratifying. The same would not be achieved in working at Chennault Cosmetics.

Chris put his hand in the air not waiting long for his father to acknowledge him. "I don't understand my purpose here. It doesn't sound like you need something from me. You know you already have my vote." He had to push back in public, remind his father, siblings, and cousin that he wasn't giving up everything he'd worked for to make his firm a top-tier entertainment group, only to get sucked into the family business.

"Actually, you are here Christopher, because I've been approached with an offer for us to become a part of a joint venture. It would be for a skin care agent that addresses both anti-aging and hyperpigmentation."

"Mergers and acquisitions are not my wheelhouse, Dad. However, I can assure you that I will find and retain the best attorney to review all contracts should you chose this path."

Chauncy got to his feet. He paced the room while everyone looked on in silence. "That won't do. I need you on this, son. The company that approached me is Noir Cosmetics." The entire room audibly gasped, but Chauncy continued. "Our history with them taints my ability to trust so I need to make sure that if we do this deal, the contract is ironclad. You're genius at that."

"Noir?" Both Chris and Chloe stood at the same time, challenging their father.

Chris wasn't sure if this was the reaction his father wanted—to drag him back in. However, going against everything his mother stood for while she was alive was a sure way to reel Chris in. Claudette was his weakness, and Chris wouldn't allow her work to be tainted by his father's wild ambitions. Therefore, he wouldn't sit idle, considering this bold move.

"The people that pushed your father out after everything Great-Grandad Cyrille started, and tried to steal the formulas you and Mom created?"

"Mom wouldn't agree to this." Chloe's nose flared, golden skin turning a deep shade of red.

"She would not," Ms. Carolyn echoed Chloe as she cast a hate-filled gaze on to their father.

Chauncy ignored both his children and Ms. Carolyn, then sat back in his chair. His attention went to Mr. Ben. Both Chris and Chloe followed his line of sight and watched as the older man set his tea down.

"She would if she knew the financial trouble they were in," Mr. Ben stated. "When your father told me Melvin approached him—"

"Wait a minute," Chris interjected. "Is that what the tiff at the ball was about?"

Their father nodded then gestured for Ben to continue. "After Melvin approached him, I did some digging into Noir's financials. They've been struggling to turn profits. Their pipeline has dried up...which makes sense because they were beholden to what Cyrille and Alphonse started the company with. Minor evolution with Charles and Edouard, and then of course they lost access to your father and mother's revolutionary ideas. Noir hadn't had anything great until a mascara about two years ago and a fragrance this year."

Chris was already tuned in. However, he perked up, learning that Carrah's ingenuity had probably helped to keep the company afloat. The logic he often applied in his business dealings took the driver's seat and he deduced that Carrah might be trapped because she was desperately needed by her family to save their crumbling empire.

"I hear the youngest daughter engineered both," Ms. Carolyn announced. "The girl is said to be the only one of Melvin and Camille's children that took his science gift."

"Yes, Carrah is her name. Melvin told me she had been working on a skin-correcting formula," Chauncy confirmed and Chris hated that his instincts were on par as usual.

"Mm-hmm, though it seems as it has taken her longer than expected to develop it, and the shareholders are not happy. I'm hearing rumors of a takeover."

"Then why do we want to go into business with them?" Finally, a question from Carter. Only it revealed his naiveté and the need for his business killer instinct to be honed.

"Because"—Chris had a sinking suspicion as he looked his father dead in the face—"Dad is going to take it back."

Chauncy chuckled as he leaned back in the chair and crossed his legs. "I am. They are desperate right now. We will use their vulnerability to our advantage and acquire them. Revenge is long overdue."

Chapter 19

CARRAH YAWNED, SHRUGGING into a lab apron. Last night...
last night. She couldn't stop thinking about it. It was the reason she'd left the second dawn broke. Being alone with Chris
induced insomnia while challenging everything she ever
thought she knew about him. Behind that stern demeanor was
a man with a sense of humor who believed in his work and
loved his family. The efforts he'd taken to preserve his mother's
legacy, be present for his father, and help her navigate a place in
the publishing world revealed a side of Chris she never should
have known.

Because now she wished for things she didn't know she
wanted. Sitting on a couch next to him before they both fell
asleep watching *Dirty Dancing* stirred desires she wasn't
allowed to have. Their last names drew lines in the sand that
neither would dare cross despite the fact that she'd shared her
deepest secret with him.

"Come in," Carrah called, answering the knocks that hit against the door as she turned the dial on the lab mixer.

The latch of the door clicked. She turned as she heard it open and saw both Aubrey and Beau. They entered her space as if all power were vested with them and it was simply because they were older. Add in the fact that they only understood the business of Noir whereas she knew the business and science, a chip seemed to remain on their shoulders.

"Late night." Beau folded his arms and took a wide stance. "When'd you get home?"

Like hell. Carrah snorted loudly then turned back to the contents swirling around in the beaker in front of her. Not this morning or this summer would her brother come into her lab as if they were back at headquarters questioning her like she was a child. "I guess that's for me to know and you to find out."

"Must you always be so defiant? It really is unbecoming."

"Must you always be an ass so early in the morning?"

Beau came to stand in front of her, puffing as though he were about to blow like he always did in meetings when she didn't bend to his beck and call. She let him stew. He needed her; she didn't need him. One day he'd accept that. Until then she positioned the microscope and prepped the slide to view the mixture that would be done in a few seconds.

"Carrah." She glanced up as Aubrey maneuvered her way around. Aubrey then signaled their brother to calm down and took his place, which was closer to Carrah. "We only came down here to check on you. You've hardly answered our questions. Can you please make sense of a few things? The shareholders are down our necks."

"Oh shoot!" Carrah quickly pressed the button to stop the mixer. The ingredients were failing to coagulate.

Both her siblings drew closer. "What is it?"

"I think the VC is unstable," Carrah replied, quickly sliding on a new pair of gloves before taking the beaker from the
mixing deck. "I must've used too much," she mumbled under
her breath.

"VC?" her brother asked.

"Vitamin C, Beau," Aubrey answered, backhanding him in
the chest.

Carrah nodded. "Yes, Vitamin C. For a long time it was
taboo to mix with niacinamide due to the pure ascorbic acid
concentrated in C. However, they are two powerful ingredients that if I can stabilize will be a game changer for correcting
hyperpigmentation while reducing fine lines. This has to work."

Carrah scooped contents from the beaker onto a glass slide
and then placed it under the lens. She bent over to view and
saw that the formula's suspended particles were swimming on
top. Worse was when she glanced to the beaker she saw that an
emulsion was beginning to separate.

"So what does this mean?" Beau asked as he fidgeted with
his hands in his pockets. He then came over her shoulder as
though he fully comprehended what she was observing. "We
need this product. We promised it to the board."

"Before or after you conspired a forced marriage?" Carrah
shrugged away from Beau and moved to clean the slide. "It's
not ready and it wasn't supposed to be until next year. I need
more time."

"That's not something we have. Why is it taking you so
long to figure this out?" He visibly seethed. "You presented
this idea last year, and you wait till now to test it and find out
that it will be delayed."

Carrah slammed the slide down, shattering it against the
granite countertop. "You're right, I presented this a while ago.

Yet your pride and fear of me having more influence than you stalled production."

"Right now we have a few weeks, maybe a month, to get a product in the pipeline that we can produce and launch early next year or we risk Butler Savings forcing an acquisition...and we will not be the ones acquiring. Unless you accept Trent's proposal, which buys us time for you to tinker with all of this."

Carrah froze. She looked from Beau to Aubrey. Her sister's chagrin confirmed her brother's words without her opening her mouth. They still expected her to make the sacrifice, again. The lack of awareness exercised within her brother's words demonstrated his refusal to accept Carrah's sentiments on a marriage to Trent.

It was also conveniently obvious Beau forgot that while he and their father ran the company, and Aubrey played house with her family while Dominic was away at college, Carrah had been the only one left to care for their mother. The physical and mental toll of being the main caregiver while working and then trying to remain sane had impacted her productivity.

She would not confide that she wrote for therapy and to escape the hopelessness she felt many days while caring for their mother. A confession of such would only garner more criticism not in her favor. Unlike last night at the cottage.

For the first time in a long while, Carrah had found a space safe enough to share her true feelings without the judgment. She was doing the best she could for the family. She always did, despite the overwhelming burden that rode her back to be Noir's savior. And if her time with Chris taught her anything, it was that there was a path etched into the road, waiting for her journey. She simply had to be willing and ready to own the highs and lows.

Her potential for self-discovery fueled her with the courage to speak up.

"Did you really ask me what is taking so long? Was our mother not sick, battling for her life last year? Who was her primary caregiver? And I won't tell you again that I am not marrying Trent."

"How dare you act as though you were the only one who cared about Mother," Beau retorted, disdain dripping from his words.

Aubrey stepped between Beau and Carrah. Her head turned to Beau. "You need to cool down. This animosity between the two of you will not help us out." She then faced Carrah. "I understand the role you played in helping care for Mom impacted your ability to work. I also support your decision to refuse the marriage proposal. With that said, we have still got to figure something out and fast or we risk losing the company."

Carrah looked her sister dead in the eyes. Even though Aubrey appeared to be telling the truth, Carrah still hadn't accepted that their family company that had operated for the last hundred-plus years was facing an uncertain future. "I don't want to believe you," she whispered.

Beau's face fell into his palms. When he moved them away, Carrah noticed dark circles under his eyes. "You think I've been riding you hard for my health or that I take pleasure in being the hard-nosed big brother?" He shook his head. "We are actually in trouble. You not *wanting* to believe me is irrelevant."

Carrah tightened her face, suppressing her tears, and then she spun on her heel and proceeded to leave her little lab. She had questions. The one person that should've been more distraught than any of them was their mother, and she had not mumbled a word.

Chapter 20

CAMILLE ANDREWS HAD been the only child of Edouard and Adelaide Chàvous. She was the heiress of Noir cosmetics. Her father had inherited half of the empire built by Alphonse Chàvous and Cyrille Chennault. Of course, the Chàvous family later seized all of Noir after the famous fallout between Edouard and Charles. Therefore, Carrah needed to understand why her mother had been silent in all of this.

Except she stopped mid-stride, and her mind rewound to a few days ago when Camille approached her subtly about the marriage proposal from Trent. Carrah restarted, marching over to the house with Beau and Aubrey on her heels, begging her to reconsider approaching their mother.

She couldn't. The undue stress and overwhelming expectation for her to commit all of her time to developing product lines was unreasonable…and it would hinder her from chasing her own dreams. Nothing made sense.

The generational wealth had been enough to last three

lifetimes. Before her great-grandfather even dreamed of founding a company, her white French great-great-grandfather had found a way to circumvent Louisiana Civil Code and ensure his descendants inherited all of his real estate and possessions. The real estate they held in the French Quarter and throughout the world, coupled with trust funds and various investments, made this situation improbable in her logical mind. Surely there was enough money somewhere to bail Noir out of trouble.

"I don't understand how this happened," Carrah blurted, finally responding to her siblings, "or why I've been kept in the dark."

Aubrey reached out to comfort her sister, but Carrah walked faster. "It wasn't intentional."

"Then what was it? By mistake? I somehow find that hard to believe."

"It wasn't intentional for the reasons you may think," her brother clarified, validating her point.

Carrah couldn't help the way she dismissed him just before her hand turned the knob on the door. She entered the house with rational consciousness streaming as she considered how Noir had profited tremendously during the last sixty years off of revolutionizing concentrated pigments that addressed the varying shades of melanated skin. The bold affirmation of declaring Black beauty had allowed Noir to emerge as a leader in an industry that often skipped over color palettes that complemented darker skin tones.

No way could they be in trouble after decades of ensuring Black beauty persisted. But if they really were, Carrah was selfishly more afraid of what that meant for her. How would she be able to leave? Their father was out of practice in the lab since he directed operations. Aubrey was only great at marketing, and the jury was still out on Beau's financial stewardship, given what she was hearing. Notions of breaking free seemed futile in this moment.

The quiet lingering within the walls of the Andrews house was in complete contradiction to the anxiety raging within. What, how, when, did the contract matter...were fighting in her head as she searched the downstairs for her mother in her normal spots.

Finally Dominic casually informed them as he made way to the kitchen that their mother was with their father in his office. Carrah hesitated. She hadn't counted on her father being present because she hoped to have her mother's vulnerability in discussing how the Chàvous family legacy got put on the chopping block. His presence could potentially impact her mother's answers and right now she needed transparency. Something that should have been given by her father since he managed the day-to-day operations after her mother had made the choice a long time ago to be in the home and raise the children full-time.

Carrah started walking to their father's office with her older siblings remaining in tow. She peeked in the half-closed door and saw her father, then knocked.

"Come in," he replied. He drew back, watching as the three entered, and their mother stood from her chair. "To what do we owe this highly odd pleasure?"

"Carrah—"

"I can speak for myself, Beau, but thank you." Carrah turned her attention from her brother and then focused on their parents. "The skin-correcting serum is not ready nor will it be anytime soon. Aubrey and Beau have informed me that the timeline doesn't work, and without it, Noir has accepted a death sentence. Is that true?" She purposely trapped her mother within her gaze.

Camille shifted in her chair, crossing her ankles and releasing a long exhale. "Unfortunately, yes." She avoided making eye contact. "I traded something a long time ago"—she swallowed hard—"and, well, I guess I am finally paying the price. I only wish I'd known then what I know now." She finally glanced up and met Carrah's stare.

"I will not submit to the pains of regret. Yet, had I honored my father's original will of the company I would have maintained operating control and in that you, Carrah, would not have ever played second fiddle to your siblings' jealousy." Her mother's brown eyes sliced at Aubrey and Beau then landed back on Carrah. "The innovation in the revamp of the mascara, and of course, the fragrance…it's how we want all our cosmetics to sell. Butler Savings Bank also provided that feedback in their recent investment audit in addition to restating their concerns about our liquidity while waiting for you to finish the serum for release."

Carrah's hands trembled and forced her to grip the empty chair in front of her. Had she been in the lab instead of writing…

Beau must've sensed her comprehension of the dire straits Noir found itself in and decided to take advantage. He proceeded to express his disappointment to their parents over Carrah not holding true to the timelines she had previously communicated. The banter between everyone else in the room went in one ear and escaped the other in the same way she wished she could.

"Dammit, Carrah," her father said, clapping his hands once, "I acknowledge that family circumstances slowed your work down. I truly appreciate the care you gave your mother. Yet this was something you had already been tinkering with. What took your focus away? We need it." The expression upon her father's face as he worked to steady his breath filled Carrah with uncertainties. How could she take a step forward on the path Hurston House paved when Noir's was in need of repair? Entertaining the gravity of her thoughts humbled her before her family. Carrah then moved around the chair and pulled it behind her until her knees touched the front of her father's desk and she sat. The frown upon his face softened. This had been their safe space since she was old enough to mix things together when they worked as teacher to pupil.

She took her time, slowly explaining in scientific terms how the emulsion had separated, while drawing a picture and labeling the serum's ingredients. Her mother looked on over her shoulder with approval as her siblings chimed in, seeking to cut corners on science and find a way to get the formula ready for market in enough time to quell the demands issued by the bank.

"Do you not get it?" Carrah snapped over her shoulder at Beau and Aubrey, who had remained at her back. She had to be the one to speak up since her father's patience was far longer than hers. "If we rush this then we risk consumers having a product that changes color, odor, maybe even texture."

"A terrible shelf life," Camille shot back at her oldest children.

"Yes, it's a disaster waiting to happen when compounding is not optimal. Are we willing to risk our reputation on a recall? Because beyond us not having money, we won't have a name."

The room became pin drop silent. She waited for her parents to say something and it was clear Beau and Aubrey were waiting too. When another minute passed, Carrah got up from the chair and proceeded to leave. Before she was out the door her father cleared his throat, effectively halting her steps.

"You're right," he admitted, and Camille released an audible sigh of relief. "The legacy of our family is in jeopardy."

"Everything," Camille whispered. "Everything," she repeated louder, gritting her teeth, "my family built from the ground up is at risk of a hostile takeover since Butler Savings was brought into the fold." Her mother sliced her father with both her words and gaze. "I will not rehash my conversation with your father, but I should've been made aware of the deal with Butler Savings, despite my illness. Never would I have agreed to a marriage for their money," she hissed.

"Cam—"

Her mother threw a hand up, demanding her father stop talking.

In a flash, Melvin moved from his desk and kneeled at Camille's side. His hands reached for her and a faint smile touched his lips. "I am sorry, you know that. I believe I've found us a way out of the agreement with BSB. It may ruffle some feathers, but it will save us and give Carrah time to get the formula market ready. Give me a few days. I won't let you down this time."

"Is there anything I can do to assist?" Beau stepped forward.

"Not yet. When the time is right, I will need all three of you to fall in line. This company means everything to me and your mother. I never want her to regret giving me the opportunity to run it."

Carrah nodded, acquiescing to being the good daughter. How could she even think about publishing a book when her family's entire legacy hung in the balance?

Chapter 21

THE OLD PINK-AND-WHITE house came into view as Carrah turned at the stop sign. She yawned, pulling into the closest parking space and admiring the gingerbread adorning the front porch of the town's favorite coffee shop. A lightly caramelized, almost nutty scent had found a way to escape the confines of the house and seduce anyone up early enough in downtown Mount Dora, to beat the morning rush for magic promised in a cup.

As soon as Carrah opened her car door, that caramel nut scent coupled with roasting coffee beans hooked her olfactory sense and lured her inside through the little Dutch door. The hustle and bustle of the baristas in addition to the aromas swirling around vanquished the grogginess she'd endured from the last two days of researching to find ingredients to stabilize the serum.

So much for summer, she almost said aloud while waiting for her order to be taken. Not only was she working as if she were in her lab at headquarters, but she'd skipped dinner with her friends yesterday and was considering bailing out on Reggie's game night this weekend for a quiet evening all to herself. The worst was that she was no longer sure about moving forward with the publishing contract.

Carrah suspected it would take another two or three days coupled with a miracle to balance the formula. There would be more days and weeks to invest in for reinvigorating the pipeline pending the formula's success. And that would be the beginning of restoring a semblance of hope. It was the only way out without feeling as though she'd assassinated Noir.

"Next," the boy behind the counter called, offering a kind smile while she approached.

Carrah inhaled the rich, dark delicious scent that made her mouth water as she stepped up to the register. "Morning! I'll have a London Fog with almond milk. No sugar, raw honey."

"Make that two." The depth of authority oozing from Chris did more to her than words could describe...or that she would ever admit. She released a shallow exhale then glanced over her shoulder. "That sounds good"—his light eyes locked with hers—"and I'm in the mood to try something new." He then leaned forward and tapped his phone against the payment reader before his fingers gently curled around her wrist and he pulled her away from the order line to the pickup area.

Carrah's breath quickened, her heart raced, and she had no idea that she coveted this man's touch. "Thank you," she managed to get out as he let her go. She cleared her throat. "Imagine seeing you here." She eyed him, noting the leather Armani sandals that exposed his toes, which actually appeared manicured, and boat shorts he'd paired with a classic V-neck that allowed the fine hairs on his chest to peek out. "Not working today?"

It was a legitimate question since she knew Chris maintained office hours due to his recent expansion. Besides, she needed to distract her mind from imagining her fingers playing at his chest.

He chuckled as his hands slid into his pockets. "Actually, I'm done working for the day. I wrapped my last call about thirty minutes ago." A bark of laughter escaped him as she drew back and fiddled with her phone to check the time.

"It's only eight thirty in the morning. Is that normal for you...I mean in your line of work?"

Chris nodded, answering, "The entertainment industry is worldwide. I was negotiating with a production studio in London. It's afternoon there now, and in this industry early is always better."

"Morning meetings are not my ministry." They both laughed. "Having to be cordial and no doubt code switching before eight is just crazy and seriously early."

"No earlier than you tiptoeing out my front door." Not a trace of humor was visible on his straight face, and if she were not overanalyzing maybe the small tick at his jaw revealed a hint of frustration. "Haven't heard from you since." He folded his arms and watched the baristas work. "What, it's been—"

"Two days." Carrah refocused her attention to the prep bar silently hoping they would call her order and remove the elephant he'd dropped in the room. Out of the corner of her eye she saw him nod his head. It was that cultural way of acknowledging BS. "I didn't want to wake you up after I'd already overstayed my welcome."

His brows furrowed. "Did I say that?" Carrah shook her head no in response. "Then how did you arrive at that conclusion?"

"Two London Fogs," a high-pitched voice called from behind the counter.

A sigh of relief escaped her as Chris darted forward and retrieved their teas. He passed her a cup then carved a path through the now crowded café for them to exit. "This is good!" He sipped from his drink as they stepped outside onto the porch. "Never heard of it until now. London Fog," he mumbled, lifting it back to his mouth.

Carrah couldn't resist the smile she felt curving her lips. She loved that he had taken a liking to one of her guilty pleasures. "Well, when you don't like the taste of coffee, but want something more sophisticated than hot chocolate with a pinch of caffeine." She raised her drink then took a sip and relished the sweet hints of bergamot smoothed by vanilla and honey.

He smiled at her, and dear God, it made her think of the way Billy Dee smiled at Diana Ross in *Mahogany*. She melted. Only, she knew the outcome of this. So she caught herself because falling wasn't an option.

At that moment she decided that one day after Noir was rescued and she could dream again, maybe then she would publish her story. Lord knows she wanted people to read the tale of how her star-crossed lovers waited for each other over a thousand lifetimes. She would break the news to Chris later. She wasn't prepared for him to think less of her or be upset for wasting his time.

"You know what would be good with this?" His words pulled Carrah from her contemplation and she watched him saunter down the sidewalk. He turned right, taking a few more steps, then paused as though he were expecting her to be at his side. "Are you coming?"

"Depends on where you're going," she responded while walking to where he stood.

He raised his cup and pointed in the opposite direction of her car. Most of the shops in that direction were retail. "A glazed twist would pair well with my London Fog."

"From Not Jus' Donuts?" The light rumble in her stomach confirmed that she too thought it would be good. In fact, it made her think of her grandmother Madilyn, and how the old woman often paired fresh beignets with her tea. Carrah groaned, fighting hard to resist sweet temptations that could otherwise compromise the fit of her gown for the annual June-teenth Red Party. "I can't."

"Are we back to this? First fries, now donuts." He did an about-face, came to where she stood, and then tugged her until she started walking at his side. "Besides, you owe me after I was forced to endure an insufferable romance."

"*Dirty Dancing* is not insufferable." She side-eyed him, watching as he shook his head in disagreement. Not a battle she wanted to fight today. "Do you know how many calories and carbs are in one donut?"

"I'll burn it off when I run." He glanced across to her. His lips quirked in a way that made her regret Chris was retained as her good, commonsense attorney, because damn if she didn't want more than legal advice. "Can you live a little bit, Carrah Andrews? Be like Baby, or whatever her name was in that movie. Don't stay in the corner."

His words froze her. In one evening the boy she had known from afar had deciphered the secrets of her soul. Shame flooded Carrah, drenching her in the regret of knowing that she still lived for everyone else. The last few days in the lab and reconsideration of the book's contract proved as much.

Though she would not confess it to Chris. He'd escaped the preordained path of working at his family's company, ventured out, and found his own way, which garnered much success. Someone like him would never understand how or why she was afraid to push out of a corner.

How could he? He'd never been boxed in. Carrah had been trapped a long time, and it started with her mother.

Camille had dictated Carrah's style, weight, hair, elocution… the essence of who she was for appearances' sake. Then, of course, her father had reinforced four sides of the box and given it a lid two days ago. A reminder of the trade she'd made from beauty queen to lab rat. Therefore, she was in no position to simply live a little bit. Not when her duty was to revitalize the life of Noir Cosmetics.

* * *

The second her feet became stuck on the cement, Chris regretted his words. "I shouldn't have said that."

"You watched the movie? I thought you fell asleep."

A lazy smile curved his lips. "*You* fell asleep. I was in and out," he lied. He'd watched it until the end while stealing long glances at her.

Even right now, Chris couldn't help how he studied her in those blue, hip-hugging yoga pants and formfitting crop top, which accentuated all her curves and taut stomach. It was clear she cared about her body. He'd long noticed how fit she was. Still, he had no idea why she was so hung up on counting calories and grams of sugar. Perhaps habits from being on the pageant circuit died hard.

"But you saw the part where Baby is trapped in the corner." She narrowed her gaze on him. "That's like the most important scene, and it's at the end, so I don't believe you, Christopher Chennault." Her jesting warranted a snarky reply. Only, before he made a comeback her face became pinched, making him swallow his words. "And it's okay. You're right," she muttered. "Everything is always for someone else. Me being in the lab the last few days goes against why we come to the Shores."

Again, Chris pumped the brakes on a response. If he confessed what he knew, then maybe he could help her. But then, would she really want his help? He didn't want her to reject his assistance...or him for knowing what his father had planned. A sliver of regret planted seeds of doubt.

It was unfortunate he had the knowledge of knowing her family's empire was on the brink of collapse and that she was the only one with the brains to maybe pull it out. His mind floated back to the first thoughts he had after his father presented the joint venture.

While his concerns should've been of his mother and knowing that Claudette wouldn't want their family mixed up with the Andrews, he thought of Carrah. Noir's impending ruin wasn't her fault, and having to fix it was not fair to her. Only, he understood the expectations of the burden she carried to give back to her family. Most everyone in their circle of friends had been raised to exalt the family legacy.

Beyond the frill of being a child raised in an elite Black family, he didn't want her to become a casualty of a revenge-based business deal. It would likely tarnish lines for any future reconciliation. However, the last and most concerning thought was that he wondered if her family were the ones she felt trapped by.

It made the most sense as he considered crumbs she'd unwittingly dropped. She'd definitely maintained her guard. Yet, as he heard her speak about working the last few days while in the Shores, he speculated the concerns with the family business were maybe the reason she had not responded to an email from the agent he'd referred.

"Have you been talking to my dad?" he asked, and she giggled. "He, too, doesn't believe in work during the summer. He's still upset I'm keeping hours while here this year and made our vacant space downtown into my makeshift office."

"I think I might like your father," Carrah teased, and opened her mouth to say something but stopped and then stuck her nose in the air. "Mmmm." She inhaled deeply. "You smell that, Chennault?"

A flush of adrenaline rushed through his body at the way his name fell from her lips. His face lit up like a kid's in a candy store, unsure if it was because of her beautiful wide smile or because his sweet tooth would finally get some action. "Fresh donuts!" He licked his lips, still uncertain of what he liked most. "Come on." He tilted his head in the direction of the store. It was easier than telling her that he liked the way she'd said his name.

They commenced a brisk stroll down the sidewalk, sipping their Fogs. They passed a host of shops, including the new comic stand Duncan had helped bring to downtown, Uncle Willie's and the bookstore he imagined would one day hold Carrah's book. Being beside Carrah as they wandered downtown was one of the most touristy things he'd done in a long time.

He especially liked their debate on which debutantes and escorts might hook up after the ball. It was intriguing to see how they similarly read people. They both agreed that Destiny and Xavier might as well set a wedding date. On the contrary, Alexandria and Carter were done. Alex was pretty, came from a good family, and had decided to attend Spelman, which was right across the street from Carter, who was at Morehouse. However, she was much too bossy and immature for the two-year age gap already between them.

For a fraction of a second, his breathing suspended, listening to Carrah speak so highly of his brother. She had really taken time during preparation for the ball to learn who Carter was. Chris couldn't help wondering if she would give him the same courtesy or if she would relegate him to simply being a professional service. Time would tell.

For now, he still wanted to know more about this foe he was currently aiding. He paused at the edge of the sidewalk leading to the front door of the donut shop. "Before we go inside, I want you to tell me something else I don't know about you."

"Right here?" She scanned him, skeptically debating his question and he nodded yes. "Is this a game?" He shrugged, savoring another sip of his hot tea. "It's how we bridge the distance between us courtesy of our families' feud."

Her lips pressed together and he could see her mind searching for a nugget to share. Finally, her cheeks filled as her eyes focused to his face. "I love landscape art. Mountains, the lake, a lush meadow, and sunsets...I chase them sometimes searching for a modicum of peace."

"It's why you cherish your time here?"

"Yes," she admitted.

Chris understood. Peace was always discoverable in the Shores. He found it every morning on his run to greet the sunrise as it bloomed over the lake and scattered light across the sky. His steps restarted then halted when she tugged at his arm.

"Not so fast." She giggled. "Your turn. Eye for an eye, remember?"

"I miss the beach." He couldn't help returning her smile. "I haven't been in ages."

"Why?"

A knife-sharp pain pierced him in the chest. He looked off for a second, struggling to breathe, and then finally exhaled. "Time...my mother's passing. Then there is the expansion and client demands. My ex also wasn't a fan. She hated sand between her toes," he sheepishly admitted.

"Well, I love sand between my toes. We should go. I mean, we're only an hour or so away."

Reality seemed woozy, but Carrah appeared genuine. A part of Chris believed she was. And yet, loyalty to his family demanded he think differently. It whispered against where he stood with her now, and chastised the attorney-client agreement.

Accepting her as his client introduced an unnecessary complication into his life. Instead of avoiding it, he ran to it. There was something about her that challenged his right mind. He didn't know what it was. Yet he was compelled to find out.

"Maybe we should grab a dozen to go, to take with us to the beach." He took a swig of his tea and then restarted his steps down the sidewalk. He opened the door to the shop for her, and as she was about to pass through he asked, "How long will it take you to get ready and meet me at the cottage?"

Chapter 22

THE SUN HAD yet to reach its highest point in the sky when Carrah turned down the gravel-filled path. She blew a long breath while gripping the steering wheel until her knuckles ached. What had she gotten herself into? She muttered to herself as she looked up ahead and watched Chris open the trunk of his Jeep.

She parked and noted a hint of gray clouds rolling in and wondered if they should reconsider. Her thoughts to make a change of plans had little to do with the potential of rain. This was summertime in Florida. Everyone knew the weather was fickle. Besides, most melanated folks preferred the cloud cover at the beach.

Contemplation of their impromptu excursion had everything to do with her thoughts of being alone with Chris again—and not for the reason that most would think. He was safe, easy to talk to, listened, and offered solutions. Hell, she'd already confessed her most sacred secrets of writing a novel and feeling trapped. What would she tell him next?

There was no denying she was vulnerable to the heir of Noir's longest-standing competitor. She best not forget that he was indeed her rival. Reminding herself of the constant he had held in her life since she was old enough to know might reduce the chances of her lips becoming loose and disclosing the trouble the company was in.

"You again," he snickered, opening the door to her car. His smile made the world go still while issuing regrets of a past they had no ability to change. "I honestly thought I'd be waiting another thirty minutes or so. You changed and gathered your stuff quicker than I expected." He extended his hand and helped her from the car.

"So it seems you take me for a run-of-the-mill type of girl." She took his hand, exited the car, and moved to get her beach bag and chair from the back seat.

His face tightened as he reached in first and took her bag and chair before moving to his trunk. "Run-of-the-mill girls can't get my time."

"Summer does." She bit her tongue as her eyes darted to the ground. Why did she say that? He wasn't Gav, Dunc, or Reg, whom she could be careless with and tease. Nor was he Trent, making her second-guess the woman she was because his eyes, hands, and dick wandered.

There was no rebuttal. Just Chris moving to place her belongings into his trunk. Which, in some ways, was a reply. Not exactly one she liked, but she cared not to read between the lines. What he did with Summer was his business. Still, the silent treatment was killing her. It seemed especially worse when he brushed past her and went to the passenger side of the Jeep.

"Come on, get in." His tone was clipped and impatient as he held the passenger door open. "We've got about an hour ride."

The demeanor he now demonstrated contradicted the way he was seconds ago when she arrived. In an effort to still her tongue and keep the peace she disregarded the manner in which he spoke then slipped through the door. She settled into her seat, wishing he hadn't clearly taken her comment so seriously as she watched him go around the front of the car and then slide into the driver's side.

"Jealous much." His peripheral sliced across her before he put on his sunglasses and she felt like she'd turned the shade of rage. "Never pegged you for that type."

"Because I'm not," she snapped.

"Hmmm...then why say what you said?"

Carrah gazed out the window. She honestly wondered too, and so she searched herself for the answer to his question. What she found, she didn't like, because it exposed the stains of insecurities her ex-lover had left behind. Chris was not allowed to see that damage. "Apologies. I tease Gav, Dunc, and Reg all the time about their lady friends. We aren't there yet." She swallowed hard, fidgeting with her hands before finally looking over at him.

His head ping-ponged while his gaze remained straight ahead on the gravel path leading them to the main road. Abruptly the car stopped, and without a word he got out. From the side mirror she observed him close the gate to his property. When he got back in the car he sat still as though he was in deep contemplation.

"You're right. We aren't there yet. I believe that is the point of all of this. Am I wrong?"

Anyone else being as direct as he was in this moment

might have appalled her. However, she had learned from their last few interactions that Chris didn't mince words. In honesty, it was refreshing because there were no secrets or hidden motives to uncover.

She shook her head. "You aren't wrong. I meant what I said. I want to know you…beyond the attorney-client association."

"But why?" He finally turned and looked her in the face. God willing her heart wouldn't flatline.

"I could ask the same of you." Their eyes locked and she hoped he couldn't see her unspoken desires.

"So you want us to be friends? Like how you are with Gav, Dunc, and Reg?" Carrah nodded a cautious *yes*, uncertain if he was in total agreement. Besides, this was all they could be. The two of them sharing a semblance of any friendship already went against each of their family's principles. Chris fastened his seat belt, put the car in drive, and turned onto the main road. "For the record, Summer Bradshaw attempts to steal my time. I don't give her any."

"Seems like you were when I ran into the both of you at the ball."

"I was being cordial," he exhaled with a grumble. "Besides, she's the only one that didn't give me crap about tagging you during the kickball game."

Her eyes rolled as she snorted derisively. "Oh, there's a surprise."

He chuckled then. "She's not my type."

"You have a type? I'm intrigued. Do tell." She turned in her seat, putting her back against the door to face him.

He chastised her for a few minutes on the unsafe nature of how she was sitting. After her third refusal to sit right, he sighed. Carrah grinned in his silent concession and then repeated her question.

Chris cleared his throat. "Aside from physical attraction, I like a woman who is confident, yet soft. Intelligent—and isn't chasing me. A woman begging me to slip between her legs is unattractive."

"Unless you're a fuck boy," she quipped.

"Of which I am not." He only took his eyes from the road for a second and glanced at her. "I think you know that, though, even if you don't know me all that well. Your turn."

A tense silence crept between them. This hole was much harder to avoid than the others she'd outmaneuvered in their more recent conversations. She took in a deep breath, accepting the safe space, and decided that it wouldn't be so bad to share. There was no benefit, no one for him to run and tell her business to. Most had already speculated that the relationship her parents and Trent's attempted to sell to the public was far from perfect.

"Faithful." She swallowed and turned to sit correctly in her chair. "A man who only wants me."

* * *

Chris eased his foot off the gas pedal. His head whipped to get a better look at her, sitting quiet now with a distant gaze at the road ahead. The pieces were starting to fall into place. Albeit slowly, he was beginning to comprehend that Trent had been the unfaithful fuck boy. It was perhaps the reason they were no longer a couple. However, he wouldn't dare ask if her ex got his kicks from having a side piece or two.

Without thinking, he raised the volume on the radio to ward off the silence sitting between them, and offered her full command. A thing he never did, but was relieved to see a smile light up her face as she reached for the radio. She pressed buttons, reacting to the songs that came over the airwaves. Classical music made her giddy while she hummed with the tune.

Rock was a no go, but the old school sounds of Motown got her fingers snapping. Eventually, and to his surprise, Carrah settled on a hip hop station.

This woman seated next to him contradicted the prim-and-proper girl he knew from afar. Bouncing to the beat and rapping along with one of the hottest female artists in the industry made him tease her, calling her ratchet. She laughed, and continued spitting lyrics. His discovery of her in this light was refreshing. It lowered his guard, and by the time the next song hit the air, he joined in as they rhymed in sync with OutKast.

What was meant to be a temporary distraction sparked banter between them that became lighthearted conversation for the remainder of their ride.

"Bethune Beach okay?" Chris asked while exiting the highway. He turned onto the palm tree–lined street heading in the opposite direction of the main causeway. Most people tended to prefer New Smyrna. It was the surf hub known for the Canaveral National Seashore and exploring sand dunes. However, if today was meant for him to escape, then he wanted to avoid the crowds while reconnecting with a place his family had frequented when he was young.

Carrah's hands clapped together and her smile lit up his car. "Of course it's okay! I used to dream of having a beach house out here."

Enthusiasm ignited between them as the car merged onto the only road leading into the well-preserved enclave known by many both in and out of their circle as the Black beach. While Martha's Vineyard clung to the Inkwell, the Shores had Bethune Beach. It was founded by Dr. Mary McLeod Bethune after Black students were denied access to Daytona Beach, as a result of the Jim Crow South. Bethune Beach was a place during the first half of the twentieth century that came to be a haven for African-Americans who were not allowed at any other public beaches.

No less than fifteen minutes later, Chris parked, and they were out of the car setting up a blanket, chairs, and umbrella on the shore in no time. He watched Carrah venture down to the shoreline and curl her pretty toes in the sand as he plopped down onto the blanket and looked out on the waves crashing in. He inhaled the deep salty air and relaxed. This was where the Atlantic Ocean met the Indian River, and it was pristine, quaint, and beautiful, much like his companion.

His stare remained fixed on her, wondering how he might keep his composure once she shed the crop top and shorts for the lavender bikini peeking underneath.

"I want to show you something," Carrah called to him while jogging back to where they had set up camp. He tilted his head to see over the rim of his shades and tried his hardest to ignore those shapely, caramel thighs exposed in her cutoff jean shorts. "Got time for a little science at the beach?" Her lips quirked as she reached for her beach bag and pulled out two empty mason jars, a small shovel, and a funnel.

Chris chuckled. "I think it's safe to say I have nothing but time today." He stood, accepted the jar, and followed her to the shoreline.

"After we decided to come here, I realized we'd never done anything like this before... you, me, out alone as uh—friends." She fidgeted with the top of the jar, but still continued eye contact. "You might have heard stories of me and my science experiments. I always did them with everyone else when we were little. Since you and I never had that"—she shrugged—"I thought, why not today."

The icy shield he needed to maintain melted a little more. The night they spent on the couch watching *Dirty Dancing* had taken a chunk of it and now he was uncertain if there was anything left. Emotions coupled with confusion continued to betray logic and the loyalty owed to his family. There seemed to be a meaning and purpose beyond him in finding this friendship or whatever they would call it. Carrah was unexpected, had been since the day she came into his office demanding help.

He gave a quick bob of the head. "I guess it's never too late."

She nodded and then began refreshing his memory on the concept of density while filling the mason jar with water, sand, and shells. The tangible example that varied densities wouldn't mix but stacked had been forgotten by him. Chris never pretended to be a man of science, but she sparked renewed interest with this little experiment.

After closing the lid and shaking it all up, he watched everything fall back into its place. "Like oil and water, they will never mix," he mumbled, observing the contents of his jar.

All the while thinking of how the dynamic established between the Chennaults and the Andrewses mimicked the separation. It was inevitable that after she no longer needed him, they would go their separate ways.

Carrah wrapped her fingers around the hand that he was holding the jar with and shook. "Not exactly," she chortled, stilling his hand as they both watched the water and sand swirl within the jar. "While it's true that both are heterogeneous mixtures, oil and water are chemically insoluble. They will never intersect. Whereas sand remains in the water settling at the bottom. Some scientists believe over time the sand absorbs the water."

He snickered. "Did you really just geek out on me?"

She looked up at him and then back down to the jar in her hand. "Hardly." She winked. "I just wanted you to understand that this isn't like oil and water, and neither do we…have to be."

"How'd you know I was thinking that?"

"Because it's what everybody says of our families...and I was thinking it too," she confessed before allowing a smile to slowly stretch across her face. "Turns out they are wrong. We're more like salt water and sand."

Laughter trailed behind her as she took off toward their umbrella and stashed the jar. He followed, processing her actions and then without knowing what else to say, he blurted, "Thank you."

"For what?" she asked, lifting her shirt over her head before facing him with creased brows.

"Letting me in." He swallowed hard, again fighting not to admire the top of her lavender bikini, which was now exposed. "I've never been one to feel as though I was missing out. But after this experiment"—he huffed a chuckle—"and knowing everyone else had this with you all of these years, it stings a little."

"Yeah, it does." She sighed. Her mouth opened, but then closed. No more words fell upon his ears.

The awkwardness that surfaced between them lasted less than a minute as Chris tucked his jar away, shed his shirt, and grabbed the Boogie Boards. He was done standing behind enemy lines, debating if this woman was friend or foe. There was a picture he had not yet deciphered because she was unexpected. However, he knew they were no longer rivals. He could no longer pretend to be.

He extended his hand to Carrah. "Ride the waves with me?"

"You'll have to teach me. I never learned." Her hand slid into his.

He held it, wondering when to let go as they ran toward the water together.

Chapter 23

SALT WATER FILLED her mouth and she spat it out through giggles while crashing onto the shore. She jumped up off her belly and stood then turned to look back out to the sandbar from where they had launched. She spotted Chris, riding a wave in, and then adjusted the bracelet linking her to the board and ran to where he ended.

"You cheated." He chuckled, squinting the salt away from his eyes as he got to his feet.

Her laughter was uncontainable. She'd bested him in no time. "Did not. Guess you're a good teacher."

The push and pull of the tide shifted her feet, forced her forward, and she slammed into his chest. It was hard, warm, and safe. She stayed there a second longer than what she probably should've before stepping back and meeting his eyes. They were deep with need, protecting some hidden emotion that she was desperate to uncover.

"Two London Fogs!" the barista called.

The smile filling Carrah's cheeks relaxed. The memory from two days ago was on a constant loop, popping into her mind whenever it was idle. She scrambled to grab her head from the clouds and rushed to the counter while closing out of an email that had come in from Olivia Grimké, a popular literary agent out of New York offering representation.

True to his word, Chris had said he would help if she let him. He'd made that affirmation when they escaped to the beach, and again yesterday at their morning meet. It seemed the man was determined to unlock her hidden fantasies and make each one come true.

Where was he? She scanned the café not seeing him and picked up their drinks. As she exited she checked her watch noting that he was already ten minutes later than he had been yesterday. Once on the porch she placed the cups down, eased her phone from her bag, and pressed his contact. There was no answer. She messaged him, waited a few seconds, but got no reply. Finally, she called his office. She cleared her throat as Shayla answered the phone.

"Morning, Shayla, this is Carrah Andrews. Is Chris available?"

"Not at the moment." Her response was crisp, but not cold. "Would you like me to give him a message?"

No, she didn't want that. Carrah didn't even want Shayla to tell Chris she'd called the main line since he'd told her to do so only if there was an emergency. "No," Carrah replied. "Can I swing by real quick and drop something off for him? I don't need to see him if he's busy."

There was no response. Carrah held the phone away from her ear to see if Shayla had hung up. A blowing noise came through the other end. "I should not be telling you this, but…Chris had a rough morning. He was only in the office half an hour before he left, said he needed to go clear his head."

Words repeated in Carrah's head twice before the light bulb went off. Chris told her the first time they went to the cottage that it was a place he came to when he wanted to escape or clear his head. "Thank you, Shayla. I owe you."

They disconnected and without hesitation she moved to her car. On the way to his cottage she made a pit stop at Not Jus' Donuts and grabbed his usual glazed twists. After the way he'd made her laugh and forget about the cares of the world the last few days, it was the least she could do to help chase his dark clouds away.

When she finally arrived at the cottage, the gate was closed. Yet there were fresh tire tracks...and he'd said this was where he came to escape. She pulled off the road and parked in a grassy patch on the side. Once she was certain her car was safe she grabbed her keys and the little pastry bag.

The second she climbed over the gate she noted his smooth, black Bentley. Instant relief flooded her in that she hadn't been wrong or wasted her time in locating Chris. She stepped on the porch and knocked on the front door. After no one answered she tried the knob and found it locked.

Again, she called his phone and got no answer. Her hands went to her hips, thinking of a way to get in as she scanned the property. Carrah took the steps down from the porch and ventured to the side of the house. Her mission to find Chris was almost distracted by the bright purple butterfly bush that grew under the umbrella of an old oak tree. She remembered Mrs. Caldwell stating the flower shied away from the sun, and so it made sense that it was nestled in a spot shaded by the house and ancient tree.

Temptation to pick a few stems was strong. However, her desire to find Chris and be there for him like he had been for her was stronger. She restarted her steps and not even ten paces away she saw him standing with his hands in his pockets still dressed in business clothes underneath a large magnolia.

Carrah approached slow and quiet, wanting to surprise him. "Are you hiding from the world?"

His back stiffened before his head began to shake. "No, just the reality that my mother isn't in it."

Pain laced with sadness quieted his voice. A moment of indecision caught her footsteps before she moved to his side. She gazed out onto the lake and understood why he came here to escape. It was a breathtaking serenity, sweet with the scent of blooming magnolias and orange blossoms that came from remnants of an orange grove to the left. The sun rising against the lush hills, tall cypress, and unspoiled nature surrounding them was hard to find anywhere else.

"I'm sorry, Chris." She thought of taking his hand. He had taken hers the other day when he led them into the water. Except this was different. She saw that he was vulnerable and didn't want to assume or take advantage of the proximity they were establishing.

"Why?" He finally looked at her. However, it was only for a fleeting second. "It isn't your fault she isn't here."

Carrah didn't know how to respond so she didn't. She stood there patiently waiting until the crumpling of the pastry bag reminded her of the twists she brought him. She extended her arm offering him the bag. After he took it she lowered herself to the ground and sat crisscross. To her surprise, he dropped down beside her in his designer slacks and crossed his long legs that were capped by Prada dress shoes. His taste was impeccable.

"Humor me."

She glanced across to see she was being offered a glazed

twist. While she was waving a hand to refuse, her head went back in laughter. "Are you trying to make me fat? I had a funnel cake and ice cream with you at the beach. Strawberry shortcake yesterday. Your sweet tooth is endless."

"Your body is beautiful." Their eyes locked. "Why do you worry about what you eat so much? Pageant habit?"

Avoiding the sincerity he spoke with, she turned away from him and focused back on the tranquil landscape of lake water and blue skies. She wished it were simply an old-habits-die-hard sort of thing. It wasn't. In the years she'd dated Trent, he had nitpicked her being too thick or too thin. Butt too big and breasts too small.

Nothing ever pleased him, especially after she gave up pageants. He often criticized her, believing she was ten pounds heavier, and then screwed women who were model thin. One was actually more voluptuous. The point was Trent's preferences for anything but her spurred body confidence issues that were as real as the new day. Chris would never know how much she and her ego appreciated his declaration.

"Critical ex-boyfriend." She exhaled, getting it off her chest while hoping she would not become full of self-doubt. That tended to happen when she rehashed the hurt she'd endured, especially in the company of a man as handsome as Chris, who made her hyperaware of her appearance.

A loud harrumph escaped him. "You mean stupid ex-boyfriend. You are as André 3000 rapped, the prototype."

Carrah froze, allowing the gravity of his words to sink in. The compliment was heady and completely unexpected coming from someone who had always looked the other way when she entered a space. She huffed a chuckle, playing off the mixed signals her brain failed to uncross, and maintained refusal of the twist.

"More for me then." He took a bite out of the fried dough. "Mm-mm, thanks." She nodded, and for a little while they sat in silence. Until he said, "When we were at the beach, it reminded me of the times I spent there with my family. A day trip to Bethune Beach was one of my mom's favorite things to do whenever we came to Florida. I guess I'd found reasons to avoid going because—do you know what it's like to watch your mother become a shell of herself?"

The spirit of the human condition humbled Carrah. She understood more than he knew. It made her contemplate how much more she would let him in. Sharing family secrets with the one man who could use them to his advantage was risky. Except her intuition whispered against her thoughts.

"Actually, I do." She cleared her throat. "My mother suffered an uncommon, aggressive flare-up with her lupus. Her body was ravaged to the point that none of us expected her to be alive to see this summer."

"You're lu...cky." He paused, swallowed hard, and then focused on something in the distance. "My mother woke up one morning and had stage four triple negative breast cancer. Then in what seemed like the blink of an eye, she was gone." His voice trembled.

"I've never felt so lost, Carrah. She was my guide. My go-to. My father stays upset with me for establishing my firm. But my mom didn't see it like that. She encouraged me, challenged me...believed this path I made was worth traveling. Today was one of those days where I would've called her up, given her an earful, and then asked for advice."

"I can't replace Ms. Claudette, nor will I try. I can be all ears, though."

*   *   *

His distant gaze settled upon Carrah. "What if it's about you…amongst other things?"

Chris reclined back to his elbows and observed her. He was unable to articulate what those other things were, for he was in no position to divulge wanting his mother's opinion on his guilty conscious regarding his father's revenge scheme against the Andrews family. Nor could he explain to Carrah that losing his mother brewed chaos within him that created doubts about sacrificing duty to his family for his career choice.

"Me?" One, maybe two seconds passed before she looked over her shoulder at him. "Because I'm you're client? Let me guess, you would ask her if you were wrong to accept me?" She swallowed hard and turned her head away from him, folding her arms.

He'd observed in previous interactions that whenever her arms crossed her chest, it was in response to something she disagreed with and it was normally accompanied by a pout. Other times he thought it was cute. Right now, not so much.

Carrah was just as aware that beyond the rivalry their grandfathers had started, their mothers had barely tolerated each other. Societal niceties from the various organizations they both held membership in was the only reason they ever even exchanged greetings. Therefore, he had other questions for his mother.

Questions that may yield answers to help him get rid of the confusion warring in his head between loyalty to his family and Carrah Andrews. Their time at the beach, the morning tea meetup, and even now, did him no favors. He'd spent the better part of last night second-guessing everything, including keeping his distance from the woman sitting next to him.

"Well…glad you know what goes on inside my head." Sarcasm dripped off his tongue unintentionally. It was hard not to think of all the ways he still desired to help her despite their jaded past.

Carrah clambered to her feet, brushing off her bottom after being seated in the grass. She started past him without a word and he grabbed her hand. Chris let go of her feeling the tug against him. "You're going to leave like that?"

"Why wait for you to tell me that our business arrangement is a mistake?" A myriad of expressions ran across her face before she schooled it to appear free of emotion. "Go ahead, say it, Chris. It's for the best anyway. I can't honor the contract with Hurston House. You can let Olivia know."

Pretending to be surprised might have worked if he didn't care about Carrah's success. He had been prepared for something like this after learning her family was in trouble and the impact she made on the company. Ever since the day she waltzed into his office demanding help while confiding her aspirations, he'd felt indescribably linked. He knew her dreams and wouldn't allow her to stop reaching for them. Besides, it could only get worse if Chauncy exacted revenge.

Chris pushed off the ground in one fluid motion and met her face-to-face. "Is that why you came here…to tell me you quit? How dare you give up on something you want because you think you know what's in my head," he gritted through his teeth. It stung a little but he had to say it. "You truly don't know anything about me."

"Maybe not…I tried to know you." She blew a breath, fidgeting with her hands before she fisted them on her hips. "I'm here even after you stood me up, because I have this feeling that had it not been for our family history, we could've gotten along like everyone else. And as for everyone else, I would've found them to see what was wrong and be a friend in their time of need."

His weight shifted from one foot to the other and so did his demeanor. It reminded him of the Hulk reclaiming his life as Bruce Banner. "For the record, I would ask her, my mother, how was it fair that you and I didn't have a choice in all of this?" The hardness of her face became soft. Her hands dropped from her hips and she focused on his face. "We have been in each other's orbits since toddlers in Jack and Jill, young adults in the Lakeside Debutante Ball, and now as full-on grown people. From Louisiana to the Shores, our spheres have never not intersected and yet they made us enemies. Is it not too late to change things? And I'm sorry. My head was—I didn't mean to stand you up."

She blinked twice. "I didn't come here to quit." Oddly, she avoided him, looking down to the ground. "In all honesty, I don't want to give up. The problem is, I don't know how to do both."

"What is both?"

Everything around them seemed to have her attention except him. He squeezed her hand, firming the grip to hopefully help her understand he was there to help. He needed to. Guiding her was the only way he no longer felt lost himself.

Her lips pressed together and parted more than once before she explained. "My family...the business. Noir needs me right now and I don't know how to work on the book and be in the lab. I can't do both."

"Answer me truthfully." He peered down into her eyes. "What do you want to do?" A deer-caught-in-headlights expression was the answer he received. Had he pushed too much? He hoped not. "What's wrong?"

Her head shook no. He was so confused by this woman until she opened her mouth and said, "No one has ever asked me what I wanted."

"I—"

"Don't take it the wrong way. Thank you for helping me realize the things I desire are important." He nodded. "I want to publish the book. Hopefully write more."

"Done. No turning back." He dropped her hand, uncertain if he meant the contract to write the book or them no longer being rivals, and went back to his seat in the grass. "Don't leave. You like landscapes. The view is pretty today." Carrah squatted back down beside him. The battle within him seemed to quiet. "Thank you for checking on me."

"Seven a.m.," she replied.

"I don't follow."

"That's how you pay me back," she softly giggled. "Seven a.m. tomorrow meet me for tea. Maybe chat about my options so I don't breach the contract you negotiated, Attorney Chennault."

A smile curved his lips. "Sounds good. Now, since I have you here...tell me something I don't know about you."

"That game again." They both laughed. "Well, if you must know, I hate fishing."

Laughter surrounded them. Chris latched on to it and the happiness it invoked.

Chapter 24

"WE BID SEVEN and a possible," Reggie stated after Gavin said he had one book.

"What!" Carrah shot back, studying her hand. It was nothing to brag about. Hopefully Ava had been luckier than her or they were about to get their butts spanked. After her meltdown on the kickball field, Carrah didn't want to reveal her tendency for being a sore loser at the card table. A glimmer of hope taunted Carrah when Ava winked at her. The problem was she knew Ava didn't know how to play spades. "What you got, Aves?"

Ava fumbled the cards around in her hand confirming Carrah's fears. The people Carrah would've partnered with hadn't been invited. So Ava it was for the night. "Uhh…maybe two. What other cards are considered trump?"

Reggie and Gavin burst into laughter as Carrah sank in her seat. This was about to be a disaster.

"Give up your Black card, Ava," Gavin said mockingly and then took a sip of his Hennessy. "Might as well throw your friendship away too. We all know Carrah hates to lose at the card table."

Ava peered over at Carrah and gave her the I-don't-know-what-to-do shrug, which forced Carrah to refocus on her hand. There were thirteen possible books, and the boys were saying they had eight. Probably more if they were banking on Ava's rudimentary skills to sabotage Carrah.

"I don't play with cheaters." Carrah folded her hand and turned it face down on the table.

"Whoa, whoa, whoa! How you calling us cheaters?" Reggie piped up, visibly frustrated with Carrah's actions. Unbeknownst that this was part of her game. Get in his head prior to starting. "Ava is the one who cheated. Up here talking across the table telling you she don't know what to do. If she can't play, she needs to get up. This is a grown folks' game."

Ava pushed her chair out, stood up, and threw her cards down. "I can't do this with y'all. The game hasn't even started and three of you are acting like some Bebe's kids."

"Reese," Gavin called to the other side of the room, where she sat booed up with Duncan. "Come take Ava's spot."

"Reese don't wanna play," Dunc responded before dropping a kiss on her forehead.

"Doesn't want to play what?" Chris asked, entering the room. "Sorry I'm late. What's going on?"

Carrah's heart rate sped up. It had been calm all afternoon. Now, it was back to racing like it had earlier at the café when they met for tea. She had to get herself under control, vanquish idle thoughts that would leave her looking like a fool and a turncoat to her family.

"Come take Ava's spot." Gavin nudged Reggie, reminding him of Carrah and Chris's tumultuous rapport.

Carrah ignored them and how they were acting. They

didn't know she and Chris had moved past coexisting from a distance. It wasn't like they could announce their rivalry was suspended because they'd entered a business agreement. In fact, they would never tell their friends for risk of bringing unwanted attention to their arrangement.

"What y'all playing?" Chris asked again.

"Spades," everyone answered.

Chris came to the table. His eyes seemed to avoid Carrah on purpose, like he wanted to remain hidden behind their secret wall. "I'll play. Who's my partner?"

The room became silent as the night before Christmas. Everybody started looking at each other and then nowhere to evade replying. Carrah sat up in her chair, but didn't take her eyes off the table. If he had avoided acknowledging her when he arrived, there was no telling how he might react now.

"I am," she finally said.

Chris sat in the chair Ava abandoned. He picked up the stack of cards left behind and let out a long whistle. "You ready to whip these boys' asses, partner?"

Carrah perked up. Her heart stopped as she met his gaze from across the table. The wink he gave her made her smile so hard, her cheeks hurt.

"What the hell?" one of their friends drawled. She couldn't make out the feminine voice. However, she registered the surprise.

"What?" Chris and Carrah said at the same time.

Quinn came over to the table and looked from Chris to Carrah and then to Reggie and Gavin. Her jaw was slack as she stood there saying nothing. "Y'all know what." She har-rumphed. "The two of you on a team—working together—it's a tad bit creepy."

Howling laughter escaped Chris as he scanned the room

and then gave Carrah a look of knowing. "Teamwork makes the dream work. I got your back."

She nodded, accepting the sincerity he extended to her from the other side, for Carrah understood he wasn't only talking about cards. Over tea they'd discussed her exit strategy from Noir, right before she had him proofread her response to Olivia, accepting representation. After which he offered his cottage to her as a quiet place to write so she could meet deadlines. She trusted him.

"Then let's do this. How many books you got?"

"Three and a possible," Chris responded to her while sorting his cards.

"I've got three, solid. Safe to say six?" Chris accepted and Carrah scribbled the number 6 onto the score sheet.

An arrogant cackle louder than normal came out of Carrah as she set her sights on Reggie and Gavin. The twisted expressions marring their handsome faces as they began recounting their hands made Chris taking Ava's place more than worthwhile.

"Ah shit!" Duncan chortled and came hoovering by the table. "This about to be good."

Chris reared back to look at Duncan and then made eyes with Carrah. In the time they'd spent together, she could tell without asking that he wanted to know what was happening.

She giggled. "Tweedle Dee and Tweedle Dum bid seven and a possible. We just bid six. I'd like to see their asses get set."

"Play to win." Chris side-eyed Gavin and Reggie, who sat at his right and left sides. It was nothing personal, just once one sat at the spades table, allegiance was only to your partner. "You're lead off, Gav."

The room became intensely quiet. Gavin contemplated his hand then mumbled as he threw out an ace of diamonds. Chris followed suit, throwing off a high card, which made Carrah aware he had no more diamonds. She eagerly waited for Reggie to play, and after he did, she pulled the deuce of diamonds from her hand and tossed it at the pile.

Gavin reached to retrieve the book and stopped as Chris's hand covered the stack. "What's trump, Gav?" Chris's laughter was drowned by expletives from the other two at the table as he collected the book.

Carrah loved the sound and planned to keep it going. She followed the next set with dropping the big joker and then sat back, enjoying the way Reggie and Gavin squirmed while Chris talked trash.

By round five, patience was beginning to wear thin for Gavin and Reggie since they had managed only one book. After Chris threw out a low card, Reggie cut him with a spade. From the corner of Carrah's eye, she watched Gavin's face curl into a malicious grin. He pulled a card and began tapping it on the table by the played pile. Of course, Gavin being a seasoned player was baiting her, trying to garner a reaction since he figured she would probably cut Reggie.

The second she threw out another spade to trump Reggie's, Gavin stood up and slammed his card on top, making him the victor of the book. "Not today, Ms. Andrews." He gloated, slapping fives with Reggie before he claimed the book.

"You should be thanking me for giving you that book," Carrah snipped at Gavin. "The rest are ours," she said across the table to Chris.

He snickered, pretending to bow to her. "Your wish is my command."

Chris and Carrah won the next book. The ones that followed belonged to them too. No less than thirty minutes later, she and Chris fist-bumped across the table, claiming the victory while ignoring their opponents' disgruntled commentary. Eventually Reggie and Gavin acknowledged their win. However, they didn't miss the chance to call Chris out for breaking bro code.

"Hey, everybody!" Summer entered the parlor along with Peyton and wasted no time coming over to the card table. "Who won?"

"Chris and Carrah!" Reese giggled. "The irony."

Everyone laughed except the two of them, who remained locked in each other's gazes from across the table. If someone would've told Carrah before the summer started that an old family foe would become a friend, she wouldn't have believed them. Those light eyes stared back at her, piercing her soul while unmasking the desires of her heart. She wished things could be different.

"It is ironic." Summer's nasally voice removed Carrah from her contemplation. "Considering how you don't like her." She plopped down into Chris's lap.

Unexpectedly, anger clashed with jealousy inside Carrah and she struggled to keep it cute. All her life she'd deceived herself into thinking she didn't like Christopher Chennault. The last few weeks revealed a lie. She had always liked him, and that was why she wanted to be his friend when they were kids. Only, he had rejected her. Made her feel unimportant, and that was what she'd done to him all these years to suppress a spark she wasn't allowed to light.

So to watch a woman like Summer Bradshaw sit in his lap and then make a mockery of the way they had interacted with each other for over twenty-years stung. No one could know, though, especially Chris. Remaining true to who she was, Carrah got up from the table and left the parlor.

* * *

"Really, Summer?" Ava roared before she darted out behind Carrah.

Chris got to his feet, dumping Summer from his lap. All of his instincts screamed for him to run behind Carrah. Instead logic won. No one knew he was representing her or that they'd warmed up to each other...or that he'd somehow had a need to protect her. If they did, then that meant their families might have questions neither was prepared to answer.

"Why would you say that?" Chris's attempt to remain calm felt futile while ten sticks of dynamite exploded inside him.

Summer gave a wry smile before she tried closing the gap between them. "Well, it's true."

"Maybe it is. We don't say it," Gavin clipped. "Thanks for making things weird again."

"Oh my God!" Summer stomped her feet. "It seems like it was just yesterday they were at odds over a kickball game. I could keep going. It's always been weird."

"No," Quinn barked as she started moving closer to Summer. Peyton came off a stool at the bar and grabbed her. "No, it wasn't weird. For as long as I can remember, Chris and Carrah have always shielded this friend group, which you technically are not part of, from their families' differences. They coexisted from a distance"—Quinn glanced at Chris—"or whatever they call it so we could all still have each other. You just made the shit weird."

"Because she likes Chris." Reese stretched her claws out like a little cat. "You have since debut. Admit it," she hissed.

Chris didn't need Summer to admit a damn thing. He knew she had an interest in him. He simply never had any in her. Perhaps if he'd been clearer about that he wouldn't be standing here now with egg on his face and Carrah gone.

His jaw twitched as he eyed Summer. "Who invited you anyway?" He took off to find Carrah, no longer concerned with what people might think.

Summer gasped, reaching for him while attempting to offer an explanation. Chris ignored her and kept going, taking the direction he'd watched Carrah walk away in. He came to the end of the hall and could either turn right or go outside. Thinking back to Carrah sharing that she loved landscapes and then seeing the breathtaking views of the lake against the twinkling lights made him go to the French doors. A crack in the door confirmed he'd chosen wisely and he stepped out into the Caldwells' backyard.

He skimmed over the yard not seeing anyone. He then pulled his phone to call Carrah, but stopped when he heard voices. He stepped off the lanai and followed the cobblestone path to where it ended at Mrs. Caldwell's greenhouse. The voices became louder, and before he got to the entry he had distinguished both Carrah and Ava.

He tapped the glass door and then pushed it wider. Ava greeted him warmly. Carrah, on the other hand, folded her arms and turned the other away. Her sadness ate at him, making him wish that they weren't having to hide behind the antiquated animosities of their families.

Chris tabled that thought for later reflection and moved closer to where they stood within an almost overpowering scent of flowers. An awkward silence settled between them. For once in his adult life he was fresh out of words that needed to be spoken.

"What the heck?" Ava guffawed, turning her head from Carrah to Chris and back again. A breathless giggle escaped her. "Oh my God, you two did bump uglies."

"No!" Chris and Carrah shouted at once.

Ava assessed him then Carrah. "Then what's going on between you two, and don't say nothing because clearly it's something." Neither offered a reply. "Did you make him take you on as a client, Carrah?"

"No one makes me do anything I don't want to do," Chris responded.

"And yet we stand in Ms. Caldwell's greenhouse inhaling the most potent gardenia—"

"Rocket trumpet," Carrah corrected.

Ava shrugged. "Fine, rocket trumpet…But we're here because Summer pissed Carrah off and you came to comfort her?"

Chris didn't avoid Ava's directness. It was the one trait he'd always appreciated about their friendship and he wouldn't be upset at it now because she had figured them out. "We have an attorney-client relationship. I do not dislike my clients."

"Got it." Ava's tone was lofty. "Well, I'm going back up to the house. Don't worry, I won't say anything." She squeezed Carrah's shoulder then patted Chris on the arm. "You need to tell Summer you're not interested." She slipped by him and left the greenhouse.

Chris maintained his distance. After everything that had been said this evening, he wasn't exactly sure of her head space.

"You can skip the part where you apologize for what Summer said. We both know it's true. We can't hide behind the attorney-client relationship pretending to like each other."

"So you're pretending to like me?" He closed some of the distance between them. "Because I was not."

She cut her eyes at him and hugged herself tighter. "Neither was I," she confessed. "But—" A pained expression stole her words right before she took a deep, steadying breath.

"The only thing ironic about us getting along is that our

families don't. They haven't for a long time but that doesn't have to be us."

Carrah's arms unfolded and she faced him. Her contemplation to let him stay in was evident by the way she swayed and laced her fingers. "Today after I left you, I went home and immediately accepted that I'd left my dream and reentered reality. I never even opened my book. Have you ever felt like you're giving everything to everyone else and you may have nothing left to give yourself?"

Chris swallowed hard. He knew all too well. He'd watched his mother do it for years. For now, he chased those painful memories of his mother working so hard that the stress of the company came before her health.

"No, but I've seen it happen." He sighed. "My mom, she was always giving to everyone, including me, and everything one hundred and fifty percent. When it came time for her to give the same to herself…she literally couldn't. Her body was too exhausted." He cleared the words attempting to choke his throat. However, the water welling in his eyes didn't remain concealed.

It was obvious she saw by the way she slowly approached. She didn't stop until the space between them was nonexistent. Yet full of something that pulsed around them and whispered to his unspoken desires.

He inhaled her scent. The one he'd come to know that he couldn't get out of his head. It was heady and enchanting at once, reminding him of flowers that bloomed at night and citrus groves that used to grow near his grandparents' cottage when he was young. In this moment he finally understood what he desired most, and it was her. Why had it taken him so long to realize that he didn't have to hate his rival; he wanted to champion her.

"I wish I could've known your mom." Her words were soft, stroking the hardened parts of his heart. "Sounds like she meant a lot to you." He nodded and she continued. "I don't want the same fate. Only, I don't know how to escape it."

"I will help you, Carrah Andrews." Their gazes locked for a moment in time.

Her breaths stuttered as she shook her head. "You can't," she panted, "because…I'm afraid of falling for you."

"Then, we'll go off the deep end together." Instinct over-rode logic. He pressed his lips against hers. A primitive desire seized his heart, and he clasped her face between his hands and kissed her to the depths of her soul.

Chapter 25

"THREE O'CLOCK," CARRAH sighed, spotting the night table clock. She turned over in the covers for the umpteenth time until she was back on her belly. She stuffed her arms under the pillow and blew a loud breath.

For a while she stayed in that position, kicking at her duvet till it fell from the bed. First she was cold; now she was hot. Back, belly, or side, nothing induced the sandman to grant her sweet dreams. Finally she sat up and scooted back to her upholstered headboard, drawing her knees into her chest.

She contemplated life, as though it wasn't about that kiss Chris had laid on her lips hours ago. *Would a kiss that made you forget the world make you suffer insomnia?* "Yes, apparently so," she mumbled although no one could hear her since she was safe in the confines of her room.

The world she knew no longer made sense, and after that kiss, it never would again. How could it when the forbidden was what she wanted? The sense of security that enveloped her as they connected awakened something deep inside that had been waiting to be set free.

Only, her family could never know. Not while Chennault Cosmetics continued to dominate the industry they were clasping by threads.

Her lids began to droop. The circles Chris ran in her head began to slow. She glanced over at the clock and saw that it was now five thirty. A few hours of sleep were all she needed before she would find her way into her father's office to debate her most recent discovery for possible solutions to balance the serum.

Carrah pulled her cover from the floor, slid back down into bed, and rested her head on the pillow praying for sleep to come.

The ringing of Carrah's phone forced her eyes back open. At a turtle's pace she reached to her bedside table and picked it up. Through blurry vision she read CHENNAULT GROUP on the caller ID. Her eyes closed for a second.

No matter the push and pull between her brain and desire, she was in no position to avoid Chris. They had to talk about what had happened and reestablish boundaries.

"Hello," she answered, trying her best to sound like she wasn't still in bed.

"Good Morning, Ms. Charles!" The chipper voice gave Carrah pause. One, why wasn't Chris on the other end of the phone? Two, she had to get used to the whole pen name thing. "This is Shayla from Mr. Chennault's office. I'm calling because Chris mentioned that you signed with Ms. Grimké, and there are a few documents requiring your signature. Our digital signature software is experiencing issues and I really need to get these items processed today. Are you able to come by the office and get things situated?"

This was inevitable. It wasn't that she didn't want to see him or be held in his arms again; it was just that the dynamics of their relationship had changed. Those confessions from last night could lead to scandal, heartbreak—

"Yes." Carrah abruptly cut her racing thoughts and replied to his assistant. Chris had told her the story of his mother. Hiding from him and what they'd done would be to please everyone else, not her. "I'll be there sometime around noon today."

"Great, I'll see you soon."

When they disconnected the call, Carrah saw that Chris had sent her a message in between the time she fell back to sleep and now. This was good, right? She opened the message and read:

Last night...

His text was only two words, but it was loaded with innuendo. The warmth that tingled up her spine before it rushed her body in Mrs. Caldwell's greenhouse had returned. It was as if she were again reaching up to wrap her arms around his neck. One kiss seemed to have the power to erase the world that had pitted them against each other.

Pure fantasy. They were living in a reality where the morning after could bring regrets. What if he were second-guessing, feeling her out to make sure he avoided a land mine? Carrah was not interested in playing her cards. She'd done that last night. Right now, she had to maintain some of her guard. There was a world surrounding them that dictated who and what they had to be to each other. So, her reply was simple too.

...It happened.

There was no reply. After she showered and dressed, there was still no response. Either she had struck a nerve or the warring thoughts doing battle in her mind were doing the same in his. They could talk about it once she got to his office.

Half past noon, Carrah pulled up to the Chennault Building. She quickly checked her hair and makeup while rehearsing what she would say about not hearing from him. She got out of her car, adjusting the straps of her sundress as she made it through the entrance. She opted for the stairs to tame the restlessness she was experiencing.

As she approached the suite door at the top of the stairs, her belly flopped. She took more than a few breaths then turned the knob to enter. Shayla greeted her the moment she walked in and ushered her down the hall. It was as though anticipation was doing the rocket launch countdown as they made their way to a door that was across from where she remembered Chris's office to be.

"On a call?" Carrah asked Shayla while pointing at the closed door to his office.

Shayla laughed. "Normally, yes. Today, no. He's traveling." She opened the door to a small conference room and motioned for Carrah to have a seat. "Urgent business on the West Coast had him catch a red-eye out last night so he could be there for business first thing this morning."

Well, at least there was a reason for why he hadn't responded back to her message. "Does he travel like that often?"

"He hasn't traveled much since May. Since I've known him, he's kept a rule that May through July are off-limits since he comes to the Shores. The expansion hasn't allowed him to be as liberal. Are you the same?"

"If you mean come here during the summer, yes. Although this summer I've been forced to work a little."

"I hardly can call any work done here in this cute little

town work." Shayla chuckled then proceeded to divulge her family's excursions as they explored the town.

Carrah recommended the yacht club's sailing regatta, Renninger's Flea Market, launching kayaks from Dorian's Cove, or taking a day trip to New Smyrna Beach. The woman's face lit up with excitement, reminding Carrah of how she felt every year she sat packing for the Shores. She deeply resented the position her family had placed her in.

"So you work?" The quizzical expression upon Shayla's face reminded Carrah of all the times her mother had encouraged otherwise. She tried not to hold it against the woman. Except her face must've told a different story because Shayla then said, "Sorry. I didn't mean to offend. You, uh, you just don't seem like the type. I mean you're so glamourous."

Although Carrah couldn't see her own face, she fixed whatever ill expression was upon it with a smile. "You thought I was a kept woman?" She snickered, knowing that could never be her despite it being the life her mother raised her to lead as a beauty queen. Not to mention it was the one Trent had begged her to keep so that she could be a prize on his arm at political functions. Never. "I'm actually a chemist. I formulate makeup, skin creams, perfume, and stuff like that."

"Oh, like what his family does? Is that how you know each other?"

Carrah glanced down to the table, hating that her grandfather had backstabbed Chris's and tried to sell the company from under his nose. It was the nail in the coffin that triggered the fallout and split of the company. Chàvous kept Noir, and the Chennaults founded Olina Chennault Cosmetics. They'd been fierce competitors since then to the point where she and Chris had abandoned any hope of a friendship until now.

"Our families are business rivals. They have been a very long time. It's complicated." Carrah offered no more and firmed her face to make the point.

"Hmm, he said the same. And because I know how to mind my business." Shayla dismissed the convo and pulled a stack of papers from a folder that was sitting on the table. "He also told me that you needed to sign these documents."

They both sat at the table. Shayla explained each document requiring her signature before she signed. On the last few pages Shayla read notes highlighted by Chris, clarifying agent fees before pointing to the line for Carrah's signature.

Shayla gathered all the papers and placed them back into the folder. "I'll let him know you completed the signatures. Copies will also be sent over to the agent." Shayla scanned Carrah for longer than what seemed reasonable. "I'm glad he accepted you as a client."

"Me too…but why do you say that? Or is this something you say to all his clients to make them feel good?"

"You challenged him to think differently." Shayla got to her feet and looked Carrah in the eye. "That first day when you were here, I knew there was something special about you that could help him find his way again."

If she'd known Shayla longer, she would've asked her to explain. Maybe in time she would understand what the woman was saying. Right now, Carrah couldn't fathom the Chris she'd been getting close to as a man who was lost.

"Anyone here?"

Both Carrah and Shayla jerked their attention toward the door. The muscles in Carrah's body tensed. She looked around the room and saw only one way out. Why was Summer here? More important was that Summer couldn't know she was here.

"One second," Shayla called.

Carrah shot out of her chair, pressing her index finger against her lips, and moved to where the older woman stood. She pulled Shayla away from the door and shut it. "She can't know I'm here," she whispered.

"Who is she?"

"A girl that he and I have known for a very long time."

Shayla's eyes narrowed on Carrah. She pursed her lips, but then nodded and left the conference room, closing the door behind her. Carrah began wearing a path around the table, spinning in circles as she waited for Shayla to return.

Thanks to Reese, Carrah already knew Summer had her sights set on Chris. However, Carrah didn't think it was to the extent that Summer would pop up at his office...or was it? Now she wondered if this was Summer's first time here or if this visit was a happenstance? The clinginess exhibited by her at the ball and then the way she'd plopped into Chris's lap last night made her consider if more had transpired between them.

The insecurities that Trent had bred in her rode in like a witch on a broom after they were supposed to have been vanquished with thousands of dollars in therapy. His damage had its lingering effects.

"She's gone." Shayla cracked the door and effectively ended Carrah's pacing. She reentered the room discharging a dismissive wave followed by a snort. "Although I'm sure she'll be back. Her kind always is."

"Summer has been here before?" Carrah stiffened as she asked the question. Shayla shook her head no. "Then what do you mean?"

Shayla gave Carrah the girl-are-you-for-real look. "Ms. Bradshaw has called here a thousand times for Chris. At least five this morning, which means he's not taking her calls. Her unannounced visit is also proof. He's had several women do this sort of thing when they think their time with him is about to expire and want to hang on a little bit longer."

"Oh," was all Carrah managed to say.

For over twenty years she'd known who Chris was, but had not been within his inner circle. Therefore, she had no idea of what his reputation was with women beyond what he'd told her at his cottage. It was still shocking, considering his best friend was a certified dick slinger.

Chris was also handsome beyond compare, smart, accomplished, and extremely wealthy. Carrah had already wasted more than enough time with a man who had similar traits. The only difference was Trent had never promised her anything. She had to believe Chris was different. At least she wanted to.

"Doesn't seem as if you fall into the same category," the woman said, regaining Carrah's attention. "You're different. That's why he likes you." Carrah looked off as a flush heated her cheeks. "Chris has never taken a client, let alone a woman to his grandparents' cottage. That's his sacred space, and yet you were there."

Chapter 26

THE WHEELS TOUCHED down on the tarmac. Chris cracked open his eyes, gripping the armrests as his body shook slightly. The plane's lengthy taxi to disembark gave his body time to wake up and become alert for the light commute he would make to get back to the Shores.

The moment the flight attendant authorized use of cellular devices, he powered his on. After a six-hour, three-time-zone flight, he was greeted by a ton of messages. All of which he had no intention of replying to except one. He scrolled to the three-day-old message from Carrah that had almost made him walk out on a deal of a lifetime. It happened.

Damn right it happened. He'd abandoned who they were and crossed the lines their families had drawn in the sand. They'd both been willing and equal participants. Hell, she'd wrapped her arms around his neck and kissed him back in a way no woman ever had. If her message had come after the Summer Bradshaw pop-up Shayla had informed him of, then maybe he would've understood her off-putting tone. But it didn't.

He took a deep breath and finally typed back: What is that supposed to mean?

Instantly those three little dots populated his screen.

Wow, 3 days later.

Chris scoffed at her message and pocketed his phone. What was he really doing? He had to search himself for answers because maybe he had got caught up in a moment. This level of frustration over a woman who was not his wife, girlfriend, mother, or sister was not a part of his summer plan. Between the expansion and the joint venture his father was considering with Noir cosmetics, he didn't have time to be playing a cat-and-mouse game. He'd already proved that in ending things with Heather.

After he was off the plane and on the way to the parking garage, his phone vibrated. It was another message from Carrah. He moved to the side of the busy walkway and swiped to her message.

Guess no reply means another 3 attorney Chennault?

He cupped his neck and rolled his head as he let out a long breath. If he had ever sent another woman the text he sent Carrah, he probably would've garnered an invitation to her bedroom. Instead he was being tried and convicted for what, not responding to her flippant message. This woman was unlike any of the women he'd dealt with in the past.

It was clear the lines had been blurred, feelings were hurt...at least his were, and he couldn't help wanting to kiss her again.

Chris tamped down his annoyance and went into his photo library. He selected a picture of the magnolia tree they sat under at his cottage. He captioned it Meet me here in an hour and pressed send. He didn't wait for a reply before sliding the phone back into his pocket. Either she came or she didn't. Time would tell.

Fifteen minutes shy of an hour, he turned down the dirt road. The cares of the world faded away as his cottage came into view with Carrah sitting on the swing at the front porch. His breath hitched and his grip on the steering wheel tightened as though it would steady the unexpected rhythm of his heart.

Chris schooled his face to be absent of the happiness that had seconds ago induced a smile. Carrah wasn't allowed to see this far behind his veil.

Once he parked and got out of the car, he inhaled the fresh morning air, which smelled of the lake and orange blossoms that weren't far from his property line. It reminded him of when he first got to his grandparents' house in the Shores for the summer. He knew he was coming to something good.

He gazed back up to the porch before his feet began crunching the gravel as he made his way to the house. He invited the warmth surrounding him at the sight of her to seize his heart. She was a dream sitting pretty in a pink dress that highlighted her tawny skin while maintaining immaculate posture as she swung. She was the epitome of a Southern debutante with beauty, intelligence, class, and sophistication. The kind of woman that was more than a prize on a man's side, for she was a gift made to be cherished.

"Are you done being bossy, Mr. Chennault?" She stood, taking his breath away while making him understand why he had always looked the other way.

"For now." His lips quirked. "You're here so there's no need." Although she was not at all ready to find out how bossy he could be. He watched as she fidgeted with the hem of her dress. "I am hungry, though. I got off the plane and came straight here. Have you eaten anything this morning? We could go into town and grab breakfast at Mama's Place."

Her brows furrowed and she turned away for a second. "Our families would know before we got hot plates. Have you forgotten how fast gossip spreads around here?"

Chris hadn't forgotten. He just didn't care. This was their path. Besides, it was only a matter of time before the joint venture. Soon, the world would know that the Chennaults and the Andrewses were on speaking terms if they were able to do business. However, since she didn't seem comfortable, he said, "It's fine. I'm sure Ms. Watson has the fridge stocked. I can make something." He moved toward the front door.

"Wait!" She scurried past him. The sweet scent of night flower lingering behind entreated him to unchaste thoughts as he watched her go to her car and retrieve a basket. "Your seven a.m. meet-me-in-an hour text didn't seem like it included breakfast." She began taking the steps back up. "So I brought something just in case."

Her smile made him turn away and dig in his pocket for the key. Had he continued looking at her, he might've kissed her again. And based on the last correspondence over the topic, he was uncertain if that was something she wanted. He pushed the door open and allowed her to step inside first.

She went straight to the kitchen and set the basket on the counter. He was two steps behind watching her move about the space as though she had committed it all to memory.

"I hope you like it." She took out a large pastry that resembled red velvet cake, but smelled like cinnamon, sugar, and toasted pecans, and set it on a plate. "Already prepping for the Red Party?"

Giggles filled her cheeks. "I've not thought of Red night since Quinn brought it up at my mother's party."

"It's going to be lit." He winked then clapped his hands and sat at the place setting, licking his lips. "What is it?" His sweet tooth would one day get him into trouble.

Another giggle escaped her. "A red velvet cinnamon roll. Seeing as you always lose your mind in that donut shop, I thought you would enjoy this."

"Mmmmmm," he groaned, and then took another bite. "You made this? 'Cause if so, I need to make you my wife." He chuckled then got up to grab milk from the refrigerator and poured a glass.

Carrah burst into laughter. "Guess that won't be me. Baking isn't my gift." The laughter between them faded after he brought his glass back to where he was sitting and took another bite out of his treat. "After mixing chemical ingredients all day baking seems tedious. Besides, I struggle with my work now as it is."

There was a note in Carrah's voice that captured his attention. It wasn't sadness, nor was it happy.

"Because you're in the lab over summer?" His question was genuine.

Her fleeting smile became a straight line. "Chemistry was always my escape plan." They looked across at each other. "I hated being all dolled up for people to judge the way I spoke or appeared in a bathing suit." She sighed and pointed to his plate. "You know how long it's been since I had one of those for fear that I wouldn't be able to fit a dress right or wear a bathing suit without feeling bloated?"

He chugged down his milk, gulping hard. If he hadn't, he may have confessed that her body was made for sin. Of course he had not forgotten how sexy she was in that two-piece lavender bikini the day they went to the beach.

"Anyway, after years of the pageant scene and enduring the pressures of winning Miss Xavier and then Miss Louisiana, I quit. I refused to be a Miss America contestant that would cater to superficial standards that did nothing to elevate Black beauty, and unlike a lot of girls, I actually loved science and studying compounds.

"Knowing I had my father's full support to work in the lab at Noir after getting my degree allowed me to further my advocacy to diversify beauty standards in the industry and positively reinforce that Black women and other women of color are beautiful.

"Only, the company's other priorities took precedence over my product innovation and market suggestions...until now. What I used to escape is trapping me."

His hands dropped to his lap and he turned on the stool until he could stare her in the face. "Sounds like you're telling me that you haven't done anything with your manuscript. Did you at least start with the changes the editor mentioned in her comments from the offer?"

"I told you before," she sighed, "doing both is hard...My family needs me to balance the serum. Everything depends on it."

"I know what you told me. Bottom line is, are you going to take a chance or remain trapped?"

* * *

"I took the chance. That's why I'm here with you." Carrah looked anywhere except at him. His face, those eyes, that scent of spicy earth and rich amber was irresistibly masculine and had been driving her wild from the moment he got out of the car. There was nothing she could do to subdue her racing heart after the sincerity he'd shown.

A moment of silence rested between them. She sensed hesitation that had not been present the last time they were together. Had she said too much, allowed him too far in to see it was no ordinary box built around her?

When Carrah finally glanced up, she met a smoldering stare that burned her body as if she were on the stake. This might be the one thing she didn't care to escape. Yet, she knew she probably should because being trapped by her attraction to a man who was a sworn rival of her family couldn't end happy. So why was she continuing to test the limits as though this were an equation that could be solved?

Chris cleared his throat. "You make it sound like I'm a risk. Is that how you see me when I only want to help?" He inched to the edge of the stool, closer to her.

"The other night..." Carrah swallowed hard then looked off for a second to catch her breath.

"It happened." He folded his arms, arching a brow.

She jerked off the stool and began pacing behind where he sat. "I didn't know what else to say."

"Maybe"—his deep voice was deceptively calm as he spun the stool until he could see her—"tell me that you liked it or that you didn't. How hard is it for you to say what you feel?"

Carrah effectively stopped the anxiety that was causing her feet to char the wood floors. She narrowed her eyes on him. "Oh, so what you should've done! Instead you were trying to feel me out for an answer. How did I know you hadn't changed your mind? Maybe even regret what happened and then I'm stuck confessing my innermost thoughts."

Chris stood up. Each step he took toward her made her take one back until she bumped against the wall and his arm caged her in. "Is that what you want to know, my innermost thoughts?" His gorgeous eyes cast down as his mouth hovered above hers. "I've been dying to kiss you again. My fingers itch to caress your skin until you're glowing in my arms. This pink dress"—he tugged at the bottom half—"I'd rather see bunched up around your waist so I can have permission to cup that luscious ass of yours.

"The rest of *my innermost thoughts* spawn X-rated fantasies in my head that simultaneously contradict my loyalty to my family." He closed his eyes, groaning, as he pushed back from the wall.

Carrah watched his chest visibly pound against his shirt. She understood because hers was doing the exact same thing. Their hearts raced toward an attraction that was set on a course to collide. There was no control.

"Just say what you feel," he managed through strangled breath.

She rushed him, went on her tippy-toes, and stole a kiss that left her searching for air.

The ringing sounds of their phones made them come apart. Carrah stepped out of his hold, but was pulled back for him to reclaim her lips once more. For the second time their kiss was cut short by their phones. This time they both moved to retrieve their devices.

There was a missed call from her father. It was probably about missing their meeting this morning.

"Shit!" Chris brought the phone to his ear. "I'll be right back." He left her in the cottage and went out a sliding glass door.

She then quickly dialed her father. He answered. "I need you home within the hour."

"Is something wrong...is Mom okay?" She couldn't help

if her mind went there. They all knew a relapse was possible even though it was not expected. After her father confirmed his request had nothing to do with her mother, he reiterated she get home ASAP.

She grabbed her key off the kitchen table as Chris reentered the cottage. His entire demeanor seemed to have shifted. "Everything okay?"

He glanced to the front door, a tick prevalent in his jaw. "No, I need to leave."

"So do I." He nodded and began cutting off the lights. "Do you want me to put the cinnamon rolls in your microwave?"

"Uh, no, I'll take them with me." He took the basket from Carrah and then ushered them from the house. He walked her to her car and held the door open for her to climb inside. "Carrah." She turned to face him, meeting his eyes. He looked off for a second. "I…" The tension battling to be loyal or give in to whims fueled by desire would pull him under. "Never mind."

Family won. The quizzical expression shaping on her face demanded he give something better. Something that she might be willing to forgive for after the next time he would see her. "The next time I see you"—he gave a fleeting look to the sky—"promise not to hold it against me."

"Promise."

Chapter 27

WHEN CARRAH TURNED into the driveway of her parents' home, there were two cars she didn't recognize and one in need of a tow. Trent's continued forced insertion into her life triggered pain and resentment for her parents. She wasn't a fool to the rank he pulled at his family's bank, and she knew they weren't either. However, she was done relegating her life for other people to accomplish their dreams while hers died. And she felt the same for Noir.

No longer could she pretend that what she wanted didn't matter. Chris had opened her eyes and heart to the possibilities and made some of her wildest dreams become realities. Going back to life as it was before him was unimaginable.

With one last woosaah, Carrah exited her car. Her defenses locked and loaded as she turned the knob on the utility door to enter the house. Long gone was the use of good manners. A flair for the dramatics was necessary to end Trent's attempts.

Raised laughter filled the downstairs, and she noted that house staff moved about as though they were prepping for something. Whatever was happening, she had intentionally been left in the dark about it, she thought as she ventured to the other side of the house to see who all were present.

She peeked around the corner and saw her father, and siblings including Dominic, dressed as though they were at headquarters. The house staff was serving drinks to two current board members, Sandra Butler and Edward Willis, and the general counsel, Marcus Peabody, who was also dressed in formal business attire. Trent, the only one in traditional summer wear, was seated at the table, which had been set for a meeting. If this was why she'd been paged, then they were in for a colorful morning as far as Carrah was concerned.

"Carrah!" her father called, moving in her direction as she passed through the archway to enter the library. "You look beautiful, darling." He kissed her cheek. "Where did you go off to so early?"

She recoiled. Maybe he didn't notice, but she sure felt her eyes go wide like a deer caught in headlights. No longer was she ten, needing something from him, or incapable of making her own decisions. Therefore, she didn't owe him an answer.

However, he owed her one. Why were corporate officers infringing on their family's summer? It was already bad enough she'd been spending her days in the lab.

Before she could ask, her father cleared his throat. "Would you mind changing into something more professional?"

"Why, and why are all these people here? I thought the Shores was our sacred time. You already have me spinning wheels for a formula I can't solve."

"Lower your voice," he growled through his teeth. "Now please, go change and hurry back down. We will be starting soon."

When he turned on his heel, she signaled for Beau. He was sometimey and as of late he'd been on her ass over work stuff. However, she hoped he would fill her in. "What is this all about?"

Her brother shrugged, panning the room before looking her in the face. "I'm in the dark like you. Dad hasn't said anything to Aubrey either. Apparently this is a surprise announcement."

"I don't do those well." Carrah folded her arms, scanning the inside of the library again.

"Nor do I," he sighed and walked off.

Carrah relinquished her hesitation and proceeded upstairs to change. She pulled down a chic blue blazer with matching trousers. After she had dressed, she stood in the mirror noting that her lipstick was gone. Her fingers went to her lips. She closed her eyes and her mind replayed the moment she decided it would be all or nothing and kissed Chris.

The man had spoken to her core existence, whispering his innermost thoughts, which mirrored hers. Never had she craved a thing that was the base root of conflict. And yet, it set her free, unleashing her passion and fueling her desires. It was a power she never knew she was capable of owning after serving at the beck and call of Camille and Melvin's expectations and her duty to Noir.

Once whatever her father needed her to do was done, she planned to reach out to Chris. She had to make sure he was good anyway since he left in a completely different mood than what he'd arrived in. For now she pressed pause on those thoughts and dashed back down the stairs.

There was no laughter seeping out from the library this time as she approached. However, she did hear voices. More than what she remembered before going upstairs. The second she passed through the archway to reenter the library, it was like the day the earth stood still. Chris Chennault was there standing amidst the company of her father and his.

*　*　*

A strange sensation whirled around Chris, and the hairs on his arms began to tingle. The thoughts in his head went silent, and as if he knew Carrah were there, he gazed over his shoulder and found her standing in the archway. Their eyes met across the room.

Her body tensed before she avoided him by glancing off in another direction. He had wanted to tell her, wanted to confess he would see her again soon, which was why he made her promise that she would not hold this moment against him. Although he was certain she had no way of knowing he meant now.

Carrah turned away and started to leave, but her sister caught her by the hand and led them deeper into the room. Chris tamped down his base instincts to go to her. It was a contradiction he had no remedy for, and it forced him to return his attention back to the old man who was the general counsel for Noir while turning his back on Carrah.

Nothing the man said registered. Not when Carrah was behind him probably thinking less of his character. Only, he wasn't able to break his father's confidence. Nor would he because they'd kissed. It was the very reason he'd avoided discussing family business. He didn't want to taint what existed between them when the lines were already blurred. This morning was confirmation.

"Christopher," his father called to him. Chris schooled his

face, suppressed emotion, and walked to where his father stood along with Carrah and Melvin. "I'm certain the two of you know of each other."

"We do," they said at once.

Their glances met for a second before Carrah snapped her head away. He still couldn't help looking at her, willing her eyes to connect with his again. He'd misjudged this entire situation.

"Good then," Melvin said with a dry smile. "Well, Chauncy, if you're ready?" Chauncy agreed and then Melvin announced for everyone to take seats at the table. Chauncy then gathered Chloe, Miles, Ms. Carolyn, and Mr. Ben. "Ah, Camille!" Melvin turned all attention to his wife as she floated in.

Mrs. Andrews reminded Chris of his mother in the way she walked with confidence and sophistication at once. She made a business suit appear elegant instead of corporate, and she commanded the attention of everyone. Without a doubt he understood how his mother had been the woman's friend at some point in time. Mrs. Andrews stopped in front of his father. Her face revealed a myriad of emotions before she offered her hand.

"Good to see you, Chauncy." She clutched his father's hand as a mother would her child's. "It's been a long time." Chris stretched his eyes to Miles, who stood at his side when they both reached in and embraced like old friends. "I still can't believe Claudette is gone." Her words hung in her throat. "She was the best of us."

Chauncy nodded, perhaps afraid to say anything and risk a bout of depression in a place that was not home. "You've met my oldest, Christopher?"

She smiled at Chris, and they shook hands. "Of course, a

long time ago. He's the only one of your children that took Dette's eyes."

A light chuckle escaped Chauncy. "I haven't heard anyone call her that in years." Both their gazes scattered to the ground. Chauncy lifted his head. "And this is my nephew, Miles."

"This is Hannah's son?" The woman's eyes rapidly scanned Miles. She then glimpsed over her shoulder in the direction of her husband before shaking Miles's hand. "It's nice to meet you, Miles." She continued staring into his face. "I never knew Hannah had a child."

Chauncy cleared his throat. "Hannah never much cared for the Florida heat. My sister prefers Oak Bluffs, after spending so many years in the North. Miles is his mother's child and shares her sentiments."

"How old are you…Miles?" Camille concentrated on his cousin, almost dismissing any context his father offered.

"Thirty-four, and it's nice to meet you as well, Mrs. Andrews." The woman reared back as she clutched her chest. "Are you okay, Mrs. Andrews?"

"Yes." She stumbled forward, forcing a smile. "I'm fine. Let's take our seats."

Once everyone was at the table, Chris noticed that Carrah was seated closest to her father while her siblings came after the general counsel and board members. He considered it an interesting dynamic given that in his research of the company he'd learned the older brother was the CFO and the sister was the COO, while Carrah oversaw research and development.

His attention was grabbed by Melvin when he stood at the table and cast his gaze over everyone. "Thank you all for coming. You've been invited here to witness a feat I never thought possible in my lifetime. As you all know, Noir Cosmetics and Olina Chennault Cosmetics started as one over eighty-three years ago. Since then each company has revolutionized Black skin, hair, and cosmetics care. As consumer preferences have evolved, so must we."

The man directed his gaze at his family. "A few weeks ago, I approached Chauncy with a proposal to bring the world's two largest Black-owned cosmetics companies together again." Gasps from the Andrews side of the table bounced off the walls while Chris's side sat patient as monks. "Therefore, we"—he gestured to Chauncy—"are pleased to announce a joint venture in an effort to pioneer a skin-correcting foundation serum."

Camille's face became as hard as a statue. Carrah had some slack in her jaws, but her siblings and the board members displayed full-on outrage. The only ones who seemed content were Melvin and the attorney.

"Why a joint venture?" Beau scowled, perching in his chair.

"The joint venture allows us to work on this one specific project together. We pool the best of our resources, people… Carrah and Miles will collaborate to develop something we believe could become a global phenomenon."

"There are risks, are there not?" The oldest sister spoke. Her shifty eyes were a sign that she was not in favor of such a strategy.

Their attorney cleared his throat. "There are risks associated with any business deal. Your father and Mr. Chennault have drawn up a contract that splits everything down the middle. The rewards from the product's success are shared. This is also true for any loss should it fail."

Carrah stood. She took a deep breath, swallowed hard, and stared her father in the face. "So my idea—that's been researched and tested, nearly eighty percent ready for market trial." Her head cocked. "You now want to punt it over to Olina Chennault?"

An ache formed at the pit of his stomach and Chris wished he wasn't present to witness her hurt. In the same breath, all it did was make him more determined to help her get out. The fact that her father had not confided his plans to her or anyone on the other side made him suspicious to the point where he questioned his father on the deal. Except, knowing his father's business sense meant the manipulation they were witnessing was all a part of his plan. He would use the seeds of dissention to take Noir down at the knees in the same way Melvin had done years ago. This time there would be no second chances, only ruin.

"Why is that, Mr. Andrews?" Trent piped up. Everyone focused on him. "It seems Carrah is offended by being made to relinquish her intellectual property, and as my family has a say in our investment and Carrah is to be my wife—"

"What?" Chris, Carrah, and Camille lashed out at once.

"Our engagement is postponed," Trent murmured acidly, rising to his feet.

Chris made the motion to push up from his chair. His father gripped his hand and steadied it into the armrest. Chauncy cut his eyes at him and then gave a barely noticeable shake of his head.

Trent's mother whispered something to him and he sat down. Her scrutiny went from Carrah to Melvin. "I've been clear, in fact more than accommodating, in allowing you additional time to get the product ready. It was never a secret that those repayment extensions were made considering Carrah and Trent's relationship."

Chris couldn't stop staring at the beautiful girl who'd been waiting on his front porch this morning. Forget how she kissed him back and had been welcome to his innermost thoughts. She had softened the rough edges that had formed around him after his mother's death and made him consider things beyond expanding his firm or negating duty to his family. He dreamed and thought of things the way he used to. Until now he had not realized how lost he'd been.

Trent was a mistake. He wanted to stand up and shout. Any man who used money to demand affection of a sacred promise was. Control faltered and he inhaled a tight breath to keep from telling Trent and his mother to jump off a cliff because Carrah was his—

His. Shit. This was so bad.

"Trent proposed and I said no." The strong will of Carrah's voice contradicted the fleeting glance she gave Chris.

Sandra then got to her feet and Camille did the same. "Just yesterday, your father and brother assured us that you were coming around."

Both Carrah and her mother whipped their heads to Melvin, still standing at the head of the table. Instead of responding to Sandra, Carrah left. Every fiber in Chris's being screamed to go after her. The only reason he didn't was out of respect for her because he no longer gave a damn about the bad blood between their families.

Chauncy lifted his hand off Chris and leaned into the table, steepling his hands. He focused on Melvin. "Is your daughter unwilling to work with Miles?"

"Or marry my son?" Sandra countered. "Carrah's agreement dictates how the bank proceeds."

"Our daughter is not a child. Nor is she a commodity to be traded." Camille threw daggers at Melvin, then turned like a graceful ballerina and exited the room, leaving all eyes on her crestfallen husband.

In Chris's line of work negotiations were an everyday occurrence. This one in particular was compromised, and for once, he was happy about it. Carrah would never be able to meet the deadlines for her book while spending hours in a lab to create another product for two multibillion-dollar organizations.

His father finally got to his feet. "It seems you need time to chat with your stakeholders, Melvin. We'll be in touch."

Everyone on Chris's side of the table followed suit and found their way out. Before he was outside, he pulled his phone and messaged Carrah. She didn't reply. Once more he tried as he got into his car and received nothing. After being on the inside of her box, he saw the intricacies that could keep it closed. Only, he'd promised her, and he would do everything in his power to help her find a way out and achieve her dreams.

Chapter 28

CARRAH PULLED INTO a parking space in front of the Chennault Building downtown and glanced up to the second floor. She hoped Chris would forgive her for being radio silent. There had been a lot to process after she'd last seen him in her parents' home.

One week had gone by since she was humiliated by her father in front of mixed company. If ever there were a time she was made to suffer the stereotype of the dim-witted beauty queen, it was then. She sighed, wishing to forget the shock of Chris being present to witness her father exploit her for Noir's gain. Daddy Dearest hadn't bothered to inform her or ask permission. He simply took and gave to the company because it always came first.

Her happiness and what she wanted in life would never matter. The tempered chill inside the Andrews house for the last week was proof. Oddly, she didn't care to induce a warmer climate. Carrah used the cold shoulder treatment running like a wild vampire to her advantage and stayed in her room, where she prepared for a meeting with her agent and her editor.

Being immersed in a world she created was beyond compare. There were no morning labs, no strict guidelines, no expectations, and she chose what happened. In that world... she chose Chris. There was no denying that she missed their morning tea meets, his deep chuckle, encouragement, and simply sharing life.

It was why she now sat in the parking lot gazing up at his office. For the last week she'd ignored every one of his texts and calls for fear that his glimpse into her life would make him pity her. He was a man who possessed the courage to defy family tradition and find his own way. A man who promised to help because he'd read her potential in a manuscript and believed she had dreams worthy of coming true.

Therefore, Carrah didn't want his pity. She wanted something else although she didn't know exactly what that was. The only thing she did know was that she owed him an apology for the distance that had sat between them the last seven days. Once upon a time it was normal. Now, it felt like a crime.

One last pep talk was all it took before she was out of the car, up the elevator, and turning the knob to enter his office suite. Shayla's stank-faced, dry hello bloomed another bout of insecurity within Carrah. She had been cordial in the emails they had exchanged during the week, but now she wondered if Shayla knew.

"Hi, Shayla, is Chris available?"

"Let me check." Shayla moved from her desk and disappeared down the hall.

Carrah claimed a seat in the lobby. Her fiddling thumbs went still and her body began tingling with anticipation when she heard footsteps that had to be his since there was no click-ing of high heels. He passed the desk, stepping into the lobby looking oh so sexy in tailored gray slacks and a button-down shirt that skipped the neck closure.

"Chris." She struggled to find her breath. God, the man was fine and those eyes lit up the world. She got to her feet and attempted to close the distance between them.

"What do you need?" He checked the time at his wrist and then pushed her back with his arresting stare.

Take one, no words came out. She took a deep breath and tried again. "Uh…nothing. I, uh, just wanted to come by and say hello."

A dry chuckle escaped him. "A phone does that job well. Maybe try checking yours. While at it, return calls and respond to messages?" His jaw tensed before his hands slid into his pockets, shifting his stance in a manner that made it hard for her to concentrate. "Is everything okay?"

Her eyes went to the floor first and then she looked around the room and saw that Shayla was not at her desk. It was just them. "Are you asking because you feel sorry for me or for your family?"

Chris's body went stiff as his nostrils flared to life. "Nei—enjoy the rest of your day. Call me if it pertains to our business arrangement. I'm going to get lunch."

In a blink of an eye he went out the suite door. Carrah darted behind him. This was worse than she'd imagined.

"Wait," she called, taking brisk steps to catch him. She slowed when he stopped in front of the elevator and punched the call button with his thumb. "May I come with you? We need to talk."

He cut his eyes at her then stopped when the elevator dinged. "Well, there's a genius idea." He stepped inside the open doors, leaving his sarcasm to grate on her nerves as she followed.

The second the doors closed, he grabbed her and pushed her against the wall. The rhythm of their pounding hearts stirred chaos and yet delivered calm as his eyes stared down into hers, bewitching her into his charms. He pressed his lips against hers demanding affection she willingly returned.

The elevator stopped and he stepped back. Carrah struggled to stand upright. Her knees wobbly, breath shaky, and the ache between her legs begged for attention. She thought the last time they'd kissed, she'd lost her damn mind. This time he'd robbed her of all conscious and reasonable thought. No one compared and all she knew was that she wanted more.

"Are you even hungry?" he asked once they got outside and she nodded yes. "What do you want? There's a lot in walking distance."

She cleared her throat, still fighting for composure and mad that he wasn't. It wasn't his fault she lacked experience. Besides, he was a little older and she knew he had the reputation of being somewhat of a playboy. Her assertions about him were not exactly wrong all those nights ago at his cottage.

"I'll eat whatever you want."

A sly smile curled his lips. "Sure about that? What I want isn't on the menu at any of these restaurants." His eyes roved over her body before he snatched his gaze away. "Lucky Dill?"

She nodded again. Her mind was still playing catch-up, and to avoid saying, *No, let's go to your cottage*, it was better to agree in silence. They took a few steps together before she looked around and remembered where they were. Luck and early morning had been on their side when meeting for tea.

The lunch hour was riskier. Many of the ladies who worked

in the restaurants were employed by the summer crowd, and there were just more people out and about. They could easily become the gossip of the day. It was like white on rice in the Shores, and the very last thing they needed after everything that happened last week.

"Maybe one of us should stay behind for a few minutes. Make it seem like it's a coincidence instead of popping up together."

*   *   *

Chris froze. "Is this because you're betrothed to Trenton?" he asked mockingly, still hating it was even a possibility.

"I just kissed you." She was cute when she pouted. "I wouldn't have done that if I were engaged to another man."

He took her by the hand. "Then stop being afraid of what people say or think." They began crossing the street. "You do realize there will be people who will not like your book. Are you going to stop writing because they criticize you unfavorably?"

Carrah didn't answer him right away. He saw that she was processing, attempting to understand the bed of roses she'd been confined to fostered her complacency while providing guard. She had to find the strength he knew she had and use it to be brave on the outside of the box she seemed desperate to escape.

"No," she finally responded as they arrived at the deli. "I won't stop. But I also don't want to provoke unnecessary criticism." She let go of his hand.

An emptiness he hadn't expected, but had felt since she'd pulled away last week, cut him down at the knees. Her tenacity was admirable. However, her worrying about the perception of others was problematic. Still, he understood so he conceded.

Growing up the old guard way meant that at a young age you became aware that there was an image and reputation to uphold—and it was everything. Especially when you had a prominent last name that commanded power and wielded prestige. This was the way of the Black elite, and old, ingrained habits died hard.

Besides, if the way she kissed him back in the elevator was any indication of how she felt, then he was doing just fine.

"Compromise," he said, opening the door. "We order and go back to my office to eat?"

"I'd like that." She smiled at him then strolled past to go inside.

After managing to beat the lunch rush by mere seconds, they were able to get back to his office with two fried egg salad sandwiches, Parmesan fries, sweet tea, something sweet, and a giddy Carrah. At his desk they sat catching up on the last week while he tried hard not to hold a grudge. Beyond the typical gossip, Gavin demanded a rematch, anticipation for the Red Party was at an all-time high, and the old lodge had been submitted to the city as the site for the youth village. They talked about everything except the meeting between their families.

"How's it going with Olivia?" He sat back in his chair, sipping the sweet tea that was like his grandmother's. It was the main reason he loved the Lucky Dill so much.

"She's amazing. Although in fairness, I have nothing to compare it to." She continued rambling on about her upcoming meeting with her agent and editor.

All the while he tamped down his urge to ask her if this thing between them was good until the book published. He had to know because he didn't want this to always be a secret. The questions gnawed at him. However, he wouldn't push. He got the sense that Carrah was being tugged and pulled more than necessary by her family. She had already been riding the seesaw with regard to their client-attorney relationship, and he didn't want her to shut down on him again.

"Oh my goodness!" She shot up in her chair, watching as he unboxed a strawberry cupcake. "You're not full? I'm stuffed." Her hand wrapped around her stomach as she leaned back in her chair. "I've seen the Lucky Dill for ages, but had no idea it was so good."

"As my grandfather used to say, good things come to those who wait." He took a bite out of the sweet treat, savoring the fresh-baked taste and from-scratch frosting. "Blame it on Dunc. He took me there forever ago for one of these"—he held up the cupcake—"and I make it my business to drop in at least once a week."

Carrah burst into laughter. "Your sweet tooth is insane."

"It is well documented." He chuckled, taking another bite out of his dessert.

She giggled a few minutes more, watching him polish the cupcake off. All of a sudden her smile fell flat. She stared at him from the opposite side of the desk while it appeared as though she were searching for words. "When we left your cottage that day...did you know you would see me later?"

A part of him was fine with her avoiding this conversation. He'd grappled with it ever since she ghosted him the last week. If he told her the truth, she might disappear for another seven days. If he lied, he was delaying the same outcome because it was inevitable she would find out. Their lives were too close.

"I did," he confessed. "I wasn't allowed, but not because of my family. Your father requested the strictest confidence. He explicitly stated that his children were unaware. At the time I was certain he was illustrating his definition of confidentiality because no one knows we talk. Most think we are still running around the same circle of friends avoiding each other."

"I wish I could say I didn't understand. I do. I just…I mean, if you could've—"

"No." He breathed heavily, for he already guessed she had thought this. "I refuse to bring the business between our families into this." He moved his hand between them. "I'm already in a bit of a pickle anyway."

Her face softened. "Care to explain?"

Chris had to explain, make it clear for them so they could land on the same page. He unlocked his computer, filtered to all the emails associated with Carrah, and then turned his screen so she could see. "All of these emails are about you. The ones flagged have my attention. They have moved up your release date and Olivia has even inquired about my review for a contract of a film agent.

"You've mentioned revisions. Soon they'll want a detailed synopsis of book two. I'm not seeing how you meet your deadlines and collaborate with my cousin in a lab. I also don't see how you will enjoy the rest of summer, but that is a drop of water in the larger bucket."

Her gaze fell to her lap and stayed there for longer than a few minutes as she twiddled her thumbs. He allowed the quiet to spin around them and give her time to think about the commitments that lay ahead. Carrah was new to the entertainment world, and whereas she might wield some control at Noir, she didn't have that same power at Hurston House yet. If she made a list, a popular book club, and gained crossover appeal, maybe. For now she had to prove herself and he wanted her to be a success.

"You really are the best, huh." She finally looked back up

and focused on his face. "You know everything I've never told you."

"You're my client. It's my job to know and anticipate. I'm also on both sides of this, which is the pickle I mentioned. Normally, I'd recuse myself. I can't and won't because it would raise suspicions and abandon my promise to you."

A small smile curved her lips. "Your mother raised you to have honor in your word." Chris nodded. He would never forget Claudette's creed. "Thank you," Carrah said, slightly above a whisper. "For not forcing or telling me which one to choose. That is rare in our world."

"Oh, to be a family within the old guard." He returned her smile. "You did more for my brother than you'll ever know...and...me too. You grounded me. I didn't realize how lost I'd been since losing my mother until I committed to helping you."

Chapter 29

CHRIS SAT INSIDE his father's study. He had not endured a stare-down competition such as this since voicing his desire to pursue interests outside the family business when he was nineteen. All he'd done was walk into his father's office to explain why he canceled their round of golf this afternoon. No longer thirteen, and too tired from the day for these chastising games, Chris threw his towel in the ring and proceeded to leave.

"Before you go"—Chauncy's full kingmaker tone gave Chris pause—"what is the Andrews girl to you?"

Chris faced his father. He hadn't validated a friendship since middle school. Then again, none of those kids were children of his father's business rival. "I don't understand your question."

"I think you do, Christopher." His father got up and came from around his desk, meeting Chris where he stood. He looked him square in the face. "I tried ignoring your...response to her that day we went to their home. The way you watched her, almost came out of your seat over Trenton's remarks, and then seemed out of sorts on the ride back home."

His father moved past him to the wet bar and poured a glass of cognac. "Video surveillance showed her at the office as far back as a month. So I ask you again. What is she to you?"

Chris carefully watched the man who taught him how to play chess. It was like they were sitting at the board and his father had moved his king's pawn, and then he did the same, hasty to shorten the game. This time Chauncy played the queen's knight and was patiently waiting to checkmate him.

Almost two weeks had passed since Chris had sat in the Andrews house, and over a month since Carrah first ventured to his office in search of help. Although he no longer cared about the forces that deemed the Chennaults and Andrewses as rivals, Carrah did. He wouldn't be goaded into exposing her against her will.

"She is nothing to me." The lie strangled him. Carrah was something. He just hadn't worked through what that was yet. "What are you looking for me to say, Dad?"

"The truth," he replied pointedly then sipped from his glass. "The two of you had lunch from the Lucky Dill on Monday, and then today takeout from Mama's Place. I believe there was also a coffee run and a convenient dinner gathering for Roland's daughter the other night."

Chris's throat was dry, his vision blurred. This was the behavior that had taken his mother to an early grave. The anxiety in his gut twisted in pain. "Are you seriously having me followed?"

"There is a multimillion-dollar deal at stake. Her family's finances are in ruins and you are the heir. Like it or not, one day you will run this company."

"That is not what I want. We had a deal—Mother—"

"Your mother is no longer here with us, son," his father yelled. "She's gone and you're all I have left."

"That's. Not. True." Chris raised his voice a decibel. "There is Miles. Chloe and Carter."

His father scoffed and slammed his glass down. "Miles is not my son. Your brother and sister are far from ready, thanks to you." Their gazes met. "I delayed them learning the business for fear that they might abandon me like you did."

"Jesus, Dad, stop criminalizing the choices I've made." He refused to control the tone or the volume of his voice out of parental respect. "While I understand your sentiments on Carter and Clo, I'm not to blame. They were old enough to see Mom work until she collapsed across her bed countless nights. There were even times that she wouldn't take her meds for fear that she would fail her fiduciary duty to the company. Her weight to prove herself to you and Grandmother was too much to bear. My brother and sister blame Chennault as much as I do." He balled his fists.

Chauncy grabbed his chest. He took a winded breath before his knees buckled underneath. Chris darted to his side and caught him. "Help!" he shouted.

"Shh…" His father blew as he sat in the winged back chair. "I'm fine. My pressure, it's been high lately, and this talk about your mother…" He sighed.

"Your pressure?" Chris waved Ms. Watson and Carter away as they entered the room. "Maybe I should be the one asking if there's something you need to tell me."

A weak chuckle escaped Chauncy. "Cut it, smart guy."

Chris took the seat beside his father. He sat for a few minutes until the empty desk in front of them became too much after what had just happened. He got back up and kneeled at his father's side. "You can't quit on me yet, old man." They both laughed. "I know you're not one for promises. However, can you reconsider your position on Miles? I don't want to lead Chennault, Dad."

A grimace flattened Chauncy's lips before he looked away from Chris. "That is more complicated than you'll ever know."

"You helped raise him. He's like my brother."

"Only he isn't." Chauncy pushed on both armrests and got to his feet, and Chris did the same. Chauncy took another deep breath. "In the meantime, sow your oats with the Andrews girl if you must. But be careful—the women of that family are known to trap things."

It was an unflattering characterization he thought. He wouldn't debate it, but hopefully he could alter his father's prejudiced viewpoint. "A person desperate to escape doesn't set traps."

"They are the worst ones."

The stare down they began with was how they ended. Except this time it was more warning than reprimand. Either way after he checked to ensure his father felt fine, he hurried out. When the door closed behind him, he texted Carrah.

Escape with me

Where are we going?

He smiled then texted, You tell me

Surprise me

Meet me in 30?

More like an hour. I've been summoned for a family meeting (:

(: Just had one of those. Message me when you're done.

okay

* * *

Minutes floated by before Carrah eased off her cloud. She refocused back on her computer, where her hand began trembling as it hovered above the keyboard. She sucked in a deep breath and then pressed send on an email back to her agent committing to revised deadlines. There was no turning back now.

The alarm on her phone rang. She closed her laptop and scrambled downstairs. She was second to the table behind Dominic. Her mouth fell open and then she narrowed her eyes on him. Rarely did he engage in family business unless there was something he wanted.

"What you want, Nic?" No need to hesitate understanding her brother's motivation for being present on an evening that he could be out with friends or one of the many girls who had been chasing him.

"Nothing much." His lips pressed for a second. "Just need Dad to get off my ass. I flunked a class and now he's pissed. Talkin' 'bout cutting my monthly stipend." He scoffed. "I never asked to be an attorney. Maybe I liked mixing shit together like you."

"You're bad at math."

He shrugged. "Don't matter. I should've had a choice. Didn't you? Beauty queen or chemist?"

Carrah almost fibbed like she did when they were little to make him feel better about the control their parents wielded over them with an iron fist. Maybe if she told him that chemistry had been the exit plan he'd feel better about the space he was in. Only, her genius in science and math had trapped her more than she'd ever imagined. She hoped her brother wouldn't meet the same fate.

Doubtful, given that they were sitting at a table at five o'clock in the evening for a business meeting instead of summering in the Shores.

Nic's confession triggered the realization that she had

never once stopped to consider the choices stricken from her siblings. Maybe if they'd rebelled, the expectation to conform would be less overwhelming.

"You must want something!" Aubrey giggled, staring at Dominic as she crossed the room and came over to the table with her husband.

Before Dominic could reply, the rest of their clan excitedly marched in, chatting away along with the company attorney and claimed seats at the table. For a second, it didn't seem they were here for business since Aubrey shared her excursion to the zoo with Zoe, followed by each family member highlighting their day. Of course, Carrah didn't confess that she had snuck off with Chris early in the morning for their London Fog run at the café. Instead she lied, and used Ava as a cover since their mothers were not chatty.

Perhaps if the joint venture was approved, the rival lines she and Chris stood behind could be erased. It would be nice not to hide from a relationship they both seemed eager to discover.

A quick pivot to the necessary business at hand was made by her father. His position remained the same as it had the last few times they'd gathered to discuss details of the venture. Albeit cautious, he affirmed it was the only way to ensure the longevity of Noir. Beau, on the other hand, still disagreed for two reasons. The first, he was uncomfortable that Olina Chennault was investing a bit more. Second, he had reservations with only Carrah communicating and collaborating with Miles to bring the product to life.

All eyes shifted to Carrah. She didn't know if it was her big brother's heavy-handed comment or the unspoken question she knew they wanted to ask: Would she be able to finalize the serum? Truth be told, she had little bandwidth to coddle her brother's insecurities. Most important, she had to finalize the serum before her planned exit.

Chris might frown upon her revised deadline schedule. Only, Carrah knew Noir depended on her. She had to see this through before fully embracing something that was hers and hers alone.

"What exactly do you need from me?" She schooled her face to appear the epitome of Miss Congeniality.

"Your cooperation in working with Chauncy's nephew is a must," her father replied pointedly. "I hear he is as genius as you are alchemically."

Her mother's tongue clicked like the old Creole women who sat on their front porches while gossiping. "Did you know Hannah had a son?" Her gaze sliced into Melvin.

"Not until a week ago." Melvin rubbed his neck. A thought appeared to cross his mind, but then he tucked it away. "At any rate, Carrah, you'll need to allow Miles a chance to review your research, including the notes we exchanged as you were attempting to coagulate the integrity of the formula. Chauncy mentioned that Miles studies interactions at the molecular level and reverse engineers. Perhaps you'll learn something from him that we can use later, after the venture is complete. For now, focus on working together to make the blockbuster product we need."

Carrah scoffed. "Reverse engineering? That takes time." More than what she planned to give after her sacrifices to the company.

"In my father's infinite wisdom, he had the foresight to see we may hit a stumbling block. Attorney Peters"—Camille gestured to Mr. Ben sitting a few chairs from her—"informed me of a fund that was created for situations such as this. We will give BSB their money, fund the venture, and use PR to build anticipation. We have more time than we did yesterday." Her mother's sigh matched the vacant expression resting atop her face. Carrah would need to ask if she was feeling okay. Camille had that look she wore when she battled for her life last year.

Aubrey slowly raised her hand and waited for their father to acknowledge her. "Will the Butlers go away so easy? It wasn't simply the money." Her sight slid to Carrah.

Carrah bit her tongue, looking in the opposite direction of her sister. What was her endgame? Because the way Aubrey presented her question contradicted the sisterly bond they shared.

Carrah leaned into the table to tell her sister to go to hell with gasoline panties on when Dominic sat up in his chair, clearing his throat.

"Time-out." He gestured the same with his hands. "Ole boy been hopping from bed to bed since we been here. I'm a saint compared to Trent. My sister deserves better, and if he thinks otherwise, the public can decide. Press of his philandering ways will make his political run hard."

"Thanks, Nic." Carrah reached over and squeezed his hand, and he did the same in return.

"Agreed," Camille chided. "Melvin, make sure you give the news to Sandra yourself...or is that something else you'd like to do behind my back?"

Shock rushed through the room, tapping Carrah and her siblings on the shoulder before they watched their mother get up and leave without another word. Oddly, their father didn't follow. He reclined back in his chair, face turned to the ceiling, ignoring that they were in the room.

Carrah tried to care. She didn't. She slipped into the void left by her mother and sprang from the room. After grabbing a few things, she texted Chris.

Done. Meet?

She held her breath, hoping he still wanted to link up. Three little dots popped up.

An uber will be to you in ten minutes. It will bring you to me.

A smile filled her cheeks until they hurt. She replied okay, and then took off. She couldn't wait to see him.

Chapter 30

THE UBER DRIVER pulled up to the tall iron gate guarding the Chennault estate. All these years Chris and Carrah had lived so close while in summer residence but had been kept apart. She couldn't escape the irony that had foreshadowed their entire existence. Especially now as the gate opened and Chris strolled toward the car.

He opened the rear door. Carrah pushed away from the seat to get out, but then froze. The same thoughts she'd had moments ago as the car slowed and turned up to the gate flooded her head. She still wasn't supposed to be here.

His family might see her. Her family would find out, and then what? The venture hadn't repaired the fracture. Her father wanted nothing more to do with the Chennaults than for them to help Noir escape their current crisis.

"Don't overthink it." He peered inside. "My father went to dinner at the country club. Both Chloe and Carter are out with friends. No one will know you were here." He offered his hand to her and she took it.

An unyielding satisfaction set the butterflies loose in her belly. They kissed her insides and made her knees weak. Once she was out and next to him, he dismissed the driver and closed the gate. She gazed up to the immaculate Tudor revival–styled mansion and instantly understood.

The steeply pitched roof, beams, and elegant stonework set against Lake Dora possessed unmistakable charm, like the man before her. His entire family had always carried themselves in a distinctly uncommon way that many envied and few attempted to copy.

"Your family's home is beautiful." She was breathless, exhausted from chasing her restless heart.

"*Ma chère*." His thick Nawlins accent made a guest appearance. "You flatter me." His lips quirked into a mischievous smile, and dear Lord, take her to the water. Not for a refreshing dip but for washing away the sins of her mind that featured him. "I've known this house my entire life so I never quite looked at it as you do. Come." He pulled her by the hand.

Chris and Carrah disappeared down a path hidden from plain sight as their laughter filled the air. Once they emerged from the dense canopy of trees and shrubs, they were only a few feet from the bank of the lake. He continued on, leading her to the dock where one of the boats had been lowered into the water. They boarded with Chris taking the helm, and Carrah at his side watching as he launched from the dock.

The breeze was gentle, the water smooth, and salmon rays were beginning to melt at the horizon. Seeing the sun dangle over the wide-open water, the symphony of color exploding with blue, yellow, orange, and green before fading to black, had always been one of her favorite parts of the Shores. It was a peaceful conclusion to the day, and it seemed even more perfect that it would happen beside him.

"Sooo this is your surprise?" Both their heads turned to face each other. He lifted his shades and their eyes met for a second. She was so damn doomed.

He lowered his shades and focused back to the water. "You told me you liked landscapes, sunsets. I want us to chase it."

Tilting the wheel, he accelerated the speed on the bow rider as it glided along the shoreline of Lake Dora. In no time they were coming up the backside of downtown. Hill House Bed and Breakfast stood prominently to the left before he curved around and zoomed by the yacht club. The old lighthouse at Grantham Pointe was a bright riot of color competing for attention. He promised to come back by when it was night to see it fully lit.

After which he steered toward the channel linking the chain of lakes. There were so many places they could end up by taking this route since it flowed into a thousand waterways. Carrah appreciated the surprise and welcomed the intrigue in discovering where they would end to say goodbye to the day together.

*   *   *

Chris cut his eyes across to Carrah, hearing her giggle as the water sprayed them. She was the sunset he was chasing. This time alone with her out on the water sharing one of his favorite parts of the day warmed his soul in a way he had least expected when the summer began.

He reduced the speed on the boat, following the signs as they entered the canal. Luckily the waterways were clear or else he might run out of time getting to the spot he wanted her to see.

"Have you done this before?" Her question seemed

hesitant, almost accusatory. "Like, is this something you do with women?"

"What did he do to you?" The words slipped out of his mouth before he could stop them. He stole a glance and saw that she'd folded her arms and turned away. "I'm sorry. I didn't mean to—yes, I've done this before.

"A thousand times. It's a moment in the day that brings a sense of calm. Allows me to reflect on life and most times leaves me breathless." He scanned her, wishing she would turn back and face him. "And no, this is not something I do with women unless you count the times I've come out here with my mother and sister."

She didn't move and he wouldn't pry. The best he could hope for was to give her a sunset that was worth more than words. He upped the speed once they exited the bypass and entered open water.

"Look!" he called to her.

The next thing he knew, she was standing next to him as he steered on toward the horizon.

"It's everything I never imagined." Her arms flung into the air and she closed her eyes. "*Merci!*" She pecked his cheek and then threw her arms back up.

He chuckled, slowing the boat until it was in the middle of Lake Beauclair. There was the illusion that if they reached up, they may be able to catch the golden ball and wish for everything they ever wanted.

Chris wanted her. He knew it with certainty the day she came to check on him at the cottage. However, Carrah still seemed to be straddling the fence even after he'd invited her into his world.

Instead of focusing on his bad timing earlier he reclined back in his chair and tuned into the nature around them. He heard the bass break the water and the song of small birds. Frogs croaked, and he imagined them hopping on top of the lily pads. The bellowing of gators in the wild tossed him back into reality. Carrah, however, remained silent and so did he for fear of saying the wrong thing again.

After a while she faced him, biting her lip between her teeth as her hands fidgeted. This was that rare side of her that contradicted everything he'd ever known about her being a spicy, stand-her-ground kind of girl especially when she sat at a card table talking trash or standing up to her father in a business meeting.

"He...Trent, never made me...feel like this." She sat back down in her seat, staring straight into the sunset. Chris didn't know how to respond to her confession, only that it warmed him, and just maybe she was ready to jump over that fence. It seemed she had more to say so he waited patiently. It was easy given where they were. "But you—what's that old song?" She paused again, thinking, then hummed an old seventies ballad before saying the words *"You make me feel"* in the rhythm of the song.

"Brand new," he sang. *"I sing this song 'cause you..."* Their eyes locked for a moment in time. He would never forget the way she made him feel. No woman had ever tapped into this side of him. While plenty had asked for and desired his attention, none had ever made him want to give it until now. "The Stylistics sang that, I believe. My parents loved that song."

"Mine too," she murmured, still searching him with wide eyes. "You sing...Tell me something I don't know about you, Christopher Chennault." She positioned herself in the chair so that she remained facing him.

"There's a lot you don't know about me." He stared into her beautiful brown eyes and knew he would certainly sell his soul to her even if it was against the rules.

"Stop being so mysterious." She giggled, breaking the tension, and swatted at him. "Waiting on an answer."

"Fine," he groaned. "My grandmother was a music teacher. She taught us all how to play the piano and carry a tune or two. Chloe is actually the songbird. Your mother as well. She was trained by my grandmother. Did you know that?"

Carrah drew back in her seat. Her face tightened and then she said, "I did not. Do you think the venture will restore what used to be between our families?"

Why did her question seem to match the darkness that was rolling in uncommonly fast this evening? He restarted the engine, not sure of what to say. He knew his father saw the venture as an opportunity to exact revenge and he didn't want any part of it. But he could never betray his family by telling her.

"Can we change the subject? I'd prefer that we not discuss the business of our families. I don't want this to be complicated by them." His response was sincere. Though he wasn't sure how she would take it, and he couldn't look over to see given how rapid his visibility on the water was changing.

"You're right, sorry. I shouldn't have brought that into us."

Us? He couldn't help but steal a glance. What were they? Attorney and client didn't seem to fit anymore. Not after he'd kissed her twice, and was now here with her like this. Yet it was safe. And it stayed that way as they made the ride back.

The night fishermen crowded on the boardwalk, and the twinkling lights that came from the houses in the hill held her attention until it seemed she got lost in her own thoughts.

"Where are we going?" She sat up and looked at him.

He guided the boat along a back channel and reduced the speed, pointing up ahead to the well-lit dock. "The cottage. By now my father will be back at the main house. My Jeep is here. I'll take you into town and call an Uber to drop you off at home."

"Guess I'm not the only one that cares about creating a family scandal." Her words taunted him.

Chris barked a laugh without amusement and concentrated on docking the boat. He'd stopped caring a long time ago about what people thought. It was the only way he stayed sane after shirking legacy status at his parents' alma mater and then removing himself from the family business. The only reason he attempted to comply with the standards set within their elitist crowd was because his father still cared and he was a Chennault.

He hopped off the boat onto the dock and began wrapping rope around the cleat. "Are you attempting to gaslight me?" He went back to the steps of the boat and helped her out. "You care much more about what people think than I do. It's why no one knows we're friends."

She reached for his wrist and stilled them on the dock. "Is that what we are?"

"What else could we be?" He gently pulled away and gestured for her to exit the dock, and he followed as they cut through the backyard and up to the back porch.

Chris didn't mean to be a smart-ass. He'd been on the opposite end of the rope with Carrah, enduring the tug-of-war between their attraction and longtime rivalry. Her reluctance was understood as was the hesitation he witnessed earlier to get out of the car. It made his question valid for both of them.

She abruptly stopped and faced him before they could enter the French doors of the cottage. "I don't know. But I can't stay in this limbo with you." She took a deep breath and released a stuttering exhale. "Not when I think about you all the time, wondering what you're doing and when I'll see you again. I crave something more than our birthrights will ever allow... Maybe you can't give me that but it's what I want."

He scanned her, eyes wandering to the deepest crevices

of her soul. He sensed vulnerability that he wouldn't take for granted. He took a few steps to close the distance between them and a deep breath to steady the rhythm of his chaotic heart, then he stared down into her eyes. "I told you I had jumped off the deep end. Been waiting for you to join me."

"I can barely keep my head above water," she confessed and then went on her tippy-toes and pressed her lips to his mouth. "I want to stay…with you…tonight."

Chris threaded his fingers in her hair, his lips pressed to hers, and he closed his eyes. He'd captured his sunset and now a part of him was stirring, awakening to an explosion of emotions that had been nestled deep within, searching to break free and occupy his heart.

He broke the kiss. Her eyes were still closed, lips puckered, and before he claimed them again, he had to confirm her words. There would be no mistakes with Carrah. "Define 'stay tonight.'"

Her chest rose and fell like it was collapsing, and then her eyes fluttered open. There was an innocence about her that he'd never noticed until now. She reached for his hand and laced their fingers together. "Is the door open?"

Chris unlocked the door then pulled it open. She led them inside. Her lips gently landed on his once more before she pulled at the short hem of her dress and lifted it over her head. Almost instinctively one arm moved to cover her breasts while the other traveled lower. He reached in and stopped her.

"Don't hide." He stared her in the face. His gaze roved over her body, taking in the full breasts and hourglass shape that made him wanton with need. "You're so fucking beautiful," he growled, and wrapped his arms around her, holding her tight as he kissed her until they were breathless.

Chapter 31

THEY CAME APART, hostage to each other's gazes. Each searching, wondering, and unsure of what should come next.

"Are you sure you want this?" Chris asked.

Carrah nodded. How could she not want this gorgeous man who believed in her dreams and made each one come true? "I want you," she panted. "I've never wanted anything more."

He grabbed her by the hand and moved them away from the doors in the family room down a hall and then into a bedroom. His eyes seemed to glow at her in the dark before he snatched off his shirt, flaunting incredible washboard abs. His delicious golden skin pressed against hers as he reached around and undid her bra. His body on her body was a chemistry set about to explode.

Oddly, he drew back and all those insecurities Trent had given her came rushing in. Were her breasts not big enough, was she too light, not thick enough, or too thin? The courage she'd found to even come into his house and take her clothes off was quickly evaporating.

"Shit!" He pulled his wallet from his shorts pocket. "I don't think I have any protection."

"Do you have some here?"

He gave a vigorous head shake of no. "I've never brought a woman here. Nor did I plan to." Another expletive shot from his mouth as his head turned up to the ceiling.

The apprehension that had attempted to creep in on her vanished. She moved to Chris, and tickled her nipples against his chest. He groaned, and looked at her with the hungriest eyes.

"Pull out?" she suggested. "I'm clean. I've only had one partner and that was over a year ago."

"I'm clean too. I've always worn protection. This is... unexpected." He caressed her cheek. "I can pull out."

Carrah was back in his arms, her mouth covering his until the bulge against her belly begged for her attention. She looked down and then up to him. That panty-teasing smile was on full display.

"I told you there was *a lot* to learn about me," he teased then pushed her against the wall. His hand slid inside her panties and his fingers began massaging her clit. "By the time I'm done with you..." She moaned, loving the way his thick digit worked into her. "You'll be wet enough to take all of me. I can't wait to make you scream."

Chris planted a kiss at her neck. He then trailed to her breasts, belly button, and by the time he was at her thighs, he was on his knees. He pulled her panties off, hooked her leg over his shoulder, and drove his tongue into her hot center.

A tingling sensation coursed over her body in a way she

had never known. Of course, she'd heard of pleasure, but she'd never experienced it this way until now. Sounds she didn't know she could make filled her ears before she called his name, channeling the flames of ecstasy that filled her up then burst and made her knees buckle.

Before she fell to the floor, he caught her and placed her in the center of the bed. "I'm not done with you yet." He grabbed her by the ankles, spread her legs wide, then stood back at the edge of the bed, staring at her wet pussy. "You really are delicious." His husky voice seduced her into a state of euphoria. "Touch yourself."

Her panting breaths became shallow as their eyes met in the dark. His sensual command compelled her to abandon inhibitions and latch on to the sexiness he'd given her free rein to control. She closed her eyes, widening her legs, and allowed her fingers to journey to her apex.

* * *

Had he taken it too far? It was a fleeting thought that was once again fading as he watched Carrah's body bow off the center of his bed. She'd made him lose control, let him look inside her soul, and now he wanted to devour her.

She was more beautiful than he could've ever imagined. The willingness she had to engage his dominance made him weaker than he'd ever been, and he was willing to give her anything she desired while committing every nook and cranny of her luscious body to memory.

Chris shed the rest of his clothes, climbed onto the bed, and stilled her hand. She groaned in protest, panting out of frustration as he pinned her hand to the bed and hovered above her. "Open your eyes," he whispered, fighting for control as the heat of her pussy licked the head of his manhood.

"Your eyes are so beautiful," she whispered as her lids fluttered open.

His heart caved, his cock stiffened, and he dismissed logic. He kissed her and slowly pushed forward, parting her wet pussy lips with his rock-hard cock. "Mmmm," he moaned, having never felt a woman so tight.

Her breath hitched as her hand cupped his jaw. "It's..." she panted, "soo...mmm."

"Are you going to take it, Carrah?" he whispered, pausing mid-stroke. There would be no regrets. She nodded. "You have to say it."

"Yessss."

Chris cradled her leg over his arm and then thrust all the way to the hilt. He relished the moans that escaped her and wouldn't stop until she found release.

Chapter 32

A BRIGHT LIGHT played at Carrah's closed lids. She turned in the bed and found the other side empty and cold. She rolled to her back and began recounting last night. Seconds had become minutes, and then turned to hours. Time lapsed into what felt like infinity within Chris's hedonistic rapture.

Her body heated up, thinking of all the naughty things he'd made her do and how much she had enjoyed it. Never had she felt so sexy, empowered, and in control of her sexuality.

"Does she always wake with a smile?" His deep voice created an ache between her thighs as he entered the room smelling like a fresh meadow in the spring.

Her nipples hardened and desire bloomed between her legs at the sight of his well-defined arms, chiseled chest, and washboard abs carved into his golden skin. The heat was almost unbearable. However, after six rounds with the last ending at daybreak, she wasn't certain if her body parts could take him again.

"Depends." She pulled the sheet up to hide evidence of her musings and the fact that she wanted him again.

"I've seen it all. No need to cover up now." He tugged the covers. His eyes went to her breasts and a tent began to pitch under his towel. "Because I am a gentleman and have had the pleasure of making you cream all over my dick, I know you need rest. Just believe me when I say it is taking everything in me to stay here while you lie there."

Carrah giggled, but he was serious. The same way he had been last night flexing his dominance while exposing her to things she'd never done before. "What if I don't want you to stay there?"

He shook his head. "You risk not going home today." He reached to untie his towel when the house phone started ringing. His attention darted past her to the nightstand, where the phone rang again. "I probably should get that." He moved to the other side of the bed. "Few have this number and no one calls me here unless they haven't been able to reach me." He picked up the phone. "Hello," he answered.

Carrah rolled from the bed to give him privacy and went down the hall to the bathroom. When she first came here, she had no idea it was a one-bedroom, one-bath dwelling, for it looked much larger on the outside and the front living space was classically proportioned. She very much appreciated how the old blended with the new since it was clear that renovations had been done to accommodate the vessel sink vanity and rainfall shower.

Another piece of her heart melted seeing that he had already set out linens and toiletries, including a shower cap for her use. After last night, how could they go back to pretending they were rivals? She pushed the unwelcome thoughts from her head, brushed her teeth, and then hopped in the shower.

Hard as she tried to focus on the million other things she needed to be concerned about, Carrah stood in the mist of the shower wishing the conflict between their families away.

"Did you get lost?" The shower door opened and Chris entered in all his naked glory. He was the incarnation of Zeus and Nefertiti's son, golden, chiseled, beautiful, and powerful.

"In my thoughts, yes," she answered honestly.

He took the washcloth and soap from her and began scrubbing her body. "Don't get stuck there. Live in this moment with me."

"Moments are fragments. They don't last long."

"No, but memories can live forever." He fingered her chin up and looked into her eyes.

"So is that what we are to be, a summer memory?" Carrah rejected his notions and turned her back to him. God, she hated how this man made her feel, and yet she loved it because she knew there was the audacity to hope for more than the life her parents and Trent had assumed of her. "I don't need you to have summertime memories in the Shores."

"I asked you last night what else could we be and you never answered me, Carrah."

She swallowed hard. "I gave myself to you in a way that I never have with any other man."

He grabbed her by the shoulders and made her face him. "So then, what are we? I'm done caring about my dad or your parents. If we want this, then nothing else matters."

"I don't know what this is," she confessed. "But I want it… want you, as unexpected as it is."

"So do I." His forehead pressed against hers. Their chests were rising and falling in unison. "Time didn't steal this away from us. It was what we needed to find whatever this thing is between us."

Carrah nodded her head, acknowledging that it hadn't, and then his mouth slammed down against hers. His tongue thrust desperately between her parted lips, greedily taking her affection. He came up for air and stared into her eyes. "I remember, once when we were little, we all went swimming at Reese's. You forgot your swim cap, and when you came up from under the water, your hair was curly. Does it still do that?"

She allowed her mind to go back in time. "I...my mother and—" She cleared her throat. She wouldn't say another man's name while she was in his arms. "Straight hair is—was— preferred for pageants and certain appearances. I rarely wear my hair in its natural state."

Chris dragged the shower cap off her head. He smiled as the water began hitting her hair. "Unless you count the Red Party, I don't believe you're prepping for a pageant or an appearance. You're supposed to be working on a book." Their laughter ceased when he lifted her up, gripping her ass and then slid her down his steely cock. "Besides," he groaned, "now I don't have to feel guilty for getting your hair wet."

* * *

By late afternoon, Carrah was home at her desk attempting to complete the serum brief for Miles. Only, last night was on a constant loop. The warmth of Chris's kisses claimed her heart while his touch set her soul on fire. Her body had confessed the secrets she was too afraid to speak.

There were no regrets. She had never felt more alive, free, or so seen in her entire life. She wanted this chance with Chris. This unexpected path that gave her everything she ever wanted. There were no doubts in her mind until she heard shouting downstairs.

Camille was broadcasting her reservations about the

venture, her distrust of the Chennaults, and she reminded Melvin that Noir belonged to *her* family. Unlike her siblings, Carrah refused to linger outside the study door eavesdropping. She went back to her room to grapple with how lust, attraction, and something else sitting at the base of her heart had betrayed her mind. Her family wasn't ready to discover she'd bedded the enemy.

"Come in," she called as knocks rapped at her door. Her little niece, Zoe, bounced in ahead of her sister, who appeared as though she hadn't slept all night. Carrah got up from her desk and gathered Zoe in her arms before showering her with kisses.

"I like your hair, TT Carrah!" Zoe patted Carrah's curls.

"This is not the time for you to rebel. Mom is on a rampage. You need to call the salon and get an appointment." Aubrey appraised her in a way that would have normally made her feel as though she'd broken a rule. She then moved to Carrah's side and frowned, pulling at the natural coils. "I mean, I like it. I'm just saying you know how our mother is about image and with Senator Roland hosting the annual Red Party tomorrow…"

Hand to face. In submitting to Chris's hedonistic rapture, Carrah hadn't considered the Red Party, which kicked off the weekend's Juneteenth festivities. For a second she contemplated calling a stylist to blow her out. Except, she looked in the mirror. A long time had passed since she saw this girl staring back at her, and she loved her. It wasn't just the hair. She felt whole, confident, appreciated, and loved.

Unexpectedly Chris had come along and helped her tap into a power that was always hers.

"My image is fine. I'll be ready tomorrow. I have my red attire, and my social graces remain intact. What else could Mother ask for? Hair doesn't define me."

"Geez, forget I said anything." Aubrey cleared her throat. "Anyhow, as you've heard, Mother has reservations on the venture. She wants you to spend some time with Miles Chennault to determine if he's truly capable."

Aubrey proceeded to explain that Miles was on his way over to collaborate with Carrah in the lab. She then disclosed that their mother seemed to have an unhealthy obsession with him, and his involvement had triggered her reservations.

"This is silly." Carrah had more to worry about than their mother liking Miles. "I don't have time for this, Aubrey."

"He looks like a younger version of Dad, Carrah," Aubrey blurted out. "They were all friends at one time. Haven't you ever really wondered what happened? I have always thought that there were holes in the story of how the two families fell out. And I'm wondering...Haven't you noticed the cold shoulder Mom's been giving Dad? They've never argued like that in front of us."

In truth, Carrah had not noticed. She had been caught up in her own affair and was now processing how she and Chris would navigate the Red Party tomorrow after the blatant disdain expressed by her mother downstairs.

"I hadn't noticed."

A grimace formed on Aubrey's face. "Try paying attention when he gets here."

No more than an hour passed before Carrah was being paged to come downstairs. It was too late to pretend she hadn't heard what Aubrey said earlier. As a result, she found herself engaged in the scrutiny of their guest.

Miles's eyes were dark like their father's with a golden complexion customary of his Chennault kin. His nose was thin, and his ears were similar to hers. He seemed familiar as they worked in the lab and sat discussing hypotheticals.

"Miles." Camille entered with a faux smile. "Did you figure it out yet?" He laughed along with Carrah and divulged a few theories he had for the serum failing to stabilize. "Interesting. Well, tell me, where did you get this genius from? Hannah hated science."

"Still does." He chuckled. "She says it comes from my father." He shrugged. "Except I wouldn't know. I've never met him."

Camille moved closer, analyzing him with each step. "Do you—"

"Mom," Carrah interjected, seeing that Camille had no filter on her quest to find something she probably would regret knowing. "We're almost finished here." She met her mother's gaze and saw more pain than she could have ever imagined. "I'll bring Miles up to the house after we get these notes into the brief."

Camille hesitated. She nodded then turned on her heel and left Carrah with a man that reminded her of her father. Naturally Carrah now wondered if Miles was the real reason that lines had been drawn between the two families.

Chapter 33

THE ANNUAL RED Party in honor of Juneteenth had long been the most anticipated event of the summer. From the time Chris was old enough to vote, he was expected to attend, for it was the one event that had never drawn boundaries between the Andrewses and the Chennaults, or their kind of people, from the local townsfolk. Everyone of African descent attended to pay homage to the bloodshed of their enslaved ancestors through the transatlantic slave trade and then celebrate freedom from bondage.

Chris fastened the button on his double-breasted burnt red coat, which he'd paired with gray slacks, then helped Chloe from the car. They waited for Carter and his father to make their way around and entered the event as one. Once upon a time the sea of red had been overwhelming. The food and drinks were that color as were the décor and everyone's attire. Finding the perfect fit for this coveted event used to be a chore. Now he looked forward to it and this evening more than usual since he couldn't wait to see Carrah again.

Their night together made him want the moon and stars with her at the center of his universe. Never had he dreamed of wanting someone like this, and maybe it was the poison his mother had warned him about all those years ago because he was weak with need for Carrah. He scanned the perimeter, not seeing her, and then separated from his family to go where Gavin, along with Quinn and her brother Roland, were hanging by the water.

"Evening." Chris extended greetings to both Quinn and Roland while Gavin looked at him as though he had something on his face. "'Sup, man, why you looking at me like that?"

"You got on the wrong colors, frat." Gavin chuckled, then gripped him up in their secret handshake. "Hell, we all do." He tugged at his red sports coat.

"Watch your mouth!" Roland laughed, flashing his fraternity sign. "Red and white trumps black and gold any day."

"So the Nupe said." Chris chuckled and hit fives with Gavin.

Quinn cleared her throat. "Have y'all seen my girls?"

They all looked around and then responded with head shakes. "Are they ever on time? Reese and Peyton are notorious for being on CP. Carrah is always on her own time, Miss Grand Entrance, and Ava ebbs and flows," Gavin offered.

"There's Reggie with Reese and Dunc," Roland said, waving to them as they made their way to where they stood.

The party of four became a party of seven, which grew again when Lockhart and Trent invited themselves into the circle. Chris checked the time at his wrist then stepped away from everyone and moved closer to the rail. He gazed out onto the dark waters of Lake Dora and wished he could be back at the cottage with Carrah.

"You've been MIA lately." Gavin stepped to his side. "She keeping you busy?"

Chris felt the crease form between his brows and told himself to play it cool. Gavin knew him inside and out, and would sense something was up if he acted any other way. He slid his hands into his pockets and asked, "Who's keeping me busy?"

"Heather, Summer, work? Hell, I don't know. I assumed a woman with the way you've been moving lately."

"Neither," Chris scoffed.

"Then why is she looking for you?" Gavin tilted his head to the lower lawn where Summer stood alongside Chloe, waving to them.

"I'm straight." Chris didn't bother to return her wave before he gave Summer his back. He'd given her a million hints that he wasn't interested.

"Damn, that girl wants to give it to you bad," Gavin teased. "Ain't nothing wrong with accepting what's freely given."

"Gentlemen," Reese called to them, waving good-bye before she kissed Duncan and started in the opposite direction.

"Reese!" Her voice was unmistakable. Chris moved back to where everyone remained congregated. "Wait for me."

Chris himself felt hypnotized as Carrah strutted their way, sparkling like a ruby in her plunging neck wrap dress. The way her thigh peeked out of the slit of her dress was much too high for his liking, given their current company. Worse was that the sexiness enveloping her had him contemplating actions that would have him quickly judged. He loved how her tawny skin glowed, calling to him as her wavy hair accentuated her beautiful face.

Carrah was nothing less than a Miss America, Miss Universe...Mrs. Chennault. His heart stopped. She was everything he ever wanted and didn't know it. In chasing her dreams, he'd unexpectedly discovered his. He found his breath but the rhythm of his heart was lost, and it didn't restart until he locked eyes with Carrah from afar.

"Gav, Reg, Dunc, Chris." Carrah's gaze lingered on him before she smiled at all of them. "Trent, Lockhart," she muttered. "The boys clean up nice." She giggled, joking with Reese.

"Mmm-hmm," Reese seconded. "Gucci, Boss, Armani, McQueen," she pointed out, going down the line from Gavin to Chris. "All latest collections too— But Ma'am!" Reese's entire face lit up. "You. Are. Rocking this hair! I haven't seen you wear it like this in a long time."

Trent laughed. "Rightfully so, it's wild." His hands swirled around his head. "Big. Guess you decided to tap into your roots tonight." He sneered then moved to be at her side but she jerked back.

Chris saw that shadow of doubt cross her face. It had happened a few times when they were together. Now he witnessed firsthand what that jackass had done to her. Boys like Trent dimmed lights they felt would steal their shine. He wouldn't allow her spotlight to be ruined.

"I think it suits you. You look beautiful, Carrah." Chris looked her in the face, not caring that anyone else was around.

The entire circle went silent. Reese had slack jaws, Duncan scratched his head, while Gavin clasped him by the wrist as though he were about to run interference. Chris recalibrated, unsure of how to process the way his emotions flew off the handle. Never had he allowed his feelings to impact his actions. It was the first rule of law. Carrah was the exception.

Carrah looked away for a second, attempting to hide the flush staining her cheeks. "Thank you, Chris." She cleared her throat and then waved to Quinn, who was calling for them to join her on the lawn. "Ready, Reese? Quinn's going to kill me for being so late." They linked arms with each other and started off. "Catch y'all later," Carrah called over her shoulder then looked back at him one last time before they faded into the crowd.

"They are truly the prettiest girls in the world," Reggie said before turning to look over the balcony where all of them stood below in the garden. "I mean, the whole group is fine."

Duncan cleared his throat. "Watch your mouth, man. Reese is taken."

So is Carrah, Chris wanted to say but couldn't. Not yet. He wouldn't risk exposing them to their friends since she had asked for time to break the news to their families first.

"Carrah's taken too." Trent provoked Chris's attention, forcing his eyes to tear away from where Carrah mingled with her friends. "She just needs to get over herself."

The icy words chilled Chris to the bone while his right hand tightened into a ball and contemplated disregarding social decorum and punching the other man in his face. "Taken by whom? I thought she was single."

"So did I," Gavin chimed in, side-eyeing Chris before refocusing on Trent. "Word on the street is she turned down your marriage proposal."

"She did." A sardonic smile stretched across his face. "I can't help that I love ass or that my girlfriend hung on to her virginity until grad school. I'm a man. What'd she expect, faithful? We ain't have no rings on our finger." Trent's derisive laugh made Chris want to punch him again. "Carrah doesn't even know about all of the women. Only two, that's how many she found out about and it was enough to ruin everything." He gazed into the distance, eyes on Carrah without a trace of remorse.

Reggie shoved Trent. "What's wrong with you? I mean, I know she can be spicy as hell, but Carrah's beautiful and crazy smart. What man can't keep his shit in his pants for a woman like that?"

The frown upon Trent's face contradicted his shrug. Only, the despondence Chris noted as the man broadcasted his infidelity lacked sincerity.

"Carrah's not spicy." Trent walked into Reggie's face. "She's a Goody Two-shoes that will do anything to keep her parents happy, and that includes marrying me. She'll come around. Her parents need my family's bank and I need her on my arm for this political journey. Besides, I'm her first, last, and my dick will stay fitting her like a glove."

Chris cracked his neck and took a step closer to Trent. "Must you always be so damned crass? *Besides*, your comment is only true if you are, in fact, the last."

Trent lunged at Chris. Gavin stepped between them, halting any possibility of an altercation. He gave Chris a knowing look that communicated he finally understood why he'd been absent this summer while urging him to back down.

"Do I have something you want, Chennault?" Trent popped his collar. "I thought it odd the night of the ball when you were with Carrah on the balcony. But then, I saw the way the two of you looked at each other at Melvin's meeting. Tonight, you stand defending a girl that has historically been your enemy. So tell me, what more is there between you and my future wife?"

Laugh. That was what Chris did to avoid saying something that would further complicate the way he felt about Carrah

Andrews. The woman meant something to him and he wasn't about to betray her trust and what could be over a pissing contest with Trent.

"You're a clown. I need a fucking drink." Chris turned away from the group. His departure was halted when Trent grabbed his arm. He snatched it away, took a few steps back, and was grateful Duncan and Gavin jumped between them.

*　*　*

"What's going on up there?" Ava pointed up to the balcony where the guys were.

Carrah, Reese, and the rest of the girls all glanced up to see Trent take a swing at Chris and Duncan catch him by the arm. Carrah yanked the hem of her dress into her hand and moved like lightning to get back upstairs. No less than twenty minutes ago, everyone seemed fine. How did it get to this? She ran on her tippy-toes as the volume of their voices increased.

"It's okay to want what's mine," Trent spat at Chris while Lockhart held him back.

Carrah rushed to where they stood, slipped in front of Trent, and then shoved him. "What are you doing?" She shot a quick glance over her shoulder to check on Chris. He remained dignified in contrast to the man in front of her, even as his pensive stare made her heart sink.

"Get outta my way, Carrah." Trent attempted to brush her to the side. She disregarded him and remained firm.

"No! Is something the matter with you? Why are doing this?" she hissed, and then took a few steps back until she bumped into Chris. She turned to face him. She wanted to kiss him, except she couldn't. He didn't deserve this after helping to make her dreams come true. So she settled on helping him save face. God forbid his image get tarnished because of Trent Butler. "Are you okay? What happened?"

Chris dismissively waved his hand then lowered it as he pressed his lips together. "I'm fine."

A pained groan escaped Carrah as Trent seized hold of her arm, digging his fingers into her skin. Before he could pull her, Chris moved in and created a divide. He secured Carrah behind him and was face-to-face with Trent.

"Is he why you won't marry me?"

"What?"

"You heard me, Carrah." Trent stretched his neck to peer around Chris. "What's Chennault to you?"

She knew the answer to this question. She'd contemplated it since their night together and came to the undeniable conclusion that Chris was *everything*. Somewhere in between her becoming his client to them becoming friends, she'd fallen head over heels in love with Christopher Chennault.

Only now she was on the spot. It wasn't just their little summer crowd. Her parents, his father, their siblings, their friends, plus others were watching. How could she answer and not make a mess of their lives?

"I…he…" She struggled to find the words.

Chris turned to face her. His gorgeous eyes scanned her for a minute before they locked to hers. "Let me help you." He brushed past her and began walking away.

A second, maybe three or four, passed before she registered his actions. She went after Chris, leaving all the gossip and stares behind and called to him, but he kept going. After the third time of him ignoring her, she yelled, "Why won't you stop?"

He froze, keeping his back to her. She walked until she could stand in front of him.

"I'm sorry...I...I didn't know wh—my parents, your dad—"

"I don't care about any of them. What did I tell you?" Her gaze fell to the ground. He leaned down until he found her eyes and she lifted her head. "What did you tell me? You said you wanted this, us." He motioned his hand between them. "So did I, but never as a secret. I won't be your dirty little secret not when I know with certainty that I'm in love with you."

Water welled in her eyes. Carrah had never expected to hear those words. In this moment her heart battled to be whole and withstand the cracking pain of knowing she was unworthy of his confession. "What would you have had me say?"

"More than what you did, Carrah." He drew back. "You put the lid back on your box. I should've expected it...My mother said you were poison, and I fell for this wicked-ass game you played."

"That isn't true!" Her insides detonated, finally shattering her heart into a thousand pieces, knowing that she'd hurt the one person who made her believe in herself and the possibilities life had to offer. She closed her eyes, pleading with the saints, and took a step closer to him. She swallowed hard then opened her eyes and focused to his face. "Tell me...tell me something I don't know about you."

His lips quirked into a fallen smile. "That along our journey all I wanted was to give you everything you ever wanted, and more if you would've let me."

"I know," she choked over a sob, and he took a step back.

"And yet you still can't do it, can you? Stop living in their box and acknowledge this unexpected thing between us?" He released her from his penetrating stare and looked off for a second. "Do you remember the summer you passed me a note in church asking if we could be friends?"

"Yes." She wiped tears from her eyes. "You were mean about it. Tore it into pieces then left it on the church pew after making an ugly face."

"I said no because of this. I didn't want to like you as a friend and then be told I couldn't be your friend especially when I already thought you were pretty and knew my mom didn't like yours. Basically, I didn't want to get hurt…You did it anyway."

He brushed past her to leave then whipped back around. "I guess this is why you write happily ever afters. You're too afraid to live your own. Goodbye Carrah."

Chapter 34

"I SHOULD'VE STOPPED it when I learned you had taken her to your cottage. Instead I ended up watching my son in a cock-fight." Chauncy's heels clicked against the wooden dock before stopping at the bench Chris sat on. "Mind if I take a seat?" Chris slid to one end and gestured for his father to sit. "The laws of attraction don't adhere to the rules of man, Christopher. Two caged birds set free can find each other in the wild."

A moment of silence came and sat between them. It wasn't uncomfortable; it was needed right now for Chris to process the emptiness Carrah had gifted him when she was a coward to her feelings for him. He had felt broken like this only once before, and it was after his mother had passed because he was utterly powerless to control his range of emotion. It was the same now. Was he mad, sad, or stupid? He felt all three.

His father pointed past the dock to the dark water. "The night hides everything and so do the depths of the water. Only for a time, though. You sat in my office the other evening pretending that young lady was what, a friend? Maybe still our rival? The day we went to Melvin's, I saw your secret. As unexpected and unsettling as it was, I knew I couldn't change it. The way the two of you looked at each other. It was the way I looked at your mother. However, it's best if it not go any further."

"Why?" Chris finally spoke. "The rivalry started because of a business deal. You are now embarking on a joint venture with them. This should change the way our families view each other."

"I'm afraid that will never happen." Chauncy got to his feet. "Our fallout with Melvin's family was never simply about him manipulating a business deal to cut us out. The how and why are much more grim. Another secret that will hopefully remain buried at the bottom of the lake."

His father moved away from the bench and began retreating. Chris couldn't let him go yet. He needed answers. The woman he loved was still forbidden to him, and he had been willing to break all the rules—even befoul his mother's memory—to have her.

"Dad, I can't let you walk away from this like that. You once told me that being with Mom was like breathing fresh air for the first time. I feel like that when I'm with Carrah," Chris confessed, and he saw the tightness in his father's face fall.

"Ever since Mom died, I've felt like a part of me was locked away…lost. Carrah brought it back to life. I stopped only thinking of myself and expanding the firm. I watched Carrah be willing to sacrifice her own dreams to ensure Noir survived. Now, my mind lingers on the choices I've made regarding our family, Chenault Cosmetics, legacy…with her. So, for me to walk away from this…feeling, I need to understand why the relationship between our families is irreparable."

His father came back to where he stood. He seemed to assess Chris as though he were screening him to determine if he deserved top secret clearance. Finally Chauncy let out a long sigh. "Melvin didn't always have the money he has now. When I first met him in college, he sometimes didn't know how he would make it through the week. Yet he was smart, resourceful.

"He befriended me. We became fraternity brothers, room-mates, and ultimately were best friends. When I went home for the summer, I brought him so he, too, could intern at the company and make a little summer money. He displayed his genius to your grandfather and was offered a job at Noir.

"Coming from where he came from to seeing our wealth and way of life created a hunger in him, and he desired to have the same. So much so that he began seeing your aunt Hannah, whom he fell in love with."

His father shook his head. The anger that crossed his face would've made Chris believe this tale had happened yesterday. "At some point Melvin realized he would never assume any-thing more than a good job, despite marrying into the fam-ily. So he entertained advances from your mother's then best friend, Camille Chàvous, heiress to fifty percent of the Noir empire. She was an only child and her father craved a son, which he found in Melvin.

"Camille abandoned her friendship with your mother and aunt, and in no time she married Melvin. However, he left my sister very pregnant with Miles."

"What?" Chris shot to his father. "Miles is Melvin's son? Does he know?"

"No, he does not. That was your aunt Hannah's choice. It's the reason Miles never summered here. He resembled Melvin a lot as a child and that would've been too much scandal for a social family like ours. So, as you can see, Melvin not only took liberties with Noir. He did the same with our friendship and my sister. Your grandfather's intuition feared he may attempt to manipulate Miles to gain access to Chennault Cosmetics, and prohibited all interaction as a condition of Hannah's inheritance."

Okay, so they had skeletons in the closest. What family didn't? Everyone was grown now, and the animosity was no longer justified. "Miles should know who his father is, and Melvin should know he has another child who inherited his scientific genius, like Carrah."

"Miles is only a few months older than their oldest daughter. Camille would be hurt. She transferred all of her power to that man to make him love her. Exposing her deal with the devil could cost us everything we've worked hard for."

"Then why the venture, Dad? It makes no sense," Chris scoffed, sliding his hands into his pockets as he intentionally pried to understand his father's motivations.

"Revenge, Christopher. I have it on good authority that they are bleeding financially. The Butlers won't give them any more money. Hell, they want some of it back. Melvin realizes they don't have the resources alone to see this project through, and with Carrah declining a union with Trent, the gloves are off. Noir will be ours again. Now do you understand why it's best you leave the Andrews girl alone?"

Chris glanced at the ground. He was ashamed of his father's actions. Perhaps because of what he and Carrah had shared, and he understood her unwavering loyalty to her family. However, he knew there was little he could do to change Chauncy's mind. Once his father spoke plans into existence, they happened. His mother often complained of the tactic she had spent the majority of her life fighting.

"Dad." He pulled his head back up and met his father's eyes. "Revenge won't change the past or the fact that Miles has a father in this world that he should know about." The brows of Chris's face furrowed while the light bulb turned on. "This is why you never found Miles suited to run the company?"

His father nodded and then proceeded to leave the dock. Chris remained in step with him. "I cannot pretend to understand your logic, and I'm not sticking around to see how it turns out. I'm leaving in the morning."

Chauncy's steps broke. His jaws slack. "There is a month and some change left before the summer is over."

Chris shrugged. "I care not to be here." They continued their way up to the house. "I've neglected some things the last few weeks. I need to refocus and get back on track. Might be a good time for you to reconsider your feelings on Miles and leadership. I won't be part of your revenge schemes."

Chapter 35

TWO DAYS HAD passed since the Red Party, yet it still felt like it happened a second ago. The memory of Chris walking away, the family blowout, and the condemnation by their mutual friends was all still so raw. It almost overpowered her ability to reminisce on the time that they shared.

Those moments...Carrah wanted them back. She was unsure of how to get them as she sat scrolling on her phone, hoping a message from him would pop up. He hadn't responded to any of her messages. Still wouldn't answer her calls.

Carrah wondered if the angst and turmoil of sleepless nights accompanied by crying fits would go away if she could apologize, try and make things right between them. No longer having the patience for time to tell, she went to his office. It was closed.

Locked up as if he'd never occupied the space this summer. Desperation took over and she journeyed to the outskirts of town to his cottage. The gate was down to the dirt road. There was only one place left to go, and the last time she went to the Chennault mansion, Chris was expecting her. After the scene she'd caused at the Red Party, she doubted anyone inside the walls of that home wanted to see her. Still, she had to try.

The courage Carrah held evaporated the moment she pulled up to the mansion's gate. To her surprise she was instantly buzzed in. She drove down the long drive and stopped in the circle where Carter emerged from the front steps and she quickly got out of the car.

"What are you doing here?" His snippy words raised the hairs on her arms. She had not anticipated this reception from him.

"Carter." She walked around the car to meet him where he stood. "I need to see Chris. I want to apologize for what happened."

"Which part? The fact that insults were hurled at him over you by scheming-ass Trent Butler, or that you hung him out to dry?"

She deserved that slap in the face. "I care about your brother. Is he home?"

"You know, I thought you were different. He warned me. I didn't listen." He turned away and started back to the house. "You can leave. My brother is gone."

"Where?" she pleaded, but he kept going. "His office is closed. The cottage gate is chained."

Carter faced her. "Chris took you to my grandparents' cottage?" She nodded as he scanned her over with hard eyes. "Maybe you should come in," he mumbled.

They went into the Chennault home, and it couldn't compare to any other home she'd entered in the Shores. Not only did you see opulence, you smelled it, or at least you thought you did. Polished wood floors, an Italian marble staircase, and furnishings fit for the monarchy.

"Wait here." He left her in the foyer and disappeared.

She paced back and forth. What would she say? How would she start her apology? There was so much to say now that her head finally understood her heart. The laws of attraction needed a disclaimer. The agreements of love required an interpreter.

"Carrah." The older man's voice startled her. She turned to see Mr. Chennault standing before her while Carter was a few paces behind. "I understand you're here for Chris."

"Yes sir, I am."

"Chris isn't here, Carrah. He returned to New York the day after the Red Party."

The beat of her heart skipped then scattered, searching for its rhythm. She clutched her chest, hoping to pull away the ache; unfortunately it spread. Her eyes closed instantly replaying the last time she saw him walking away from her. A hand rested on her shoulder and she opened her eyes to see Mr. Chennault at her side.

He guided her to a chair where she inhaled then fought to exhale. Her eyes closed again while her ears rang and she found herself clawing back to the surface.

"Here," the man said, forcing her eyes open for a second as he shoved a glass of water into her hands. She drank and then felt her body begin to calm. "Are you all right?" he asked, taking the glass from her.

Carrah opened her eyes and saw both Carter and Chloe standing behind their father with another older woman now holding the glass she'd drunk from. She stood on wobbly legs. "I'm fine. I'm sorry I bothered you all. I should get back home."

"Wait," Mr. Chennault protested. "If you aren't in a rush, I thought we could talk for a bit?" She nodded, more curious than anything to learn what the man had to say. "This way."

Carrah followed him down a long hall and up a short flight of stairs that led into a study. An oil painting on the wall of the Buffalo Soldiers first caught her eye. Then there was a rendering depicting the life of a free Creole in French New Orleans. On his desk she noticed *The Isis Papers* and *Soul on Ice*. There were also original album covers from Motown's greatest artist and an ode to Prince. The eclectic mix of art and culture between extravagant mahogany shelves that paired with earthy-toned furnishings created a warm space that encompassed the duality of Black history and Black achievement in America.

They took seats across from each other at the empty fireplace.

"The cottage on the outskirts of town," he smirked, "my parents left that old place to Chris. Before our kind of people were able to purchase land on Lakeshore, my mom and dad created a little lake haven. Chris loves it there in that one-bedroom shack. You've been there?"

So many times..."Yes."

The man's assessing eyes peeled back whatever lies she might have told and he simply asked, "How many times?"

"A few," she admitted. "There we didn't have to worry about becoming the topic of gossip. We didn't have to hide from the fact that our families couldn't get along."

"It wasn't always like that. In fact, we used to joke that since the attraction bug skipped me and Camille, our children would unite two of the oldest bloodlines of the *gens de couleur*."

Carrah perked up. "Wait, you and my mom...were supposed to marry?"

The old man chuckled. "No. Our parents were quite progressive and did not believe in arranged marriages. Although I'm certain they would have loved it if Camille and I had fancied each other. It definitely would've made things less complicated with the business and preserved the friendship that had been established by our grandfathers."

"Until my grandfather betrayed your father and changed everything," she sighed.

"You mean your father." Chauncy gave her a pointed stare. "Your grandfather took the blame so his only daughter could have what she wanted, and that was your dad. Your mother gave Melvin what he'd wanted, which was relevance, position in our world, and the keys to Noir. Your father has sacrificed everything and everyone to sit atop an empire. Sort of like now."

It was. Although she couldn't agree out loud. Her father had unknowingly sacrificed her dreams, the wishes of her mother, Beau's vision for the future of the company, and there was probably more. Carrah could not ignore that her father was possibly exposing the company to risk. He'd disregarded everyone's opinions for the belief that a joint venture was best for Noir.

"Do you say that because I'm turning over top secret formulas to be reviewed by your nephew? Is your plan to steal then produce without us?"

"I am not *your* father," the older Chennault bit back. "That was him who tried to steal the formulas Claudette and I created...amongst other things." He paused as though searching for the right words. "My son confessed to me the way he felt about you. I made the mistake once of watching your father's greed ruin beautiful things. I can't allow it to happen again."

"What do you mean?"

The man got up, went to a cabinet, and pulled a box out. He came back and handed her a square-like item heavily wrapped in old newspaper before reclaiming his seat. Carrah unwrapped the newspaper and then allowed her eyes to focus on a picture of what was likely a very young Claudette Chennault along with Mr. Chennault, her father, and another woman she didn't know.

"Who is this?" Carrah asked another question, this time hoping for a verbal reply.

"My wife and I, along with your father and my sister, Hannah. We were thick as thieves. Your father almost became my brother until he made a choice that complicated the relationship of our families forever."

"I don't understand."

He sighed. "You may not. However, I believe your mother suspects. She's been asking a lot of questions lately. But that's not why you're here." He paused, assessing her with a piercing brown stare. "How do you feel about my son, Carrah?" The sincerity of Mr. Chennault's question forced her to confront what she'd been allowed to escape the last few days since the night of the Red Party.

Hiding from her feelings didn't seem to be a viable option with the misery that had followed her ever since Chris cut off all contact.

"I…I'm not supposed to love him, but I do." Her vision was of the floor beneath her feet. How could she look this man in the face after knowing the unfiltered history of her father and the havoc it had and still wanted to wreak over so many people's lives?

"I assumed so." He chuckled, and she looked up and stared in his face. "You would not have come here otherwise. When do you plan to tell him?"

"He won't answer any of my calls or messages, and you just told me that he's gone. Maybe it's for the best."

"Of my children, he is the most logical but unfortunately the most obstinate. Give him time to rationalize what happened. I'm sure you two will have a chance to talk. My advice to you is, strive to achieve your dreams or they will be lost and become figments of your imagination. What you did the other night was cater to the whims of other people. Me included."

Chapter 36

I miss our morning tea...

Chris swallowed hard, staring at the text message from Carrah. His thumbs hovered above the keyboard. He missed meeting her at the café too. Her beautiful eyes, fresh face, and thoughtful attitude always brightened his day.

Instead of typing back he cut his phone off and tossed it on his desk. He sauntered over to the floor-to-ceiling windows of his corner office where he was greeted by Tribeca's historic waterfront and the Hudson River Park. For most, the view was spectacular. He would never deny the fact. However, it couldn't compare to the Shores.

Or her...

He released a long breath while taking the landscape in. She'd loved landscapes...but apparently not the idea of them enough to choose the happiness she deserved. Which was why he decided against responding to any of Carrah's calls or texts. If what had happened between them had been purely physical, then maybe he could reply. He'd never had a problem viewing sex as sex. Hell, he knew the rules.

But that wasn't what it had been between him and her that night. The memory haunted him of the way their bodies entangled as she kissed him, touched him, and accepted his pleasure without complaint. She had given her all to him from dusk till dawn, and it was then he realized he had already fallen in love with her.

The phone on his desk rang, decapitating memories he wished were nonexistent. He moved back to his desk and saw Gavin's number on the caller ID. Shayla's failure to announce the caller illustrated her heavy-handedness in forcing him to connect with what he had left behind. "'Sup, Gav," he spoke into the receiver.

"You tell me, man. You ain't never left the Shores early."

"Don't pretend you don't know why." There was no reason to beat around the bush. The pissing match with Trenton Butler was well documented…and he wouldn't allow his heart to be Carrah's punching bag. So it was best to transition back to that alternate reality where their rivalry permitted her to be the dutiful daughter while pretending he didn't exist. "Anyways, what are y'all getting into today?"

A snort came from the other end of the line. "That shit won't work, bro. You and Carrah were legit knocking boots behind everybody's back. Now you're gone and she's isolated herself. Won't come to anything, and she's usually at every event. Everything is weird. It doesn't feel like summer anymore, and I don't know if it ever will after all of this. Too many lines were crossed."

Chris cursed under his breath. "Sorry, man. I…I should've kept my hands to myself." It wasn't his goal to upset the dynamic of their group, and he hated that Carrah had to hide to avoid ridicule.

"Takes two to tango. Both of you needed to keep your damn hands to yourselves. Why didn't you tell me?" His teeth smacked. "My duty would've been to keep you away. Women like Carrah make men forget who they are. You see Trent. The man been cheating with all the ass in the world and yet he won't let her go. Guess that famous voodoo queen great-grandmother of hers didn't just pass down looks."

A light chuckle slipped from Chris. Leave it to Gavin to lift his spirits. And yet his words held truth. Carrah had made him forget he was her enemy, that his mom didn't approve, and that he wasn't looking for love. She was the lady he wanted in his life, despite knowing he could never have her.

It was then that a fantasy entered his mind. For a moment he wondered what it might have been like if they'd beaten their star-crossed odds. They both knew on some level that they were playing with fire. It was obvious neither expected the third-degree burns they now suffered. His jaw tightened as he rubbed at his chest. The ache deepened.

"She says you aren't answering her calls." A pause hung on the line. "I don't see this as a hit-it-and-quit-it sort of thing so why won't you talk to her?"

Gavin was his best friend. He had been for a long time, which meant Chris knew where all the bodies were buried. Therefore, it rendered this line of questioning hypocritical, given the many women Gavin never gave consideration to after he spent time between their legs.

"There is nothing left to say." Chris meant it. Carrah had been unable to be honest with her feelings toward him when it mattered most. This was his punishment for falling for her—for being a traitor to his family.

A loud, strong harrumph came from the other end of the line. "Try that on someone who doesn't know you. The fact that you moved as discreet as you did and then stood ten toes down against Trent when he spoke ill of her contradicts the way you left. And to find, what, distraction with your work?"

Maybe. It still didn't matter. His mind was made up.

"Riddle me this"—he couldn't see Gavin's smirk but he heard it—"how does the thought of Carrah being with another man make you feel? That will become a reality if you stay stuck on your ego, Chennault."

Chris gulped hard and sat absently staring up at the ceiling. He didn't know how, but he knew he would never fall for another woman in the way he'd fallen for Carrah. For all their lives they'd been around each other dancing a jig, pretending it was because they hated one another. The more he peeked behind the scenes, the more he understood that he and Carrah had both been suppressing a forbidden attraction. Subconsciously it must have turned into hate since they were not allowed to act on it.

As he ended the call and placed the phone in the receiver, a solemn mood clouded him. He couldn't control how he wanted to not feel for her. And as bad as he wanted her, he refused to put himself in a position to be hurt by her all over again. He'd laid all his cards out to her once, twice, maybe three times. He didn't have it in him to do it again.

The handle on the door to his office clicked before it opened and Shayla walked in. She stopped in front of his desk, holding a stack of papers and eyeing him much longer than normal. "What did Gavin say? Is Carrah okay?"

Without looking up at her, he replied, massaging his temples. "Gavin seems to think she's isolating herself from everyone. He says it no longer feels like summer."

"Yeah, no, it doesn't. I would give anything to be at the boardwalk right now. Unfortunately, we're back in the concrete jungle." She then set the documents in her hand on his desk. "You should go back."

"No." His voice rose a decibel.

"Why wo—fine!" She threw her hands in the air. "I know this look, your vibe, whatever you want to call it. You don't have to discuss it with me, but you should know your mood has been barely tolerable." He turned his gaze sharply on Shayla. "You're miserable without her. The entire office knows something is off with you.

"They think it's because Gerron got booted from his show. Only, I know it's because of your situation with Carrah, which is worse in my opinion because there's no legalese to erase what happened. So if you think coming back to New York to work ungodly hours is the answer, you're wrong."

Chris felt his jaw twitch with irritation, but he still refused to offer a response. He was certain Shayla took it to mean he was done talking by the way she walked out of his office. He cursed more than a few times then finally picked up the phone and dialed Carrah's number.

"Hello," her soft voice came through the other end, effectively clenching his heart.

His eyes closed while his chest rose and fell with the vigor of a man who had just endured a twelve-mile run. "Carrah, this is Chris. I—"

"Hey." She was breathless. "How—"

"Is everything okay?" He cut her off, unintentionally injecting a stony tone, but understanding he needed a shield of protection. This was a bad idea. He couldn't relapse this easy. "Might there be something regarding your contract needing my attention?" Never again did he want the lines between professional and personal to become blurred.

* * *

A long pause filled the line with silence. His frigid tone took her back to the very first time she went to his office. The question stung. She was sure he'd seen her messages. None of which mentioned their business arrangement.

"Everything is fine," she lied. She wanted to say, *I'm miserable…I love you but you probably no longer love me…and I wish we could start back at the beginning.*

Since that night when they'd debated time travel her stance had changed. Hindsight revealed that she would use it to go back, start all over again, and confess her feelings to Chris at the Red Party. Maybe even alter the dislike between their families so he could've been her beau at debut. Perhaps then they could've discovered the thing that lingered between them.

"Fine," he drawled.

"Yes, fine." Defense mechanisms kicked in, making the reply lofty even though tears were stinging her eyes. "I appreciate the call. I have to go." Without saying bye she hung up the phone.

Her face went into her palms, capturing her tears. She heaved in her disappointments and blew out her regrets. He'd already said goodbye three days ago and she didn't want to hear it again.

Once she felt she had her feelings under control, she sat upright on the couch and met Reese's and Ava's concerned stares.

"Why didn't you tell him?" Ava's somber voice consoled

Carrah before she made it to her side and wrapped an arm around her shoulders. "How hard is it for you to tell that man you fell in love with him?"

Reese flanked her other side. She looked Carrah in the face and frowned. "You're much too stubborn. Don't be like me and miss ten years with the man you love, Carrah. It's hard to make up that time. No matter how many beach-in-a-jars you make."

"Neither of you heard him." Carrah sniffled, unable to withstand the way her heart began breaking all over again. "He was all business, cold, and—"

"You did that," Ava said matter-of-factly, and got to her feet. "How was Chris supposed to act after you threw away everything the two of you shared this summer? Just like you sat on that phone and lied to protect yourself, he did the same. Only"—Ava's nostrils flared and she blew out a harsh breath—"he has the right. You don't!"

Carrah's head snapped up to Ava. Her friend always seemed to take up for Chris more than anyone else. "You like him." She whispered her accusation.

Ava's arms folded, melting her frustration from sight. "A long time ago I had a crush on Chris. But I've always seen the way he looked at you, Carrah. Especially when no one was watching."

"And the way Carrah looked at him when she thought we weren't paying attention." Reese side-eyed Carrah, chiming in and helping to soften the glare that was set on Ava. "It is clear that something is between the two of you, regardless of your families' drama. I mean, Chris disregarded societal decorum and stood up for you in front of everyone."

Thoughts, words, they were all bogged down by the memory of him protecting her from Trent on the night of the

Red Party. Before Christopher Chennault, Carrah had been trapped inside a gilded cage. He'd freed her by championing her dreams, keeping her secrets safe, and giving her someone to love. Through him she was allowed a chance to discover a new path. And though it was full of complication, heartache, and uncertainty, it ended with him. She knew she would never love like this again. He was her happily ever after, and she was no longer afraid to fight for it.

Chapter 37

KNOCKS STRUCK AGAINST the door to Carrah's bedroom before it opened and Dominic popped his head inside. "You rang?" Carrah shushed her little brother and pulled him inside her room. "Where are you going?" He strolled over to the foot of her bed where she had a duffel bag packed to the brim.

"New York," she whispered over her shoulder before taking off to the bathroom and coming back with a few more toiletries she stuffed in her bag as Dominic watched with big eyes. "I need you to take me to the airport this evening."

Before Dominic had the chance to respond the wall speaker crackled. "Carrah, Dad wants you to come downstairs now, please."

They both gave an audible sigh as Carrah's attention went to the bag by her bed. She truly didn't have time for this. She needed to get to Chris. After the last few days and then hearing his voice yesterday, going to his New York office became her mission. He deserved to know that she loved him and could not imagine life without him.

"Do you know why I rarely attend or chime in at family meetings?" Dominic asked, and it made Carrah refocus.

"Because you don't care?"

"Actually, I do. I wholly know if I answer, then it's always expected of me regardless of what I want." He sighed. "You want to leave but can't because you're expected to be at this meeting. Oh, and FYI, when I was downstairs earlier, neither Dad nor Mom were in good moods since most of their friends keep asking what happened at the Red Party."

A huff escaped her as she gathered her bags and placed them by the door. "Well, there's a surprise."

"Ahh, but it is." Dominic gave Carrah a foolhardy grin. "They never expected you to be the one to bring scandal. That was my job." He winked and Carrah couldn't help laughing while hating that anything associating her with Chris was perceived as a scandal. "Don't not go, Carrah. Stop denying your happiness for a company that only takes. You've given Noir everything. It's okay to have something for yourself. Let me know when you're ready to go to the airport."

Dominic left imparting wisdom that she never counted on coming from her younger brother. A few minutes later, she followed after making herself presentable. Beau and her father were waiting along with her mother in the study.

"You wanted to see me?" She stepped in, garnering the three's attention.

"Yes." Her father smiled and pulled her deeper into the room. "We've just heard from Chauncy and his attorney. They want to meet to discuss the venture. Miles is attending as well so we think it would be a good idea for you to come and be ready to present or speak on any questions they may have. We need to get this finalized."

Carrah dropped her father's hand. Whatever it was they wanted to say about a so-called scandal was pushed to the wayside. It no longer had a bearing on their ability to execute business as usual. Once they solidified this venture she was done. She could no longer be a pawn in a game while watching her life turn into figments of an imagination, as Mr. Chennault had warned. Besides, her memory of Chris owed him more. She couldn't have reached this point without him.

"Is something wrong, darling?" her mother asked, and came to her side. "You seem unhappy."

Four days later her mood was finally noted by her mother. Not a one of them seemed to consider that maybe she was hurt. She would return the same uninterested energy once she gave her farewell to the company. "I'm fine. When is the meeting?"

"In a few hours at their building downtown." Beau's words spun her around, making her relive the times she'd been there with Chris. She closed her eyes and counted to three. "Are you okay?"

"Why wouldn't she be? That blunder at the party is water under the bridge. Chauncy doesn't seem to be holding on to any grudges, so why should we? It's time to focus on the future of Noir."

"Is that all you care about, Dad?" Carrah finally pulled through the fog and looked at her father. She wouldn't miss her flight tonight or the chance to be the captain of her heart. "It's forever and always about Noir. You never bothered to understand what happened at the party or how I felt about it. Only that I made a spectacle with our family's rivalry that garnered unsavory attention.

"But now it seems that rhetoric has changed since the

Chennaults are still agreeing to collaborate with you on a product I created...oh, but wait, it isn't mine because it belongs to Noir."

"Carrah, I beg you to stop." Her mother stood and came to her. She took her hands. "We need to close this deal, and we need you to do it. Nothing has changed between our families. This is business."

"Is that how you compartmentalize the fact that Miles looks like Dad?" She eyed her mother and then glanced to her father, who remained staunch. She feared more than ever that the words of his longtime rival had been spot-on. "I will do my part for this family as I always have. However, once the deal is cemented, I intend on resigning." She turned away from her family and left the study to prepare for meeting the Chennaults.

* * *

After hearing Carrah's voice on the other end of the phone yesterday and then learning from his siblings that she had come by their family home, he realized that the world he'd created in which he was attempting to forget her collided with the one that needed her. However, it wasn't enough. The courage she gained to find him would leave again if her parents had their way. Proof was in the fact that her agent had called and made him aware that Carrah declined to sign an updated deadline schedule. A problem for him to navigate since she was still, in fact, his client.

And now this. The SOS his father sent late last night demanding his presence today for an unexpected meeting with the Andrewses over the joint venture had him on edge. He'd left the Shores to get away from Carrah and now a meeting like this would pull him back into her orbit. It was a place he didn't care to be for fear of losing himself again.

He pulled up to the downtown building about ten minutes later than the meeting's start time and quickly exited his car and went up to the suite. The temporariness of the suite mocked him, reminding him of how his time with Carrah had been the same. Voices from the conference room lulled him from that dark place. He invoked the teachings of his mother, remembered this was business, and put on his game face.

People hurt you only if you wore your heart on your sleeve. A mistake he'd made with Carrah Andrews, and it was not to be repeated.

"Christopher," his father boasted with natural pride as he stopped in the door. The players at the table were different this time around. Not as many and not less important. Carrah was present with her parents, brother, and their attorney. His father had only brought their attorney. "Here, take your seat next to me."

Chris greeted everyone purposely avoiding eye contact with Carrah, and sat between his father and their company attorney. When he glanced up, she was staring at him from across the table. She was beautiful as ever with glowing skin and those almond eyes that seemed to pierce his soul. His heart couldn't take the punishment, and so he focused back on his father.

"As I was saying," Chauncy continued, "I am glad we could meet before drawing up the formal paperwork. Present-day circumstances have forced me to dwell in the past for much longer than I should." He directed his attention to Melvin. "I in good conscience cannot submit to a joint venture with Noir Cosmetics."

"May I ask why?" Melvin shouted over the audible shock that bounced around the room.

Chris perched up from his seat and focused on his father. He was intrigued by this sudden change of heart.

Chauncy's gaze darted into the other man. "My intentions of this transaction were not honorable. I planned to take advantage of your financial situation and exact revenge for the way you tore Noir apart and treated my sister. My son disagreed. His shame over my actions reminded me that revenge wouldn't change what you did or the fact that my nephew, Miles, is yours and Hannah's son."

Camille clutched her chest, shaking her head. She scooted her chair out and then went to Chauncy. "When I first saw your nephew, he reminded me of a younger Melvin, and it hasn't sat right with me since. Now I know why." She fingered a tear from the corner of her eye.

Chauncy pointed to Melvin. "He couldn't keep his hands off my sister even after your daddy gave him keys to the kingdom." Chauncy then softened a bit and looked Camille in the face. "Claudette and Hannah never forgave you for intentionally breaking his and Hannah's engagement, Milly. The unwed pregnancy stained my sister's reputation and created a rift between her and our parents."

Camille's face melted into tears. Her sobs became louder before Carrah stood and went to comfort her mother. "All this time I believed Hannah ended things with you. I lost two best friends. Is it true, Melvin?" Her father didn't answer. "Is it true?" she screamed.

"That I loved Hannah and continued to see her after we were married, yes." Guilt clung to him. "That I knew she was carrying my son, no."

"How old is Miles?" Camille's voice trembled.

"A few months older than Aubrey." Chauncy remained astute, and Chris finally understood why revenge was his father's answer for Melvin's crimes. Still he didn't agree because it would not change anything, only bring more pain. "Miles is unaware. Hannah thought it best due to Melvin's nature to manipulate situations for his benefit and greed."

Melvin got to his feet and moved around to where Chauncy stood, then walked up into his face. "Neither you nor Hannah had a right to keep this from me. Now you want to deny a business venture because I have a son I didn't know about?"

"You see, you keep making this about you. Look at them." Chauncy pointed to Chris and Carrah, who were lost in each other's gazes. "They are why I cannot exact revenge or keep the fact that you and Hannah have a child a secret any longer. It will ruin us all. My son and your daughter don't deserve to reap sins of the father."

Camille cleared her throat. She straightened her dress and primped her hair after dabbing a wet sheen from her eyes. "I was a fool back then to how much you loved Hannah. I thought my family's money and status within the old guard was enough. I was wrong, and though it happened a long time ago, I can't turn a blind eye to your infidelity or the way our daughter looks at a boy who never had to be her rival." Camille glanced at Carrah and then followed her line of sight back to Chris.

"Milly," Chauncy started, "if Claudette were here, I'm not sure what she would say. What I do know is that somehow in the midst of all our bullshit, our children found a way to mean something to each other. They've given both our families back a lost legacy that is worthy of rebuilding. I will gladly work with you to restore Noir to its greatness."

She considered his words then stole another look at Carrah

and Chris. "Our fathers would celebrate our children, Ace. They did what neither you nor I could and reclaimed the bond that has existed between the Chennault and Chàvous lineage from before we were born." A smile curled her lips, "Thank you. We are not too proud to accept your help. You and I will work together since, effective immediately, I'll be resuming operating control of Noir."

Melvin fumed. "Wha—"

"I missed you," Carrah proclaimed as though she were speaking from the top of the mountain to people in a valley. She was done avoiding what she needed to say to Chris. He didn't shy away, nor did anyone else. They were all watching her. "I called to tell you I was sorry a thousand times, but you never answered. And then when you called back...it wasn't you."

That business shield of armor cracked. The sincerity of her words coupled with the way she looked at him made him acutely aware of the truth she spoke and the stronghold she had over his heart.

He cleared his throat. "We can talk after." Chris didn't want an audience to witness his hurt. She'd broken a promise and that lingered.

Melvin took about four steps back. "So the rumors are true? He is the reason you won't entertain Trent's marriage proposal? Had you accepted, I wouldn't have even stooped to ask for this joint venture."

Beau glanced from Carrah to their father. "That is not the reason. You know that. Carrah told us why she doesn't want to marry Trent, and I support it. Her happiness should mean something to us."

"It should," Melvin shouted, "but Noir—"

"Has always come first, Dad." Carrah fidgeted with her hands. "I'm choosing me this time."

"As you should, Carrah." Camille squeezed Carrah's hand. "I'm sorry it has taken me this long to understand. Your happiness is important. So tell me, what does Christopher mean to you?"

Carrah stared at Chris, hoping their hearts could find that secret place that had set them both free. "I'm in love with you, Chris."

A tear slid down her cheek as his heart filled like a balloon in his chest. Words that he never wanted to hear from a woman had become music to his ears because she sang the song his soul recognized. Only, bitterness had settled within the crack of his heart from where she'd broken it.

"What helped you come to that realization?" His father nudged him under the table as Chris met her gaze.

"You told me once that I was afraid to live my happily ever after. I'm not afraid anymore. I'm here, right now, trying to fight for it because I love you…need you." She broke into tears, and he pushed away from the table and went to her, pulling her into his arms.

"Perhaps we will leave you two alone." Neither Chris nor Carrah acknowledged his father's words.

Silence surrounded them like the sounds of darkness hiding secrets that needed to be set free. Maybe he had been a hardass for asking her to confirm her love. However, he needed to know, needed to be sure, before he submitted and confessed how utterly lost he was without her.

"Nothing else mattered without you. I didn't breathe again until I saw you at that door." She swallowed hard, fighting back tears as she clutched him tighter. "It took me longer than you to understand that I couldn't be hostage to a rivalry that had existed since before we were born."

"I know the feeling." They came apart and he laced his fingers with hers. "You came when I least expected, but somehow needed." The beat of his heart would have made a deaf man hear. The time he spent with Carrah had taught him how to give love without conditions, and he planned to do just that for the rest of his life. "You helped me breathe again. I was suffocating without you."

He looked down into her eyes, and took her hand. He placed it against his chest. "Do you feel that?" She nodded and his forehead touched hers. "My heart belongs to you. I'm unexpectedly yours, Carrah Andrews."

"Ditto," she whispered. "I had packed my bags and bought a plane ticket to New York. I would have been on your doorstep this evening, begging you to forgive me and start over."

He chuckled. "Oh, so you're bold now."

"For you, yes." Her bashful admission made him weak. "You set me free."

His brow arched, highlighting curiosity, as he pushed a wispy hair behind her ear. "You never told me that." He scanned her quizzically. "Tell me something else I don't know about you."

She held her breath for a second and then closed her eyes before she said, "I don't want to spend another summer in the Shores without you." Without hesitation, Chris leaned in to seal her heady declaration with a kiss. Carrah reclined back, targeting him with a side-eye. "Fair exchange, Attorney Chennault."

Chris nodded, enchanting her with those beautiful eyes. "I dreamed you were my wife."

Their lips touched then teased and parted before he

deepened the kiss, reaching to the essence of her soul. They were finally free of an unkind past, and now the way was paved for a future where he saw them starting a life together.

"Well," she whispered, breathless against the flushed heat of his skin, "I can't wait to see you make that one come true."

"I told you that I wanted to give you everything you've always wanted and more. I mean that. I love you more than you could ever know."

Acknowledgments

There will never be enough words to express how grateful I am for my family and their unwavering support and encouragement. To Mark, my love—you are everything. To my Marz, you challenge me to make love stories cool. Love you, Pookie! To my B-Man, I love your hugs. Thank you for always making sure I'm okay. To my mommy, if there is ever darkness, you are the light. Thank you for always sending me in the right direction. To my baby sis, you keep me on my toes, challenging me to think different, you millennial. To my brother, Horace, you speak to me from heaven above, reminding me that life can be short so live—I miss you. To Diana Neal, LaQuette, Reese Ryan, Tamara Lush, and Dylan Newton, I daresay you author gals are lifelines in these literary streets. To my aunts Vivian and Carolyn, your support and encouragement endure in the Williams name, xoxo.

To the unofficial Hype Crew, Shauntae, JaNiece, Ms. Debbie, Alisha, Alesiah, Trishana, and Aunt Sharon—thank you for always supporting and bringing gorgeous vibes.

To my amazing agent, Latoya Smith, looking forward to what comes next.

To my awesome editor, Kirsiah Depp, thank you for loving this as much as I do.

To all the beautifully talented authors writing romance featuring Black Heroines and Heroes—keep writing! The world deserves to see our excellence as we defy stereotypes and show that everyone is worthy of a Happily Ever After.

To my readers, thank you. I hope you enjoyed returning to the Shores. Be on the lookout for the next HEA set in this charming town.

About the Author

C. Chilove is a Southern girl writing sexy, thought-provoking romance that explores the human condition while proving love transcends societal clichés. Her characters are strong, witty, and prove that diversity is beautiful. When she's not writing, she's living out her personal happily ever after by rockin' the stands for her volleyball star, cheering on her future MLB slugger, or celebrating date night with her hubby.